SPECIAL MESSAGE TO READERS

THE ULVERSCROFT FOUNDATION
(registered UK charity number 264873)
was established in 1972 to provide funds for
research, diagnosis and treatment of eye diseases.
Examples of major projects funded by
the Ulverscroft Foundation are:-

- The Children's Eye Unit at Moorfields Eye Hospital, London
- The Ulverscroft Children's Eye Unit at Great Ormond Street Hospital for Sick Children
- Funding research into eye diseases and treatment at the Department of Ophthalmology, University of Leicester
- The Ulverscroft Vision Research Group, Institute of Child Health
- Twin operating theatres at the Western Ophthalmic Hospital, London
- The Chair of Ophthalmology at the Royal Australian College of Ophthalmologists

You can help further the work of the Foundation
by making a donation or leaving a legacy.
Every contribution is gratefully received. If you
would like to help support the Foundation or
require further information, please contact:

THE ULVERSCROFT FOUNDATION
The Green, Bradgate Road, Anstey
Leicester LE7 7FU, England
Tel: (0116) 236 4325

website: www.foundation.ulverscroft.com

Luca Veste is a writer of Italian and Scouse heritage, currently living on the wrong side of the River Mersey. He is married with two young daughters, and is himself one of nine children. Luca is currently a mature student, studying Psychology and Criminology in Liverpool. He is the editor of the Spinetingler Award-nominated charity anthology series *Off the Record*, which raises money for children's literacy charities. He also has short stories in numerous publications. A former civil servant, actor and musician, he now divides his time between home life, university work and writing.

You can discover more about the author at:
www.lucaveste.com
Twitter — @lucaveste

THE DYING PLACE

DI Murphy and DS Rossi discover the body of known troublemaker Dean Hughes, dumped on the steps of St Mary's Church in West Derby, Liverpool. His body is covered with the unmistakeable marks of torture. As they hunt for the killer, they discover a worrying pattern. Other teenagers, all young delinquents, have been disappearing without a trace. Who is clearing the streets of Liverpool? Where are the other missing boys being held? And can Murphy and Rossi find them before they meet the same fate as Dean?

Books by Luca Veste
Published by Ulverscroft:

DEAD GONE

LUCA VESTE

THE
DYING PLACE

Complete and Unabridged

CHARNWOOD
Leicester

First published in Great Britain in 2014 by
Avon
A division of
HarperCollins*Publishers*
London

First Charnwood Edition
published 2015
by arrangement with
HarperCollins*Publishers*
London

The moral right of the author has been asserted

This novel is entirely a work of fiction. The names, characters and incidents portrayed in it are the work of the author's imagination. Any resemblance to actual persons, living or dead, events or localities is entirely coincidental.

A catalogue record for this book is available from the British Library.

ISBN 978–1–4448–2569–5

Published by
F. A. Thorpe (Publishing)
Anstey, Leicestershire

Set by Words & Graphics Ltd.
Anstey, Leicestershire
Printed and bound in Great Britain by
T. J. International Ltd., Padstow, Cornwall

This book is printed on acid-free paper

For Angelina 'Angie' Veste
11/04/1936 — 07/05/2014
My nana. My nonna.
She loved her family and her family loved her.

Acknowledgements

As ever, this book would not have been possible without the support of so many, many people. I would like to show my appreciation and say a massive thank you to the following people:

Nick Quantrill, for his endless backing and friendship. My turn to visit the KC next season. Eva Dolan, for her constant encouragement and for all the great ideas. Steve Mosby, for being a continual source of inspiration and faith. Helen FitzGerald, for just generally being awesome and a better writer than most could ever hope to be. Mark Billingham, for *that* quote and for also sharing an incident outside an Indian restaurant in the middle of London (who knew people called dogs Luca?!). Characterisation, characterisation, characterisation. Stav Sherez, for the rack conversation and also for all the support with *Dead Gone*. Pete Sortwell, for the late night laughs and tears over all the things we could never work out. Tracey Edges, for being a fantastic supporter of *Dead Gone* in the early days of release.

Neil White, Linda Moore, Liz Barnsley, Col Bury, Paul D. Brazill, Susi Holliday, Mark Wright, Anne McLauchlan, James Everington, Mel Sherratt, Mark Edwards, and Jan Russell, for all the online support. You make it worth the procrastination of just checking Facebook and

Twitter one more time.

All the readers who contacted me after reading *Dead Gone*. Hands down my favourite part of the process is hearing from people who read and enjoyed the book. Thank you.

My agent Phil Patterson, for being not only an incredible source of knowledge on anything and everything, but also one of the funniest, most random people I've ever had the pleasure of knowing. This book doesn't exist without you, Sir. Thank you for continuing to change my life for the better.

My editor at Avon, Sammia Hamer, for being not only a great believer in me and my writing, but also a friend I hope to have for a long, long time. You always made things better. I, and everyone who enjoys the violent and gory parts of my books (which you always, always wanted more of!), will miss your input. I promise not to let you down. Good luck in the new job. You'll be as awesome as ever.

Katy Loftus for taking over editing duties and adding even more to the process. You're going to be a huge success story at Avon. I know these things.

Everyone at Avon and HarperCollins for their support during these first two books. Although sad to move on, I'm extremely grateful for all that you have done in the past couple of years. You all rock.

Keshini Naidoo, for being a fantastic copy-editor. You contributed so much to this book. And bobble is probably too colloquial . . . you're right.

Uncle John 'Murphy' Kirkham and Gina Kirkham, for, well . . . everything.

My parents Alan Veste (I am the one who knocks!), Tracy Veste (and I turned around and said . . .), Sue Kirkham (Orlando soon!), John Brisk (I'm going to need a new bookshelf soon, big man), Carole Woodland (all right, you're not *that* posh really), and Alan Woodland (one more whisky?). Yes, I collect parents like Panini stickers. Thank you for always being there if needed.

My siblings were promised an actual naming in the acknowledgements this time around, so here goes . . . deep breath . . . Beverley, Chrissie, Colin, Mike, Jemma, Daniel, Natalie, Alex, Alice, Joshua, Santino, and Vincenzo. I'm incredibly lucky to have the most amazing brothers and sisters anyone could ever wish for.

The Hales/ Carnabys/ Robertsons, Perry, Cath, Andrea, and Jay. Your determination in making me a household name in Newcastle knows no bounds. Thank you.

Peter Veste (and Brian!), Izzybella Veste, Joanne Johnson, and Andy Veste, for . . . you know. You made the whole *thing* bearable. *Vi amo tutti*.

Finally, my wife Emma Veste and daughters Abigail and Megan, for always being there for me. Abs and Migs — Daddy did it again. Promise not to visit every shop in a thirty-mile radius to look at the book on the shelves. Just the twenty this time. Emma — I promise to finally get my driving licence. Although I know you'll still want to drive me everywhere. Your love and grounding is all I ever need and is more appreciated than you'll ever know.

Now

No one believes you. Nothing you say is the truth. They know it every time you open your mouth and start speaking, hoping to be believed. Everything is just a lie in disguise, dressed up nice, trying to be something it's not.

Mutton dressed as lamb.

That's just how it is. You go down the social — or the jobcentre as they call it now, although that'll probably change to something else soon enough — and try to explain why you're still worth sixty quid a week of *taxpayers' hard-earned money*. Trying to justify yourself even though you haven't worked in years. Get that look which seeps into you after a little while.

I've heard it all before, love.

There's no let-up. Being judged at every turn. Lucky enough to have more than one kid? Unlucky enough to lose your part-time job working the till at some shitty shop? For your fella to piss off with some slag from around the corner? Doesn't matter, shouldn't have had more kids than you can afford. Doesn't matter that you're a single parent — I'm paying your benefits.

You live on a council estate, on benefits, and that's it. You're scum. Do not pass go, here's a few hundred quid to pay some dickhead landlord who thinks five ton isn't too much for a terraced house that's overrun with damp. Mould growing

1

on the walls if you dare put any furniture too close to it.

Your kids then become scum as well. Shit schools, shit kids. Bored with life, constantly pissed off because you can't afford the latest frigging gadget that Sony or Apple put out. Every six months without fail, something new that every other kid in the school has, that they can't be without.

You try. You really do. But it's never enough. Sixteen hours working in a supermarket, a few hours doing cleaning. Bits of crap here and there. Never enough.

No one believes you.

Your kids get older. Get in trouble. Bizzies knocking on your door at two in the morning, hand on the back of your fifteen-year-old son.

He's had too much to drink. Could have got himself into a lot more trouble. Should keep an eye on him more, love.

That judgement again. Always there, surrounding you.

You try and explain. Tell them he'd said he was staying at his mate's, or staying at his uncle's house. With his cousins.

Get that look back.

I've heard it all before, love.

You want to scream. You want to pull the little bastard into the house by his stupid frigging head and beat the shit out of him. Like your dad would do to your brothers if they ever got caught doing stupid shit.

You try your best. Every day. It's never enough. The crap wages you get for working two, three, different jobs barely matches what you were getting on benefits. So you think, what's the point? You're tired. You want to be lazy. Exhausted by the sheer weight of being alive. Everyone else around you seems to be doing sod all. You want to do that for a while.

The kids get worse. All boys, so the house is either deathly quiet whilst they're all out, getting up to God knows what. Or, it's a cacophony of noise. The moaning, the groaning. The smells of teenagers on the cusp of manhood, burning into your nostrils, hanging in the air.

No one believes you.

When one of them doesn't come home for days, you shout and scream as much as you possibly can, but no one cares.

They think he's just done a bunk. Gone to see a girl. Gone to get pissed, stoned, off his face somewhere. He'll turn up eventually. They always do.

Your kind always does.

You try and tell them it's different. That your lads have always been good at letting you know where they are, or if they're going to be away for any time at all. That they wouldn't just leave without saying anything.

They give you that look.

I've heard it all before, love.

You try and get people interested, but no one cares. The papers aren't interested. Thousands of people go missing every year. No one cares about your eighteen-year-old son, missing for weeks . . . months.

You believe he's okay. You make yourself believe it.

3

You know though. As a parent, you know. Something has happened to him.

It's not until you're watching his coffin go behind the curtain — fire destroying everything that made him your son and turning it into ash — that they start to believe you.

It's too late now, of course.

Sorry, love.

Before

It wasn't supposed to happen this way.

The plan hadn't been for him to be in this position. Not yet, anyway. He was supposed to be there to see it through. It was his idea, his design. None of them would have thought of doing it without him. He was the catalyst, the spark that brought them all together.

That's the problem with making plans . . . the master in the sky laughs.

Flat on his back in the street outside his own home, a ghost of a smile playing across his face. Clutching his chest as his heart threatened to beat its way out, his vision going blurry. Not being able to see if there really was an elephant sitting on him, which was how it felt — crushing weight bearing down, strangling him, cutting off his breath.

He should have known he was too old for it. Not that it would have made a difference. As soon as they'd come around to his plan, he wasn't going to hide away whilst all the fun went down without him. He should have just stayed inside with a small whisky and some shite on the TV. Relaxed. Then maybe he would have had a few more years.

They'd come back again. Laughter and voices penetrating the walls from outside. No respect for people's private property. Just sitting on the wall outside his house, throwing their empty cans into his little front garden.

He'd checked the time on the clock that took pride of place on his mantelpiece, a beautiful old-fashioned gold carriage clock which had been a retirement gift from a client.

Half past midnight. Way past his usual turning-in time. Early to bed, early to rise. An old motto, but one he stuck to usually.

Something that lot out there wouldn't have a clue about.

He had noticed the area changing around him for a while. What used to be a nice area of West Derby was being overrun with those yobs. Complete with their strange bastardisation of the Scouse accent. Couldn't understand them most of the time, which was probably just as well. Couldn't imagine they'd have anything of value to say.

Back in his day, if you left school with no qualifications — as was the norm, to be fair — you took whatever job you could get, and got on with it. He'd left school at fourteen and went straight to work, doing odd jobs here and there. Joined the army a few years later, ended up in Korea. Got back home and worked for over forty years painting and decorating. Set himself up with a nice little business with enough customers to always have a bit of work on the go. Put a bit of money aside for the retirement years with the missus. They could have lived quite well for a good while.

And then he was alone.

Those lads wouldn't know the meaning of work. Not employed, in education or training, as

6

they say. A million of them apparently now, according to the papers. No jobs, you see. Whole world has gone the same way. It seemed like he'd blinked and the next minute everyone was saying it was better to live in China than anywhere else. Who'd have thought that would ever happen?

She was ten days off sixty-five when they got to her. Walking back from the post office. Doctors told him it was probably a coincidence. Didn't matter that she was left in the street for dead, she could have gone at any moment. He never believed them.

He would go for a walk every day, tried to keep fit. Walked up to the village, into the county park. Past the red church sign he always stopped to read.

Church of England
St Mary The Virgin
West Derby

St Mary the Virgin. Odd name to give to a church. But then, he found most things about churches odd.

He'd walk up the lane which ran alongside it, trees crowding in on each side. He'd find his bench, have a nice sit down and watch the world go by. Chat to people every now and again. Most people just walking on by, or smiling politely whilst thinking about their quickest escape route.

The first time they'd showed up outside his house, he thought a quick word would do the trick. Not a chance. He'd given them an hour, until the shouting had become too much. So

7

loud he couldn't even hear the TV properly. Just a quiet word, he thought, let them know someone lived here, that he wasn't going to let them take over his front. As soon as he'd walked out he could tell it wasn't going to have any effect. The attitude of them . . . Christ. They hadn't listened to a word he'd said. Just laughed at each other, whispering and turning their backs to him. He'd given up with a shrug of his shoulders and a hope that they wouldn't be back anytime soon. That they'd find someone else to bother.

He'd been wrong.

The plan was supposed to change that.

Forty years he'd worked. Up and down ladders nine hours a day. Hard work, but going home to Nancy and the kids made it worthwhile. He'd met Nancy when he was getting into his mid-thirties, her fifteen years younger. The mother-in-law had hated him from the start. Taking her little girl away. They'd had the last laugh on that one. Happily married for almost fifty years. Three children, two of them boys. When they grew up and had their own, they would have some of the grandkids over for tea once a week. Then they grew up as well.

His only regret with the children was that they weren't closer. Brothers and sisters should be there for each other, but there was always a distance between them.

It would have been okay though. Whiling away their later years together. They would've had little trips here and there. Bingo once a week at the social club. Visits to see the offspring.

The end of Nancy's story began and finished with two boys, barely in their teens, wearing hooded tops and balaclavas. They'd grabbed her bag, but she'd held on. They'd found bruises up her wrists and arms where they'd tried to prise her hands off it. A broken nose, which the CCTV showed happened when the taller of the two delivered a straight fist to her face. She'd died weeks later, but even if they'd found the yobs who did it, they wouldn't have been charged with murder. She'd died due to other complications, they'd told him.

He knew they were to blame though.

He checked outside again, looking through the curtains. Four of the little buggers. No older than sixteen or seventeen, he reckoned. He could feel the anger coursing through him, wishing he was a few years younger. Back in his army days he would have taken the four of them on and had them running home for their mothers. He wasn't one of those old guys who believed everything was better back in the day, like the moaning gits at the pub, but he also couldn't remember sitting outside someone's house drinking cans of lager, shouting and swearing. Life moves on. Things change. Not always for the better.

The fireworks were the last straw.

It had been late. Gone midnight. Explosions ripped through the silence which had accompanied his sleep. Downstairs, the direction of the noise made no sense in his confused half-asleep state. Korea. It was sixty years ago, but the slightest thing could send him back. He wasn't to know some little bastards had thought it

9

would be funny to stick a few fireworks through his letter box. Sweat dripped from his forehead, down onto the wisps of grey hair on his chest. His chest. Constricting. Tight. Everything pulling inwards. Choking him. The phone was in reach, which probably saved him that night. Couple of days in the Royal. Told to take it easy for a few days, but he should be fine. Simon, his youngest son, had gone mad, wanting to protect his supposedly frail father. Called the police, but they couldn't do anything without evidence. Said they'd look into it, but everyone knew what that meant.

A week later, the plan had begun to be formed.

The faces of war. The noise . . . explosions, gunshots, cries of anguish. The forgotten war is what they call Korea. He'd never forget it. Waking up silently screaming has that effect. It'd been a long time since he'd had the nightmares, but they had come back since the firework incident.

He wanted to get back at them. Not just that though. To show them the error of their ways.

Brazen as you like, sat on his wall, chucking their empties into the front garden Nancy used to spend hours tending to.

He lifted the phone. Dialled and said a few words.

He opened the front door and they didn't even turn around. Reached his front gate and stepped onto the pavement next to where they were gathered. They started laughing amongst them-selves as he tried to get their attention.

It happened faster than he'd expected. He gave them another chance, tried being cordial with them, asked them to move on, but they weren't having any of it. He tried explaining about the garden. They responded by laughing. Like a pack of hyenas, spotting the easy prey. He could feel his heart racing — bang, bang, bang. Beating harder than it had done in years.

He wasn't going to back down. Not this time. Things were different.

Two of them walked off behind him, sniggering under their black hoods as he held his hands out wide, palms to the darkened sky. He heard the distant sound of a car towards the end of his road and turned towards it. A shuffling sound to his left made him turn back.

Thunk.

The sound reverberated around his head. The clatter of tin on concrete brought him back to his senses, just as another beer can pinged off his head.

'What the . . . '

The laughing had grown louder. Surrounding him, constricting his breathing.

'You little shits . . . '

They were grouped together, pointing at him, nudging each other hard as their laughter grew and grew.

'Come 'ead lads', the tallest one said between fits of laughter, 'let's get down to Crocky Park. See if the girls are about.'

He stared after them as they left, mouth hanging open as they sauntered off, hands down the front of their tracksuit bottoms. Looked

11

around at the mess they'd made of his garden and the pavement in front of his house, before reaching up to his head — damp where dregs of beer had splattered onto his hair.

The van parked up his street shifted into gear and coasted towards him. He felt as if his chest was stuck in a vice, his breathing becoming shallower. He staggered backwards and sat on the small brick wall.

He lifted his head up as the van came to a stop a little before his house, squinting into the bright lights on the front of it. The passenger side door opened and he looked at the figure which got out.

'You okay auld fella?'

'Fine,' he replied between pants of breath, 'the tall one. That's who we want.'

'You sure?'

The old man swallowed and made a *go ahead* motion with his hands. 'It's time, son. One isn't enough. We're going to teach them a lesson. We're going to teach them *all* a lesson.'

* * *

Goldie felt buzzed — a bit light-headed even — but not properly pissed, which annoyed him. Even worse, that little slag Shelley hadn't let him do anything more than have a feel of her tits before pushing him away. Not that there was much there to feel. Now all he wanted to do was get home, smoke a bit — just to zone him out, like — and then have a good kip.

He smiled to himself as he remembered the

auld fella from earlier on in the night. Probably a fuckin' paedo or something, so he didn't feel bad. Not like there were any laws against sitting on someone's wall anyway. Next few weeks, he planned on making sure that auld bastard realised who Goldie was.

Lost in his half-pissed thoughts, he didn't hear the van slowing behind him. Didn't hear it come to a stop, the side doors opening. The first he realised something was wrong was when he was pushed hard in the back, his balance not what it would have been earlier in the day. It happened so quickly, he couldn't free his hands to stop the fall.

He remembered thinking the pavement was fuckin' hard, smashing into his face with nothing to brace against it — harder than even his dad had hit him that one time, before he fucked off for good. He turned around on the floor, using his tongue to feel around his mouth. One of his front teeth jutted forwards into his top lip. His left eye was going blurry as something wet dripped down his face. Blood, he guessed.

He tried to regain his senses, determined not to go down without a fight. Probably some Strand fuckers, hoping to put him out of action. He turned onto his back, raising his hands to cover himself, waiting for the kicking to start.

He looked up, confused in an instant as he saw the men standing over him.

They were old. Forties, fifties. He could tell from the greying hair, rather than facial features. All of them wearing masks.

Shite . . .

13

'You're coming with us, kid. Gonna teach you some respect.'

Goldie began kicking out, but rough, hard hands grabbed at his legs. Strength he wasn't used to from the other lads his own age. Fingers dug into his flesh as they pulled him along the concrete.

'Get the fuck off me you fuckin' twats. I'll fuck you all up. Do you know who I am? I'm gonna fuckin' kill all o' yers.'

Then the world went black as something was forced over his head, pulled tight across his face, no amount of thrashing around making it come off. Hard metal slammed into his stomach, taking the wind out of him completely. He felt a weight on his legs as he realised he was now in the back of the van, hands holding his head to the floor as they began to move. The hood over his face was loosened a little so he could breathe.

'Duct tape.'

The voice was hardened, Scouse. Proper old school, like his dad's.

'No. Don't you fuckin' dare . . . ' Goldie tried to shout, the hood muffling the sound.

The hood was lifted to his nose, before tape went across his mouth. Shouting behind it had no effect. He tried kicking out again, but the hands holding his legs and arms down barely shifted.

'Stop messing about, or we'll just dump you in the Mersey now. Relax. Nothing is going to happen to you. We're going to help you.'

Goldie tried answering back, but it was useless.

One leg got free.

Goldie didn't think twice. Just swung it back and aimed for anything he could. The satisfying clunk as his foot found flesh made him redouble his efforts.

Shouts, cries, as he struggled free, the hood over his face keeping him in darkness.

'Stop the van.'

The same voice as before, still calm, still low.

Goldie tried to stand, but the van pulling to a stop made him rock forward, off balance.

'I told you to relax.'

Goldie spun, but wasn't quick enough. His hands caught in mid-air as he tried to remove his hood. Strong grip on his wrist. Starting to twist.

Explosion in the side of his head as something smacked against it.

Then, as he fell to the floor, he wished for the complete darkness of unconsciousness — not just the vision of it. As the punches landed, the kicks and boots flew into his stomach, his ribs cracking one by one.

That tight grip on his wrist. Still there. Twisting, turning.

He cried out behind the duct tape sealing his mouth. No use.

The crack as his wrist snapped.

'That's enough. All of you.'

The blows stopped as he lay on the floor of the van, trying to hold his body together. Coughing up God knows what behind his gag. Trying not to choke. Trying to breathe, every intake of air through his nostrils not enough.

It somehow got darker behind the hood as his

head lolled backwards.

The last thing he remembered was the voice again.

'Start it up. Let's get to the farm. Now.'

PART ONE

Take the coward vermin to the nearest safari park. Shatter one of its knees. Hamstring the maimed leg, then kick the disease out of a van in the middle of the lion enclosure. No cat can resist a limping, bleeding thing. Film it and show it daily at prime time for a month. I'd pay good money to watch this show happen live. It wants to live like an animal? Let the subhuman abortion die like one.

I suppose when a judge says something is 'wicked' he presumes the accused will wilt under the 'tirade'. They may see the ugly side of life, but they simply do not understand it. Well, something that cowardly piece of rubbish would understand is a rope — or better still, piano wire. So what is wrong with visiting upon him the horror that family have gone through, doubtless are going through? Come on PC crowd, how are you going to side with this one?

**** **** and his type are not human. They are far, far beneath human. They are parasites who cause nothing but misery for real humans. People like this should be sterilised so their poisonous DNA is knocked out of the gene pool. What is it about these nasty folk who just roam around being vile? What can they possibly contribute to society other than destruction and misery?

Top-rated online comments from news story of teenage murderer

1

More sleep. Just a little bit more . . .

Detective Inspector David Murphy hit the snooze button on the alarm for the third time, silencing the noise which had cut through his drift into deeper sleep once again. He refused to open his eyes, knowing the early morning light would pierce the curtains and give him an instant headache.

A voice came from beside him.

'What time is it?'

He grunted in reply, already knowing he wasn't going to float away into slumber now. A few late nights and early starts and he was struggling. Age catching up with him. Closing in on forty faster than he'd expected.

'You need to get up. You'll be late for work.'

Murphy yawned and turned over to face Sarah, away from the window. Risked opening one eye, the room still brighter than he'd guessed. 'Do I have to?'

Sarah sat up, taking his half of the duvet cover with her and exposing his chest to the cold of the early morning.

'Yes,' she replied, shucking off the cover and pulling on her dressing gown. 'Now get up and get dressed. There's a fresh shirt and trousers in the wardrobe.'

'Five more minutes.'

'No, now. Stop acting like a teenager and get

19

your arse in gear. I've got work as well, you know.'

'Fine,' Murphy replied, opening his other eye and squinting against the light. 'But can you at least stick some coffee on before you start getting ready? I tried using that frigging maker thing yesterday and almost lobbed it through the window.'

'Okay. But you have to read the instructions at some point.'

Murphy snorted and sloped through to the bathroom. Turned the shower on and lifted the toilet seat, the shower tuning out the noise from downstairs as Sarah fussed in the kitchen.

He needed a lie-in. Twelve or so hours of unbroken sleep — now that would be nice.

It wasn't even work causing his tiredness. Nothing major had come through CID in the previous few months. Everyone at the station was trying to look busy so they weren't moved to a busier division in Liverpool. All too scared to use the 'Q — T' word. It was just *slow* or *calm*. Never the 'Q' word. That was just an invitation for someone to shit on your doorstep. A few fraud cases, assaults in the city centre and the usual small-fry crap that was the day-to-day of their lives in North Liverpool. Nothing juicy.

Murphy buttoned up his shirt and opened the curtains to the early May morning. Rain. Not chucking it down, just the drizzle that served as a constant reminder you were in the north of England.

The peace in work was a good thing, he thought. Just over a year on from the case which had almost cost him his life, he should have been grateful for the tranquillity of boring cases and endless paperwork. At least he wasn't lying at the bottom of a concrete staircase in a pitch-black cellar, a psychopath looming over him.

He had to look at the positives.

Murphy left the bedroom, stepping over paint-splattered sheets, paint tins and the stepladders which festooned the landing.

The cause of his late nights.

He'd gone into decorating overdrive, determined to have something to do in his spare time. Started with the dining room, which hadn't seen a paintbrush since they'd bought the house a few years earlier. Now he was back living there, reunited with his wife after a year apart following his parents' death, it was time to make the house look decent. Sarah was often busy in the evenings with lesson planning and marking due to her teaching commitments, so he would have otherwise just been staring at the TV, and he'd done enough of that when he lived on his own.

Sarah had started teaching just as they got married. Her past put behind her, a successful degree course, and a clean CRB check was all she needed. That, and a large amount of luck, given her ability to never actually be arrested for any of the stupid stuff she'd done in the past. Murphy had never expected that last bit to hold.

Murphy entered the kitchen just as Sarah was pouring out a cup of freshly brewed coffee. 'Cheers, wife. Need this.' He brushed her cheek with his lips as she slipped past him.

'I've only got half an hour to get ready now,

21

husband. Work out how to use the thing yourself, okay? Or we're going back to Nescafé.' She stopped at the doorway. 'Oh, and remember you promised we'd go out tonight.'

Friday already. The week slipping past without him noticing. 'Of course. I've booked a table.'

She stared at him for a few seconds, those blue eyes studying his expression. 'No you haven't. But you will do, right? Tear yourself away from your paintbrush, Michelangelo, and treat your wife.'

Murphy sighed and nodded. 'No problem.'

'Good. See you later. Love you.'

'Love you too.'

They were almost normal.

★   ★   ★

The commute was shorter now than it had been in the months he'd lived over the water, on the Wirral — the tunnel which separated Liverpool from the small peninsula now a fading memory. Still, it took him over twenty minutes to reach the station from his house in the north of Liverpool, the traffic becoming thicker as he neared the roads which led into the city centre.

After parking the car in his now-designated space behind the station, Murphy entered the CID offices of Liverpool North station just after nine a.m., the office already bustling with people as he let the door close behind him.

Murphy sauntered over to his new office, mumbling a 'morning' and a 'hey' to a few constables along the way. Took down the note which had been attached to his door as he pushed it open.

Four desks in a space which probably could have afforded two. Their reward for months of complaining and reminding the bosses of the jobs they'd cleared in the past year. A space cleared for Murphy, his now semi-permanent partner DS Laura Rossi, and two Detective Constables who seemed to change weekly.

'Morning, sir.'

Rossi looked and sounded, as always, as if she'd just stepped off a plane from some exotic country, fresh-faced and immaculate at first glance. It wasn't until you looked more closely — and in a space as tight as their office, Murphy had been afforded the time to study her — and noticed the dark under her eyes, the bitten-down fingernails, and the annoying habit she had of never clipping her hair out of her face.

He said his good mornings and plonked himself down behind his small desk, checking his in-tray for messages. A few chase-ups on old cases, a DS from F Division in Liverpool South who wanted a call back ASAP. Routine stuff.

'Anything new overnight?'

Rossi looked over from her computer screen, eyebrows raised at him. 'Nothing for us.'

'Come on. There must be something? I'm bored shitless here.'

As Rossi was about to answer, the door opened, DC Graham Harris sweating as he rushed in and sat down, shoving his bag under his desk. 'Sorry I'm late. Traffic was murder near the tunnel.'

Murphy debated whether to give him a telling-off just to kill a bit of time, before deciding against it. He yawned instead, waving away his apology with one hand. 'Where's the other one?'

'Not sure,' Harris replied, removing his black Superdry jacket. Murphy had priced one of those up in town a few weekends previously. Decided a hundred quid plus could be put to better use.

'Doesn't matter. Not like I've got anything for him to do.'

'Still quiet then?'

Rossi winced and turned in her chair, almost knocking over the single plant they had in the office. 'What did you say?'

Murphy leant back in his chair, smirking as he watched the young DC as he realised his mistake.

'Er . . . nothing. I mean . . . nothing new?'

Rossi moved towards Harris, 'You said the fucking Q word, *che cazzo?* Say it again, I dare you. *Cagacazzo.*'

'What? I don't . . . I didn't mean . . . '

Murphy sat forward, palms out. 'Calm down, it's just a stupid superstition. No reason to start anything, okay?'

Rossi turned towards him, her features relaxing as she saw his face. '*Va bene.* It's okay.' She sat back in her chair and went back to her computer screen.

Murphy worried that Rossi calling a DC a dickhead in Italian was going to be the height of excitement for the day.

He needn't have.

A few minutes later the other DC who was sharing the office with them came bursting through the door. New guy, just transferred. Murphy had enough problems remembering the names of those who'd been there years, without new ones being thrown into the mix.

'We're on. Body found in suspicious circumstances outside the church in West Derby.'

Murphy jumped up out of his seat at about the exact moment Rossi turned on Harris.

'What did I tell you? You had to say the word, didn't you. *Brutto figlio di puttana bastardo.*'

Murphy knew Harris had understood only one of the words Rossi had spat at him as she grabbed her black jacket from behind her chair. 'Knock it off, Laura.'

Rossi muttered under her breath in reply to him. He had to hold back a laugh. 'Come on. Let's just get down there. You know how these things can turn out. It's probably nothing.'

Which was perhaps a worse thing to say than the Q word.

2

Dead bodies. Decayed or fresh. Crawling with maggots, flies buzzing around your face as you examine them in light or darkness. Or, a serenity surrounding them, framed in a pale light as if time has come to a stop for them. There's no tangible difference, really. They're all the same, each with their own tale to tell, how the end has come.

It doesn't matter how many times you see one, it never gets easier. Not in reality. You can kid yourself; pretend that you're immune to it, that it doesn't affect you any more. That's all it is though — a pretence, a deception. A way of getting through it.

There was a simple answer in Murphy's opinion. Seeing death makes you contemplate your own . . . and most people spend their lives actively trying to avoid their own death. Even those risk-takers jumping off cliffs with a tea towel as a parachute are only giving themselves the thrill of cheating death. They'd leave the tea towel behind if they really wanted to die.

Once the initial shock kicks in, an unconscious mental process clicks into place and professionalism takes over. Makes you forget about what it is you're dealing with. That's the way Murphy thought of it. He imagined a shutter going down in one part of his mind, thoughts and feelings closed away and a detachment appearing.

The only time it took a bit longer for that process to occur was when they were below a certain age.

This one was on the cusp.

West Derby is a small town just past Anfield, around fifteen minutes from the city centre. Only a few minutes away from the more infamous estates of Norris Green and Croxteth, it was also the home of Alder Hey Hospital and Liverpool F.C.'s training ground, Melwood.

Now it would gain its own little piece of notoriety.

Murphy stood in the gravel entrance to St Mary's Church in West Derby — Croxteth Park off in the distance — having arrived a few minutes before the forensic team and pathologist, by some miracle. On the steps leading into the church lay what they'd been called for. A young white boy, or maybe a man. He could never tell age these days. Laid on his side, one arm tucked beneath him, the other draped across himself. Eyes closed over a destroyed face. A mask of smeared blood — an attempt to wash it off, perhaps? — which did little to deflate the impact. Open wounds on the cheeks, skin splitting on numerous areas. Red flesh on show above his mouth, his nose misshapen and swollen. Eyes puffed up under the swelling. A faded scar just below his eyebrow was noticeable only as it seemed to be the lone part of his face that was untouched. The grey-silver of healed skin stark against the surrounding reds, browns and blacks.

Rossi finished talking to a uniformed constable

and walked back towards Murphy. 'Well?' he said as she reached him.

'Two twelve-year-old lads found him. They were walking through the park to school and spotted him. Thought it was a tramp at first, but looking closer they saw his face and realised he wasn't breathing. They pegged it, right into the vicar, or whatever they call them, who was arriving for the day. He was the one who called it in.'

'They notice anything?'

'They're a bit shaken up, but adamant they didn't see anything else. They walk past here every day apparently.'

Murphy finished snapping on a pair of latex gloves, his faded black shoes similarly covered, and bent down to look at the body closer up, wincing as he looked at the victim's face.

'How old do you reckon?' Rossi said from above him.

'Not sure. Can't really tell with these kinds of injuries to his face. All these kids look much older than we ever did at that age.'

'That's probably just us getting old.'

Murphy grunted in reply and went back to studying the face of the male lying prostrate on the ground. A thick band of purplish red around his neck drew his attention.

'Fiver says it's strangulation.'

'I'm not betting on cause of death, sir.'

Shuffling shoes and shouted orders inter-rupted Murphy before he could respond. He looked up, trying to effect a look of innocence as Dr Stuart Houghton, the lead pathologist in the city of Liverpool, bounded over. The doctor had grown even larger in the past year, meaning he moved slowly enough for Murphy to pull away from the body before Houghton arrived on the scene.

'You touched anything?'

'Morning to you an' all, Doctor,' Murphy said, avoiding meeting the doctor's eyes.

'Yeah, yeah. What have we got here?'

'I thought you could tell me that.'

A large intake of breath as Houghton got to his haunches. 'We'll see.' He snapped his own pair of gloves on and began examining the body.

'How long?' Murphy said after watching Houghton work for a minute or three.

'Rigour is only just beginning to fade. At least twelve hours, I'd say. Body has been moved here.' Houghton lifted the man-boy's eyelids, revealing milky coffee eyes staring past him, the whites surrounding them speckled with burst blood vessels. A thin, cloudy film pasted across them.

Murphy stepped to the side as Houghton's assistant finished erecting the white tent around him. 'Anything on him?'

Houghton finished fishing around the pockets of the black joggers which the victim was wearing. 'Nothing at all. Was expecting a psalm or bible quote or something, given where we are.'

Murphy shrugged. 'Could be nothing religious about it. Something we'll be looking into, obviously.' A religious nut or someone with a grudge to bear against the church. Murphy didn't like the thought of either.

29

'He's been laid here on purpose, in this manner. Almost looks peaceful, just curled up. Like he just came here, lay down and went peacefully. As always, first glance is deceiving. Looks like he was strangled with some kind of ligature. Not before he was quite severely beaten.' Houghton paused, rolling the torn T-shirt up over the victim's flat teenaged stomach. Wisps of fine hair tracing a line towards a recessed belly button, barely visible behind angry red markings turning purple and black. 'Bruises to his abdomen. Some old, some new. This boy was beaten severely before death. I'm guessing four . . . no, five broken ribs. Pretty sure there'll be more broken bones to find as well. Also, there's his face of course.'

'This has been going on a while then. The older bruises, I mean.'

'Could be. I'll have more answers after the PM of course.'

Murphy nodded before beckoning over a forensics tech from the Evidence Recovery Unit — ERU — towards him. 'Prioritise this one, Doc. The media will be all over us before we know it. Dead teen in suspicious circumstances and outside a church, with these injuries? Easy headlines.'

Houghton sighed at him in response, but before he could give a fuller answer Murphy moved away to meet the ERU tech — a white-suited woman with only her deep green eyes on display before she removed the mask covering the bottom half of her face.

'Yes?'

30

'I want a fingertip search of the whole area of the church. Inside and out. Pathways which run alongside it as well. I'll see how far we can cordon the place off.'

'We know the drill. Just make sure none of your uniforms get in the way.'

Murphy attempted a smile, which obviously looked more sardonic than he'd meant, judging by her reaction — a roll of the eyes and a turn away. He was always making friends.

'Laura?' Murphy called, Rossi lifting a finger which told him he was to wait whilst she finished talking to Houghton. She'd always got on well with the doctor, annoying Murphy no end. He still wasn't exactly sure what he'd done in the past to piss off the old bastard, but was now so used to it he wasn't sure he was all that arsed.

Rossi eventually finished her conversation a few seconds later, straightening up and strolling over to him.

'What do you want to do first?'

Murphy finished removing the latex gloves, walking away as he did so. Rossi followed him. 'Interview the priest, vicar, whatever he's called, first. Then the kids who found the victim. Tell the uniforms to take them back to the station. Inform the parents, get social services to meet us. They might need counselling or whatever.'

'Okay. Anything else?'

'Door to doors,' Murphy replied, looking up towards the main road at the bottom of the gravel drive which led to the church. 'Although there aren't that many in the immediate vicinity.'

'There's more houses on the other side of the

church; Meadow Lane leading into Castlesite Road. Close enough. There's some flats above the shops on the main road as well.'

'Okay, good. Make sure the uniforms know this is a murder investigation. I don't want them thinking it's just some scally who got in a fight.'

'Sir?'

'Call it a gut reaction, Laura. Some of those bruises are old, fading. Signs of abuse. Something's not right.'

Rossi nodded slowly, writing down the last bit of info in her notebook before looking back at him. 'That it?'

'Yeah. I'll see if the vicar can accommodate us.'

The Farm

Six Months Ago

Goldie was alive, there was that at least. When he'd first been grabbed off the street, beaten until he could barely breathe without feeling the pain all over his body, he'd felt for sure that was it. That he'd pissed off the wrong person once too often and was now going to pay the price. He'd heard stories about the gangsters out there in the city and what they could do to you if they wanted.

He was expecting the end. Tried to work out which dealer he hadn't paid properly or what he'd promised that he hadn't delivered, but couldn't think of a thing.

When he was dragged along the muddy track outside, a sawn-off shotgun pointed at his chest the whole way, Goldie was thinking about all the things he was about to lose.

It amounted to very little.

There was his family, he guessed. What was left of it, anyway. One brother locked up, doing at least fifteen years for manslaughter. Hadn't seen his dad in years — didn't much care.

Now there was just him and his mum. And whoever she was seeing at the time, of course.

That was all gone. All he had now was the large room they'd shoved him in, the darkness within masking its real form. He ached from the

33

ride in the back of the van and the beating inside. His breathing was shallow, as the adrenaline he'd been feeling earlier began to wane and he became used to sucking in full lungfuls of oxygen again.

That's the thing they never showed you on TV. When your mouth is gagged, you have to breathe through your nose. Goldie's had been broken a few years before that night, which had left it resembling one of those shit paintings he'd seen in art, by the bloke with one ear or something. Or that other one. Art wasn't exactly his strongest subject. That earlier injury had left his nose skew-whiff, at an angle. Bone blocking one nostril, so breathing with his mouth closed became difficult after a while.

He waited a few minutes, just kneeling down in the dark, breathing in and out. Wondering why they'd left him there.

'Hello?'

The voice came from across the room as a whisper, shitting Goldie up big time. He scrabbled back, only being stopped by the solid wall behind him and the pain that resulted from hitting it.

'Who's there?'

The voice was a little louder now, more hiss than whisper. Goldie sensed something behind it.

Fear.

He felt the same way.

Goldie stood up, his eyes still adjusting to the pitch black, and began slowly feeling his way forwards. Arms out in front of him, sweeping his legs back and forth.

'I'm Goldie, mate. Where are you?'

'Over by my bed.'

Goldie stopped as he heard the reply come from a couple of feet away from him to his left. His eyes were adjusting now, the shape and form of things becoming clearer. He could make out a bed, two in fact, on his left. Mirrored to his right. That was it though. No other furniture.

He could smell piss coming from further away.

'What's your name?' Goldie said, coming to a stop at the bed opposite.

'Dean. Just got here?'

Goldie nodded, before thinking better of it. 'Yeah. What's going on? Why do you keep fuckin' whispering?'

There was a creak from the bed as Dean moved, Goldie imagined rather than saw.

'Because they're out there, listening all the time. You don't want them to get mad. Believe me.'

Goldie barked a laugh. 'You're paranoid, lad.'

He wouldn't find it funny after a while.

★ ★ ★

Things were calm for the first few days. They'd drop meals off for the two of them. Dean told him he'd been there for a few weeks at least. Two men had taken him, he thought. He wasn't sure, as it'd happened fast and he'd been a bit stoned.

Goldie didn't believe the things he said had been done to him since then.

Light got into the room during the day. Not

35

enough to be comfortable, but at least they could move about without worrying they'd bang into something in the darkness.

Boredom was the problem in the beginning. Goldie decided to fill his time trying to find a way out of there, examining every part of the room.

By the third day he'd given up. There was nothing to find. Every inch was solid, reinforced.

The only way out was through the door which he'd come in.

He began watching them as they dropped off meals. Food in sealed packaging. None of the stuff he was used to eating, proper horrible stuff like tasteless rice and salad. He would have thrown it back, but he was starving after the first day.

Every time they came inside was the same. The door would be unlocked, more than one lock on the outside, Goldie noted, the door swinging open, light rushing in. The eight times it had happened, there'd never been less than three of them. Two of them had either a sawn-off or a bigger gun, like you'd use on *Call of Duty*. Assault rifle, Goldie reckoned. He'd told Dean that, but not really got anything in response.

'Dean,' Goldie had said on day four, whilst they were eating a meal of some kind of mashed potato and meat, 'we should rush them when they drop the food off.'

'No . . .'

'Hear me out, lad. We could get either side of the door and surprise them. Have them over and then get the fuck out of here.'

'It won't work. And then you'd have to go on the rack. Trust me, you don't want to go on that.'

'What's the rack?' Goldie said, his brow furrowing.

'You don't wanna know . . . '

'Pretend I do,' Goldie replied, an edge to his voice. The look on Dean's face made him pause though. The lad had started sweating, his hands shaking a little . . . then more.

'I . . . I . . . No. They told me not to say anything.'

'Like I give a shi — '

'No,' Dean's voice echoed around the room. 'I'm not saying nothing.'

Goldie considered pushing harder, but Dean was now sitting on the bed, knees drawn up to his chest with his arms wrapped around them, silently rocking. Whispering to himself words which Goldie couldn't hear.

Goldie recognised what just thinking about the rack had caused in Dean.

Terror.

★ ★ ★

Day five was when it started. Three of them arrived, with Goldie expecting the same process as before. Food dropped off, no questions answered. Any movement met with a point of a weapon.

It was different this time though. No food. Two of them came towards him as the other aimed a rifle at his chest. Strong hands gripped each of his arms and pulled him along.

37

Helplessness. That's the effect a bullet can have on you. It wasn't the gun so much. Not after he'd got used to it being pointed at him. All he could think about was what it contained. Tiny little things that would rip him apart. Kill him in a second.

They led him out of the building he'd begun to get used to, out into the cold winter air of December. He could see his breath as he exhaled, hoping that would continue as the memory of his mouth being gagged came back to him.

'What's going on?' he asked, chancing it. Not wanting to talk too much.

There was no response. Goldie measured himself up against the two people in balaclavas holding onto his arms, deciding he could probably take them if needs be.

If he could work out a way of doing it before being hit by a bullet, he'd do it. He didn't want to turn into Dean back in the room. Scared for his life. Not yet.

He was led back inside another building, a large desk in a room, someone in a black balaclava and a suit sitting behind one side. It wasn't so much a desk, Goldie thought as he was dumped onto the chair opposite the man, as a long table. A red cloth covered the surface, barely hanging over the edges.

Goldie stared across at the balaclava-suit man, not willing to break eye contact. Two of those who had brought him here left the room, leaving only rifle man and the weird get-up sitting across from him. There was something so odd about the combination of a bally and a pristine suit, which Goldie could tell was no Burton's Menswear special. Nah, this was money. Made to measure, he thought.

'Nice suit. Wanna tell me what the fuck you think you're doing?'

His voice sounded exactly as he wanted it to. Hard as fuck. Don't-fuck-me-about hard.

'Be quiet. Learn to speak when spoken to, understand?'

Goldie forgot about the gun being pointed at him for a second. 'Fuck off. Don't talk at me like that.'

He heard, rather than saw, the whipcrack as Bally-Suit man raised and struck his face with something. A few seconds of nothing, before the pain cut in.

Stinging, burning. His face on fire, from ear to nose in an almost straight line. Goldie pulled his hand away from his cheek where it'd flown in reaction, looking at it as if it wasn't his. Blood, thin lines of red. Broken skin, broken face.

Burning.

'This is something my dad gave me. He no longer had any need to use it, so passed it down. I only ever got it once, that was enough. I deserved it then as well.' Bally-Suit man was standing now, his accent softening as he spoke. 'It's like a riding whip, what you'd see a jockey using. Only this is worse. Thinner, more pliable.'

Bally-Suit man moved around the table-desk and came close to Goldie as he held his face with one hand, trying to decide if punching this dick now or later would be preferable.

'You're going to learn some manners, young man. And learn them quick.'

Goldie took his hand away from where he'd been stroking the burning, turning to face Bally-Suit man. 'Fuck you,' he spat.

Bally-Suit man sighed through the covering and shook his head at him.

The crack came again, quicker than Goldie could react. Across the other side of his face. As he went backwards, away from the pain, Bally-Suit man kicked at his chair, sending him flying. Goldie's head cracked against the floor, making him dizzy for a second or three before his senses returned, his fists balling and swinging.

Laughter rang back at him as he punched thin air, then pain flared across his thighs as the crack hit there. Then all the wind rushed out of him as a boot flew into his stomach. He tried to get up, one arm across his middle, but a boot on his neck stopped him.

'Stay down. I don't want to have to put you on the rack first day.'

Goldie glanced towards the table-desk as the cloth fell from it, revealing something he couldn't work out. Restraints and wood. In any other setting it would have barely caused a second glance. Seeing it there, Goldie began to breathe quicker, trying to swallow.

Goldie shook his head clear, tried moving again. 'Am I fuck lying down for you,' he said, pushing away the boot from his neck.

His voice wasn't as good as before. The hardness was already going, leaving him, getting

40

the fuck out of there while it still could. If he wasn't alone, maybe it would have been different; with his boys backing him up, things wouldn't be the same at all. As it was, Goldie was on his own, and the prick in the bally-suit was standing over him with some whip type of thing that was causing him a lot of pain and he couldn't even see it coming.

'You don't understand, do you?'

'Understand what?' Goldie said, pulling himself onto all fours as the man backed away from him.

'You're under our control now. You'll do as we say, or there will be consequences.'

Goldie spat out a long drool of saliva onto the floor, eyes widening as he saw the redness of fresh blood mixed in with it. 'You going to kill me, is that it? What for? I ain't done nothing to you.'

Bally-Suit man laughed at him. 'Course you have. You and all your mates. Everyone like you. Young boys with big mouths.'

A boot flew into Goldie's stomach, flipping him over onto his back and making him cry out in pain before his breath caught.

'You're disrespectful, arrogant and nothing but a stain on this city,' Bally-Suit man said, standing over him. 'Well, that's going to start changing. *You're* going to start changing. Starting now.'

Goldie closed his eyes to the pain which was beginning to kick in from the beating, as Bally-Suit man crouched down and leant closer.

'And if we're not happy with your *progress*, well . . . let's just say you'll be begging for a little

41

roughing-up like I've just given you. I have many ways of making you accept change.'

Goldie opened his eyes, but the man was no longer there. Just the two in balaclavas holding guns as before.

He got up with some help, and allowed himself to be led back to what he would soon call the Dorm.

And hoped it wouldn't be the last place he could call home.

3

Reverend. Not vicar or priest. The Church of England always confused Murphy. Catholic guilt was much more his forte, forever cursed to carry that around with him. Sister Margaret Mary rapping your knuckles for getting a line wrong in the Stations of the Cross, or a proper beating for anything closely resembling *impure thoughts*. Every bloke Murphy's age who had grown up Catholic had the same stories. Thankfully, his parents had grown out of religion before too long. C of E always struck Murphy as more tea and biscuits than the hell and eternal damnation his own church had taught him.

Reverend Andrew Pearson. Wild haired, with a grey, bushy beard and bright blue eyes which seemed to dart in every direction at once. Murphy imagined he was usually much more expressive, but today he was sombre, one hand clasped over the other in his lap as if to restrain himself from making any sudden gestures. With the interior of the church currently out of bounds whilst it was searched for evidence, they had convened in one of the marked police vans which were now at the scene — Murphy and Rossi sitting on one side, facing the reverend.

'Sorry about the less-than-comfortable sur-roundings, Reverend,' Murphy said, already feeling the strain of sitting in a confined space. Being six foot four had its drawbacks. 'Hopefully this won't take too long.'

'Not a problem,' the reverend replied. Murphy noticed the accent wasn't local. From outside the city, he guessed.

'I'm Detective Inspector David Murphy and this is Detective Sergeant Laura Rossi. We just want to ask a few questions about what happened this morning. Okay?'

'Of course. But I did tell the other officers I don't know all that much. Just the boys running towards me, looking like they'd had the shock of their young lives. I guess they probably had.'

'I see. What time was this?'

'Around half eight. Bit later than I usually arrive to the church, but I was delayed this morning. A few phone calls I had to make regarding an upcoming event. If I'd been on time, those poor boys wouldn't have had to go through the shock.'

Murphy stretched his legs out slowly. 'Do you live close by?'

'Yes, the vicarage is only around the corner.'

'And you weren't disturbed overnight? Anything you can remember at all?'

The reverend shook his head. 'I'm afraid not. I went to bed around eleven and slept through until seven. Didn't hear a sound.'

'Did you recognise the victim?' Rossi said after a few seconds of silence.

'No. We don't see many teenagers in the congregation, I'm afraid. Especially males. We have a choir, with a healthy number of boys, but once they reach eleven, twelve, thirteen, they seem to find much more interesting things to be

44

doing. We try our best of course, but there's too much pressure from outside.'

'I guess,' Rossi replied, writing in her notebook. 'Did you enter the church after finding the victim?'

'Only to use the phone in the office.'

'Anything out of place?'

The reverend made a show of thinking for a few seconds before answering. 'Nothing I can think of. It was still locked up and there wasn't anything obvious to indicate anyone had been in there. I imagine your people will be able to tell if that's the case or not.'

Murphy nodded, thinking the fingertip search he'd ordered of inside the church might prove to be a waste of time. 'Better to be safe than sorry.'

'How long do you think this will take, Inspector? Only we're supposed to have midweek services this evening.'

Murphy raised an eyebrow at Rossi before turning back to the reverend. 'Forgive the bluntness, Reverend, but as long as it takes. At the moment, the church is a crime scene, and the most important thing is ensuring that we gather all the evidence we need.'

Reverend Pearson brought his index fingers together and bounced them off his chin, nodding slightly at the answer. 'Of course. I'm sure the congregation will understand.'

'Thank you. We'll keep you up to date with what is happening.'

'I appreciate that,' Reverend Pearson replied, bringing his palms down and smacking them onto his knees. 'I will be praying for the young man and your investigation.'

Murphy shot Rossi a look as she choked back what he hoped sounded like a cough to the reverend, rather than the laugh he knew it was. 'Yeah, thanks for that. We appreciate *any* help we receive.' He took a card from his wallet and handed it over. 'Just in case you have any further questions.'

★　★　★

'Not religious then, Laura?'

Murphy was leading them back to where the victim's body was in the process of being bagged up to be taken to the morgue for the post-mortem. The mood amongst the various technical officers and uniforms was more solemn than usual. Murphy guessed it was the setting, rather than the dead body.

'Not in the slightest. All a load of rubbish, isn't it? *Cazzata*,' Rossi replied, tying her hair back as she spoke.

'Thought all Italians were religious?'

'Probably more so back in the old country, but once they were outside — over here — my parents never bothered. Much to my nonna's delight of course.'

Murphy snorted. 'Well, let's hope this isn't a religious thing then. Can't imagine you'd be much use.'

Rossi stopped, placing a hand on Murphy's arm. The height difference meant she was almost at his wrist, when she was probably aiming for a bicep. 'No, don't get me wrong. I might not be religious, but I know my stuff. Religion is fascinating. Especially sociologically speaking. I just don't believe in the magic man in the sky bit.'

Murphy looked down at her and smiled thinly at the echo of his own thoughts. 'Probably best to keep your voice down a bit. You're standing on hallowed ground here,' he said, motioning towards the church before walking on.

'Yeah . . . I'm about to get struck down by God's wrath any second now,' Rossi muttered under her breath, just about loud enough for him to hear. He bit on his lip in order to stifle the laughter.

'You're not, are you?' Rossi said, as she caught up with him. 'Don't mean to offend, if you are . . . '

Murphy shook his head. 'No. Not really. It'd be nice, I suppose, but I think I've been doing this too long to believe.'

Rossi looked away, nodding. 'Anyway,' she said finally, 'what next . . . the kids?'

'Yes. Have they been taken to the station?'

Rossi looked around and beckoned someone in uniform over. 'I'll just check.'

Murphy left her to it, turning to watch as the tent cover surrounding the body was pulled back and the trolley which would transport it to either a van or ambulance was taken closer to the scene. The victim was now completely covered in black for its first step in the journey of a murder investigation.

Well, almost its first step. What happened to the boy before it had arrived here was the beginning, really.

47

'The lads are at the station. Parents are meeting us there,' Rossi said, appearing at his side. 'But, more importantly, we've got a name for the victim.'

'That was quick,' Murphy replied. 'Thought they didn't find anything on the body?'

Rossi shook her head, grinning slightly. 'Didn't need to. A uniform recognised him. Reckons he's had a few dealings with him in the past.' She pointed to an officer who was sitting on the small outer wall on the perimeter of the church. 'PC Michael Hale.'

'I've seen him before somewhere,' Murphy said, walking towards PC Hale, Rossi in step next to him.

'Same here. Can't place him though. Probably some other scene.'

'Hmmm. Possibly.'

They reached the PC, who broke off from speaking to another officer to greet them

'Sorry about that,' PC Hale said, once the officer had left.

'It's no problem,' Murphy said, looking Hale up and down. 'I've been told you know the victim?'

'Yeah,' PC Hale said, stroking a leather-gloved hand over his face. Three-day stubble, intentionally shaped and clipped. 'Had the *pleasure* of his company over the years. If you know what I mean . . . '

Murphy waited, the silence growing between the three of them until Rossi filled it.

'Well? What are you waiting for?'

'Oh, sorry. His name is Dean Hughes. Lives

48

over in Norris Green. Part of the crew there. Always in trouble for something or other. Those gangs are the bane of our lives — in uniform, you know. One of the reasons I'm trying to move over to work with you guys.'

'Right,' Murphy said, trying to decide on his first impression and finding it wasn't good. 'And you can tell, even with what's happened to his face?'

PC Hale nodded. 'I've seen him at his worst, after fights and that. It's definitely him.'

'So, how old is he?'

'Think he's eighteen now. Not sure. Haven't seen him around for a while, so thought he'd either been banged up without me knowing, or got some girl pregnant and was trying to go straight. Never happens though.'

'What doesn't?'

'Going *straight*. Those types . . . they're always up to something. Can't help themselves. Doing normal stuff just doesn't come natural. Waking up early, going to work, doing an honest job . . . they can't handle it. Rather sit at home on their arses and go on the rob at night. Looks like someone might have done us a favour here, if you ask me.'

Murphy knew the sort PC Hale was referring to — even had some sympathy for the bitterness which had crept into Hale from years of dealing with this type — but he still decided his first impression was right. Hale was a prick. 'Is that what your dealings with Dean were mainly about . . . robbing, that sort of thing?' Murphy said, aware of Rossi bridling beside him.

'All sorts, really. Street robbery, violence, drink, drugs . . . '

'Drugs?' Rossi interjected, just as Murphy was taking a breath.

'Yeah, only a bit of weed and that. Nothing major. I'm sure you'll see his record soon enough, but I imagine it wasn't just me who was picking him up most weekends. Proper little scrote. Used to take him home to his mum and she'd be just as bad. More pissed off with us than the little shit we'd took home for her. The state of that house as well . . . Jesus. Five kids, probably five different dads, I reckon. None sticking around for more than the two minutes it took to get her up the duff. You know the type. What do these people expect if that's how they're brought up?'

Murphy couldn't help but glower at Hale a little. 'Well thanks for the speech, PC Hale. Good to know a bit of background about the victim . . . you know, the dead teenager?'

Hale focussed past Murphy and Rossi at the church behind them. Murphy followed his gaze. 'Yeah,' Hale said eventually, 'no problem.'

'Let's go,' Rossi said, pulling once on Murphy's arm before walking away. 'I can't hear any more *merda* right now.'

Murphy said goodbye for both of them and turned towards the church entrance where they'd parked up earlier, and walked quickly to catch up to Rossi. Heard PC Hale ask a fellow uniformed officer what *merda* might mean, and smiled in spite of himself.

'You sorted here?' Murphy said, as he reached

50

his car — Rossi leaning against the passenger door, waiting.

'Of course.'

'Let's get back then. See what these kids have to say and then make plans.'

4

The car journey back to the station was silent, broken only with long sighs from Rossi who sat beside Murphy. The four miles back to the city centre should have taken fifteen minutes but was taking much longer due to traffic going back into town.

'Okay. I give in,' Murphy said, as they stopped at yet another set of traffic lights. 'What's up with you today?'

Another sigh. 'Nothing.'

'I know that means something. Come on, open up. You've been in a frigging foul mood all morning. I haven't heard this much swearing in a foreign language since I last went to an away match in Europe.'

'Just family stuff.'

Ah, Murphy thought, should have guessed. 'Which is it this time . . . job, love life?'

'The second one, nicely tied with the first this time around. Wanting to know why I haven't settled down yet. They've started blaming the job.'

'Surely you're used to it by now?'

Rossi examined a nail and started biting it. 'You'd think, but no. Anyway, it doesn't matter.'

Murphy sneaked a glance, seeing Rossi with another finger in her mouth. 'I'm sure they'll ease off a bit eventually. But I bet it doesn't help that all your brothers are settling down now.'

'Not all of them. Vincenzo still refuses to move in with that girl he got pregnant. And I'm pretty certain Sonny is seeing someone behind his wife's back. Apart from that though, they're all diamonds in my ma's eyes. Just me who's the disappointment.'

Murphy opened his mouth to answer, but Rossi cut him off.

'Never mind. I can't be arsed talking about it. Let's forget it. I'll try and be a bit nicer.'

A car beeped behind them as the traffic picked up pace ahead. Murphy released the handbrake again, beating the traffic lights this time and finally picking up some speed down the West Derby Road. Housing estates on one side of the A road, an endless array of shops on the opposite. Betting shops, Greggs, takeaways and those new clothes places he'd suddenly seen popping up everywhere a couple of years back. Sell your old clothes for sixty pence a kilo. Minutes up the road from the middle-class suburbs in the outskirts of the city and the differences could be seen everywhere.

Murphy didn't like to ponder too much on the endless paradoxes of his home city. Enough to send anyone mad. How could the well-off and the poor be so close together? It didn't make any kind of sense to him. He just assumed it was the same all over the country — probably more so in these post-recession times — and tried to get on with his life.

'What's the plan then?' Rossi said, interrupting his thoughts.

'Confirm the ID of the victim, interview the

kids who found him, then go from there,'
Murphy replied, spying the Radio City tower in
the distance — the signal that he was almost
in town and would be at the station before long.
'You know, the usual.'

'I almost hope we're done by the end of the
day. I know we've not been busy, but I could do
without a murder investigation.'

'Couldn't we all,' Murphy replied.

'Just let me know if it starts getting to you. We
haven't had one since . . . well, you know.'

Murphy didn't answer straight away, but his
thoughts instantly went back to the scene at
his parents' house two years ago. The violence
inflicted on them, the death. It was always there,
just on the surface of his memory, the slightest
trigger bringing it forth again. Breath going
shallow as he fought to keep the emotions down,
determined not to slip into the same situation he
had found himself in the year before. Lead
detective on the biggest murder case his division
had seen in years — a serial killer at that — but
he'd been toyed with and manipulated. Mentally
and physically.

'Sir . . . you still with me?'

Murphy blinked back the images and looked
out the windscreen towards the slowing traffic in
front of him.

'Yeah . . . I'm fine. Just . . . doesn't take much,
Laura.'

'Sorry.'

'Don't be. I'm sound. This is nothing like the
last one.'

And it wasn't. Not yet.

* * *

Murphy held his phone in one hand, comparing it to the photo which was staring back at him from the computer screen. 'I can't really tell,' he said, squinting and moving the phone around to try and see better, 'this phone keeps going dark.'

Rossi leant across the desk. 'Give it here, will you.'

Murphy allowed her to snatch the phone out of his hands. One day he'd learn how these things worked, but for now he was happy to let others do it for him. 'All right, you do it then.'

'See,' Rossi said, flashing the phone in his face before going back to studying it again, 'here's your problem. You've turned off autorotate. And you have to keep your finger on the screen to keep it backlit.'

A lot of words which meant pretty much fuck all to Murphy. 'Of course,' he replied.

'What do you reckon?'

Murphy nodded. Rossi had managed to enlarge the photo of the victim, which had been sent to his mobile a few minutes earlier, so that it fit the screen. 'Obviously can't be sure, but certainly looks like him.'

A photo of Dean Hughes filled his computer monitor. A mugshot taken during his last arrest. 'This is eight months old, but I'm almost sure it's him. Look at the scar above the eyebrow.'

'Yeah,' Rossi replied, leaning over him to look closer, 'looks like it to me.'

Murphy began reading the information which was attached. 'Arrested and then cautioned for

55

Section Five. Hughes was 'drunk and aggressive — believed all coppers to be complete 'twats.'' Sounds delightful.'

'How many arrests are there?'

Murphy scrolled down the list. 'Jesus . . . at least twenty. That's just page one. That guy Hale was right. He was used to dealing with us.'

'When was the last time we had any contact with him there?'

Murphy frowned as he went back over the record. 'Odd. Seems like he was in trouble quite regularly up until seven months ago. Then . . . nothing.'

'Weird. Was he banged up?'

Murphy checked further. 'No. Nothing about that. No court appearances scheduled or anything.'

Rossi tapped a pen against her teeth, far too close to Murphy's ears for comfort. 'What's his address?'

'Clanfield Road. Norris Green.'

'Check to see if there's anything else.'

Murphy clicked through to the HOLMES database. HOLMES 2 as it was officially called, after an upgrade during the nineties, stored information on a variety of features, most of which Murphy never had time for. Case management, material disclosure . . . it was really just a dumping ground for every piece of information anyone working in the police received.

'Here we go,' Murphy said, sitting up in his chair, 'he was reported missing.'

Rossi came back around the desk. 'When?'

'Get onto this . . . seven months ago.'

'Well, that explains things. He's been off getting into all kinds of shit, and now it's caught up with him?'

'Maybe,' Murphy replied, leaning back in his chair. 'But it didn't look like he'd been living on the streets or anything. He looked, well, normal. Like he'd been looking after himself. For someone dead, anyway.'

'I guess. I didn't really look at him all that closely, to be honest.'

Murphy drummed his fingers on his desk, thinking back to the image of the victim he'd taken in his mind earlier that morning. A snapshot, something to keep in his head whilst he was working. 'Clean fingernails,' he said, after a few moments of silence.

'What?' Rossi replied, holding her hand out in front of her and studying it.

'He had clean fingernails. I'm sure of it.'

'Okay . . . '

'We'll have to check at the PM of course, but I'm pretty positive they were clean. If he was living rough, or in some dosshouse somewhere, they wouldn't be, would they?'

Rossi looked at him with a blank face, which set Murphy on edge. He didn't like being thought of as spouting rubbish. He'd seen that look reflected at him too often in the past, and he thought he was finally getting away from it.

'I'm serious, Laura,' he went on, after waiting a few seconds for her to respond and not getting anything. 'This could be important. If he's been missing seven months, we'll need to know where he was. We can narrow the search straight off if he's been somewhere where he'd have been able to keep clean.'

Rossi finally nodded, sparks hitting her eyes as she realised what he'd been implying. 'I get you now. Good thinking, sir.'

'It's what I'm paid to do. Now, let's get a picture of him from Doctor Houghton — get it over to the family. I want an ID sorted quickly.' Murphy stood, leaving the smaller office and crossing into the wider office which housed the rest of the CID team. He strode over to the whiteboards which detailed the ongoing cases and began making a few notes underneath where someone had added that morning's new victim.

'Right,' Murphy said, turning to face the few DCs who had been watching him. 'Who's going through initial neighbour reports?'

DC Sagan raised her hand. 'Me, but there's nothing there at the moment. No one heard anything in the adjoining street to the church. Only four houses were occupied when uniforms knocked though, so there'll be more later when they're back from work or whatever.'

'Okay,' Murphy replied, eyeing a particularly unpleasant sight trundling over towards the group. DS Tony Brannon, polluting the air as he walked, eating a packet of crisps, spilling crumbs across the carpet. A pain in the arse, but one Murphy had in check, he hoped. 'Keep collecting reports,' Murphy continued. 'I want you in constant contact with the uniforms at the scene. Plus, DC Harris and DS Brannon, I want you to go down to the scene and help with enquiries.'

DS Brannon managed to pause in between mouthfuls to blurt out, 'Oh, for fuck's sake . . . '

'Don't want to hear it, Tony. Just get your arse down there. I want something before the media start getting involved.'

'Fine,' Brannon replied. 'Come on, Harris.'

Murphy spied Rossi coming out of their office, beckoning him over. He turned back to the group of five DCs still looking at him. 'The rest of you go back to what cases you were doing before this morning. See if you can get anything sorted before being dragged into this one.'

'Death notice?' Rossi said, as Murphy reached the office door.

'We don't know yet, do we?' Murphy replied, moving past her and grabbing his suit jacket from the back of his chair. 'Let's get there and find out. You got the address?'

'Yeah.'

'Okay then. Give me a minute. Want to make sure the DCI knows what's going on.'

DCI Stephens was already standing in the doorway as he reached her office, down the corridor from his own. Her office was around the same size of his, but with the benefit of being for her alone.

'Was just coming to let you know the latest,' Murphy said, realising he was still holding his jacket. He began putting it on.

'I know, I heard. Didn't want to interrupt. Looks like you've got the basics covered. ID yet?'

'Almost sure of it. Some teenager from Norris Green . . . '

'Not a frigging gang thing, is it?' DCI

59

Stephens said, running a perfectly manicured hand through her loose hair. 'That's the last thing we want.'

'Not sure yet. There's a few things not adding up at the moment. I'd stay open-minded for the time being.'

'Okay. Well, the Chief Super has taken an interest already.'

'Really?' Murphy replied, surprised to hear notice had been taken.

'Body found in church grounds? He's already imagining all kinds. Don't worry about him, I'll keep him quiet for now. You concentrate on finding out who the vic is, and how he ended up dead outside a church.'

Murphy mocked a salute. 'Got it, boss.' Received a roll of DCI Stephens's eyes in response. He walked away before she could say anything more, finding Rossi in exactly the same position as he'd left her. 'Ready?'

'Of course.'

5

Murphy fiddled with the lever underneath the passenger seat, attempting to find the right motion which would move the seat backwards, removing his knees from underneath his chin. Sliding the chair back with a sudden bang, he ignored the stare from Rossi and went back to reading the criminal record of Dean Hughes.

It could have been his own from that age, had he not been much savvier. Every time Murphy had been in trouble as a teenager, he'd managed to get away with a warning here, a run away there. Not so much as an official caution, which was handy, given that he ended up joining the dark side himself.

Not that he saw it that way. The police service had given him purpose, a grounding. He could have been another lost statistic from the Speke estate. No drive to do anything other than get pissed with his mates and cause a bit of trouble. Boxing had helped, given him a sense of discipline, but when it became clear that he wasn't going to make it above domestic level, he jacked it in. Waste of time.

Murphy remembered his dad talking to him once, dragging him out of bed at around ten in the morning, which had annoyed Murphy no end, given he hadn't got home until four. His dad then had one of those conversations with him where he asked the questions Murphy had

no answer for. What was he doing with his life
. . . was this all he wanted . . . and where's your
keep, you little shit?

Just about to turn nineteen and he had no
clue. Working every few days or so, cash in hand,
and then blowing it on cider.

He couldn't remember who'd suggested
joining the police. It had just happened one day.
He wandered into Canning Place near Albert
Dock, having passed the initial application, and
sat down to do a Maths and English test. Then it
was the physical, which he'd passed with ease,
still retaining the fitness from the boxing. Then
two years on probation.

Fifteen years later and here he was, a detective
inspector a good few years ahead of schedule,
and at the forefront yet again.

'What was the address again?' Rossi said,
disturbing Murphy's trip down memory lane.

'Clanfield Road,' Murphy replied, checking the
notes on the top of the file. 'Head for Dwerryhouse Lane and I'll direct you from there.'

'Good, 'cause I get lost in all the back roads
around there.'

Murphy sniggered, knowing what she meant.
Norris Green was a larger place than most
people expected. A council estate with one of the
worst reputations in Liverpool at that moment
— mainly for gang violence. Since the murder of
a young boy outside a pub in nearby Croxteth,
the result of a longstanding feud between rival
gangs in Croxteth and Norris Green, with the
eleven-year-old boy, an innocent bystander, shot
in the back, the area had begun to change.

Gangs had been shown on TV in exploitative *documentaries* — and subsequently shunned for revealing supposed secrets of 'street-life' — and the DIY show from the BBC had made over the local youth club, giving some kids a place to go which wasn't in danger of falling down around them.

It was still a tough place to grow up though. Not much upward mobility in those kind of estates. And not many people trying to change that.

'Take the next left,' Murphy said, as they approached the end of Muirhead Avenue — Croxteth Park off to their right, still hidden by houses — the church where Dean Hughes's body had been found that morning close by, only a few minutes further away.

'Right here,' Murphy said, looking at the derelict patch of field which lay to their left. An upturned Iceland shopping trolley was the main attraction, along with empty carrier bags, various bottles and rubbish. 'You'd think they'd do something with that.'

'With what?' Rossi replied, indicating to turn.

'That big patch of green. Just going to waste. It just looks like an eyesore, 'cause no one's looking after it.'

'You know why. They're not willing to spend money around here. Reckon it'd just get wrecked, so they won't bother.'

'I suppose.'

Rossi slowed the car, looking for the right house number. 'It's bollocks though. That argument, I mean.'

'You think?'

'Course I do. If you put people in places like this, where everything is left to go to shit, what do you expect them to do? Everything's grey, dark. That's how your life is going to feel like. It's the *Broken Windows* theory.'

'The what?'

'The theory that if the area you live in looks like shite, then the people who live there will act like shite as well.'

Murphy smirked. 'And that's how it's put in the books, I imagine.'

Rossi snorted. 'More or less.'

Murphy thought she had a point, but didn't have chance to say so as she slowed the car and parked up.

'I really wish we could have phoned ahead,' Rossi said, unbuckling her seatbelt. 'I hate just turning up with no warning. Makes it worse.'

'Home number we had for them was out of use. Everyone has mobiles these days.'

The house they'd stopped outside of didn't scream 'house of a tearaway'. A sort of mid-terrace, with light brown stone brickwork. An archway separated the house from next door, but it was still connected on the top level. There were three wheelie bins on the small driveway, a few crisp packets lifting slightly in the breeze before settling back down against the fence. It was May, but Murphy shook his head as he noticed the house next door still had Christmas decorations hanging from the guttering — the clear icicles he'd noticed on market stalls in town, the previous December.

'You ready?' Murphy said as he pushed open the metal gate, the screeching sound as it slid across the ground making his hairs stand on end. It needed lifting, fixing or replacing.

'Are you?' Rossi replied, walking ahead of him and knocking on the door. Four short raps — the rent man's knock, as his mum used to say.

They stood waiting for a few seconds before Rossi knocked again, pulling back as they heard the barking.

'*Porca vacca*,' Rossi said under her breath.

'You don't like dogs, Laura?' Murphy said from behind a smile.

'Not ones that bark.'

A few more seconds passed before they heard shuffling from behind the door. A mortice lock turning on the old-style door, the house not being adorned with one of the newer double-glazed models. It opened inwards a few inches, a face appearing in the gap.

'Yeah?'

'Sally Hughes?' Murphy said, bending over so he wasn't towering over the small-statured mother of Dean Hughes.

'What's he done now?'

Murphy raised his eyebrows at the instant recognition of them as police, even though they were in plain clothes. 'Who?'

'Our Jack. What's he done? You're either police or bailiffs. So he either owes someone or you're trying to pin something on him.'

'I'm Detective Sergeant Laura Rossi, this is DI David Murphy . . . '

'Jack was here last night . . . '

Rossi held her hands out. 'It's not about Jack, Mrs Hughes. It's about Dean.'

Sally opened the door wider, a look of resignation flashing across her face before she swiped her hand across her forehead, moving damp, lifeless hair away from her face. 'Right. Well you better come in then.'

Sally walked away from them, locking the still-barking dog in another room before going through to what Murphy guessed was the living room on the left. He went in first, wiping his feet on a non-existent doormat without thinking and following her inside. He took the few steps into the living room, some American talk show snapping into silence as he walked into the room, the clattering of the remote control on a wooden coffee table.

''Scuse the mess. Haven't had chance to tidy up yet.' Sally lifted a cigarette box and in a couple of smooth movements lit a Silk Cut and took a drag.

Murphy savoured the smell of smoke which drifted his way, before perching on the couch which was to the side of the armchair where Sally was sitting, legs tucked underneath herself.

'What's he done then? Haven't seen him in months, so fucked if I know anything about it.'

Murphy glanced at Rossi, suddenly unsure how to proceed. If they opened with the fact Dean was dead, any information that may have been gleaned from a less stark opening might be lost. On the other hand, Murphy decided if his kid was dead, he'd want to know straight away.

'We found a body in West Derby this morning,

66

Sally. We think it's Dean.'

The reactions are never the same each time. Every time a quiet difference. During his career, Murphy had experienced the whole gamut of emotions being projected in his presence; from howling tears of grief to quiet stoicism. He'd learnt to not really put much stock in the initial reaction, not to make assumptions based on them.

'Fuck off.'

He'd not heard this one before.

'Don't be fucking stupid,' Sally Hughes continued, laughing as she tried to take another drag on her cigarette, 'look how serious you both are. Sorry lad, you've got the wrong house.'

Murphy breathed in. He'd seen the overall emotion of denial before — granted, it wasn't usually accompanied by laughter, but once you got to the core of it, it was denial all the same. 'Look at this picture for us, Sally,' Murphy said, taking the blown-up, A4-sized photograph of Dean Hughes from the manila folder he was carrying. 'Who do you see?'

Sally took a cursory glance at it, allowing her eyes to only alight on it for a few seconds. 'Yeah, that's not him.'

'What about this tattoo?' Murphy said, moving to another photograph which showed a tribal symbol found on the chest of the body.

'Loads of lads his age have got the same thing,' Sally said, still not looking at the photographs for more than a second.

Rossi moved out of the room beside Murphy, one quick glance passing between them. She'd be calling for support from family liaison officers, he hoped. Murphy leant forward, taking back the picture he'd handed to Sally and replacing it in the folder. 'Sally, we think it *is* Dean, so someone is going to come and take you down the Royal to make an identification,' — Murphy held up a hand to stop her interrupting — 'and if it's not him, then that'll be it.'

'It's a waste of time, this. He can't be there.'

'Why not?'

'He's only missing. Probably getting into all kinds of shit.' She stubbed out the cigarette into a clean ashtray. 'But I'd know if anything bad had happened.' She banged an open palm against her chest. 'I'd know in here. I'm his mum. I'd know.'

Murphy watched as her hands began shaking, struggling to pass a hand through her hair to brush it off her face. Her eyes betraying her as they filmed over.

'Sally . . . '

'Don't.' She interrupted as he began to speak. 'I'll go down there, but I'm telling you, it's a big mistake. Have you got kids?'

Murphy shook his head.

'Then you wouldn't know. I'm telling you, I'd feel it if he was gone. And I'm not feeling anything.'

Murphy let the silence hang in the air, staring at the crown of Sally's head as she leant forward, both hands grasping at her hair before sliding down and crossing over so she was hugging herself. Murphy blinked, and believed she'd aged ten years since they'd walked through the door, realising quickly it was a trick.

'They're on their way,' Rossi said softly, returning to the room. 'Be about fifteen minutes. Do you want a tea or something, Sally, while we wait?'

'It's all right,' Sally replied, forcing herself upright, 'I'll do it. You want one?'

Murphy shook his head, leaning back as Rossi followed Sally through.

Denial. He was sure it was on one of those lists about grief he'd once read. He just hoped acceptance wasn't too far behind.

6

Murphy and Rossi returned to the station, leaving the support officers with the task of taking Sally Hughes to the morgue to identify her son; Murphy hoped they'd managed to make Dean look presentable at least before showing his mother the body. Murphy was relieved that the next time they'd speak to her she might be more accepting of the reality. At the moment, they had little to go on without speaking to her, other than a list of people whom Dean Hughes might have spent most of his time with. He read through it as Rossi questioned the officers who had been going door to door around the church that morning. Murphy realised how long it had been since he'd been in uniform, where you'd come across the same people, the same names, over and over. Now the names meant nothing. The people on the list would have only just entered primary school when he was in uniform in the late nineties, before the explosion of technology which seemed to have occurred a decade later. Now everything seemed to centre on a computer. Even those weren't really needed any longer, as everyone seemed to have a brand new mobile phone which did the job just as well.

Not even forty, Murphy thought as he scanned the list. Barely late thirties, and he already felt left behind.

Social media, that was the thing. Everything

70

being laid open. Murphy shunned it completely — didn't like the idea of anyone from his past being able to find him that easily. He'd been involved in a few cases in the previous years which had involved the websites — Facebook, Twitter, Bebo — so he knew enough about them that he wasn't lost in a conversation.

Twitter was the new thing, it seemed, for the genesis of such cases. The papers went through peaks and troughs with the story — usually when nothing much else was happening. Trolls, bullies, threats. Each platform gets their turn. They all get blamed, when Murphy knew the real cause.

The people.

It didn't matter which website or avenue was used, they're all just a way of exerting power.

Murphy had no doubt Dean Hughes would be on there, so he rolled his hand over the mouse of his computer, typing www.face — before the page auto-filled itself.

Scrolling down the page, he realised just how common a name it was. He tried to narrow it down by putting in Liverpool as the location, but it was still difficult to find the right one from all the results. Dean and Hughes was obviously a popular combination of names in Merseyside. He clicked on two different profiles before finding the right one. Profile picture set to a group of five lads, shaven heads on three of them, the other two with a swept-over quiff thing going on. Dean Hughes in the middle. All arms spread wide, cans of lager in one hand, teeth showing. First comment on the picture when Murphy clicked on it . . .

Gay as fuk lads!

Murphy shook his head, clicking the x in the corner of the picture and returning to the profile page itself. He waited for the inevitability of the page being set to private, which was supposedly happening more often these days. He was only mildly surprised when he was able to start scrolling through Dean's wall posts. Most of the youngsters — or teenagers he should say — he'd had reason to investigate this way seemed to revel in the lack of anonymity. Everything was left open for public viewing and consumption.

'What you on?' Rossi said, swivelling her chair around the desk and stopping as she reached his side.

'Dean's Facebook page. Look at this — *Carnt be assed wth dis. Ned 2 gt stned lads* — how do you misspell 'need'?'

'No one gives a toss online.'

Murphy grunted in reply and carried on scrolling, only pausing to read the various status updates. 'Last one was seven months ago. Which ties in with the theory of him disappearing suddenly.'

'Anyone posted on his wall recently?'

Murphy scrolled back up to the top, looking to the left side of the screen. 'Few here. Mainly when he went missing. People asking if he's all right. Nothing of interest really . . . wait.'

'What?' Rossi said, leaning forward.

'Same name posting a few times. Gets more and more angry. Paul Cooper. Dean owed him money by the looks of it.' Murphy made a note of the name.

72

Murphy's phone rang before Rossi had a chance to reply. 'Sally Hughes has finally confirmed it's Dean,' he said once he'd finished the call from Dr Houghton's assistant. 'Post-mortem starts in an hour.'

'We'd best get over there then.'

★ ★ ★

Naked, stark light shone above the body as Dr Houghton began his work. Murphy had begun to find the whole process quite boring. Once you'd winced and felt your stomach turn over the first ten or twenty times you attended a post-mortem, it became more methodical.

'I count sixty-three different contusions and marks. Some inflicted close to death, some occurring days or weeks before. The worst of those are concentrated on the torso and arms,' Dr Houghton said, speaking into a digital recorder as well as for the benefit of Murphy and Rossi. 'Healing contusion to the eye area, around a week old, I'd suggest. Bruising to the neck area, asphyxiation a possible cause of death.' He pressed the stop button on his recorder before turning towards Murphy. 'He was beaten severely and then strangled by a thin ligature. It's pretty obvious.'

'Rule out suicide then?' Rossi said.

'Unless he's worked out a way of hanging himself whilst lying down, then yes. He was on the ground when he died.'

'What was used to beat him?' Murphy asked, before Rossi had a chance to swear at the doctor in her mother tongue.

'There are three different distinctive markings,' Dr Houghton said, turning the body over with a sigh, before his assistant moved quickly to lend a hand. 'On the back here is a marking from some kind of heavy object, a bat or plank of wood maybe. On the front, something thin like a whip or something similar. And then here,' Dr Houghton pointed to the left-hand-side rib area, 'half a boot print. He was stamped on so hard I'd guess there are a few broken ribs in that area.'

Murphy tried and failed to keep the grimace off his face. The memory of the injuries he'd sustained a year earlier — broken arm and ribs after being pushed down concrete steps which led into the darkness of a basement — was still fresh. The breathlessness of having your ribs broken in more than one place. The look on the doctor's face in the Royal Hospital — only a few floors above from where he was standing now — as he'd explained to Murphy that they had to heal on their own. It was a couple of weeks before he could even stand walking any kind of distance.

Still, the sick pay was nice. Plus, he'd suddenly become more accepted around the station again, which made things much easier than they'd been previously. The snide remarks and sideways glances, just waiting for him to screw up, had pretty much ended that day. Injured in the line of duty had that kind of effect on petty differences.

Murphy absent-mindedly rubbed at his

74

right-hand side as he replied, 'Think you can get a print off that?'

'I imagine so,' Dr Houghton replied, sounding amused by the question. Hiding a grin behind his mask, Murphy assumed. 'Wonders of modern science. We have scrapings underneath the fingernails as well, which I imagine are from the back of the hands of the person who was strangling him to death.'

'Good. Full report?'

Dr Houghton sighed. 'In the morning at the latest.'

★   ★   ★

Murphy kicked at a stone in the hospital car park, watching as it jumped up and hit the side of someone's Ford Focus. He didn't move slowly enough to check if he'd chipped the paintwork as he continued to trot towards his car.

'Who interviewed the kids who found him?' Murphy said, turning to Rossi who was, as ever, struggling to keep up.

'Harris and some other DC I can't remember the name of. They're basically interchangeable at this point.'

Murphy smirked, knowing exactly what she meant. Local cuts to the police service meant that constables in CID were being sent all over Liverpool to fill in where and when needed. It meant there was no kind of consistency on who was working at St Anne Street from one week to the next. Once you got used to one face, they were sent over to the other side of the city to fill

75

in on some other case. Murphy didn't even want to consider the mind who had thought up this gloriously stupid way of working.

'I'm guessing nothing came of it, otherwise you would have told me?'

Rossi shook her head. 'Just found him and ran. Didn't see anyone at all. Nothing from door to doors either really. Other than a neighbour who thought she heard an argument near Castlesite Road. Wasn't sure of the time because she was half asleep. Could have been dreaming, for all we know.'

'CCTV any good?' Murphy said, pressing the button on his keys to activate the central locking.

'Not sure yet,' Rossi replied, opening the passenger door and getting into the car. 'I know there's a few cameras around the cross near the Sefton Arms pub, but not the other side. Depends which way they came in. It's not like we could tell if he was killed anywhere else in the area, unless there's blood.'

'Doesn't mean we don't look,' Murphy said, turning the ignition. 'We need to organise a bit of a search, I think.'

'Seems like a lot of effort. Probably going to turn out to be an argument got out of hand.'

Murphy drummed his fingers on the steering wheel as he waited for traffic to pass so he could pull out onto the main road. 'I'd usually agree, Laura, but there's a few things wrong here. The fact he's been missing over six months. The placing of the body at the church . . . '

'Like an unwanted baby,' Rossi murmured.

'Sorry?'

76

'When you hear about these abandoned babies, you know, where the mother is too young or whatever, they leave them outside churches, don't they?'

'I'm not seeing your point.'

Rossi sighed, pressing the button to half open her window. 'It could be that Dean Hughes was left at the church because they thought he'd be looked after there.'

'Possibly. I think the damage was already done though, don't you?'

Rossi shrugged and turned to look out the window. Murphy stared ahead, trying to get the cogs within turning.

Concentrating hard to stop the demons coming back in.

The Farm

Five Months Ago

Goldie had become used to life there pretty quick. It was the same all the time, really. Days spent in the quiet, waiting for the evening, when the 'fun' would begin. Three meals a day. Anything they wanted to read.

Okay, there was no TV, PlayStation, or even Xbox. No iPhone, Samsung . . . fuck, he'd take a Nokia at some points, just to be able to speak to his mum or something. He reckoned he'd even phone her first, rather than check Facebook or Twitter.

His muscles ached in so many places, he'd given up trying to work out where it hurt most. He'd caught sight of his face on one trip into the farmhouse. It was becoming harder, older.

Scarred.

Goldie was inspecting a fresh mark on his right thigh when they brought in the Bootle lad. Just dumped him in there, without a word.

They'd been getting a bit more light in the Dorm than in the first couple of weeks, so Goldie could see him fine. Dean, the other lad, wouldn't have seen shit. He was in his usual position — lying down on his bed, facing the wall, pretending to be asleep. He'd barely spoken two words to Goldie in the month he'd been in there with him.

Just shut down.

'All right lad?' Goldie said, standing up slowly, his thighs burning from overuse, his calves numb. It seemed too little a thing to say, but what the fuck else could he say? The lad had no idea what he was in for.

'Who the fuck are you? What's going on?'

Goldie held his hands out in front of him. 'Calm down mate. It's them out there you want to be pissed off with, not us.'

'Us? Who else is here?' the lad replied, standing up fully now. 'Youse best tell me what's fuckin' goin' on, or there'll be fuckin' murder, you get me?'

Goldie put his hands down. Curled them into fists instead. 'Look,' he tried a softer voice, but it didn't really work. 'Look, we're in the same boat. I'm Goldie, the lad over here is Dean. We've been taken by a bunch of nutters who want to give us some kind of army training or some shite . . . '

'Well, I'm MC Cray-Z. And MC Cray-Z doesn't take any shit, you get me?'

'You're called what? Where you from?'

'Bootle. What's it to you?'

Goldie shook his head. 'I'm not calling you MC Fucking Shit. I'm just gonna call you Bootle for now. That all right?'

'This is bollocks . . . '

'No,' Goldie replied, taking a few steps towards him. 'It's not. It's as fucking real as it can get. But you need to calm down, otherwise . . . '

'Or what? What're you gonna do about it?'

Goldie almost smiled. It had been a long time since someone had spoken to him like that when a gun wasn't being trained on him.

'Listen. I'll give you one warning,' Goldie said, stepping closer, five yards away from Bootle now, taking in his full five foot five figure. Small man syndrome exuding from every pore. 'One warning, given what you've been through. But I won't give you another.'

Bootle took a step forward, hands shaking, sweat on his forehead.

'Do something,' Bootle said as he stopped in front of him.

Goldie smiled then.

★   ★   ★

Gamma spoke first as they watched the camera feed from inside the Dorm. 'We might have a problem here . . . ' she said, nudging Delta.

'What do we do?' Delta replied.

Gamma looked around at the only other person in the small monitoring room. Tango chewed on his bottom lip for a second or two, then spoke.

'Get Alpha.'

A minute or so later, Alpha bounded in, forcing his way in front of Gamma and staring into the screen.

Gamma cleared her throat. 'Should we go and stop it?'

Alpha stepped back, rubbing at his face before folding his arms.

'No. Let's see what happens.'

Goldie didn't know where the lad had got the strength from, but he was starting to tire already. It was probably down to the endless drills he'd been forced to do in the previous weeks. Muscles not having been given a chance to heal properly, now screaming for him to stop. Lie down and don't move.

Bootle had his small hands wrapped around his throat, trying to choke him but not succeeding. Goldie had his chin ducked down low, meaning he could suck in air. All the time, he was concentrating on trying to prise away the grip.

It had started as it normally did for Goldie whenever he was in a fight. Quick movements forward and a closed fist punch to the side of the other lad's head. That usually put them down, then he could jump them. Put the boot in and end it.

But this time he'd miscalculated, and only skimmed the top of Bootle's head. Then he'd been surprised by the force of the little bastard's rugby tackle as he was forced backwards onto the floor.

Goldie stopped trying to prise the hands away. Drew back his fist as far as he could, and drove it into the side of Bootle. Kidneys. Instant pain. Bootle's hands loosened and Goldie took his chance. He pushed him away, letting him fall to the side, before punching him in the jaw, hearing a click or snap — he couldn't tell which one — in his right hand. He ignored it, punching again, hearing the satisfying thump of flesh on flesh as he carried on. Bootle's face started turning red as knuckles met skin, cuts forming around his eyes and cheekbones. Blood mixing with sweat and tears.

Goldie left him coughing and retching on the floor, stood up, and began stamping on the cunt.

He was in his socks, so he wasn't doing as much damage as he'd have liked, but it didn't lessen the pain he knew he was inflicting. Drawing his leg up, smashing his heel right into Bootle's stomach. Then a volley into his bollocks, to really take his breath away. Then he moved up. He had a wicked right foot on him, when he'd played footy instead of getting pissed or stoned with his mates, and he lined up Bootle's face as if he was about to fire in a free kick in front of the Kop.

Bang.

The sound was deafening in the small space, making Goldie jump and lose his footing.

A soft voice from the corner, that's all he could hear after the ringing had stopped.

'No . . . no . . . no . . . '

Goldie looked over the broken body of Bootle towards the door. The main guy — Bally-Suit — stood there, backed up with two others. Holding the rifle level with him. The bang had come from one of the other two rather than him, Goldie guessed. Bally-Suit wouldn't have fired a gun without it being pointed at someone, Goldie reckoned.

Goldie realised he was shaking his head, moving backwards all the time. The fight disappearing from him.

He was in the shit.

Bally-Suit man had offered up the name Alpha as he'd tied him to the rack. It suited him. Better than what Goldie had come up with.

Alpha. He was the one in charge.

Goldie tried not to pay much attention to what was happening. Thought he could zone out of whatever they did to him, think above the pain.

It didn't — couldn't — work like that. He was restrained so he couldn't make any movement at all. Every possible part of him was strapped down, tied together, and immovable. Lying spreadeagled in just the black boxer shorts he'd been given a pile of at some point — fucking Asda brand; he couldn't believe he was putting his junk into something so shite — exposed and useless.

'It's a shame it's come to this,' Alpha said from somewhere to his left. Goldie couldn't move his head to check for certain. 'I knew you'd end up here at some point, but it is really a damn shame it was due to this. We simply cannot tolerate you lads fighting each other. It will not happen again. I hope the next couple of hours convince you of this.'

Goldie shivered as a cold breeze snuck under the wooden door that he could just about make out. Just the ridge at the top, if he really tried looking down. Otherwise it was just strip light, which burned into his eyes if he looked at it too long. Lighting up his face even when his eyes were closed.

'We call this a rack, but it's not like the old

racks they had hundreds of years ago. Those ones . . . Jesus. You wouldn't believe the pain they could inflict. They'd tie you down and stretch you out, tightening the ropes and making your bones dislocate and break. Destroying your limbs. Tearing them right out.'

Goldie started shaking . . . as much as he could, anyway. He tried again to move, but it didn't matter. He could move a finger — maybe two — but not much more than that.

'Don't worry. I'm not going to stretch you out or anything like that. No. This is purely about instant pain and punishment. But also . . . hopefully . . . redemption. I don't want to destroy you. I want you to get better, understand?'

Goldie opened his mouth to answer but was cut off by the gag which was shoved in his mouth as he opened it. His vision was obscured by a thick piece of sock-like material being placed around his eyes.

'Good. Then we'll begin.'

Goldie tensed as he heard the flick of a lighter. Clenched his eyes tight and tried to block out the pain.

Burning on his chest. Fuck, his chest was on fire. He tried to see, but the harsh light overhead stopped him. Screwing his eyes shut, he thought of home, of his streets, of anywhere but there.

He tried screaming, but the gag inside his mouth turned it into a mumble in the darkness.

Some sort of vice was attached to his head. Goldie felt it tightening, the bones of his skull being forced together, screaming in agony as he thought of his head exploding. Alpha seemed to

84

know the limits though.

It wasn't his first time, Goldie thought at one point. Oh fucking shit — *it wasn't his first time.*

The needles were the worst. That's what he guessed they were. Sharp, piercing pain in the skin between his fingers and toes. A bang as he imagined the thin pieces of metal being hammered through, then more agony as they were removed and covered.

He cried behind the covering over his eyes. Goldie hadn't shed tears in as long as he could remember, always believing nothing could break him.

He was wrong.

After a while, the torture stopped and the numbness which had crept over him disappeared, bringing fresh waves of nausea as the pain kicked in once more.

'That's probably enough, Alpha . . . don't you think?'

The voice came from further away, but even in the agony-induced state Goldie was in, he could hear the fear behind it.

'Not nearly enough for this piece of shit.'

'Okay . . . it's just, well . . . we're not really equipped for putting him right if you go too far.'

Goldie listened, barely able to match the words being spoken to a real conversation.

'Would that be so bad?'

'Of course it would. We're not here for . . . for that. Are we?'

Goldie heard a sigh.

'It'll do for now, I guess. What do you think, Mr Gold?'

Goldie tried to nod his head, but it screamed in response as he tried to move it. Alpha tutted and removed the blindfold from his eyes.

'Good. Well, Omega here will clean you up and have you back in the Dorm in no time at all. I hope we won't have to do this again anytime soon. I trust you'll behave yourself from now on?'

Goldie tried blinking, but the strip light above him refused to allow him respite from the pain as it burned into his eyes. He kept his eyes partially closed as he squinted above him, Alpha's covered face looming into view.

'I think we have an understanding now, don't we? We're not messing around here. You will be taught how to behave. It's a shame your parents have failed so badly in this area and that we have to resort to such extreme measures, but it takes time and punishment, you see? Probably not now, no, but soon. Soon you'll all see.'

The dark face moved away then returned, closer this time. Whispering into his ear.

'The next time, I take a finger. Then we can really start to see what you're made of.'

He moved away again and a few seconds passed before another masked face replaced him. Goldie wanted to believe he saw pity in the eyes of this one, but he didn't know the difference any more.

He didn't know anything.

7

The first day was winding down, the light fading outside in the early May evening. Murphy and Rossi crossed the incident room, heading back towards their office. There'd be a short meeting before they left for the day, but other than the list of names they'd accrued, there wasn't much else they could do. Overtime was currently a dirty word in the station, and unless the DCI suddenly got pressure from above, Murphy couldn't imagine they'd change that for a single victim. Especially when he knew what most minds in the hive would be thinking.

Some scally kid had got what was coming to him.

It still troubled Murphy. Any death still had that effect on him. Sometimes he wondered if he had been born in the wrong era. It seemed to Murphy that there were more victims than ever that supposedly deserved their fates, in a growing number of people's opinions. Even if they were only a few years on from being nothing but kids. Not having a clue what the reality of their actions could eventually lead to.

Murphy had been there. Growing up on a council estate in South Liverpool, the line between making something of your life and screwing it up was thin. Sometimes even blurred.

Murphy took out his phone as they reached their office, the silence he'd been hoping for denied due to DC Harris sitting behind the desk speaking into his mobile, his back to them. He turned as they entered, redness creeping up his neck. Private call then, Murphy thought.

'I'll call you back,' Harris whispered into the phone, which made little difference considering the size of the office. 'I don't know when, I'll just ring in a bit, okay?' He stabbed at the phone, slamming it down on the desk with more force than Murphy thought he'd intended.

'You all right?' Rossi said, taking her jacket off and placing it over her chair. Murphy was already taking his phone out of his pocket.

'Yeah, just . . . doesn't matter. Boring shite.'

Rossi went to reply but stopped herself as Murphy shot her a look. Domestics. Best not to get involved. Murphy went back to texting.

Body this morning. Won't be late though. Bit knackered, so can I just pick up an Indian?

Murphy hesitated before pressing send. He hoped Sarah would understand that he wasn't taking her out, but he could never tell how she'd respond. In many ways they were still treading on eggshells with each other. Learning how to be with one another after they'd spent the best part of a year apart, following the death of his parents and all that had brought with it.

'Just send it,' Rossi said, interrupting his thoughts. 'She'll understand.'

Murphy smirked. And they say women's intuition doesn't exist. 'Supposed to be taking her out,' Murphy said, phone still in hand, the screen darkening. 'Forgot to book a table though, so now I've got a perfect excuse.'

'She'll be fine. Take her tomorrow or next week. All the time in the world,' Rossi replied.

Muttering came from Harris's direction, accompanied by a loud sigh.

'What's up with you?' Murphy said, sending the text as he spoke.

'Nothing,' Harris replied. 'Just, you know, they're not always as understanding as that.'

Murphy shared a smile with Rossi. 'I'm sure it'll work itself out. Don't let it get to you.'

Harris shrugged in response. Three of them in the office and Murphy realised his relationship was probably the most secure. A strange feeling, given what had happened the previous couple of years.

He was mentally admonishing himself for allowing a crack to appear in the veneer of stability. Allowing work to affect things. He couldn't let that happen again.

His phone buzzed on the desk in front of him.

Glad you said that. I'm knackered. Get home in time for 8 out of 10 Cats.

Murphy allowed himself a small smile before checking the time. Almost six p.m. Just enough time for a conversation he was dreading.

★ ★ ★

'Where's he been? That's what I want to know. Where's he fucking been for over six months,

89

while you all sat on your arses doing nothing?'

Sally Hughes spat the last question out directly at Murphy, as if he'd been involved in the whole thing. He remained stoic, eager to allow Sally to get her initial anger out so they could move forward. 'That's what we're going to find out, Sally. It'll help us if you could tell us a few things though, okay?'

'Oh, you want to hear all about it now, don't you? When it doesn't matter any more. Fucking useless, the lot of you.'

Murphy moved the box of tissues she'd been using to dab her tears away, just in case she decided to chuck that at him, which, going by the whitening of her knuckles on the table between them, could occur at any second. 'Give us a chance to prove we're not useless, okay, Sally?'

She sat back in the chair, finally breaking eye contact with him to bury her head in her hands, tears springing forth once more. 'God, what happened? Are you going to find out what happened to him?' Sally said, raising her head and facing Rossi this time.

'That's what we want to do, Sally,' Rossi replied. 'That's why we need your help.'

'Okay. Ask me anything. I'm not gonna lie to you.'

Unlike usually, Murphy thought, before giving himself an internal slap.

'Right,' Rossi said, reading the first question off the list they'd prepared before going into the room. 'Dean went missing in the early hours of 6 October. When was the last time you saw him?'

'The evening before. He was going out with

90

mates and he came in to say bye. About half six, I think, because *Hollyoaks* was about to start.'

'And did he seem okay . . . anything different about him?'

Murphy watched her as she thought back. Memory is a stranger; it plays tricks on you. He knew they might learn more from the original report, but having scan-read it earlier, he wasn't holding out much hope. Some uniform had taken it without going into much detail. Even the follow-ups from higher-ups had been perfunctory at best.

'Maybe a bit quieter, but nothing really. It was a Friday, so I knew he'd be in late, if at all. He was nearly eighteen, so I couldn't really say anything. Not that he cared at sixteen or fifteen, for that matter. Always had his own mind, Dean. He's . . . what's the word . . . stubborn. That's it. Always was. Does things his own way and woe betide anyone who tries to stop him.'

'Did he say where he was going that night?'

'Out. That's what he always said. I knew he'd be drinking, of course. Maybe more, who knows with kids these days? But he always let me know if he was staying over at a mate's or something. Send me a text in the early hours, just to stop me worrying. When I woke up the next morning and didn't have anything from him, I knew something was wrong. Our Jason — that's my youngest one, just turned seventeen a couple of weeks ago — went looking for him on the Saturday afternoon but couldn't find him.'

'Where did he look?' Murphy said, easing into the conversation.

'Couple of lads he knew that hung around with Dean,' Sally continued, taking a lighter out of her hoodie pocket. 'I'm guessing I can't smoke in here?'

Murphy shook his head. 'Don't worry, we'll have a break soon.'

'I rang you lot Saturday night. We found out more than youse did though.'

'I've got some of it here,' Murphy replied, flipping back a couple of sheets of the report. 'He was last seen by a Steven Waites at around three a.m. Said he left him in West Derby Cemetery with 'some bird I can't remember the name of'.'

A whisper of a smile played on Sally's lips before being lost with a knock of the lighter in her hand on the table. 'We found out who that was. Some slut from up the road. Amanda Williams. Sixteen, she was. Glad I have boys, I'll tell you that.'

'And . . . '

'She was pissed. Last thing she remembers was throwing up behind some grave and then her dad pulling her into the house. Reckons Dean must have took her home.'

Murphy found the part of the missing person's report which referred to this.

Took girlfriend home.

Murphy shook his head at the lack of investigation. He knew it was down to time, resources and all that bullshit. The oft-quoted statistic relating to missing persons. Quarter of a million a year. Most turning back up again quickly. Still, a bit of effort might have saved at least one life.

'And that was it,' Sally continued. 'No one saw him again. We tried getting in the papers and that, but they weren't interested. Eighteen-year-old lad with his history . . . they couldn't care less. Just assumed he'd done something wrong and got what was coming to him. We stuck posters up and that, but when we got the letter in January, we kind of stopped and just waited around.'

Murphy looked towards Rossi, who looked back at him, mirroring his own reaction. Flicked through the report to make sure he hadn't missed something, came up with nothing.

'What letter?'

8

Murphy wrote on the board under the details of Dean Hughes's murder case. Adding the new information they'd gleaned that day, his last act before going home.

He was going to be late.

Someone had sent Sally Hughes a message. An envelope dropping through the letter box one January morning. No stamp or address on the front. Just one word.

Mum

Inside, a short note which explained how he was fine and was getting help with his problems. He'd be back soon, when he was better and ready to make something of his life. Not in her son's handwriting, but typed out.

She'd assumed he was at some kind of religious thing. Actually felt okay about it. Two words in her son's handwriting . . . *Mum* and *Dean*. And a few kisses, she'd said. Murphy shook his head at the naivety of it all. Someone sends you a message saying your son is somewhere you have no idea of until he's *better*. It was ridiculous. And all she had to show it was actually written by her son were two words in his handwriting.

He guessed what the real reason was behind her supposed giving up. Apathy. It was a neat little explanation for everything. Meant she didn't have to worry any more.

Murphy slammed the marker pen back in the shelf at the bottom of the board. Looked at his watch and decided to make a move.

★　★　★

It was becoming a ritual for Rossi to do this. Every time there was a death, suspicious circumstances or not, she went to her parents' house. She'd thought she would have grown out of it once she'd gone through the process a few times, but the draw was still there.

Rossi's parents lived near the scene from earlier that morning in West Derby. Only a few minutes away really. She drove past the church — saw a couple of uniforms standing outside the entrance, keeping away any ghouls who wanted to have a poke around, but other than that, things had quietened down now. Only twelve hours on, and already people's attention was being drawn elsewhere.

She was putting off the inevitable. The questions, the judgements. Willing to go through it all, as usual. The lure of her mama's food was a much more appetising thought, but she knew it came at a price.

She parked up her car, turned off the engine but left the radio playing some bland pop song which she couldn't help but enjoy. Rossi switched off the radio with a turn of her key and got out the car. She'd managed to get a parking spot, which was becoming more and more difficult these days. It was a mid-terrace house in a quiet road which seemed to contain every different type of house you could find. Opposite, four detached bungalows; further down, semi-detached housing; to either side, terraced houses which seemed to run the length of the street.

She rang the bell, a snippet of *Greensleeves* emanating from within.

'*Bambina! Entare, entare.* What is all this talk today? What is happening here in our beautiful city? You look hungry. *Hai mangiato?* Never mind. You eat now.'

Laura was still standing on the doorstep, waiting for her mother to finish. It was always the same. Isabella Rossi — *Mama* — didn't believe in easing into conversations.

'I'm fine, Mama, *bene*,' Rossi said, finally being allowed to step into the house and taking her jacket off. 'I wanted to make sure you were both okay, that's all.'

Mama Rossi stood, her arms folded. 'You check on us? We check on you! That is how it is. Now go through. Sit with Papa and I'll bring food. Go. Sit.'

Rossi did as she was told, moving through into the living room where her father was sitting in his usual chair, waiting for her to brush his cheek with a kiss before lighting a cigarette.

'*Come stai?*' Alessandro Rossi said, fiddling the cigarette between his fingers before flicking his Zippo and inhaling the smoke.

'I'm fine, Papa. You heard about what happened at the church?'

'Of course.'

'Looks like a bad one already.'

'How young?'

'Just turned eighteen,' Rossi replied, moving back as her mama entered the room and placed a cup of tea in front of her, before hustling back out.

'Terrible, terrible business. The whole city is changing. You should really be doing something about that,' Mama Rossi said from the kitchen.

'I'll get right on that, Mama,' Rossi replied, earning a smirk from her father.

'He was eighteen. So an adult really, but still . . . ' Rossi said, lifting the china cup her mother always served tea in. Remembering why she never drank the stuff unless she was home. Not that it had been her home in a long time.

'Bad, was it?'

'It always is, Papa,' Rossi replied, looking around the room.

Papa Rossi leant back in his chair. 'You need somewhere else to go.'

'I like coming here.'

'No. You come here to be a child again. A *bambina* running into the arms of her mama. You need something else. It'll make it easier.'

Rossi wasn't sure about that. Even less so when her mama returned with pasta *al forno*, piled high on a plate. Parmesan cheese in a small bowl.

No. This was still preferable to some bloke messing up her house.

⋆   ⋆   ⋆

Murphy pulled into the driveway, spying Sarah through the front window watching TV. He left

97

the car and watched her for a minute or so. She'd have heard him pull up but didn't seem to react. He considered, not for the first time, if she enjoyed knowing he was watching her. Wondered what she was thinking, what she was so engrossed in that she didn't turn her head and look at him through the window, breaking the reverie.

He left the car, opening the front door to the house, smiling as the blaring noise from the TV snapped off. Murphy seemed to spend most of his life asking her to turn the bloody thing down, but she always waited until he wasn't paying attention before gently increasing the volume, complaining she couldn't hear it properly. Thankfully, the only neighbour they had was on the other side of the semi-detached house. Not that it mattered much anyway. Mr Waters. Eighty-odd and happy to let them get on with things.

'Hello?'

'Did you bring food with you?'

Murphy shook his jacket off, his keys going on their own hook away from the door, so as to ward against car thieves apparently. Something about a fishing pole through the letter box.

He walked into the living room, 'Yeah, Indian,' he said, seeing the chair for the first time. 'Probably not enough for you as well though.'

'It's okay. We'll make it spread, won't we, Sarah?'

Jess. Hanger-on, pain in the arse, third wheel, and his best friend. 'Great. Don't even be thinking about nicking all the bhajis though. Go and get plates.'

98

Jess left the room, not before aiming a kick at his shins.

'She all right?' Murphy said, listening carefully for the sound of plates being removed, keeping his voice low.

Sarah grimaced. 'Problems with Peter again.'

'Ah,' Murphy replied. Murphy had known Jess over twenty years and for most of them she'd been a single parent. Murphy had chipped in over that time, even standing up for Peter as a child and becoming his godfather. Tried being a friendly uncle rather than a father figure, and failing spectacularly as Peter moved into the troubled teenage years. Murphy had fared better when he was younger, easily appeased with occasional trips to the match at the weekend or the odd trip to the picture house, usually to see some *Die Hard*-type of action film Murphy didn't really enjoy.

'She's okay,' Sarah whispered, 'think she just needs a break.'

Murphy nodded, removing containers of food from the two carrier bags. He'd got lucky with Sarah. His first wife had hated the relationship he had with Jess. Couldn't understand how a man and woman could be friends, never mind as close as Jess and he were, without any semblance of romantic feelings. Sarah had accepted the fact from the beginning. Hadn't even batted an eyelid when he'd firmly told her how things were. Since getting back together a year earlier, it seemed like Murphy was becoming the extra person in the threesome. Sarah and Jess saw much more of each other, as his re-dedication to work became more time-consuming.

'Didn't get your big plate,' Jess said, carrying plates into the room, cutlery strewn across the top of them. 'You look like you need to lose a few more pounds before getting that back out.'

'I'm allowed a night off. And anyway, you'll have most of the food down your gob before I have a chance.'

'Whatever,' Jess replied, moving Murphy out of the way to take over removing the food. 'Sar, you all right with sharing the masala?'

Sarah nodded, smiling at Murphy, knowing he was already relenting. 'Korma for me,' he said, removing a plate.

'You're a fucking soft git you are,' Jess replied, tucking away the foil container holding the bhajis behind her on the coffee table.

Minutes later, there were half-full plates of curry, naan bread and poppadoms perched on their laps, and they stared at the TV in the corner. Murphy leant back in his chair.

'What's the matter, babe?' Sarah asked. 'Eyes too big for your stomach?'

'No, just thinking is all.'

Jess mopped up the last of her sauce with a piece of naan bread. 'New case?'

'Yeah,' Murphy said, attempting another forkful. 'Eighteen-year-old in West Derby.'

'Heard about that on the news. Found on the church steps?'

Murphy nodded. 'Yeah, beaten and then strangled by the looks of it. Don't think it's religious or anything, but you know . . . can't be too careful.'

100

Sarah dropped her fork on her plate, reaching over for the last onion bhaji. 'Between her with her lawyer stuff,' she said, using the bhaji to point at Jess, 'and you with your murders and shite, it's getting a bit dark a conversation for this time of night. Can we change the subject please?'

Murphy rolled his eyes at Jess, before lifting his plate off his lap to avoid a kick from Sarah. 'Okay, okay. What's going on with Peter then, Jess?'

This time it was Jess's turn to roll her eyes. 'Typical teenager bollocks. Seventeen years old and thinks the world owes him a favour.'

'We were all like that once.'

'I know,' Jess replied, 'but he's just annoying me now. Hasn't been going to college, so fuck knows how he'll get on with his exams. More interested in going round his mate's house. Keeps reminding me he'll be eighteen in a few months. He's at his dad's tonight and I've had a word. See if him and the new bint can do anything to knock some sense into him.'

Murphy swallowed a chewy bit of chicken and winced. Not as good as usual. 'Want me to have a word?'

Jess shook her head. 'It's all right. He's not done anything too bad really. Just being a mother, I guess.'

Murphy heard a sigh from beside him. Sarah, looking pointedly in his direction.

He knew what conversation they'd be having when Jess finally left.

9

Murphy headed for DCI Stephens's office, suppressing a yawn on the way. A late night was probably the last thing he'd needed on day two of a murder investigation. The half cup of coffee that morning wasn't kicking in yet. The office was mostly empty — the night shift clearing out in preparation for the day crowd to take over. He glanced at the murder board he'd set up twenty-four hours earlier, the same details from the previous night plastered over the surface.

He peeked in his office without entering, frowning when he saw it was empty. He'd expected to see Rossi inside, working away on something or other. She was usually here before him, especially when they had a murder. He glanced at his watch, giving her the benefit of the doubt when he saw that it hadn't long gone past eight a.m. It was a Saturday, after all.

Murphy knocked on the office door, hand on the handle waiting for the signal to enter.

'Come in.'

DCI Stephens hadn't seemed to have lost any sleep at all. Immaculately turned out, as usual. Always the first one here, well before the detective constables desperate to climb the promotion ladder.

'Roped in for weekend work as well, boss?' No *marm*, or any of that. She preferred boss, and that was fine by him.

'Only half a day,' she replied, motioning for Murphy to sit down in the chair opposite her. 'Super wanted to make sure we're making progress with this dead kid case.'

'He was eighteen. Hardly a kid.'

She made no sign of noticing his correction. 'What's the plan?'

Murphy steepled his fingers. 'We have a number of friends we have to question. We need to find out where he's been for the last seven months. Nothing from the door to doors, no witnesses. So unless forensics have pulled anything, that's our best bet.'

'We don't like the religious aspect to this case, David. Have we ruled that out yet?'

Murphy met her gaze. 'You know it would be wrong to do that at this point. Best we keep an open mind.'

Stephens waved a hand away. 'Of course, but the Super was very insistent that we don't overstep the mark. Last thing we need is to cloud the issue. Have you spoken to Matrix?'

Murphy mentally added that to the list. 'Not as yet.'

'Well, get on that. Eighteen-year-old kid with a history . . . best to discount anything gang related.'

'Right. Of course, boss.'

'It's quiet out there. I want you to galvanise the troops when they're in. I won't be in the morning briefing, so make sure the message gets across that we're treating this with utmost importance. I don't like the idea of kids — and eighteen is still young enough to call them kids,

David — disappearing off the streets and turning up dead. That clear?'

'Crystal chandelier, boss.'

Stephens smirked before checking herself and going back to stoic. 'Good to have you here, David.'

★   ★   ★

Murphy shushed the group of six DCs, one DS, and a few uniforms which had congregated in the meeting room. He motioned for a straggler at the back to close the door behind him, scanning the room again as if he'd missed Rossi hiding in a crevice somewhere. She was still nowhere to be seen, even though it was now five past nine.

'Okay,' he said, banging the table in front of him once, 'let's get started.'

Murphy ran through what they'd learnt so far about Dean Hughes. His mother's positive ID and list of friends. He reiterated the need to stay near the scene, directing this foremost at the uniforms, before giving the DCs he couldn't remember the full names of some menial tasks to attend to.

'Harris, you speak to Matrix. See if they have any info on Hughes. Also ask about these names.' Murphy rattled off the names of those most active on Dean's Facebook page. 'Don't bugger off on a quest if anything pops up. Let me know first.'

The door opened slowly at the back, Rossi poking in her head before entering and sitting down swiftly. The bottle of Lucozade Sport she was holding was sucked dry in a few swigs as Murphy finished up with the rest of the team.

'Boss wants me to remind you to treat this with importance.' Murphy paused and gave a stare at the PC who had made the first ID the previous morning, as he muttered something under his breath. Hale. He logged the name again in his head. He'd obviously wormed his way onto the briefing by overestimating his influence to his superintendent. 'Won't be long before the media are involved, even if it's just local for now,' Murphy continued, moving his gaze to the rest of the room. 'And the last thing we need is for anyone to say the wrong thing.'

A raised hand from the one of the DCs. 'Yes, Kirkham, is it?'

'Sir. I heard the parents received a message a couple of months after he went missing?'

Murphy nodded. 'Just the mother. Father's not around and unlikely to be. She received a letter through the door a few weeks after he went missing. You've just volunteered to go pick it up. It's a long shot, but it needs to go to forensics all the same.'

Kirkham didn't seem annoyed about the forced volunteering, which impressed Murphy. He was used to quiet moans and rolling of the eyes. He finished up the meeting with a bit more geeing up of the troops, with only a couple of them realising he was putting on a show. Murphy waited for them all to leave, Rossi staying behind as he knew she would.

'Late? Unlike you.'

'Yeah, sorry,' Rossi said, taking aim and

throwing the empty bottle across the room and into the bin.

'Not affected your aim though.'

'Not that kind of late night.'

Murphy hesitated, unsure if it was the best time to ask what she'd been up to. Decided against it. 'Forensics back in yet?'

'Don't know. Came straight in here.'

Murphy walked away into their shared office. 'Best go and check then.'

He heard the chair scrape behind him as he went to check his email. The subdued murmurs of the main office instantly shut off as Rossi closed the door to their internal workspace. She'd acquired another energy drink from somewhere and started glugging it down as soon as she sat behind her desk.

'Do we have addresses for all the names yet?' Rossi said, in between swallows.

'Harris is sorting that as we speak, aren't you?' Murphy replied, directing his question to the hunched-over DC in the corner.

'Almost done.'

Murphy checked his email, the latest message proving to be the report he was waiting for.

He read over the first couple of pages, Rossi walking around her desk to read over his shoulder.

'A couple of cigarette butts and a shoe print. That's it?' Rossi said.

'From the general vicinity. At least that's something. Look here though . . . DNA. Someone else's blood was found on the clothing. That's a break.'

106

'No matches though,' Rossi replied, leaning back on a filing cabinet. 'Won't know until we've got him that it's him.'

'True. Which is why it becomes the new thing we ask people at interview. Anyone who refuses to give a sample deserves to be looked into a bit closer.'

'The usual then. Best read my own copy of it, I suppose.'

Murphy went back to reading over the rest of the report. No defensive wounds or skin under the fingernails — the normal place for them to find DNA. However, no evidence of any restraints used either, which struck him as odd. Dean would have surely known he was about to die, and if someone was strangling him he would have attempted to extricate whatever was being used.

'Unless he was being held down . . . '

'What's that?' Rossi said, looking up from her own copy.

'No evidence of restraints being used. If you want to asphyxiate someone alone, without the worry of them clawing at you, there's three things you can do. Wash them thoroughly afterwards to remove any traces of DNA; drug them so they're unconscious whilst you work; or you have help. I can't see any note of traces of bleach or something in here. And there's no drugs in the victim's system.'

Rossi looked away from him. 'So, either he had someone to hold them down, or there's something we're missing.'

Murphy pursed his lips, 'Could be.'

Harris had turned around in his chair, watching them as they spoke.

'Any thoughts?' Murphy said towards him.

'Not right now. But I do have something. One of the names on the list. Paul Cooper.'

'What about him?'

'I know where he is. Right now as a matter of fact.'

Murphy smiled. 'Well . . . come 'ead then. Where?'

'Walton Lane nick.'

10

Five minutes away from Goodison Park, which the blue half of the city calls home, on the main stretch of Walton Lane which leads around Stanley Park and Anfield Cemetery, lies Walton Lane Police Station. The small station was twinned with the larger St Anne Street building which Murphy worked from. It had been a base of sorts until recently, the main traffic going through St Anne Street until the new crime commissioner began delegating more bodies there. The area around had suffered from an influx of professionals in recent years, those looking for cheaper rents and bigger homes, but who still wanted the security of the nicer areas. They didn't like to be reminded that they were living on what was essentially a tarted-up housing estate, but the money wasn't coming in from their wages to cover the cost of living in the more upmarket areas of the city. Hence the petitions, the pressure, the community spirit directed at those in power to do something — not to help those that they deemed to be a 'problem', but directed at getting rid of them. Those 'others'. So the new-fangled position of crime commissioner came into its own, announcing more patrols, more bobbies on the street. Never mind that the role of crime commissioner was never seen as anything more than a political appointment by the uniforms on the ground, as well as CID bods like Murphy and Rossi.

'You want to see him in his cell or in an interview room?' the desk sergeant said, addressing Murphy but not tearing his gaze away from Rossi. Murphy read his name badge but then instantly forgot it as soon as he looked away.

'Room please. More dignified.'

'Yeah, course.'

There was still no actual CID working out of Walton Lane, but more uniforms since they'd gone back to twenty-four-hour opening, locking up people in the old cells down below. Mostly for public order offences away from the city centre, where the vast majority of those crimes occurred. Mostly young people as well.

'He's in for assault, but he's due at magistrates in an hour.'

'On a Saturday morning. Poor lad,' Murphy replied. The new trials of flexible opening hours for certain courts around the country had of course included Liverpool.

'He was here last week as well,' the sergeant said, leading them towards the interview rooms. 'That was for threatening behaviour.'

'Sounds lovely,' Rossi said, keeping in step with Murphy, in order to keep away from the sergeant, rather than dropping behind.

'Should see the state of his head.'

'Think we're about to.'

Paul Cooper entered the room ten minutes after they'd sat down and accepted the offer of coffee, Murphy already regretting his decision. As soon as it was in front of him he knew he'd drink it, lamenting the fact he also knew it was going to taste awful.

Cooper sat down opposite them, eyes bleary from lack of sleep. His head was shaved to a close zero, the stubble short enough to almost be classed as bald. All the better to show off his battle scars, Murphy thought. A mass of intertwining white spidery lines across all parts of his head, no doubt from numerous fights which would invariably have seen a bottle or six flying across the place. Or the result of too many headers into walls or onto pavements when too drunk to care about walking upright like a normal person.

No handcuffs, not like on TV.

'We'll be outside,' one of the constables said, leaving the room.

Murphy waited until the door was closed before eyeing up Cooper. 'Paul, is it?'

Cooper didn't meet his gaze. 'Only me ma calls me that.'

'What would you rather we call you then?'

'Whatever. Not bothered.'

'Okay then, Paul,' Murphy said, noticing the beginning of a smile appear on Cooper's face before it swiftly disappeared. 'Just want to ask a few questions, nothing major.'

'Haven't done nothing.'

'I haven't said you have yet. Can you at least wait until I do before you start denying everything?'

Cooper leant back in the chair, arms folded and expression vacant. 'What do youse want then?'

'Dean Hughes.'

The reply was instant. 'Don't know him.'

Murphy held back a chuckle, nudged Rossi with his elbow. 'You owe me a fiver.'

Cooper raised his eyebrows, but caught himself and went back to studying the ceiling tiles. 'Prove it.'

'You know how the Internet works, Paul?' Rossi said, Murphy leaning on an elbow and watching. 'It leaves a trace. Everything you do on there is recorded. It's not even that hard to do, you know. Find a list of people who have something in common with someone, interactions between them, conversations, that sort of thing. Especially as all you divs seem to do it out in the open.'

'And what?'

'And that means we know you know Dean Hughes, that's what. So let's stop messing about here and you can just answer the questions we ask, that sound all right with you?'

Murphy was surprised to see Cooper tear his eyes away from the ceiling and finally look towards them. 'I'm not a grass,' Cooper said.

'Never said you were.'

Cooper looked upwards once more before dropping his head to his chest. 'Go 'ead then.'

'How do you know Dean?'

Cooper shrugged. 'Just from around and that.'

'How long have you known him?'

''Bout a year. It's not like we're best mates or anything. He's just always around with the same people I'm with.'

Rossi shifted some paper from inside her

112

folder as Murphy paused.

'He owes you some money?' Rossi said, reading from her notes.

'Yeah, but no one's seen him for ages.'

'How much does he owe you?'

Cooper shrugged, bit on his lower lip and shrugged again. 'A few ton.'

'A few hundred quid?' Murphy said, affecting a little surprise into his speech. 'Do you lend all your 'not really mates' that kind of money?'

Cooper was struggling under Murphy's gaze a little. 'Nah . . . '

Murphy guessed at what was holding him back. 'You didn't exactly lend him the money, did you? He was supposed to pay for something, am I right?'

'Something like that.'

'So you were just trying to get that money back?'

'Yeah. I sent him some messages on Facebook and that. Knocked at his house but his mum said he'd done one. To be honest, I'd forgotten about it.'

'Lose face a bit?' Rossi said, still not lifting her gaze up from her notes.

'What do you mean?' Cooper said, bridling at that.

'With the lads. Maybe even the girls as well. Paul Cooper getting ripped off by some lad he barely knows? Can't have been good.'

Murphy watched Cooper carefully for a reaction, something which they could possibly use.

'Well, I didn't do anything. Couldn't find him,'

Cooper replied, shifting his gaze back to Murphy. 'Why are you asking me all this now anyway? He's been gone for fuckin' ages and no one has said anything before.'

Murphy shared a look with Rossi. Gave her a nod.

'Dean Hughes is dead, Paul. Severely beaten and then strangled.'

This time Cooper's reaction was easier to read.

'Fuck . . . '

Murphy took over. 'So you understand now why we're a bit more interested in him. Why we might be interested in people who might have a reason to be angry with him?'

'No . . . '

'People with violent records, perhaps? People with a history of losing their temper easily and getting themselves into trouble.'

Cooper sat back, running both hands over his shaved dome. 'No way. I'm not getting done for this. I haven't even seen him in months. And anyway, I know when to stop.'

'Do you, Paul?' Rossi asked, flipping over a page. 'Would Stephen Fowler agree with that, do you think?'

Cooper looked between them both, an incredulous look plastered across his face. 'That was . . . nah, I'm not having this. That was years ago and the fuckin' prick deserved it.'

'Really?' Murphy said, tone lowered and controlled.

'Yeah, he tried to hurt my sister. The knobhead was lucky.'

'And was Dean Hughes deserving of your particular brand of justice?'

Cooper was sweating, the globules of moisture springing forward on his forehead. Murphy wasn't surprised. He'd dealt with so many of this type before. Cocky little wankers — until something serious landed on their doorstep. Then it's shitting bricks time.

'No, no. That's not me. I wouldn't go that far, honest.'

'Right,' Murphy said. 'Good to know. We'll take your word for it, obviously.'

'Really,' Cooper said, relief washing over his face.

'Of course not, you dopey git. We'll need to know where you were Thursday night. All night, of course.'

A smile. Just a flash, and the tension visibly lifting from his shoulders. 'Thank fuck. I was at me bird's all night. Her ma is away, so we had the house to ourselves, like. We didn't exactly go to bed early, if you know what I mean.'

'And her name is?'

'Rachel. Rachel Thompson.'

'Her address?'

Cooper rattled off an address, which Rossi wrote down.

'Right well, we'll have a word with her. Lucky boy, Paul. Usually people don't have ready-made alibis just like that.'

'It's proper D. She's a good girl. She'll be well pissed off that I've been locked up again, anyway.'

'So is there anything you can tell us about

Dean? You must have tried looking for him.' Murphy kept his tone low, but with a bit more relaxation in there now. Friendly.

'I did, but no one had seen him. I mean, he wasn't hanging with us all that much anyway, once the youthy opened.'

'The youthy?'

'Yeah, that youth club that opened on Lower House Lane. Last year. He was going there all the time.'

Murphy looked towards Rossi, who was chewing on the end of her pen. They knew the youth club in question. Opened in a burst of fanfare the previous year, funded by two local charities. Meant to get kids off the streets and doing something, but so far hadn't seemed to be working.

'Did he ever talk about it?'

'Not much. Tried asking us to go once, but none of us were into any of that crap.'

Murphy weighed it up. As a lead, it wasn't much, but it was better than nothing.

'Is that it then . . . can I get off now?'

Murphy snorted. 'Haven't you forgot, lad? You're up in court this morning.'

Realisation hit Cooper's face as he remembered why he was there in the first place.

'Shit. Bet I get remanded for this one.'

11

Murphy drove them out of the station car park, joining the busy A road back towards town. Goodison Park loomed over them, in dire need of being renovated but in keeping with the rest of the area. All terraced housing and main roads. Housing estates, with traffic included these days.

'Why do you think Dean's mum didn't mention the youth club?' Rossi asked, elbow propped up on the edge of the passenger window, chewing on a nail.

'Maybe she didn't know,' Murphy replied, following the road around Everton Valley, onto Kirkdale Road. Scotland Road was ahead, but he indicated off to run parallel to it. Quicker route back to the station.

'Seems like our mate back there thought he was right into it. The youthy, that is. Would have thought that'd be something you'd let your mum know you were doing.'

Murphy mused as they passed the big gym on the tree-lined Great Homer Street. The traffic was much quieter this side, away from the main roads which ran into the city centre. 'Maybe he didn't want her to know.'

'Why would that be, do you reckon?'

'Could be something going on he knew she wouldn't approve of. Could have been using it to do anything. Lot of kids going there aren't looking to play games and be enrolled onto courses.'

117

'Suppose. Only one way to find out.'

'Of course.'

They were making a quick stop at the station to update the team and formulate plans. Tomorrow was Sunday, so things would slow down, inevitably, but they couldn't be seen to be doing so. Especially with the local media now getting involved. A Monday morning press conference, Murphy assumed.

'It'll be open this afternoon, I bet. I'll give them a ring when we get back.'

'Sound,' Murphy replied, passing the big light shop as the roads changed from Great Homer to St Anne. *Liverpool's Largest Light Store*, the sign outside proclaimed, and Murphy had to admit that even when Rapid was still open, the shop was probably still the biggest. Not that he'd ever been in there. Sarah was much more of an Ikea type.

He slowed as they reached the station, took in the drab brown block which looked more like an office building from the seventies than the home of the busiest division in Merseyside Police.

Rossi lagged behind as he walked through to the CID offices, stopping as she reached the vending machine. Murphy kept walking, keen to get on. He should have been at home, getting on with the decorating, which was already causing friction between Sarah and him.

Murphy thought back to the previous night — the moment when he knew that as soon as Jess left there'd be interminable silence before he asked the one question that always led to trouble.

'*What's wrong?*'

Jess had been discussing her son Peter, the problems he'd been having and how she was dealing with them. A throwaway comment he'd made had earned a look from Sarah, one she made sure he'd notice.

'I don't know how you do it . . . I don't think I have the patience to deal with that sort of thing. Don't think I'd want it.'

They'd been talking about having kids for a few months now. Always the same conversation. At first Murphy placated her with *now not being the right time*, before changing tack and going for what he really felt. The 'I'm not sure I could do it at all' talk.

The previous night, after Jess had left, Sarah had asked outright if he ever wanted kids. He thought of Dean Hughes instantly — imagined himself being his father, having to study his parenting and decide if he could have done things differently. Dean was eighteen, old enough to make his own choices, but it wouldn't stop Murphy questioning himself. He was sure every parent would be the same.

He thought of all the young people he'd come into contact with in his previous years — all the wannabe gang members, the scallies, the thugs. Thought of the respectable homes he'd visited, containing parents who just didn't know what they'd done wrong, their faces drawn and old before their time. The homes where the parents had long since given up on caring. Then there were the young victims. Trying to make sense of what they'd done to end up on the wrong side of those others.

They'd flashed before his eyes in an instant. That's all it was. Sarah had taken the hesitation for what it said on the surface.

This case wasn't helping, Murphy thought. Maybe if Dean Hughes had been in his eighties, he wouldn't have hesitated at all. Would have had a better response than the one he'd given.

'I don't know.'

The office was busier now, the various detectives working on different cases. The boards from that morning looked untouched as he stood before them.

He added the name of the youth club and Paul Cooper's name on a side list which was headed *Persons of Interest*. They had no suspects as yet, but Murphy wasn't put off.

'How are you getting on?'

Murphy turned to find DS Brannon standing just behind him, looking towards the board, squinting even though he was only a few feet away. 'Not bad. Slow, but a few things have come up already. We'll get there.'

'Saw the mum yesterday,' Brannon replied. 'I know a couple of her lads. Doesn't surprise me one of them's turned up dead. His older brother is the worst. Dale. He's got a trial coming up in Crown. GBH, wounding with intent. Should have been attempted murder.'

'Yeah, well . . . that's only interesting if it has something to do with my case. You got anything on that, Tony?'

Brannon scratched at his head, bits of dandruff landing on his shoulders. 'That youth club. I know the guy who runs it, Kevin

120

Thornhill. Used to go to school with him.'

Murphy brightened. 'Good stuff. Still in contact with him?'

Brannon smiled. 'Yeah, he's married to my brother's wife's sister's mate. See him at family dos and that.'

Murphy tried working out the familial connection in his head, but got lost. 'Good. Our vic was a regular at the youth club before he disappeared. Would be good to speak to Kevin about that, see if he remembers anything.'

'No worries, I'll set it up. He works weekends, I think. I'll give him a bell now.'

Murphy watched Brannon waddle off. Sniffed and went back to looking at the board. Rossi joined him, eating a Boost and flicking the cap off another bottle of energy drink at the same time.

'How late was it last night exactly? And why don't you drink coffee like a normal copper would?'

'Gone off coffee. And late.'

Murphy raised his eyebrows, earning a frown from Rossi.

'What?' Rossi said.

'No judgement here, Laura. What you do on your own time is none of my business.'

'No. It's not, so let's drop it.'

'Right,' Murphy said, holding his hands up in mock-surrender. 'I give in.'

'Yeah, cheers. Anyway, what did Brannon want?'

Murphy led them away from the board towards the office. 'He knows our youth club

121

manager. Married to his sister's wife or something.'

'What?'

'I didn't really follow,' Murphy replied, pushing into their office, noticing it was empty before dropping into his seat. 'Not the point anyway. He's sorting out a meeting for us. In the meantime, we need to find out where Dean's been the last seven months. Anything from those looking into his associates?'

Murphy waited as Rossi checked her in-tray and email. The door opened and DC Harris entered while in the process of removing his suit jacket, a folder being held in his teeth.

'All right bosses,' Harris said, once he'd extricated the folder. 'Want an update?'

'Of course,' Murphy said.

'None of Dean's close friends have seen him since the night the mum reported him missing. One of them thought he'd buggered off to Spain to work in a bar — her words, not mine — two thought he'd joined a cult, and one reckoned he'd got some girl pregnant and done one because her auld fella was going to kill him.'

'Names on the last one?'

'Just a rumour. He didn't know what the girl's name was or approximate times or anything like that.'

Murphy sighed. 'Right, well do follow-ups with the others. See if anyone can remember anything about that.' He removed his phone from his pocket as it buzzed and bleeped in rapid succession. He read the text message and added, 'Me and Rossi have a young girl to see.'

122

'Who?' Rossi said, perking up.

'Last person we know of who saw Dean Hughes.'

'No problem.'

This wasn't going to be an easy one, but they were used to that by now. Merseyside in general had gained a reputation of taking its time with high-profile cases. If it took a year to get the right people, it took a year.

Murphy hoped it wouldn't take that long.

★   ★   ★

The house belied its area. Expensive furnishings, down to the solid coffee table which was surrounded by a deep leather settee and armchairs. The smell of furniture polish mixing with jasmine told Murphy that Amanda Williams's parents — and his money was on the mother, given the general air around the father — had readied the house for their arrival.

'We dealt with Amanda at the time, Inspector,' the father said, who'd introduced himself at the door only as Mr Williams. 'I'm not sure what the point of all this is.'

'We just need to make sure all avenues are explored, given the seriousness of the crime,' Murphy said, eyeing the chocolate digestives on the plate sitting on the coffee table. At least the mother had offered her first name. Faye. Murphy liked the name. Filed it away. He peeled his eyes away from the biscuits, gave a small thanks to Faye, who smiled thinly and perched herself on the arm of her husband's armchair.

'They're just here to cover every angle, Jim,' Faye said to her husband, her accent buried in a veneer of clipped pronunciation. 'Let them do their job.'

'Well, I suppose that's good enough. Tell them what you know, Amanda.'

Murphy hadn't looked towards Amanda since they'd arrived. Dark eye make-up and drawn-on eyebrows. Legs clad in skinny jeans, tucked underneath herself, straining the fabric against her knees. She was wearing a large jumper which she sucked on the sleeve of, pulled against a thumb. Amanda brushed hair off her face, causing the bouffant to expand on top. Extensions, Murphy thought. Sarah had mentioned them once, but he'd baulked at the price and she hadn't brought it up again.

'Amanda, you know why we're here?'

'Yeah.'

'You realise how important it is to tell us everything you know, okay?'

Amanda nodded, eyes still on the edge of the coffee table, rather than on either her parents or Murphy and Rossi.

'Good. Did you know Dean well?'

She sniffed, 'Not really. Just from around and that.'

Around and that. Seemed a popular answer. 'Were you seeing each other?'

'Not really.' Her eyes shifted finally, looking nervously at her parents. 'He wanted to take me out, but I wasn't that interested.'

Amanda's father bristled in his chair, tutting quietly. Rossi caught the motion and cut in.

124

'Young girl like you, I bet you have a fair few lads after you?'

She shrugged. 'Suppose. Doesn't mean I do anything though. I'm not a slag or nothing.'

The tut of admonishment came from the mother this time. The father was shaking his head.

'What we need to know, Amanda, is if Dean and you were close.'

'A bit, like. Not really. We'd talk and stuff. He'd text me a lot. WhatsApp and that.'

'Did you talk the night he disappeared?' Murphy asked.

'Not much. He was just normal. Messing about with the lads, showing off, that kind of thing. I don't remember much about it, to be honest.'

'That's because you had too much to drink,' Jim Williams said, leaning forward, brow furrowing.

'Please, Mr Williams,' Murphy said, raising a hand. 'We'll get to that.'

Jim sat back in the chair, chewing his lip.

'Was everyone drinking, Amanda?' Murphy said.

'Yeah. It was a Friday, so there were a few of us. We all chipped in and got a load of cider.' She shot another look at her parents. 'I don't drink normally, but I did that night.'

'Apparently you got yourself into a state,' Rossi said, smiling, her tone on the jokey side. 'Been there a few times.'

Amanda smiled for the first time since they'd arrived. 'Yeah . . . guess I wasn't used to it.'

'So what do you remember then?' Rossi said.

'Just laughing a lot. Some of the lads were taking the piss out of one of the girls, and it was well funny. I was supposed to be staying at my mate's house, but she disappeared at some point. I reckon it was with Aaron, but she denies it.'

'What time was that do you think?'

'Can't really remember now. It was ages ago.'

'At some point you ended up alone with Dean though?' Murphy said, enjoying the way he and Rossi were in sync.

'Yeah, but I was wrecked by then. Nothing happened. We was just talking, I think.'

'Do you remember anything he said?'

'Not really,' Amanda said, stretching out her legs, the bones cricking in them as she moved. 'Just talking shi — rubbish and that.'

'Was he scared, afraid, anything like that?'

She considered it. 'I don't think so. It was so long ago. I think he talked about the youthy a bit. Wanted me to go down there in the week.'

There was something she was holding back, Murphy thought. Happy to discuss things she thought were safe topics, but there was something ringing in his mind. 'Amanda, are you still okay with your parents being here? Only, if there's something you want to tell us, but would rather do it privately . . . '

'There's nothing she can't say in front of us, Inspector . . . ' Jim said.

'I'm sure that's the case, Mr Williams,' Murphy replied, 'but sometimes a little discretion is needed.'

He and his wife shared a look. 'Five minutes.

126

And we're just in the kitchen. Don't be forcing her to say anything she doesn't want to. We know our rights.'

'Of course,' Murphy said, waiting for them to leave the room. Faye left first, the father looking behind as he walked out of the living room. 'Okay, Amanda, is there something you want to tell us?'

'I don't know . . . '

Rossi took over, sensing the same thing Murphy was. 'It's okay, Amanda. If something happened between the two of you when you were on your own, that's not your fault, we'll listen.'

Amanda sat forward. 'No, it's nothing like that.' Her voice raised upwards, into a higher pitch. 'God, he wasn't like that.'

'Okay,' Murphy said, his hands out in front of him, 'what is it then?'

'The drink. Like, we didn't exactly pay for it.'

'What do you mean?'

Amanda sighed, leaning back into the settee. 'I wasn't there though. It was nothing to do with me. I got told later. Dean and a couple of the other lads nicked it from an offy. That's what I heard anyway, later on like.'

Murphy scratched at his beard and looked at Rossi. Got a blank look in return. 'Which offy?'

'Think it was the one on the Strand.'

'Right. Anything else?'

Amanda shook her head.

'Well, if there is anything more, just let us know, okay?'

Murphy felt there was more being unsaid

— maybe about the exact nature of what happened once the two teenagers had been alone. He knew they weren't about to be told anything else right then though. Amanda had retreated back into her shell, chewing on the end of her jumper, looking years younger than her seventeen. A little girl, thrust into the world of adults and death. The shock of the real world etched across her young face.

The Farm

Three Months Ago

It was becoming almost crowded in the Dorm now, Goldie thought — what with Dean, Bootle, another new lad who had arrived the week before, and himself. Four teenage lads, none of them older than nineteen, and Goldie reckoned the new lad was lying when he said that was how old he was. Looked more like sixteen, with bum fluff on his top lip which would probably disappear in a strong wind.

Bootle had tried to be the big man again when the new lad showed up. This time he'd been ignored, rather than beaten up like Goldie had done to him. Seemed to work just as well, from what Goldie had seen.

'What's your name, mate?' Goldie had asked when things had calmed down after that first night, when the new lad had stopped banging against the door trying to get out.

'Craig,' he'd replied, from the bed he'd now taken to sitting rigidly upright upon. 'What's yours?'

'Goldie. Over there is Bootle . . . '

'It's fucking MC Cray-Z . . . '

'Whatever,' Goldie replied, dismissing him with a wave of his hand. 'Call him what you like, but I'm sticking with Bootle. In the corner, that's Dean. He doesn't say much, but don't worry,

Bootle more than makes up for him.'

Craig didn't say much the first few days. Things started happening in shifts now, their *lessons* taking place one after the other. Always in the evenings, which Goldie had begun to realise was because they, them out there, probably had jobs and stuff during the day. He thought it meant he had more chance of escape during the daytime, the idea that less of them out there made his odds better. It didn't matter though. Turned out the odds were pretty shitty when you were looking at a shotgun.

'How long have I been here?' Goldie had asked at some point.

'How long do you think it's been?' The answer had come back from Omega. Goldie had learnt all their names and could tell who was who even without being able to see their faces. There was a woman in amongst them. Gamma. Goldie had counted five of them, including Alpha. He'd been shocked at first, not thinking it was possible that a bird could be involved in something like this. Then she'd called him a lazy, thick, fat twat, and he'd stopped wondering about her.

Omega was the only one he could tell wasn't from Liverpool. Sounded more pie-eating country than proper Wool. At least he wasn't a Manc. Goldie didn't think he could handle being kept locked up by a Manc.

Goldie's days were mostly the same . . . as were all the lads'. Wake up, or rather, be woken up by the banging on the door. The door would open and food already dished out on trays would be thrown on the floor. Porridge, which ranged from being too sweet to far too bland, depending on the day. The usual argument over who was going for a piss first, before the boredom set in. The only thing to do was read the books that were provided for them. Goldie wasn't sure all four of them were exactly big readers on the outside. Dean would lie on his bed, just waiting for the evening, he guessed, whilst they sat around, sometimes talking, sometimes telling stories of the outside. Dreaming of what they'd do when they were finally let out.

'I'm gonna fuck everything that moves, mate,' Bootle would say constantly, endlessly. 'Seriously, it's going in every fucking hole, lad.'

'Surprised you can find the fucking thing to stick it anywhere,' Goldie had replied, the look of anger on Bootle's face disappearing as they heard laughter from the direction of Dean's bed.

That was about as much as they got out of him. Goldie would have been worried, but he was more interested in how he was in himself. The weight was draining from him. He could afford to lose some but didn't want to end up as some lanky streak of piss.

No one spoke of how scared they were. Scared of every bang on the door, scared that every time they left that small dorm room, it would be for the last time. Goldie had almost become used to the way his throat would close up in fear when they arrived. When they were alone it was all bravado. Just a show.

The days would drag, only broken up by the arrival of some more food during what they guessed was the afternoon. Someone would have a shit and stink the place out for a bit. Get moaned at, but then forgotten.

No one looked forward to the evenings. Yeah, it was nice to get out of the Dorm, but it wasn't worth it.

Goldie went first or second, usually. Frog-marched out, guns trained on him all the time . . . and him not suddenly becoming that bloke in those action films, Jason something, able to take out four guys holding weapons and making a run for it.

He'd be taken into a different building than the one which held the rack. This was slightly bigger, more sparse. Dirty floor and wind blowing through the gaps in the wood-covered walls. He knew the drill now. Walk to the middle, as the three men lined up in front of him. Then the exercises would begin.

Push-ups, sit-ups, jogging on the spot, star jumps. Those were the easy parts.

'I'm not doing this,' Goldie had said after he'd started feeling dizzy in the first few days.

'Then you're no use to us. We'll put a bullet in your head and bury you out there in the farmland. No one will ever find you.'

It was amazing the energy that could suddenly be found when you believed someone would have no problem with digging a hole for your dead body.

After the warm-up, it was time for the hard part, holding himself in the push-up position with just his fingers, waiting for them to buckle so he would fall face first into the floor. Then, if they weren't happy with how long you had done it for, starting all over again. Squatting down, all your weight on your thigh muscles, burning, stretching. Agony setting in quickly.

All the time, he had Gamma or Delta shouting at him for any wrong move he made. For any time they believed he wasn't putting in enough effort. It didn't matter that he never had time to rest his body, other than on the odd days they didn't show up in the evenings.

Being made to lie face down on the floor, raising his hands and feet until they told him he could put them down.

The stretching was the worst. Being forced into unnatural positions, which caused him to cry out in pain every time. Placing his hands into the small of his back and squeezing his elbows together, stretching out his chest. Then, inevitably, one of them would come over and force his elbows together.

Those were the easy parts.

'Pull your arms back.'

'You're not trying hard enough.'

'You fucking piece of shit, move.'

Voices getting louder all the time. Screaming by this point, right into his ear.

Then he'd do something they didn't like.

It started out weird. Like they were scared or something. It got worse quickly though.

Goldie didn't know how long it had taken for the first time. Maybe a week. Ten days maybe. He'd noticed Dean coming back into the Dorm, wincing a little, a little crusted blood under his nose. Goldie had put it down to not being up to the physical part of it.

133

Then he'd felt it himself. The build-up.

'Why are we even bothering ourselves doing this?' he'd heard Tango say one day. Whispered for effect. 'He's just a scally no-mark. This isn't going to do anything.'

Goldie had made the mistake of replying. 'Fucking right, mate.'

He felt a crack as he was lifted off the floor, halfway through another press-up, flipping over onto his back.

'What are you doing?' Goldie had heard the other one say.

'The only thing these pricks understand.'

Goldie tried bracing himself, but it didn't matter. A boot came into his side, making him double up. Trying to breathe, the wind taken out of him. A hand grabbing him by the ear, stretching, pulling his head up as he still struggled to get his breath back.

Tango's fist pounding into his face. Dull weight crashing into him, over and over.

That was just the first time. Now it was an excuse for a couple of blokes to do him over every few days. Working out their frustration. Him forced to lie there and take it. Not able to fight back.

At least it was just being beaten up. That's what got him through it. No one had tried to do anything else. Sexual, or whatever. He wouldn't have been able to take that, he decided.

He could take the physical part. That was exhausting but easy. It was never knowing when they were going to start. *If* they were going to start.

Being afraid wasn't easy for him.

Afterwards, he was allowed a shower, and then it was his time with Alpha. Back in the rack room. It was covered now, but Goldie knew what lay beneath the cloth. At that point, the other lads had all been on there except Craig, but Goldie knew he'd get his turn eventually.

'How are you today, Joshua?' Alpha said as he sat down in the chair opposite him. Goldie hated that he'd told him his real name, but he was sure he knew anyway. Was sure they knew all they could about him.

'I'd like to go home,' Goldie replied. The same thing every time. Hoped that one day he'd get the answer he wanted.

'Well, you're making good progress, but it's still a little early for that I think.'

Goldie sat back, folded his arms, but then let them hang loose as he earned a withering look from Alpha.

Every day was the same. Over and over, drummed into them, the errors they'd made. Some days they had lessons, of a kind. How to manage money, how to look for jobs.

'*You've got to be willing to work from the very bottom level. The nastiest, scummiest job you can think of can lead to anything you like. It's all experience. You have to get out there, show tenacity and persistence. We all had to do it years ago. There was no dossing around, living on benefits and just popping out a kid if you wanted a bit more money. No big flat-screen TV bought on HP from bloody BrightHouse or wherever. You worked hard for the luxuries. You*

135

worked hard, full stop. That's what you're going to do if you ever leave here.'

Goldie understood the message, even if sometimes they used words he'd never heard before. They made it sound easy, like he could just go out there and work his way up the ladder just by working hard. He doubted they really knew the score these days. It was shit jobs, for shit money.

He nodded along and said yes in all the right places though. Sometimes his eyes would betray him and Alpha would cock his head. That was a cue for Goldie to brace himself as the whip was used on him. Welts appearing across his face for the other lads to stare at. Occasionally his mouth would get him into trouble, but for the most part he was keeping his head down. Just waiting.

'Last night we spoke about what you had been doing since you left school.'

It was all they ever spoke about, Goldie thought.

'Yes.'

'What do you think about your behaviour now you've had some time to reflect?'

Goldie went into standard mode. 'It was really terrible, what we did to those people. I would never do it again, swear down.'

Alpha tutted in response. 'There's that 'we' word again, Joshua. You're not accepting full responsibility for your actions. *You* did these things. Tell me some of them again.'

Goldie almost sighed, but eyed the handgun in Alpha's hand — finger resting on the trigger as always — and thought better of it. 'I dunno

'. . .we . . . I robbed some kids of mobile phones. Got pisse — I mean drunk, in the street outside people's houses and then shouted stuff at them when they moaned . . . '

'Not moaned.'

'Sorry, yeah, I mean . . . erm . . . complained.'

'What else?'

Goldie had gone through the list so many times it should have been easy to remember all the things, but he didn't want to. It sounded so stupid when he said them out loud. Kid stuff, really.

'Gone on the rob too many times. From shops and that. Fuc — beat up other people for a laugh.'

Alpha shifted the gun from one hand to the other, seeming to relax a little. Goldie had waited over the previous months for a single slip, one mistake that he could use. He was always too slow though, too scared to take any chance of escape.

'You're still holding back on me.'

Goldie's eyes shifted left. He rubbed his palms together, sweat making them feel greasy.

'I'm not . . . '

'You are. And I'm tired of it.'

Goldie thought for a few seconds. Tried not to think about the worst things he'd done.

'It's written all over your face. I'll say it again. We can't move forward here until you're completely honest. So, tell me what is it that you don't want to tell me.'

Goldie closed his eyes for a second. Two, maybe. Remembered the face of the woman.

137

Grey, lined with years of life.

Then, afterwards.

'We robbed a house once,' Goldie said, his voice quiet and shaking. 'Thought it would be in and out. Only did it for a laugh. Didn't really need anything but thought we'd get a few extra quid.'

Alpha leant forward, one hand on the gun, the other laying beneath the table. 'What happened?'

Goldie breathed in. 'She woke up. The old girl that lived there. Came down and scared the shit out of us.'

'Us?'

'Just me and a couple of mates. Don't hang around with them any more.'

'What happened then?'

'She came in the living room, just as Joe was shitting on her carpet. Put the big light on and we all froze . . . well, nearly all of us. Joe carried on like it was nothing. She starts screaming at us. It'd been a laugh up until then. Just robbing a bit of jewellery she'd left downstairs, some notes out her purse and that. It wasn't like she had anything worth nicking really. That's why Joe decided to do that. Anyway, this old girl, she starts kicking off big time. Had hold of this big walking stick and is just waving it in front of her, like she was about to beat the shit out of us with it. I'm just stood there staring, 'cause I can't believe she's woken up. Joe is trying to pull his kecks up. But Chris . . . Chris is stood the closest to her. Had hold of the hammer we'd brought . . . '

Goldie swallowed, risked taking a look towards

Alpha, looking away as the man's eyes stared towards him.

'What happened then?'

Goldie put his head in his hands. He didn't want to say any of this. Never thought he would tell another person until he was on his deathbed.

'He swung at her. She just crumpled into a heap. He gave her a few more kicks when she was down, but by that time Joe had got up and was dragging us both away.'

'Did she die?'

'I kept checking the *Echo*, but it didn't show up for a few days. She didn't die. Not right away. She was old though, so maybe that was it?'

Alpha nodded a little. 'Put your left hand on the table. Spread out your fingers. Omega, come over here.'

Goldie frowned but did as he was told.

'Hold his shoulders,' Alpha said, looking past him towards Omega.

Goldie worked out what was happening too late. He watched as Alpha drew out the hand that had been underneath the table. Goldie blinked as the blade came into view. Alpha grabbed his hand.

'This'll make you always remember what you did.'

The pain wasn't instant. It was a dull siren, coming from a few streets away, getting louder by the second.

'What have you done? This wasn't sup-posed . . . '

'Be quiet, Omega.'

Goldie stared down at his hand as if it was

139

alien to him, not connected at all. The space where his little finger had been now filling with blood. Realisation hit him then. He shook back in his chair, barrelling Omega over, holding onto his hand as he got to his feet, Omega on the floor, the gun he'd been holding scattering across the room.

'What the fuck? What have you done?' Goldie screamed, turning to face Alpha.

The man in the balaclava and suit stared back at him, moving only to point the gun towards him. 'Don't do anything stupid.'

Goldie wanted to. Wanted to do something, anything. Stared at the gun and thought about how quick that bullet could travel. He was barely aware of Omega getting to his feet.

Goldie made a decision, just as the pain from his hand began to really set in. He dived to the floor, determined to get to the other gun, crawling across the room out of sight of Alpha. Heard the older man swear and start moving. Omega was slow to react, screeching out in pain as Goldie reached him standing and sank his teeth into his leg. Quick, just enough to make him move back and give him more time. He saw the shotgun at the end of the table, lying on the floor, the barrel facing him. Goldie lunged, his hands closing around the stock and pulling it towards him.

A boot crunched down onto his ankle, then the world exploded, his ears ringing. Wind passing by his face, turning away to the heat. His grip on the shotgun faltering as he blinked into the space above him.

'Don't fucking move.'

Goldie could feel the blood seeping out of him onto the cold, hard floor.

'Let go, now.'

Goldie did as he was told and closed his eyes. Thought about his now-deformed hand and allowed the pain to swell over him.

★　★　★

Omega turned on Alpha as soon as the boy had been taken away by Delta and Gamma to be patched up. Somehow. He wasn't sure how the hell they were supposed to fix a severed finger.

'What were you doing?' he said, unable to hold back his anger. 'You could have killed him.'

'And then what? What do you think we're running here . . . a nice little bootcamp where they can all live happily together?'

Omega stumbled over his words. 'No . . . I just . . . I just don't think we should be doing that type of thing. I know what the others do to them. Don't think I'm stupid. I've seen the bruises, the marks being left on those boys. But you and me. We're men of God. That's what you promised me.'

'Hebrews 9:22.'

Omega paused, remembering the verse.

'You don't remember it, *Omega?* Let me refresh your memory. *Under the law almost everything is purified with blood, and without the shedding of blood there is no forgiveness of sins.*'

Omega blinked once, twice.

141

'We're doing a good thing here. We need to teach them the error of their ways. Teach them that their sin will not go unnoticed. You heard what he said before. He let an old, defenceless woman die because of his actions. He needed to learn that his actions have consequences. He's lucky we didn't take it further.'

Omega nodded, his perception shifted. 'Okay. But please, talk these things through with me first.'

★ ★ ★

He left later that night, wanting to sleep in his own bed. Not on those single, threadbare mattresses back at the farm, but in the nice king-size one he had at home. It wasn't too late, and he had appointments the following morning anyway.

He needed to keep up appearances, after all.

Reverend Andrew Pearson fiddled with his dog collar in the rear-view mirror and then drove his car away from the farm.

From the place where sin was rife.

12

They'd done a few hours on the Sunday, but there was really no point to it. Murphy had pushed to get more done, but there were no leads. They'd tried the off-licence on the Strand in Norris Green, but the owner barely remembered the incident involving Dean, never mind bore a grudge over it. Told them shoplifting happened so often, he only made complaints just to claim on the insurance. Murphy had ended up going home in the early afternoon, losing himself to the match on the radio as he did some more decorating.

It was Monday morning, the effects of the weekend silently leaving the station. The remnants of a busy weekend in town, the logistics of policing the multitude of pubs and clubs becoming almost second nature to most of those working, but still difficult to imagine for anyone who hadn't experienced it for themselves.

Murphy stood in front of the Dean Hughes board. Examined the limited information posted on there, making sure there was nothing he'd missed. He wasn't sure what was worse ... dealing with pissheads in the city centre, coked-up and looking for a fight, or this.

At least it was only one.

Briefing was set for nine a.m., so Murphy spent an hour in his office reading over the information gleaned from the door-to-door enquiries. More information gathered from those not home the first time around. Nothing there. The body being dumped late at night, not directly in front of any houses, Murphy had expected nothing less. It was still an annoyance, especially with the preponderance of CCTV around the city. No trouble clocking him doing a few miles an hour over forty going down Scottie Road, but they never pointed the bloody cameras at possible body dumps.

'Anything?'

'*Nada.*'

'That's Spanish, but thanks for trying.'

Rossi had arrived twenty minutes after him, bearing gifts of bacon sarnies and fresh coffee. She was in his good books for the day.

'What's the Italian then?'

'*Niente.*'

Murphy pushed away from his desk. 'I think I prefer the Spanish.'

'If it wasn't for the months he was missing, we'd be looking at who he was hanging around with . . . '

'We have been.'

'Not really. The girl he was with last? The one lad already in custody? Both don't know what he's been doing. Could have been anywhere, with nothing sinister about it at all. We've had that kind of thing before.'

Murphy scratched at his beard. 'Yeah, but usually there's a pattern of behaviour before that happens. His mum was shocked he'd gone, thought there was something wrong until the

144

note arrived. And that's bullshit as well. You don't fuck off with someone and then send a note months later.'

'Maybe . . . '

A knock at the office door interrupted Rossi, the door opening without a response from either of them, and DS Brannon entering.

'Morning,' he said, perching himself on the edge of Rossi's desk, facing Murphy. 'I've spoken to Kevin.'

Murphy gave him a blank stare, Rossi pushing him off her desk.

'Okay, okay, I'm moving,' Brannon said, bringing one of the chairs from the DCs' desks over. 'Kevin Thornhill. The guy who runs the youth club your scally was seen at.'

'Right,' Murphy replied. 'Good.'

'Yeah, said we can go around this morning.'

'*We?*' Rossi said, disdain dripping forth so much from a single word that even Brannon couldn't miss it.

'Yeah. I thought since I know the bloke it was only right that I go with you. Make things easier and that.'

'Reason not to, if you ask me.'

Murphy held up a hand to stop Brannon arguing back. 'The three of us are going. We need all the help we can get at the moment.'

Brannon smirked at Rossi, earning a look back which wiped it off his face.

The briefing out of the way, Brannon drove them to the youth club, situated on the outskirts of the Norris Green estate. The long road coming down from Croxteth Park turning from

145

Dwerryhouse Lane to Lower House. The houses behind the main road grouping together to form the estate itself.

Rossi sat behind Murphy, sulking because she had to sit in the back of the car. It was hardly like Murphy could squeeze his bulk in the back, but she'd attempted a small victory by making it difficult for him to slide his chair back enough to stretch his legs out.

'That actor, David Morrissey, used to go to that school,' Brannon said, pointing towards De La Salle on the right-hand side. 'It's one of those academies now . . . whatever they are.'

'Didn't Rooney go there as well?' Murphy asked, pulling at a thread on his black trousers. Time to get another suit.

'Yeah, but he was well after. Guessing you went to Speke Comp?'

Murphy nodded. 'Gone now, though. Pulled it down a few years back. Just been left to rot. Saw a thing in the *Echo* a year or so back. Bunch of people living there were complaining because they were getting rats.'

Brannon slowed the car, indicating right to pull into Carr Lane East, the church on the corner hiding the youth club behind it. The back of the church faced onto a few small houses — the vicarage, Murphy assumed — and a large building which was opposite. The sign was loud and garish, jaunty colourful writing splashed across the front.

Norris Green Youth Centre.

The club itself was the newest building in the area, completely rebuilt from an existing run-down shack of a place. Murphy recalled the full spread given to the project in the *Liverpool Echo* — the pictures of the people who had backed the project standing proudly next to the first bricks being laid. All victims of crime. Youth crime in particular.

It seemed to be *de rigueur* for the families who had been affected by serious, well-publicised crime to go on to help the community at large. Something for those parents of children lost, or the offspring of older victims, to hold onto, to work towards. A distraction from the reality of grief. Murphy had considered it when his own parents had been murdered; setting something up in their names to keep the memory of them alive, to keep himself going. In the end, he internalised it all, placating his conscience with the thought that his mum and dad would have hated any kind of public display of their deaths. No matter that their murders had been quite the story when they had occurred. Better to let the story die than to keep raking it up.

Murphy got out the car as soon as they'd parked up, eager to stretch his legs and take in a few breaths of fresh air, away from the various smells of fried chicken mixing with greasy burgers emanating from within Brannon's car. Rossi had done the same, wincing towards Murphy as she looked over the top of the car. 'You two talk to this Kevin. I'll have a look around, see if I can jog anyone else's memories.'

Murphy nodded towards Rossi, letting her walk ahead as he waited for Brannon who was attaching a steering lock inside his car. 'What are

147

you doing that for? It's the middle of the day.'

'I know what it's like around here. Not taking any chances,' Brannon replied with a shrug.

'Like anyone would nick that piece of crap anyway. You need a new car, Tony.'

Brannon gave him a stare as he shut and locked the car door. 'Not all of us can afford a new car . . . sir.'

Murphy let him have that one.

Kevin Thornhill met them at the entrance of the youth club and led them towards a short corridor away from the main hall. His office was at the end, a few posters on the walls of the corridor, drugs and sex education in the main. Windows on the other side faced out onto the road, the fields behind the school in view. Murphy kept a few paces behind, allowing Brannon to make small talk with Thornhill.

'Do you want a drink? We've got tea or coffee,' Thornhill said, as he closed the door behind them.

Murphy shook his head. 'I'm all right, thanks.' Brannon did the same after a moment.

'No problem,' Thornhill replied, sitting down behind a small desk. The office was roomy enough for two chairs either side, but that was where the space ended. Murphy looked around, impressed by the level of clutter which Thornhill had aspired to.

'Sorry about the mess. Yearly review is coming up, so I'm up the wall with paperwork, trying to justify costs and that.' Thornhill turned to Brannon, 'Just shift that box over if it's in the way, Tony.'

'We won't take up much of your time, Mr Thornhill . . . '

'Please, call me Kev,' Thornhill said, flashing a smile that showed faded white teeth.

'Okay, Kev,' Murphy replied. 'I'm sure DS Brannon has given you a few details of why we wanted to speak to you.'

Thornhill's smile disappeared in an instant. 'Yeah, I was shocked to hear about poor Dean.'

'Well, I'm sure then you'll be keen to help us with our enquiries?'

'Of course.'

'Good. When was the last time you saw Dean Hughes?' Murphy said, removing a notepad from inside his jacket. He loosened his tie as he noticed the heat increase in the cramped office.

'Would have been last October. About six months ago.'

'And how was he?'

Thornhill leant back, a hand drifting towards his earlobe. 'Seemed normal. He was a good lad at heart, but he was always getting himself into trouble it seemed.'

Brannon removed his jacket, placing it over his lap, but stayed silent. Murphy continued, writing down Thornhill's responses. 'Did he come here regularly?'

'A few times a week up until October. We were trying to get him involved with the younger ones. The younger teenagers, I mean. I thought giving him some responsibility would bring him out a bit.'

'How had Dean taken to that?'

'Really well, I think,' Thornhill replied,

nodding his head. 'He was talking about taking a few college courses.'

'Did he have any problems with anyone here?'

'Not that I know of, but he could get a bit hot-headed. Usually he calmed down quickly, but he let his frustration show a few times. There's a few like him who come here. All looking for something to put them back on the straight and narrow. I thought he could make something of himself.'

'Were there any fights or bust-ups with other lads?' Brannon said, speaking for the first time.

Thornhill thought for a second. 'Not that I can remember. We tend to have an argument every day, but it never gets very far. They all know we have a strict policy on that sort of thing.'

'What is that policy, Kev?' Murphy said.

'One chance and you're out. You get an official warning and if you break it, you're not allowed back.'

Murphy hummed. 'Seems a bit harsh . . . '

'What you have to remember is that this is supposed to be a place these kids can come and be away from anything like that. If we allow that peace to be broken, they'll stay away because it'll be no different than the streets we're taking them away from. This place has to be special, otherwise there's no point. Plus, we're only open because we have a good investor. Can't be seen to be a soft touch.'

Murphy nodded slowly. 'It seems to be working out well. I know youth crime is down in the area in the past year.'

Thornhill smiled. 'Well I can't take credit for

that obviously, but we are very happy with the progress we've made.'

'Who did Dean hang around with here? Any friends he brought in with him?'

'Yeah, he was always in a group of three or four. He seemed to be the mainstay though. The others dropped in and out.'

'Names, Kev?' Brannon said, Murphy writing down the names as Thornhill said them. Names they already knew from Dean's various social networks and from Amanda's interview.

'Anything else you can tell us, Kev? Doesn't matter how small you think it is, we're just trying to build up a picture right now. He was gone a long time before he was found.'

Thornhill leant back again, fingers unable to leave his earlobe, pulling on it, stretching it out. 'I don't know if it's important really . . . it could be nothing.'

Brannon inclined forward in his seat. 'Kev, give us a hand here mate.'

Thornhill sighed and placed his hands on the desk. 'About a week after he was here last, someone came looking for Dean. Bit aggressive and that. Nothing we're not used to. Was moaning on about being owed money.'

'Did he say anything threatening about Dean?' Murphy said, looking Thornhill in the eye.

'Just that . . . well, it could mean nothing as they're always throwing this kind of thing around these days . . . he said Dean was going to be dead when he caught up with him.'

Murphy took out a mugshot of Paul Cooper and showed it to Thornhill. 'Is this the guy?'

151

Thornhill looked at the photo for a few seconds and then nodded. 'Think so. Pretty certain about it.'

Murphy sighed internally. Cooper's alibi was pretty watertight, so he didn't think he was involved. Murphy wrote a note to look more into Cooper anyway.

Something wasn't adding up.

★ ★ ★

Rossi let the blokes walk away, uninterested in what some youth club manager had to say. Much more interested in what was going on in the main hall.

The layout was much as she expected. A couple of pool tables, lots of chairs, vending machines and what were probably called 'activity centres', but were just trestle tables with some large scraps of paper on them. There was a place for younger kids in one corner, a few soft toys for the offspring of teenagers, she imagined.

'Who are you?'

Rossi turned to find a stout woman in what looked suspiciously like a tabard standing next to her. Pockmarked round face, with limp and languid brown hair. Grey roots showing through. Her eyes told a different story though. Rossi thought they looked like they'd seen some hard times but hadn't lost any sense of kindness behind them.

'Yeah, sorry, I'm Detective Sergeant Laura Rossi. We're investigating the death of Dean Hughes . . . '

'Terrible news that was. I was tellin' our Angela — that's my sister, she sometimes helps out here — about it before. Dead shocking it was.'

Rossi tried keeping her voice at an inside level, but it was difficult when matched up against this woman's boom.

'And you are . . . '

'Sorry,' the woman said, wiping a hand down her front and offering it up. 'I'm Margie. I kinda do all the hard work while himself sits in the back, working out how to pay for it all.'

'Nice to meet you. Tell me about the place.'

So Margie did. In great detail, much to Rossi's misplaced delight. After a few minutes non-stop talking, Rossi thought Margie was about to run out of things to say, as she told her about the experience days, the efforts going into keeping everything fresh and exciting for the regular kids who came in.

Who was copping off with whom was probably information Rossi didn't need, but she didn't mind listening.

'They're good kids,' Margie said. 'Just need a bit of guidance, that's all. Not getting it at home, so we're the next best thing. We've had loads of kids come here, been in trouble with the bizzies and that. Give them a bit of attention, a bit of support, and things change. Always my favourite part of the job when they come in and tell me they've got a job or something.'

'What's the worst part?' Rossi said, looking over at a couple of shaven-headed lads in tracksuit bottoms and hoodies laughing with an

153

older woman whilst playing pool.

'Everyone always imagines it's when one of them goes off their heads or something. You know,' Margie leant towards Rossi, the smell of cigarette smoke coming off her in a wave. 'When they get a bit violent and that. With us or each other. But it's not that at all . . . '

'What is it then?'

'It's when they don't come back. When they disappear. That's what gets me every time. Because I never know if they're safe . . . like if they've gone down the wrong path or something. It's the worry that I've failed.'

13

Thornhill showed them back to the entrance to the youth club, Murphy and Brannon emerging into the sunshine to find Rossi leaning on the car, frowning at her phone. She looked up and threw away a cigarette as she spotted them.

'Smoking, Laura?' Murphy said, shaking his head.

'Just every now and again. I swear I'm not back on them full-time.'

'Not me you have to worry about. Your ma will kill you if she finds out.'

'Well she won't, will she?' Rossi had started smoking regularly following the events of the previous year, a small tic she'd picked up, as all those involved had done. Murphy's crutch had been food, putting on the two stone he'd worked hard to shed, quicker than it had taken him to lose it. He was just getting over that. The takeaway on Friday night had been his only slip . . . apart from that morning's bacon sarnie, but that hadn't been his fault really. Rossi had foregone food or a drinking problem and gone for smoking. Something small to take the edge off. You deal with something as big as the first serial killer in your city for almost a hundred years, you're going to need something.

'Learn anything?' Murphy said, opening the passenger side door and getting into the car.

'Not much,' Rossi said, sitting in the back, the

middle this time. She looked around her for a seatbelt but gave up quickly, leaning forward between Murphy and Brannon. 'Spoke to Margie. She's the brains of the operation by the sounds of it. Good woman, you know. Also spoke to a couple of the kids in there. They liked Dean, looked up to him.'

'Did they mention anyone coming looking for him?'

Rossi shook her head. 'No. Nothing like that. Just that they'd asked about him at the youthy and no one knew where he'd gone.'

Murphy pointed right, back to the station, as Brannon reached the end of the street and threw his palms up. 'Kevin Thornhill reckons someone came to see Dean a week after he went missing, trying to find him. Owed him money, threatening.'

'Really? No one mentioned that to me,' Rossi replied.

'Showed him a picture of Paul Cooper and he was almost sure it was him. But as we know, he wasn't around that night. Plus I'm not sure he's got it in him to keep this sort of thing quiet. Something doesn't make sense. Could be there was someone else he'd pissed off. Unless he'd annoyed the wrong person and gone into hiding, where would he have been for that week? Something isn't right.'

'Could be he was found,' Brannon said, one hand resting on the steering wheel as he fiddled with the electric window. 'Let's say for instance he owed someone money. Forget Cooper for now, he's too low-scale. Maybe a proper dealer or something. Dean knows he's in trouble, so gets his head down. Moves away, something like that. Thinks enough time has passed, so he comes back to Liverpool. Only, as we know, these types of people have long memories. He's found pretty quickly and ends up outside the church, dead.'

Murphy scratched at his beard, weighing it up. It made a weird kind of sense. 'Only one thing with that . . . the letter that was sent to his mum. Where does that come into it?'

'Unless Dean really did send it?' Rossi said from the back.

'Good thinking,' Murphy replied, now thinking about the whole. 'So let's run this whole thing out. Dean Hughes goes out with his mates, cops off with some girl, but before that has run up debts with a dealer or something similar. No history of drug abuse, but we know he could have owed a whole lot of money just by doing coke at the weekends — weed in the week. He's late paying back. What happens after he takes the girl home? He's walking back to his own house and is jumped? Threatened? So he just takes off without a word . . . doesn't even go home to pack a bag or anything? Something is missing here.'

Rossi sat back in the seat in the rear of the car. Brannon drummed his fingers against the steering wheel, after finally getting his window to the correct opening. Otherwise, there was silence as they all tried to fill in the blanks.

It was a quiet trip back to the station.

* * *

The sun was shining through the windows into the main office space, bathing the incident room in golden light, with people shielding their eyes, complaining about the non-effectiveness of the blinds. Detective constables shuffling back and forth between desks, tapping away at keyboards and sometimes sharing a joke. The odd couple of people leaving or returning. Studying whiteboards and updating them.

The space around Dean Hughes's own murder board was bare. The details on there still sparse and untouched from that morning. Murphy considered it while standing a few feet away, still trying to make his mind up about how to approach it now. Fewer resources had that effect. He couldn't afford to take a multi-pronged approach, and given the little information they had, there was only really one way to tackle it.

'Laura,' Murphy called, spotting her return from the vending machine. 'Over here.'

Rossi sauntered over, ripping open a chocolate bar she'd plundered from the machine. 'Yeah?'

'We're going to have to concentrate on the money angle. It's the best guess we have right now. So I want every available effort we have going into finding out who he owed money to, I want that lad we spoke to Saturday morning . . . '

'Paul Cooper.'

'Yeah, him. He'll know more. Just have to ask the right questions. Get him picked up. He'll be on bail, I imagine.'

Rossi nodded. 'Anything else?'

'Every one of his mates. I want them all pulled in.'

Rossi blew out a long breath. 'That's a few cells being taken up.'

'Not in the cells. Interview rooms. I don't want them thinking they're in trouble or anything like that. I just don't want them interviewed in the comfort of their own homes. Let them know it's serious by bringing them down here.'

'Okay then.'

'Someone will have a name. Once we have that, everything will be much easier.'

Rossi nodded, turning away and calling DCs by name to follow her. Murphy watched her leave, safe in the knowledge that she'd dole out the tasks properly. He turned back to the murder board, staring at the two photographs of Dean Hughes tacked onto it. One was a school photo from around four years ago, according to his mum. The other photo showed little change. Taken from one of the times he'd been picked up by police, the comedown apparently. A hardening look around the eyes, perhaps. Dark circles underneath, which spoke of late nights wearing him down little by little. The hair was now shaved close to the scalp, rather than the short tousled look he'd sported a few years previously. He still looked like a child though. A man-child, eighteen, but not the same eighteen as previous generations, leaving school at fifteen and going straight off to work. Now Merseyside boasted one of the highest levels of youth unemployment

159

and an increasingly disenfranchised section of society. Murphy had been there at the beginnings of it, during the nineties, when dock changes took away the jobs there. The factories and warehouses emptying. He'd seen the increase in youth crime — always there, but not to the significant level it now was. A combination of no prospects and bad education perpetuating through the generations.

Brannon appeared beside Murphy, slipping into his peripheral vision and following his stare towards the board. 'Going for the drugs angle then?' Brannon said.

'Looks like our best bet at the moment,' Murphy replied, finally turning away from the board. 'Something along those lines anyway.'

'Always is with this lot.'

'What lot?'

Brannon sniffed, a sneer growing across his face. 'These kids today. If they're not robbing people's houses, they're killing each other over a few quid or some stupid *turf* war. Honestly, I don't know why we waste our time with these scrotes. What's the point? They're just nasty little shits who sit on their arses all day and do nothing but cause us all trouble.'

Murphy breathed in deeply. 'Where you from, Tony?'

'What's that matter?'

'Humour me.'

'Heswall,' Brannon replied, his voice now quieter. 'Over the water.'

Murphy sighed. *Over the water* meaning across the River Mersey, on the Wirral. 'Nice

160

place, that. Ever lived on an estate in Liverpool, Tony? Or even just over the water . . . Leasowe, Seacombe?'

'What's your point?'

'Let's just say you've got no idea what their lives are like really.' Murphy turned towards Brannon, looking down at him and fixing him with a stare. Leant in towards him and said in a whisper, 'And if I hear you say anything like that again during this investigation, I'll throw you through the fucking window . . . metaphorically speaking, of course.'

Murphy walked away before Brannon had a chance to respond, catching up to Rossi as she finished speaking to a couple of detective constables. He motioned towards their office with his head. The noise dissipated as they closed the door behind them.

'We've got uniforms going around to all the names and picking them up. Monday afternoon, so hopefully most of them will be at home.'

'Good. Make sure there's somewhere to put them when they arrive. I want a statement from each, so divvy them up between whichever DCs we have.'

'No problem.'

Murphy looked at his watch. 'I'm going in to see the boss, see if we can get an appeal out for *North West Tonight* later.'

'Press officer been briefed?'

'Not yet. We'll do that at the same time. Too late for the print edition of the *Echo*, but we'll get something in there for tomorrow. Someone must have seen Dean Hughes. He can't have

161

been underground for seven months.'

Rossi nodded and began walking towards the office. 'Everything good between you and Sarah?'

Murphy smirked. 'Well, it was. Now we're in a bit of a stalemate.'

'Really?' Rossi replied, her voice rising with surprise.

'Yeah. Everything's good, don't get me wrong. It's just we're having the kid conversation again.'

Rossi nodded. 'I get you. You're still digging your heels in, I assume?'

'It's just not the right time. Especially with this kind of thing going on.'

'You know what they say . . . it's never the right time. Any sane person would never have kids if they waited for the exact right time.'

'I know.'

'You sure it's not something else? It's only been a couple of years, you know. No time really.'

Murphy looked away. Almost two years exactly since his parents had been murdered; the bastard who killed them an ex-boyfriend of Sarah's who hadn't been able to let her move on. Sarah and he had broken up — well, Murphy had left and largely ignored her for almost a year. They were back together now, but Murphy continued to feel that it was still under the surface, the fragility of their relationship known to both of them.

'We'll see. First let's get this cleared so I can at least go home at a reasonable hour.'

Murphy left Rossi to get on with organising the influx of teenagers that would be arriving shortly, and crossed the incident room to DCI Stephens's office.

'David, how's it going?'

Murphy sat down opposite her. 'New line of enquiry.' He brought her up to date with what they'd learnt that day.

'Sounds promising. We find where he's been, who he's owing money to, we find our suspect. I like it.'

'I still want to know where he's been the past seven months though. Reckon we can get an appeal on TV later?'

DCI Stephens nodded. 'We've got to give them an update anyway. I'll sort that out with the press officer and release a statement. We have a good picture of the victim don't we?'

'Yes. He wasn't exactly a stranger. Should be on HOLMES.'

'Good.'

The Youth Club

Kevin Thornhill picked up the phone, dialling the number from memory. Hands still shaking from the meeting with the police. He hated speaking to people in power like that. Constantly worried that he'd be arrested and thrown in jail. Even the knowledge he'd never done anything wrong wasn't enough to calm him. It was his number one fear. Being locked up inside. Part of the reason he did the youth club thing was because he was sure he wasn't alone in that feeling.

The phone was answered within a couple of rings.

'Yeah . . . what's up?'

'Hey, it's me . . . '

'I know that. Your name comes up on my mobile. Doesn't it do that for you?'

'Yeah, course, just wanted to make sure.'

'What do you want? If you need more money, I'm afraid you'll have to wait until the next review . . . '

'No,' Thornhill interrupted, 'it's something else.'

'Pretend I'm intrigued. Go on.'

'The police have just been here. Asking questions about a lad who's gone missing and now turned up dead . . . '

'And . . . '

'I just thought you should know.'

'Listen, don't worry about anything. I'm sure they've got more important things to look into than our little youth club. Just sit back and let it play out. There's nothing there to be discovered. All right, kid?'

Thornhill breathed out. 'Yeah. Will you be around soon?'

'Not likely at the moment. Up the wall with stuff at work. Being an actual director of a large company, rather than just a name on a list, is harder than you think, you know?'

Thornhill said goodbye and hung up. Still worried. No idea why.

He just didn't like what was going on behind his back. And he was sure something was happening.

14

Seventy-six people had posted on Dean's Facebook wall in the seven months he'd been missing. Since news of his death had spread, however, there'd been many more postings. And a RIP page set up for people to express their grief in a nice, public way. What got Murphy every time were the people who posted comments without even knowing him. Hundreds of them, just aching to outpour their feelings about the pain the death had apparently caused them; the fact that someone they'd never met had died seemingly being enough for them to feel personally hurt.

It took the constables an hour or two to identify the most prominent posters and bring them in. Interviewing had been split up. All of them were told they didn't have to be there and they weren't in trouble for now. Not that it made any difference to most of their attitudes. All teenagers, therefore sullenness was an Olympic event for them. The spark in their eyes already dulled. The cliché of the slighted teenager, being forced to do something they didn't really want to, being broadcast in each interview room.

Murphy guessed from the looks on the faces of those doing the interviewing, as they made their way out of each room, they weren't making much breakthrough.

'Still nothing?'

Murphy turned towards Rossi and shook his head. 'Even if anyone knows something, chances are they won't tell us. We've got no . . . what's the word?'

'Leverage.'

'That's the one. They know they're not in any danger of being charged with something, so they're not going to tell us sod all.'

Rossi smirked. 'Keeping the spirits high. I like it.'

Murphy was interrupted from responding by a wave from DC Harris who had poked his head out of Interview Room Three. Murphy winked at Rossi and walked over towards him, stepping back as the DC closed the door behind him.

'What have we got?'

'Lucy Yates. Sixteen years old. Reckons she knows something about the youth club the victim was attending.'

Murphy frowned. 'We've already been down there. What's she saying?'

'Nothing yet. Just . . . intimating. I think she knows more than she's letting on. Thought you might want a crack at her?'

Murphy sighed, looked towards Rossi who just raised her eyebrows in response. 'Nothing I like more than talking to non-responsive teenage girls.'

Lucy Yates was almost an exact copy of Amanda Williams, the girl Dean Hughes had last been seen with. Long, platinum-blonde dyed hair, drawn-on eyebrows and immaculately painted fingernails. The pinched look on her face as she fiddled with a pen was more pronounced on Lucy, however. The pen banged against the table as she began to drum out a tune.

'Hello Lucy, I'm Detective Inspector David Murphy, this is Detective Sergeant Laura Rossi.'

Lucy's eyes flitted across at Rossi, instantly sizing her up, lingering on her for a second before dismissing her. She rested her gaze on Murphy. 'I told the other bloke everything.'

'Good. That's helpful. We just have a few more questions, that's all. You don't mind, do you? You haven't got anywhere to be or anything?'

Lucy made a show of checking her mobile phone, before shrugging her shoulders and dropping the pen. 'Suppose I've got a bit more time.'

'Good,' Murphy replied. 'DC Harris was telling me you knew Dean from the youth club.'

'Only a bit. I don't go there any more.'

'But you did?'

'Yeah, but not much. It was boring.'

'Right.' Murphy shifted in his chair. 'Is that the only place you saw him?'

Lucy flicked her hair forward over her shoulder and began playing with a few strands. 'Saw him around and that, but didn't really know him.'

Rossi leant forward. 'Why did you stop going to the youth club, Lucy?'

Lucy shrugged in response. Her voice lowered. 'Just said.'

'It was boring?'

Lucy nodded.

Murphy looked towards Rossi, before turning back. 'What are the people who run it like?'

'All right, I suppose.'

Murphy felt something then. A weight in the room. 'Just all right?'

'All those types are a bit weird, aren't they?'

'What types?' Murphy replied.

'Wanting to help people for no reason. Has to be something in it for them.'

Murphy waited a second or two to reply. 'Lucy. It's really important that if you think something was going on there, something which you maybe think is related to Dean, that you tell us. Okay?'

Silence filled the room for a few seconds. 'Nothing dodgy,' Lucy replied, just as Murphy was about to say something more. 'It was just a weird feeling you'd get sometimes.'

'A weird feeling?' Rossi said, writing in her notebook.

'Yeah,' Lucy said, the sarcasm returning. 'I can't really describe it. That's why I didn't say anything before. It's just in some of the things that were said and that. Like, about us.'

'Us?'

'Yeah, by the people there, like. They'd do like . . . what are them things called they do in big halls and that, when they talk at you for ages?'

Murphy pursed his lips. 'A lecture, you mean?'

Lucy bobbed her head up and down, leaning forward now. 'Yeah, yeah. One of them. They'd get everyone together and start, like, doing religious stuff, but without the god and that.'

'A sermon . . . ' Rossi murmured.

'And they'd just go on and on about kids today and how they've never had it that good,

169

and all that kind of thing. It was just weird, because it would come out of nowhere. Some bloke would just show up and start going on and on.'

Murphy's ears pricked up. 'Some bloke?'

'Yeah, he wasn't there all the time. He'd turn up and just go off on one. We had to sit there and listen to it all.'

'What was his name?'

'Dunno.'

'He never introduced himself?' Murphy asked.

'Probably, I just wasn't listening. I'd switch off as soon as he'd start. It was just weird.'

'Was he on his own?'

'He knew the guy in charge, but other than that, he was on his own.'

★ ★ ★

'It wasn't much, but it's something at least. A guy walks into a youth club and gives a lecture about how kids are today and all that rubbish . . . wasn't all that much on its own. Couple it with the fact one of those involved in the youth club is murdered, and it deserves a bit of looking into.'

'The word is *tenuous*, David.'

Murphy rubbed a hand across his beard, choosing not to look at DCI Stephens directly. The day was drawing to a close and the only thing they'd got from interviewing a whole bunch of teenagers from across the city was one girl's weird feelings about a bloke giving a talk in a youth club.

Not exactly the most productive of days.

'It's about all we've got, other than the possible debt angle — and that's even more tenuous. We'll have another word with the bloke who runs the place, see if he's a bit more forthcoming about this new information.'

DCI Stephens shook her head at him. 'Fine. But this investigation isn't exactly proving very fruitful at the moment. We've had half the school leavers in Liverpool down here and not exactly pulled up any trees. I need something concrete, or we're going to have to start answering some very difficult questions. Understood?'

Murphy nodded, already rising from his chair. He turned and left the room without another word, not wanting to give DCI Stephens a chance to admonish him further. He left the main office at a pace, wanting to get back to his own office and the silence which would welcome him.

Opening the door to his office, he was greeted by the sight of DS Brannon sitting at his desk.

'No such luck . . . ' Murphy said under his breath.

'Sorry,' Brannon said, standing up quickly, 'nowhere else to sit in here.'

'Doesn't matter,' Murphy replied, swiping a hand over his seat, scattering crumbs to the floor. 'Have you been eating in here?'

'Erm . . . '

Murphy sighed. 'Forget it. Need you in here anyway. I'm guessing Laura caught you up on the interview earlier?'

'Yeah. Gotta say though, don't think Kevin is

171

the type to hold anything important back from us. It'll be something or nothing most probably.'

'Well, still needs looking into,' Murphy said, fiddling with his chair to get it back to the right position. 'Get on the phone to Kevin . . . '

'Thornhill,' Rossi said, without looking up from the paperwork she was filling out.

'Right. Thornhill. Get on the phone to him and find out this guy's name. I want to know more about what he's saying to these kids.'

'Sir,' Brannon replied, snapping his shoes together and mock-saluting, leaving the office before Murphy had the chance to launch something weighty at his head.

'Press in half an hour,' Rossi said, as the door closed behind Brannon.

'I know,' Murphy said, loosening his tie.

'You going to be all right with it?'

It was the elephant in the room for Murphy. After the case the previous year — *The Uni Ripper*, as the press had so delightfully monikered it — there had been several meetings and courses on press relations. People on the team still hadn't forgiven him for the monumental waste of time it had proven to be. They all knew the score, nothing had changed. Just some depressed DI taking issue with one of the hacks. Losing his temper during a press conference hadn't been the best of decisions, but he never thought it would result in them all being made to take part in shitty courses. Something as high profile as the case had turned out to be meant lessons had to be learnt though. So they'd all had to shuffle into the stuffy rooms and be lectured at about the current climate, the twenty-four-hour news agendas, the struggle of the print media to find stories to run.

It wasn't even Murphy's fault, really, he thought. One particular little shit on a dying local paper who seemed to have it in for him. That was all.

'I'll be fine. Dean's mum is doing it separately anyway. Heard she's doing an exclusive with the *North West Tonight* lot. I'm just doing the statement.'

'Written it?'

'I'll just do the usual.'

The usual was so old hat now, Murphy wondered if anyone really listened to it these days. The platitudes of *enquiries continue into the matter* and *detectives would urge anyone who witnessed this incident or who has any information about it to contact us on . . .* never really giving anyone listening the opportunity to form a salacious story from the limited information.

Not that that would stop anyone.

Murphy stood and left the office, entering the toilets down the corridor. He stopped in front of the mirror, fixing his tie and checking the rest of his appearance. Didn't want to give off any kind of impression other than smart and in control.

Twenty minutes later, he was outside the entrance to the police station and in front of a few microphones with five or six journalists. He didn't pause to count, wanting to get it over and done with. Only local by the looks of things, and no sign of the rotund dickhead who Murphy had fallen out with the previous year.

Silver linings and all that.

'On Friday morning, police were called to a church in West Derby . . . ' He could only provide information they already had, but repeating it gave the impression the briefing was giving more than it actually was. Something which Murphy had been told actually made a difference.

' . . . Enquiries led us to the identity of the victim,' Murphy continued. 'Dean Hughes was an eighteen-year-old teenager, much loved and missed by his family.' He had no idea if that love went further than his mother, but it didn't hurt to throw something like that in. Pull on the heartstrings a little.

Murphy finished with the usual spiel and took a couple of questions. The bored looks on the faces of those dispatched to cover the briefing told Murphy everything. They'd be lucky to finish out the week anywhere near the front page of the local news, never mind the radio stations. A young lad, from a working-class background . . . not exactly good copy. Give them a fresh-faced young girl with a good middle-class family behind her and it would have been all over the place. Harsh, but that's the rub.

'Can you say if drugs may have played a part in Dean's death, Inspector?'

'We're looking into every possibility at the moment, Alice,' Murphy replied to the young *Liverpool Echo* reporter. Murphy had dealt with her a couple of times. Impossibly young but fair was his opinion. That would soon be driven out

174

of her, he imagined.

'Should the public be worried?'

Murphy kept his face straight. 'We'd like everyone to remain vigilant, but we don't think the wider public is in danger, no.'

A voice near the back muttered almost inaudibly but couldn't help itself from speaking up. 'I'm sure you said that last year . . . '

'That was last year,' Murphy snapped back. 'This is different.' His hands clenched into fists, searching for the face of the man who had spoken.

'That's all for now,' the press officer said, interrupting before Murphy had chance to say anything further. 'We'd like to reiterate the importance of any information that anyone may have . . . '

Murphy tuned out as the press liaison officer wrapped things up. The sun was still up, but the sounds of the traffic behind him heading out of the city centre told him the day was drawing to a close. Cars heading towards the Mersey tunnels, over to the Wirral, away from the non-stop nature of town.

Once back inside, the press officer giving him a reassuring nod as if to say *well done, no screw-up this time*, Murphy loosened his tie once more, riding up the lift alone, trying to work out what the next moves should be.

The lift doors opened and the short trip down the corridor towards the incident room was uninterrupted and quiet.

Too quiet.

Murphy pushed his way through the double

175

doors, expecting to be hit by a cacophony of noise, frowning when stillness greeted him.

Everyone was looking towards someone at the end of the room. He peered over a few heads which were in the way and saw her sitting at a desk that wasn't her own, holding the phone to her ear. Rossi turned, catching his eye as he looked over, the hand she was holding up for quiet becoming a gesture for him to come towards her.

'Okay . . . No, that's fine . . . We can send a car for you if that's better . . . ? It's important that you do come in though Ian, you understand . . . ? Okay, good . . . '

Murphy whispered into Brannon's ear, who was leaning on the desk behind the one Rossi was sitting at. 'What's going on?'

'One of our guys is on the phone. Rossi is talking him through handing himself in.'

Murphy sighed. A breakthrough. Then something jarred at him.

'*One* of them? How many are there?'

Rossi turned to him then, first placing a finger to her lips to shush him, then turning it to an open palm.

It took Murphy a few seconds — then he realised.

Five of them. Five.

The Farm

Three Days Ago

Goldie had noticed Dean had started going south after Bootle had been let go a few weeks earlier. Goldie thought it was because Dean assumed that as he was the first one to have arrived in there, he'd be the first one out; Dean had started changing from that moment.

Not that Goldie hadn't been pissed off himself that they'd let Bootle go. Shocked at first, then just angry. There was also the two new lads to work out at the same time. Mikey, a younger lad from Garston who hadn't said much. Tyler, another loudmouth Goldie imagined would have to be put in his place before too long.

Dean paced up and down the Dorm more often. Sometimes talking to himself under his breath. Goldie could never work out what he was saying, but none of it sounded good.

That morning, Goldie had tried talking to him for the last time. 'I'm sure you'll be out soon, mate. They're just trying to mess with us a bit. You really think Bootle was being the best out of all of us?'

Dean had stopped at the end of Goldie's bed where he was sitting up in the middle, legs crossed. 'It doesn't matter what we do,' Dean had replied. 'They're going to keep us here forever. I bet he wasn't even let go, like. We're

177

just animals to them. I can't take it any more.'

'Don't talk like that. We're gettin' out of here, we've just gotta be patient.'

Dean had turned away and carried on pacing. Goldie tried speaking to him again, but it was no use. There was no getting through to him after that. All day he was just winding himself up. Goldie was worried. And not just about Dean. When they'd finally taken the bandage off his hand, the skin where his little finger had been was now turning an odd colour. Not healing properly.

The pain had gone now. Just a weird sense of loss every time he used his left hand. Nothing felt the same any more.

That evening was when it happened.

Goldie was being led back to the Dorm, after going first, as usual, that evening. His muscles in agony after the exercises and then the beating, his mind turning over the possibilities of what might happen soon.

Bootle had been let go. Was getting on well, according to Alpha. They had people keeping an eye on him apparently. It was the first time Goldie had heard any of them mention people on the outside who might be involved, and at first hearing, he'd instantly been sceptical. Then he thought about what he'd gone through in the months he'd been there. There was no way they could set something up like this and keep it sustained without outside help, surely? It wouldn't have shocked him if this was some sort of official programme from the government or something.

He smiled to himself as Omega coughed behind him. Remembered how in his first few days Craig had thought it was some kind of reality show, like on BBC Three or ITV2 or something. Bad Lads' Bootcamp, he'd called it. Maybe even some kind of Ross Kemp programme for Sky. Bootle reckoned one of his mates was on the gangs show he did, but Goldie had laughed at him, saying the show was full of dickheads who wouldn't know a proper gang if it came up and bottled them on the street.

It didn't matter that they'd had guns trained on them from the beginning. Craig thought they were fake. The whole thing was a set-up, he said. To make good telly; to make them out to be worse than they were and fix them.

Even Goldie showing him where they'd lopped off his finger didn't make him flinch.

It was Craig's first time on the rack that had shut him up. He didn't think they'd allow torture to go on the telly.

Goldie was feeling as good as was possible in the hell he'd been going through the past few months. For the first time, he could see an end in sight — the real possibility of being free again.

Shouts from up ahead made him stop in his tracks. He turned around to see Omega tense, his shotgun trained on his back.

'Keep walking,' Omega said after a few more seconds of silence. The shouting had stopped, so Goldie shrugged and carried on walking. The noise struck up again, followed by the opening of the door to the Dorm and the sight of Gamma flying outwards.

Goldie became aware of the gun jutting into his back after a short period, but at first his attention was solely on the open door and what lay beyond.

'Get in there, now,' Omega said, teeth clenched so Goldie imagined the spit flying onto his clean T-shirt.

Goldie kept walking, faster now, eager to see what was going on. As they reached the Dorm, Gamma was getting back to her feet, brushing down her black cargo pants. Her balaclava had slipped a little, so Goldie watched as she readjusted it so the eyeholes were in line.

'That little bastard is dead,' Gamma said, as she picked up the gun which had fallen beside her.

Omega pushed Goldie inside, where the scene was laid out for him. Dean struggling with Tango on the floor, Tango's gun lying a few feet away. Goldie allowed himself to be forced further into the room, not taking his eyes off the scene which was unfolding in front of him. He sat down on the edge of his bed, tearing his gaze away from what he thought was about to turn into a bad situation, to see Craig kneeling, hands gripping the frame of the bed, ready to jump up.

'Don't,' Goldie said, shaking his head. It was enough for Craig to loosen his grip a little.

Dean had forced Tango onto the ground, his hands around the bigger man's neck, when Gamma raised her shotgun, smashing into the back of Dean's skull. The thumping sound seemed to echo around the Dorm. Dean didn't move for a second or two, but Goldie knew he'd lost his grip around Tango's neck as he heard the man start swearing and coughing.

Gamma booted Dean in the ribcage, which finally saw him teeter over and fall to the floor. Goldie hoped Dean was already out cold as he watched Gamma start again, kicking and stamping on his prone body, the sounds making Goldie feel sick. Tango joined in then, still on his knees as he punched Dean in the face.

Omega stood back, both hands on his rifle as he watched it happen in front of him. Goldie couldn't tell what his facial expression was behind the black mask of the balaclava but wanted to believe it matched the horror of his own. Then he remembered his severed finger and Omega's lack of action when it happened. Imagined a grin beneath the mask instead.

In the doorway, a shadow fell over the man and woman beating the teenager. First Gamma stopped, backing away, then she nudged Tango with her foot.

'Stop.'

Tango turned to see Alpha at the doorway.

'What's going on here?' Alpha said, his voice loud and echoing off the walls.

'He tried to escape,' Tango said, his words almost lost behind a mumble. 'He hurt Gamma.'

'Really? Is that right.'

Goldie stared at the men and woman standing over the still body of Dean. The lad from Norris Green.

'In that case . . . lads, I want you to watch very carefully,' Alpha said, the end of his sentence delivered in the direction of the other four

181

teenagers in the room.

Alpha gripped Dean's T-shirt and lifted him up into a sitting position. His head lolled slightly but then righted, making Goldie sigh a little with relief.

'You think there's a way out of here without our say-so, do you? Well, I'm sure a bit of time on the rack will sort that out.'

Goldie heard rather than saw the gob being hoicked up, and winced before Dean had even spat in Alpha's face.

'Fuck you,' Dean hissed. 'Just a bunch of fuckin' torturers and pussies. Can't take us one-on-one, so you get guns and force us to live like this. You're not hard men or soldiers. You're nothing but shit.'

Goldie realised he'd been holding his breath as Dean spoke, watching as Alpha wiped at his eyes. Dean had spat directly into that area, the only part which wasn't covered.

A good shot — or a bad one, considering how you looked at it.

Alpha didn't speak. Kept a loose grip on Dean's T-shirt with one hand, but nothing else.

Then Dean's voice boomed around the Dorm room.

'Come 'ead then! If you're 'ard enough, take me now, one-on-one.'

Alpha moved quicker than Goldie had ever seen before. With the hand which had been gripping Dean's T-shirt, he shifted up his neck, the other whipping from the side and directly into the temple of Dean's head. Then he got to his feet and stamped on Dean's stomach, almost

182

flipping the teenager over with the force. Alpha stepped backwards and Tango and Gamma took the chance to continue again, aiming kicks, boots, stamps into Dean's body as he just shook on the floor.

Goldie made to move, but caught the darkened eyes of Omega and froze. His body trembled as he imagined crossing the room, covering Dean's body with his own. Saving him.

Instead, he watched, as did Craig, Mikey from Garston and the new lad from their own beds, as Alpha took something from his belt loop and pushed away Tango and Gamma.

Alpha grabbed Dean's hair and pulled him up into a sitting position before moving behind him.

Goldie learnt something that day.

It takes a long time to choke someone to death. It wasn't quick like in films or telly. It takes a good few minutes. Time stretched, as he couldn't turn his head away. He heard someone retch and throw up from the other side of the room, but he didn't stop watching as Alpha stole Dean's life.

When it was done, nothing more was said. Just a nod to Tango and Gamma from Alpha, who took the now-still body of Dean and dragged him outside.

Goldie sat in the same position, having watched them kill someone he'd spent almost every minute of his life with for the past six months. Not a friend, not family. Nothing like that. But they were something.

And he couldn't help but think that he was next.

PART TWO

PART TWO

15

Sally Hughes was going to bury her son.

Her own child.

There'd be a funeral, in which people would pretend that a glorious young life had been taken from them. A future snuffed out too soon.

It wouldn't even be a burial, she thought. She couldn't afford that. Her son would be cremated. His ashes scattered somewhere or kept in an urn on the mantelpiece.

Her son would become an ornament.

She could put it somewhere. His favourite place, maybe. Except his favourite place was probably some park or cemetery where he could get pissed or stoned with his mates.

Probably not something she could share with people.

She was going to be one of those mums who turned up on morning TV. On the couch, being consoled by someone who used to talk to a puppet when she was younger. Fake sincerity, plastered-on concern ... for around five minutes, before they had a grand old laugh with the latest reality TV star.

They'd talk about her behind her back. All those who lived around her. That was without question. She'd heard of those parents who were blamed for everything that happened to their kids. She'd be in the papers as the mum who neglected her son and he'd ended up dead. A life on benefits which led to her kids being brought up wrongly, before finally paying for her laziness.

It wasn't like that.

She used to be different.

It had been three days since those two detectives had arrived at her door, changing her life forever. She bet they'd already forgotten about her, leaving her with some stupid woman who kept asking if she was okay. Family liaison or something. Pointless waste of space. Of course she wasn't okay. Her son had been murdered, with God only knew what happening to him in the months before that.

She'd have to live with the knowledge that she'd never find out. Not for sure. She wouldn't know how her son would have been feeling. Had he been afraid, frightened? Had he been tortured?

Had he been expecting to be saved by the one person who had always been there for him?

She'd done nothing. Not when he'd disappeared. Just sat on her arse in front of the TV, expecting him to show up. To walk brazenly through the door wanting his tea. Not caring that she'd been worried sick.

So she hadn't bothered. He was old enough to look after himself, Sally thought.

They'd argued before he left. Her last conversation with her son ended with him telling her she was *a fucking bitch*.

He left with her thinking, but not saying aloud, that she wished he'd never been born. That none of them had been. That she'd stayed single. Hadn't let that man have his way with her in the back of a Skoda when she was seventeen. Married at eighteen. Three kids and too many beatings later before she finally escaped him.

Left with three boys, a forty-a-day habit and a taste for vodka she could barely resist on a daily basis.

She didn't know how to grieve. It was only from watching TV that she knew something should be happening. She'd been sitting on Dean's bed now for over an hour. Just staring at the wall, expecting to feel something.

Instead, she was just empty.

Hollow.

Sally only had a few friends, but what there were had been there all weekend. Fussing over her. Helping her cry dry tears. Talking of revenge on the bastard who had taken her son. Talking about how this type of thing never happened when they were kids. How things were different these days.

After the first couple of days, the numbers had fallen. People were already moving on. Leaving her sitting in her son's bedroom because she'd seen some actress in an ITV drama do it once when she'd lost her husband or something. Maybe it had been a kid. Sally couldn't remember. It had seemed important. Like she'd learn something, make a plan of some kind. Just by sitting on her dead son's single bed, the fabric on the bottom of the divan flapping around every time she moved. Springs near the bottom digging into her. Crusty sheets and an old duvet.

Barely anything in the room anyway. She'd tried burying her face in some of his clothes, but

189

the only ones that were clean smelt of nothing but discount brand washing powder. She didn't want to smell the dirty clothes gathered in a pile underneath the window. They would only smell of damp.

She'd tried. Taught her boys right from wrong. Don't do this, don't do that. It never worked.

She'd tried her best. It just hadn't been enough. She'd accepted that a long time before.

Sally Hughes sat alone on her dead son's bed. Staring at peeling wallpaper that hadn't been changed since Dean was in primary school. Black mould in the corners of the room. Nothing in there reminded her of him. It was a shell, just a box where he'd slept.

Sally had cried at first, of course. Now, three days later, she didn't know what to do. Act as before? Just go back to normal? What was she supposed to do as a grieving mother . . . how was she supposed to act?

So she continued to sit upon her dead son's bed.

The face of the man who killed him lying in a pile of discarded papers and forms on his bedside table.

16

'Hello . . . Ian . . . Hello?'

Rossi looked towards Murphy, pursing her lips as she did so. Murphy moved quickly, almost snatching the phone from her hand and putting his ear to the receiver. Dead air.

'He just hung up,' Rossi said, pushing the hair back from her face. 'Didn't even give me chance to stop him.'

'Don't worry,' Murphy replied. 'You didn't say anything wrong.'

The incident room suddenly found its voice, with shouted enquiries from over the top of workstations as the other detectives began trying to work out what was going on.

'Enough,' Murphy said, his voice echoing around the room. 'Let me speak to Laura and then we'll meet in the briefing room in fifteen minutes.' He beckoned over DC Harris. 'Harris, trace as best we can. I want the area he was calling from as soon as, okay?'

Harris nodded and scuttled off.

Rossi picked up the notepad she'd been writing on during the phone call and walked ahead of Murphy as he waited for her near their office. Once inside, she flopped onto her chair and leant back, rubbing her forehead.

'You okay?' Murphy said, taking up his own chair.

'Yeah,' Rossi replied, still rubbing the tension

191

out of her head. 'Just a bit unexpected, that's all.'

'I can imagine. What happened?'

Rossi explained to Murphy what had led her to picking up the phone. A man, identifying himself only as Ian, had called the non-emergency phone line. After explaining he had information about the Dean Hughes case, he was put through to a shocked DC who had begun looking for Murphy himself. As he was downstairs in front of the media, Rossi had drawn the short straw.

'And you're sure he was involved? Not just a prank?' Murphy said.

'If he wasn't involved, I'll show my arse in Burton's window.'

'I'm not sure that's really convincing me . . . '

'Shut up. No. He knows far too much about the case for it to not be someone who was there when Dean died. Injuries, age, appearance, tattoo, where he was left exactly. The bloody scar on Dean's face. Do you want me to go on?'

'Okay. We'll go on the assumption he's one of . . . how many did you say?'

'Five. But he doesn't know what's happening now.'

'From the beginning, Laura,' Murphy said, leaning back in his chair and picking up a notepad from his desk.

'He started by saying how sorry he was that the boy died. That it wasn't the plan, and all that bollocks. On and on about how they were trying to help him, not kill him. It was repetitive.'

'Okay. Doesn't make sense, but not the first time we've heard that defence.'

192

'True. Anyway, he then started telling me what had happened since. There's a place — a farm or something — he's been living at with four other people. Didn't say where it was. They all had code names for each other, but that was for the benefit of those being held.'

Murphy held up a hand. 'Slow down. *Who* were being held?'

'The boys,' Rossi replied, pinching her eyes shut with her thumb and forefinger. 'They've been taking teenagers off the streets and trying to make them 'better', as he put it.'

'And Dean was one of these lads?'

'Yes. Only, they couldn't make him better. According to Ian, it went too far — their *discipline* of him — and he ended up dead. Wasn't meant to happen, blah blah blah . . . '

Murphy let out a long breath. 'This is . . . '

'Fucked up,' Rossi finished for him.

'Yeah. So why is he ringing now? Guilt got to him?'

Rossi shook her head. 'It all went wrong last night. He wouldn't say what happened, but he's scared. Wants to hide.'

'Who from?'

'Alpha,' Rossi replied, shaking her head. 'Whoever that is.'

⋆   ⋆   ⋆

Murphy left the car running on the driveway for a few seconds after he pulled up, listening to the end of the news on the local radio. His own voice, coming low out of the speakers as he

193

listened to what he'd told the press earlier, now seemed empty, considering what they'd discovered since. Murphy rubbed his eyes, the tiredness threatening to overwhelm him. The dashboard clock said it was just past two a.m., but Murphy was sure it was later than that. Felt as if he'd been awake for days.

The last few hours had passed in a blur. Once Rossi had explained what she'd learnt from the phone call, they'd rejoined the team in the briefing room, DCI Stephens taking a prominent position as she listened to what had occurred late in the day. The rest of the evening had been spent waiting around in the hope that 'Ian' would call back, with no joy. The tracing of the call had led them to a pay-as-you-go mobile and a possible location of the tower the call had been pinged off, near Huyton. Officers had been sent to the area, but the likelihood of them ever finding someone was remote before they even left.

Murphy shut off the engine and got out the car. He pressed the button on his key fob and heard the comforting clunk as the doors locked behind him. After quietly letting himself into his house, the lights all off as he'd expected, he crept through to the kitchen, trying to make as little noise as possible.

He wanted a drink, a proper one, but settled for a glass of orange juice. He wanted to be down the station but knew it was pointless. The night shift team had been briefed about the ongoing situation, so he took his mobile out of his pocket to check it was still charged. Tutted to himself as the battery showed less than half full. The charger was upstairs next to his bed, so any plans of not disturbing Sarah and taking up residence in his chair for the night vanished.

He padded up the stairs one step at a time, trying to avoid the creak on the third-to-last stair and failing.

'David?'

Murphy stopped on the stairs, his shoulders falling. He hated waking Sarah when he got home late. He'd sent her a text earlier saying he'd be late back but was hoping to save the inquisition.

'Be there in a sec.'

He went into the bathroom, not worried about making noise now he knew she was awake. That was Sarah . . . once she was awake, it took her a while to fall asleep again. A really light sleeper, always on the verge of full consciousness.

Once finished, he turned off the bathroom light and shuffled his way across the landing to the bedroom. Sarah had switched on the light which sat on her bedside table and was propped up on the multitude of pillows she slept upon — in direct contrast to the one single, flat pillow which Murphy used. He'd woken up a few times in nights gone by with a pillow or three lying on his face.

'You're in late?'

Phrased as a question rather than a statement. Interesting. 'Yeah. We've had a pretty busy night. Won't bore you with it.'

'Everything okay?'

'Yeah,' Murphy replied, making his way

around the bed to his side. 'Just . . . a murder enquiry, so if something big comes in, being sent home is usually not on the agenda.'

'Something big?'

Murphy sat down on the bed and began the process of getting undressed, shaking his trousers off and placing them on the chair in front of the dressing table. The shirt and tie went in the laundry basket. 'Could be. Up in the air at the moment. Could mean a few more late nights though.'

'And early mornings, I imagine . . . '

Murphy looked at the alarm clock on his bedside table. 'Yeah. If I'm lucky, I'll get a few hours in before I'm back there.'

'Well . . . '

Murphy turned to face Sarah. 'What?'

'It can wait,' she replied, preparing to lie back down.

'No, it's okay. What is it?'

'It's just Jess. She's been on the phone most of the evening.'

Murphy sighed, lying down in bed next to Sarah. 'Peter?'

'Yeah. He's going to get kicked out of college. Non-attendance for the most part, bad attitude when he turns up. He's on some kind of report, so if he messes up in the next month, he's out.'

'Christ . . . What's going on then?'

'She doesn't know what to do. Peter doesn't seem to care, according to Jess. Thinks a word might be in order.'

Murphy rubbed his eyes, fighting the urge to just turn over and go to sleep. 'Couldn't really be at a worse time, this.'

'You *are* his godfather, David.'

'I know. I didn't think that meant I'd be down for this type of thing though. Just thought I'd take him for a pint when he's eighteen or something. I'm turning into a second father for the little prick.'

'Jess could do with the help.'

Murphy shook his head. 'Hasn't she tried talking to his dad? See if he'll step up a bit more?'

'It was a very short conversation, from what Jess told me. Basically, she said he's a small-dicked knobhead who couldn't tell his arse from his elbow. Which I think means it didn't go well.'

'Fine,' Murphy said, lying down finally. 'I'll try and find some time tomorrow.'

'Good. Now get some sleep. But try and be quiet in the morning.'

Murphy turned over and kissed Sarah once on the lips. 'Night.'

He heard the light go out, Sarah getting comfortable in her pillow mountain once more, and shut his eyes, willing sleep to come quickly.

★   ★   ★

Rossi left the station at the same time as Murphy but didn't go home. She sat in her car outside her house for a while, watching the darkened windows. Half hoping that there'd be someone there, knowing there wasn't. Never was.

It was why she always ended up going home to

197

her parents. The darkness inside her own home, the quiet . . . it got to her sometimes. These times more than most.

She'd thought she'd found someone the previous year. Okay, the start hadn't been perfect — someone involved in a murder investigation coming onto her hadn't been the best timing — but it had finished about as quickly as it had started. It hadn't been great between them for a while. At least a few weeks. That was her argument. His side was that they were stuck — both unwilling to accept the status quo and battling against each other. Rossi preferred her easier explanation, that it had fizzled out and that they should probably just get on with their lives. Separately.

It was the same problem she always had in relationships. Didn't want to make enough effort to make them work, firmly holding onto the belief that when it was right surely no effort had to be made.

She'd accepted long ago that she was probably talking bollocks.

Rossi just enjoyed the beginning parts of a relationship. Where it was two people learning about each other, enjoying each other. Long nights spent talking and shagging. If she could keep that part going forever, she'd be happy. When it became 'serious' and future plans had to be made, that's when she started getting itchy feet.

Why the hell did she have to be in a relationship anyway? Just to make her parents happy? She couldn't be arsed with it. It was all right most of the time. Living on her own, not having to give in to anyone else over anything. Everything just as she wanted it.

It was only during times like this that she wanted so badly not to have to walk into an empty house. To have someone there she could talk to about things. How helpless she always felt with this type of case, where nothing moved quickly. How frustrated, just sitting there waiting to be told what to do by a superior.

Maybe she should just get a cat and be done with the whole thing. Rossi smiled to herself and got out the car, trying to think which takeaway would still be open at that time so she could order some food in. She let herself into her house and quickly turned on the hallway light.

Not letting the darkness inside.

The Farm

Two Days Ago

The smell of manure lingered, an ever-constant presence, even though the farm had last seen cattle move through its fields three years previously. It was there in the walls, ingrained in the land. The wooden boards in the sheds holding a memory of the smell for a lifetime. Tyler was sick of the place. Wanted out right now. A week in and he'd already watched someone die in front of him. He didn't think things were about to get any better. For any of them.

'I still can't get used to this stink, man.'

'Well don't bore me with it. Just fuc — just get on with it.'

'Did you just stop yourself swearing, lad? They can't hear us now, you know?'

'How do you know? They could be listening, right now.'

Tyler sucked his teeth. Paranoia. He was sure of it. The lad he was speaking to had been in there longer than him, so it was only natural. 'Does this look like the kind of place with hidden cameras and shit? I don't think so.'

'You know the rules. They've told you enough times now. No swearing. Just do what they say.'

'What? You think they'll let us go if we do that? Don't be fucking stupid. We're all locked up in here until they decide to get rid of us. Once they've had their fun, of course.'

'I've seen others leave . . . '

'You've seen shit, lad. You've got no idea what happens when they go.'

The lad opposite him, Craig, replied by folding his arms and turning away.

'Craig, listen to me. We've got to find another way. We've got to get the fuck out of here.'

Craig mumbled something before standing up and going over to another bed, sitting down with his back against the wall where the headboard would be. If it wasn't non-existent, of course. Tyler smacked his hands down onto his knees and stood up.

'You've got to get fucking real here. We're screwed if we stay. Literally. I mean, have you seen any girls other than that lezza with them here? 'Cause I fucking haven't. It's only a matter of time before they start with the paedo shit. Do you wanna get fucking passed around by a load of auld sweaty blokes before they off yers?'

'Shut up.'

Tyler turned towards the corner where the voice had come from. Goldie, the oldest of the group of three lads who occupied the shed which was now their communal bedroom.

The Dorm, they'd called it.

'You know I'm right.'

Tyler heard the bed creak as Goldie got up. Shifted nervously about as he listened to the gentle pad of sock-covered feet emerge from the shadows in the corner.

Six foot four, Goldie was. Same age as him,

but by sheer size he had them all. He bore scars, though. Some healing, some now fading to silver. Tyler tried not to shrink back as Goldie reached him but instead found himself giving away even more height by dropping back to his bed.

Goldie stopped a foot away and leant forward, whispering into his ear.

'There are rules,' Goldie said, his neck cracking as he got closer, 'and you're going to keep your mouth shut and follow them. Otherwise, we're gonna have a problem. You understand?'

Tyler swallowed, his mouth filling with saliva an instant later. 'I'm just saying . . . '

'I couldn't give a f — I don't care. We've been here longer than you. We know how it works. Unless you want us all to suffer, you'll keep quiet. Follow their rules. Become a better person. Listen, do as you're told and you might just survive.'

With that, Goldie straightened up, giving him one last stare before fading back into the shadows again.

Tyler could feel his heart beating against his chest wall, his hands shaking with adrenaline. No one spoke to him like that on the outside. He wouldn't have it. He was the one in control out there. People did what he said, when he said it. He ran the street, had done since his older brother had passed on the reins when he was thirteen. For four years Tyler had been used to being the one everyone listened to.

And he had the tools to back it up. He'd lost count of the fights he'd been in, the amount of times he'd fucked up some other lad's face, or broken a bone or two. Lost count of the times he'd been in trouble with the police. He was still paying the fine for the last conviction. Actual Bodily Harm for biting a chunk out of some dickhead's arm. Hundred quid fine — a slap on the wrist really, given he was only seventeen. Wouldn't happen the next time, but he'd hardly cared.

Before anything else happened though, he'd ended up here. Lessons, rules, discipline. This had been explained to him in the previous couple of days, but he wasn't having any of it. Not him. He wasn't a fucking pussy like the others.

Tyler was getting out of there. Fuck 'em all. He wasn't waiting.

★   ★   ★

'How's our new boy?'

'Got a mouth on him, Delta.'

Delta smiled. 'They all do at first, Alpha. That'll change after a few times on the rack.'

'I guess.'

Delta leant over, placing a hand on the black-shirted shoulder of Alpha. 'You okay?'

Alpha sighed, his shoulders slumping under the weight of Delta's hand. Delta tried to make eye contact, but Alpha was staring at the floor.

'I'm just disappointed,' Alpha said after a few seconds of silence. 'I honestly didn't think it would need to happen. Plus, not returning them even in *that* state . . . it just seems wrong.'

Delta moved his hand up, tapping it against the back of Alpha's head. 'Look, we can't fix them all. But we're doing the right thing.'

Alpha finally looked up at him. 'I guess you're right.'

'Good,' Delta replied, smiling again. 'Now go and have something to eat. Tango has made a big pan of scouse. I'll watch the boys.'

Delta watched Alpha leave, before turning back to the TV screen. The picture was quite good, not as grainy as he'd expected when they'd first set it up months previously.

Six beds, only four boys occupying them. Not even maximum capacity.

★   ★   ★

The mood had changed since they'd watched the Norris Green kid die. No late-night planning what they'd do when they got out of there, what changes they'd make.

Now it was just quiet.

Goldie knew what they were all thinking. Fuck it, he was thinking the exact same thing.

Which one of them was next.

It wasn't fair. Sure, when he'd first been picked up . . . kidnapped . . . whatever . . . he'd been well pissed off. How fucking dare they? Didn't they know who he was? No fucking respect. But the time there had gone on. The beatings, the lectures which lasted hours, it seemed. The darkness of the room. It wore him down.

Now he could see something else. Knew he

204

could make a change.

The way he saw it, life was too fucking short. And he'd been wasting his. Getting pissed, getting stoned. Wasting time on girls who weren't interested.

His mum would be made up if he got home and actually did something with his life, instead of throwing it away. She could stop fretting all the time about where he was, what he was doing. The economy was still fucked, but he could find something to do. An apprenticeship, a labouring job, something. They were always building stuff near town, maybe he could get in there somehow.

Work his way up. That's what they'd told him. How long since he'd left school? Almost three years? He could have been earning all kinds by now if he'd just got his head down.

They'd filled his head with ideas. Of things he could do. Of other things that would be stupid to try.

You wanna be a DJ? So do a million other kids. Pick something else.

In media? You don't even know what that involves. Pick something else.

Each revelation punctuated with another beating.

It was working though. He was coming around to their way of thinking. When he got out, he'd be so glad to be out of that stinking nightmare, he'd do whatever he needed to do to make sure he never went back there.

Then they'd killed the Norris Green kid. And now he knew the reality. He wasn't getting out of there. They weren't going to let him go, no way. None of them.

He had to do something. The others were shit-scared, just like he was, but there was still enough of that anger inside all of them to get out of there. Tyler would be well up for it, he knew that. But they would need someone to lead it.

Him.

★   ★   ★

'We can't go on like this. It's gone too far.'

'What do you want to do then? It's not like we can go to the police. It won't just be him getting done, it'd be all of us. Can you imagine how this would look to someone coming in from the outside . . . we'd get life.'

Gamma shook her head, leant against the back door, desperate to take the balaclava off, even if it now revealed her identity. 'It's not right. Maybe if we explained . . . '

'Explained what,' Tango replied, his voice raising, causing Gamma to look quickly behind her into the empty kitchen and breathe a sigh of relief. 'That we've been taking kids — because that's what they'll call them, you know — taking kids off the streets and beating them? And for what? Because we thought we could break them?'

Gamma sighed, itching at her scalp, the heat underneath the balaclava perched on top of her head making the sweat stick. 'We're not just beating them up. We're teaching them.'

'Listen to yourself. We've been taken for

fucking fools. It's his game. His plan. Fuck knows what he gets out of it, but the other night should have made the point well enough.'

'And what's that?'

'That he's a fucking psycho and we're all in this mess he's created. There's no getting out of it for us. We either all go down, or he goes down.'

'What are you saying?' Gamma whispered, still looking around her.

'That maybe . . . maybe it's time he went away. For good. Rather than us. We let those other four go. Then we go our separate ways. The only one who knows who we are behind these masks is him. I've got no fucking clue who the rest of these people are. He's the only one who can make a problem for us.'

'There must be another way.'

Tango chuckled, the sound muffled slightly. 'Believe me, I've tried to think of something. There's nothing. Maybe before that lad was killed, but now . . . no. If we try to go, he'll drop us in it. Guaranteed. He has enough to fit us up for that lad.'

Gamma tapped her foot against the muddy path, her shoes sinking into it. 'Have you spoken to anyone else about this?'

'You're the first.'

'Then we need to speak to the others. See how they feel.'

17

Murphy stretched out in his office chair, trying to bring some life to bones which were softening from the combination of little sleep and the few hours he'd already spent sitting at his desk. It was coming up to mid-morning, Tuesday already in full swing. The vultures had begun circling as word reached the powers that be about the phone call they'd received the previous day. He'd already been on the receiving end of two ear-bashings via telephone; first from Detective Superintendent Butler, and after that from DCI Stephens, who was away from the station but wanted to make sure the message was clear.

Rossi was still in the world of maps she'd created for herself on his instruction. The man on the phone the previous night had mentioned a farm, so she was tasked with finding possible locations — which was proving difficult, given they didn't know how wide to search.

'He definitely sounds local,' DC Harris said from his small desk off to the side, shucking off his headphones. 'Can't hear anything in the background. He's outside, that's as best as I can do.'

DC Harris had been listening to the phone call repeatedly all morning, attempting to locate something which they may have missed previously.

'How local?' Murphy replied.

'I don't know what you mean . . . '

'Like housing estate Scouse, or middle-class Scouse?'

DC Harris shook his head. 'Definitely not scally Scouse, but still hard. More on the Mel C spectrum than Jamie Carragher.'

Murphy scratched at his beard. 'Ah, the official Scouse-o-meter. We're really grasping at bloody straws now.'

DC Harris shrugged in reply and turned back around. Rossi looked up from her maps. 'I suppose you'll want an update from me an' all?'

'Of course.'

'Well . . . I don't really have one. It could be bleeding anywhere. Once you get out of Knowsley and the East Lancs Road, it's all frigging farms and woods. That's just east. North, there's more, south . . . God knows. Then you've got over the water, and half of that place is bloody green. Without a team of people checking property records an' all that, never mind physically visiting these places, there's little point. I'm wasting my time really.'

Murphy nodded slowly. 'I agree.'

'You do?'

'Yeah,' Murphy replied, standing up from his desk. 'Get your coat on. We're off out.'

The traffic was a little better heading out of town, so they reached the youth club within fifteen minutes, Murphy being keen to get there. He got pissed off trying to turn off Dwerryhouse Lane, as the traffic kept coming at them from the opposite direction, but eventually they managed to park up in the same place as the day before.

'Not sure they'll be rolling out the red carpet this time,' Rossi said to Murphy as they got out of the car.

They were turning up unannounced, and without DS Brannon, Murphy explaining on the way down to his car that he wanted to *exert* a little more pressure. Rossi had made fun of him for using the word 'exert', which eased the tension a little, but Murphy was starting to feel the strain. The possibility of there being more victims somewhere in the city and a killer walking free . . . it wasn't how he'd imagined the murder enquiry moving forward twenty-four hours earlier.

They walked into the youth club, their footsteps echoing back at them in the quiet of the building. Kids were supposed to be in school, the older teenagers probably not out of bed yet. They signed in at reception, after showing their ID cards and explaining why they were there to a different bored middle-aged woman sitting near the entrance, her weathered face seeming to sag a little more with each breath. She pointed the way to Kevin Thornhill's office, but Murphy was already walking, Rossi moving quickly to catch up to him.

'What's he like?' Rossi said, as she caught up to him, speaking low so as not to be heard.

'Seems all right. Bit smarmy, I suppose. He'd shit his pants if we turned the screw a little. All bravado.'

Rossi nodded, a smile creeping onto her face.

'That's not to say we'll be doing that, Laura. As much as I know how you like taking the piss out of men like this.'

'Spoilsport.'

They stopped outside Thornhill's office, Murphy knocking loud and hard enough that the door rattled in the frame.

'Come in.'

Murphy let himself inside, followed by Rossi, who took a moment to look around the small office whilst Murphy walked briskly across and shook the proffered hand of Kevin Thornhill. Once, up and down, firm. He sat down on the same seat as he had the day before and waited for Rossi to finish looking at the various photographs and certificates adorning the walls, before sitting down herself.

Murphy waited a few seconds for the silence to grow around them, Thornhill staring back at them with a growing look of confusion on his face.

'Sorry . . . how can I help? I did tell you everything I know yesterday.'

Murphy nodded. 'Yes, I'm sure you did. Only now, we have a bit more information.'

'Where's Tony today?' Thornhill said, his gaze switching to Rossi and giving her the quick once-over Murphy had grown accustomed to. 'Although I'm not complaining about his replacement.'

'I'm sure you're not, Mr Thornhill,' Rossi replied, shaking her head. 'I'm Detective Sergeant Rossi. DS Brannon is hard at work back at the station, helping us find out who murdered Dean Hughes.'

Thornhill's expression went from leering

smirk to grave in a millisecond. 'Of course . . . '

'We're here as we have a bit of new information since our last meeting,' Murphy said. 'We were hoping you'd be as helpful as last time.'

Thornhill threw his hands up. 'Of course, of course. Anything you need to know. Although I'm not sure what else I can tell you . . . '

'Do you have people come in to the youth club regularly to talk to the kids?'

'I wouldn't say regularly,' Thornhill replied, his hands now clasped together. 'Every now and again we have various people, charitable types from local businesses, come in and give some advice or guidance. Helps the older ones who have left school and can't find a job. We don't do any of that jobcentre rubbish about CVs and that, but it gives them something to work towards.'

Murphy pursed his lips together, looking towards Rossi who was busy writing everything down in her notebook. 'Anyone else?'

Thornhill made a show of thinking on his answer, tapping the edge of his desk with his forefingers. 'Sometimes we have someone come in, like an ex-prisoner or something. Someone who has turned their life around. Inspirational to the more *troubled* teen we get here. But that's all very well-organised, so there's no problems or anything.'

'How about religious types? You're situated directly behind a church. Does that type of thing go on?' Murphy said, watching every move the increasingly nervous Thornhill made.

'No. We have a policy that we don't have anything like that here. We'd lose the kids' attention, for one thing. No, we don't have any of that going on.'

'Right. I have to ask, Kevin, because we've been hearing some stories. Can you tell me about a man who talks regularly here?'

Thornhill wiped a hand across his brow. 'I'm not sure who you're talking about . . . '

'I think you do,' Murphy replied, staring across the desk. 'One who comes in every few weeks or so. Very evangelical, so I've heard . . . '

There was silence for a few seconds, as Thornhill sweated a little more. 'I'm not sure I know who you mean . . . '

'I think you do, Kevin,' Rossi said, without looking up from her notepad.

Thornhill's shoulders slumped a little. Acceptance, Murphy hoped.

'Okay. But, please, he's one of our biggest donors. Without him, we wouldn't be able to stay open.'

Murphy leant back in the chair. 'Don't worry. We'll make sure we're careful.'

'He's harmless really. He just made it a stipulation of his annual donation. I didn't think there was anything wrong with it really. He just wanted to talk to them every few weeks or so. Okay . . . sometimes it could be a little uncomfortable, but it wasn't like I had Jimmy Savile here. He was just . . . what's the word . . . '

'Passionate?' Murphy said.

'That's right.'

213

'What was he talking about exactly?'

Thornhill sighed, now slumped a little in his chair. 'Just how things were back in his day, the importance of respect. That kind of thing.' The last part was almost mumbled, Thornhill's voice growing quieter by the second.

'Okay,' Murphy replied, sitting forward and placing his hands on the desk. 'I'm going to need you to be more specific than that. Did you even listen to what he used to say?'

'Of course I did.'

'Well then, what would he say? Why would it make people . . . children, for the most part, uncomfortable?'

Another large sigh from opposite the desk. 'Because he was quite forthright in his views. It would get a bit . . . heated. This guy is very sure of his convictions.'

'And what are they?'

'Well — and understand this isn't a view shared across the board — that kids needed more discipline. That we needed to be harder on them. Sometimes he said some things that went a bit far, but I had a word with him and he toned it down.'

'What's his name?' Murphy said.

'Alan Bimpson.'

Murphy made sure Rossi wrote the name down, mentally logging it himself. It didn't ring any bells with him, but Liverpool was a big city.

'What's he do?'

Thornhill shook his head. 'I don't know. He mentioned property development, but nothing more than that. I think I have a number

214

somewhere.' He began sifting through paperwork on his desk.

Murphy looked towards Rossi and raised his eyebrows. Received a shake of her head in return.

Thornhill scribbled a number onto a scrap of paper and handed it over to Murphy, Rossi reaching over and snatching it before Murphy even had a chance to lose it.

'Good, thanks for that. If we need anything more, we'll let you know.'

'I want to help, I really do. I'm just worried about the youth club, that's all,' Thornhill said, his hands clasped together. 'We're like a family here. It's important to me.'

Murphy eyed the photographs on Thornhill's desk. 'I understand that. But this is a serious investigation . . . '

Thornhill raised his hands up. 'I know, of course. It's just . . . you do anything for family . . . you just hope it works both ways.'

They showed themselves out, Murphy putting sunglasses on as the sun decided to show itself.

'What do you make of him?' Murphy said, getting into the car.

'Shifty. Definitely hiding something. Also, unquestionably a tits man, rather than an arse one.'

Murphy sniggered and started the car up. His feeling matched Rossi's, apart from the arse thing. Thornhill was hiding something, his gut told him so.

He just had no clue what it could be.

18

Murphy drove Rossi back to the station, leaving her with instructions to have as many people as possible look into the whereabouts of Alan Bimpson. Murphy left the car behind the station, opting to walk into town rather than trying to find an overpriced parking space. It was a ten-minute walk at most from there towards Liverpool ONE shopping centre, past the old museum and the back of St George's Hall, down Whitechapel and the main bus station. Town was busy, even for a Tuesday. A mix of suits, both professional and track, and smart skirts and short shorts. Those working and on their lunch breaks, others not working, a day off, a week perhaps, just to get some shopping done. Tourists being conned into another Beatles-themed souvenir shop. Or the unemployed, looking for something to do.

Murphy walked past yet another new shop, this one apparently offering designer clothes at discounted prices — the day it was shut down by trading standards nearing by the second — the McDonald's on the corner already looking like it needed another refit less than a year since the last one, and turned right. He was heading towards the northern part of town, where the buildings became older, where the office workers were found. The old merchant buildings now housing insurance firms, estate agents and shipping companies barely hanging in there.

The cafe on the corner opposite the courts was busy, but Murphy managed to find a table near the back. One of those new bistro type places which, bizarrely, had an alcohol licence. The sight of a worn-out bloke in an expensive suit chugging on a bottle of Corona turned Murphy's stomach, so he stuck with a coffee, pretending to read the menu for something to eat.

'Was hoping I'd beat you here. Now I'll have to sit with my back out to people.'

Jess plonked herself down opposite a smirking Murphy. 'I've come from further away as well. No excuses.'

'Is it table service?'

Murphy nodded and stuck a hand up to get a waitress's attention. The same one never served you twice for some reason. A bouncy young girl came over, all smiles and sunshine. 'What can I get ya?'

Jess ordered a coffee, which received a blank look in return. 'What kind?' the bouncy girl replied.

'Just coffee.'

'Yeah, but we do all different kinds.'

Murphy sipped on his own latte, trying not to laugh as he watched Jess become more irate.

'Just coffee-flavoured coffee.'

'Ask for a latte, Jess,' Murphy said, growing bored of the exchange.

'I don't want a latte, I want a coffee.'

'Americano?'

Jess sighed, admitting defeat. 'That'll do. And

a tuna mayo sandwich.'

The bouncy girl did what she did best and bounced off.

'How's the murder going?'

Murphy laughed as the man on the next table almost choked on his bottle of lager. 'Inside voice, Jess.'

'Yeah, yeah,' she replied, checking the sugar bowl with the spoon left in there and rolling her eyes. 'Well?'

'Few interesting lines of enquiry. Hopefully we'll have it sorted soon enough.' Murphy always lied when talking about his cases. Especially to those around him. The idea that he would tell them the truth — that the case was becoming more and more fragmented by the day — was ridiculous.

'Good.'

'So what's going on then? I need to speak to that son of yours I gather . . . '

'Sarah spoke to you then?'

Murphy eyed Jess before taking another sip of his latte. 'Of course. Isn't that what you'd hoped would happen?'

'I guess,' Jess replied, moving her purse so a different waitress to the bouncy girl could lay her cup of coffee on the table. She emptied in a packet of sugar she retrieved from the next table. 'I just don't know what to do about him.'

'You're doing the best you can. It's not like his dad is helping matters much.'

'I know. I just don't want him going down a bad path. I can see it happening. He's smoking weed, I know that much.'

Murphy raised his eyebrows. 'Really?'

'They all do it these days. It's not like we can say anything, is it?'

Murphy tutted then nodded his head. 'Guess not. Still . . . '

'You don't want them making the same mistakes you did, I know, I know.'

'There's more though?'

Jess stirred her coffee for longer than required, staring into the cup under Murphy's gaze. 'I think so, yes. I'm not sure though. I overheard him talking to one of his mates on the phone. Laughing about someone being hurt or something. I couldn't really tell. I don't want him becoming one of those lads, Bear.'

'What did you hear exactly?'

Jess dropped the spoon on the saucer and began blowing softly on the coffee, the steam dissipating above it. 'I heard him say 'did you see his face when I smacked him', then laughing.'

Murphy mused for a few seconds. Could be just a typical teenage boy, looking for something to do, boredom setting in. Fighting was something everyone seemed to get into around certain areas. 'You don't know the whole story though, Jess. No need to jump to conclusions yet.'

'Yeah, well I'd rather nip it in the bud now, you know. I think a strong word from his Uncle David is in order.' She smiled, finally looking across the table at Murphy. He saw now the tiredness behind her eyes. Not only from her job — a defence lawyer in the city — but weariness.

She'd coped on her own for almost twenty years.
He could share the burden a little.
'Where will he be now?'

* * *

Murphy pulled up to Jess's house, a detached three-bedroom new-build in Crosby, to the north of the city. He checked his watch, the afternoon now in full swing as it got closer to two p.m.

He shouldn't be doing this . . . there was all kinds going on at the station, but he was out there, checking on a seventeen-year-old with an attitude.

Priorities as excellent as ever.

He checked his phone was on — Rossi was on strict instructions to phone him the second there was any movement — and got out of the car. He could already hear the music before reaching the gate leading up to the house. The bass was surely deafening the neighbours if they were home, threatening to dislodge the brickwork. Murphy shook his head and carried on walking, the perfectly manicured front lawn the work of a gardener rather than the able-bodied male who lay within. Maybe Jess was too lackadaisical with discipline, he thought, preparing himself for the door not to be opened on the first try. He banged against it, the noise echoing around the small close.

He counted to ten, then tried once more.

Three more tries and he began to circle the house, finding the boy on his first move. Through the blinds looking into the living room,

Murphy saw him sprawled out on the couch, PlayStation controller in his hand, open can of lager on the carpeted floor near his head.

Murphy rapped on the window a few times, Peter not exactly springing to life when he finally noticed him peering in through the window. The music was switched off as Murphy walked back to the door.

'Uncle David. What are you doing here? Mum's at work.'

Bleary-eyed, hair unkempt, pointing at odd angles. Murphy wasn't sure if he'd just woken up or if it was intentional.

'Came around to see you, Peter,' Murphy replied, stepping past him into the house. He heard the door close behind him as he entered the living room. The game was paused on the big-screen TV in the corner of the room, a frozen image of some cartoony character with a gun.

'Not in college?' Murphy said, perching on the opposite settee to the one Peter had been occupying.

'No. Day off,' Peter replied, scratching at his head, his hair flattening back into shape for a second before bouncing back up.

'You have many of those?'

Peter was silent for a few seconds before leaning back into the settee. 'Spoke to me mum then. I've not heard from you for ages, so it figures.'

'She's just worried about you, lad. What's been going on?'

A shrug was the extent of his answer.

'Only a couple of months until your

221

eighteenth,' Murphy said, 'any plans?'

'Dunno yet. Probably go into town and that.'

'Then what?'

Peter didn't answer. Just stared at the screen in the corner as if it was about to magically spring into life.

'What are you doing with yourself, Peter?'

'I just don't see the point.'

Murphy leant forward. 'The point of what?'

'Going to college and that. Not like it's going to get me anywhere.'

'Course it will,' Murphy said, trying to catch Peter's eye and failing. 'Get some qualifications under your belt and you'll be much better off.'

'Will I though? You didn't need anything like that and look at you now. It's just a waste of time. I may as well wait until I'm eighteen and then join the police . . . '

'You don't want to do that . . . '

'Or the army,' Peter continued, without acknowledging Murphy's interruption. 'I couldn't sit in a call centre and I'm not going to get much else. There's no proper jobs out there.'

'How do you know? Have you looked into it at all?'

'Course I have. I've got mates with NVQs coming out their arses and they can't get a job around here. It's all call centres and fast food stuff. I'm not doing anything like that.'

Murphy sighed. He'd heard the refrain often, repeated over the years from so many young people. Everyone wanted the perfect career.

'You were doing well in school. Maybe you could do an access course like your mum did all

222

them years ago. Go to uni.'

'I'm not good enough for that. You know it, I know it, Mum knows it. I'm just not made for that.'

'Well, you can't live your life like this Peter. Getting up to all kinds of trouble . . . '

'I'm not getting into anything . . . '

'It doesn't matter,' Murphy said, his hands up in a placating stance. 'I'm not judging or anything. God knows I got myself into enough trouble when I was your age. I'm just saying, you don't want your mum worrying herself, do you? You need to get sorted. If college isn't working for you, find something else. You can't lie around here all day and then mess about with your mates at night, getting into all kinds.'

'Yeah . . . '

'Believe me, I've dealt with enough teenagers who have chosen the wrong path over the years. You're better than that.'

'Am I though? What have I got to look forward to, Uncle David? I'm nearly eighteen, and because I can't do all that maths and science shit, I'm stuck at college doing some worthless qualification, for no reason.'

Murphy shook his head. 'You're young. You've got plenty of time to decide what you want to do with your life. You're not going to find that out smoking weed and getting pissed every day though. For one, your mum will eventually just cut you off. No more pocket money.'

That brought a small smile to Peter's lips, which was quickly shut off.

'Look, son. If you're serious about the police,

then we can talk about it. Just stop doing stupid shit, and your mum can stop worrying. Get your head down and finish college . . . ' Murphy held up a hand to stop Peter interrupting. 'I know, I know, it's *pointless*, but it'll keep your ma off your back for the next couple of months. We can work this out, okay?'

Peter blew out a long breath. 'Yeah, okay. I'll go back in this week.'

'Good lad. Now I've got to get going. Believe it or not, you're not supposed to take time off in the middle of the day when you're in the police to talk with your godson.'

Murphy said goodbye, giving Peter an awkward half-handshake, half-hug at the door and walked back to his car. Felt a little relieved as he drove away. The kid was messed-up enough without having him put his foot in it.

His phone broke the silence, chirruping away in his pocket. He removed it and placed it on the hands-free kit Sarah had bought him, fiddling with the wire whilst keeping one hand on the wheel.

'Murphy,' he said, once he'd answered the phone.

'It's Laura.' Rossi's voice echoed around the car through the speakers.

'What is it?'

'You need to get back here now.'

The Farm

Two Days Ago

'It's not right. We shouldn't have done that, shouldn't have done that . . . '

'Hey, don't get like that. Not now. We need to keep our heads, now more than ever. If we start losing it, the whole thing will crash down around us.'

They sat in a rough circle around the kitchen table, the fire crackling in the hearth behind them providing a little heat, which was making them sweat. The air was thick with tension, eyes darting back and forth, each of them checking to see if the others were feeling the same as themselves.

Guilty.

Except one of them. He was more controlled, fixing his stare on each of them in turn. Alpha. There wasn't supposed to be a leader, but he was the one in charge, they all knew that — the choice of code name a big clue.

Omega wiped a sleeve across his forehead, it coming back damp. He turned away from Alpha's stare and looked towards Delta.

'What should we do?'

'This wasn't supposed to happen,' Delta replied. 'We had no plans for this.'

'Hey, we all knew what we were getting into here,' Omega said, his arms spread wide. 'I've

225

thought about this long and hard. More than any of you, I'd guess. And after much contemplation and prayer, I've come to one conclusion. It must've been part of His plan. There wasn't anything any of us could've done about it. This is just how it was meant to be. It was coming. We're all complicit. Us, the boys themselves. All of us. There was no other way. Simple as that. He's someone else's problem now.' Omega crossed himself as he finished speaking.

'Beating the hell out of them is different than actually killing them,' Gamma said, her voice quiet and steady. 'When you laid him out on those church steps . . . it suddenly became very fucking real. We need a new plan, because this one clearly isn't working.'

All the while Alpha sat still, just watching them. Delta could feel something behind those eyes. Almost grey, piercing. He was sizing them up.

Gamma was the only female there. Delta was pretty sure she was related in some way to Tango, but wasn't certain. That was the deal with them. Everyone used a code name; that way everyone was safe.

It was bullshit. They all knew enough about each other if the time came that they needed to tell someone outside the circle what had been happening. Who had been involved. They knew what each other looked like, how they spoke. The way they thought, in so many ways.

That's what happened down a pub, you picked up only the parts of the story that you actually wanted. That fit with your view of the world as it

226

was. You'd slowly get pissed, putting the world to rights with some like-minded people over a few pints and whisky chasers. The real reasons life was all going to bollocks.

They were, all of them, lonely at heart. That was the only reason he could find for the fact they'd all latched on to each other. The quiet pub, even quieter since the smoking ban (political correctness gone mad . . . or health and safety bullshit, he couldn't remember which one), became a safe place for them. Drawn together, all of them knowing what was needed.

Then those drunken plans become sober reality. The first time it happens, you feel alive. Taking one of the little bastards off the street feels like real power. You're doing something about the problem. The bizzies aren't doing fuck all, so you're doing what's needed.

★ ★ ★

They had to make new plans. Alpha supplying them all.

No one talked about what would happen if it didn't work. If they didn't listen.

No one talked about death.

Now Alpha listened to them all speak, argue, go around in circles. There was doubt there, no matter how much Omega tried to placate them.

It was all going to shit. Everything they'd planned, carried out, all of it. It was one moment, the whole process coming to its natural end, yet people couldn't handle it.

He'd known they'd have to do it at some

point. It was a natural progression. Some of them wouldn't accept the help they were providing. It was an inevitable outcome when you thought about it logically. Looking around at the other faces though, he should have known they wouldn't have thought that far ahead. It was all a game to them. Just something to get their frustrations out. They didn't really have a cause, unlike him.

They still had four of them in the Dorm. Four minds that were changing, slowly, but getting there. It could still work, but he couldn't trust the others. They were all having second, third and fourth thoughts about the whole thing. He could feel it emanating from them. The shared glances, the looks they gave each other when they thought he wasn't looking.

Like he was crazy. Like he'd lost it.

They should have known. All of them were in too far to back away now, so they should have been willing to take this process to its natural end point.

They had enough blood on their hands that a little more shouldn't matter. He honestly couldn't see what the problem was. It was logic, pure and simple. That's how he worked. How he'd always worked. It was sad, he supposed, but that was it.

He needed them back onside. He couldn't let the situation get out of control any further. He needed to exert his power — the power he'd had from the beginning.

A meeting. That would be right, would be good. They could get whatever they needed off their chests and move forward. They'd see he was correct. Know that it was just an unfortunate side-effect of what they were doing. They knew they were doing all this for good reason, they just needed reminding of it.

Boys. That's all they were really, even though they'd tried to get them a bit older. All heading towards the scrapheap. Not now, though. Not now he was involved in their lives. Now they'd have purpose. As long as they listened.

And if they didn't . . . well, that was the side-effect.

Alpha walked out of the kitchen as the others continued to talk. Listened in the darkness as the voices became lost the further away he walked. Shook a cigarette from its box and lit up. Lifted the balaclava up further away from his face and savoured the first drag as he blew it out, sensing rather than seeing the smoke swirling around him. The only light drifting from the main house, fifty yards behind.

Silence consumed him, cocooning him from reality. It wasn't the time. Not yet. He was right. He was on course. They just needed to be set back on track, that was all. They'd understand the need to be together on this. He didn't want to do this alone, not yet.

He didn't trust himself. The hate inside him was coming to the surface. Starting to affect those around him.

They didn't know the true meaning behind all of this. They were just as hateful as he was, but they didn't understand why. Striking out was just their default setting. Taking back what they believed they'd lost.

He was the one who had lost.

The one who was lost.

★ ★ ★

Something was different. They could all tell. Overnight the mood had changed, leaving them in the lurch as to what had happened. When he thought about it, Goldie knew it was the Norris Green kid dying which had started it all. As much as they'd taken them all aside one by one and explained his death had been a consequence of his own actions, Goldie knew they hadn't all believed it to be so.

It was only the main guy, the one in charge, Alpha, who had said it with any meaning. Not just with his words but with his eyes as well. Which was handy, as that was the only part of his face they'd ever seen in all the time they'd been in there.

Goldie had known some mad bastards in his life, some fucked-up nutters who would stab someone for looking at them wrong, that kind of thing. Some even worse than that. He'd known a lad once who had kicked the shit out of some kid because he didn't like the colour of the coat the lad had been wearing. Laughing as he stamped on the kid's head, blood streaming out of various cuts to his head and face. Goldie had remembered laughing along at the time, but now the memory made him sick. It was horrific violence for no reason. Passed off as no big deal. Now though, he'd had time to think more deeply

230

about things like that. About the effect such an action would have on someone.

The lessons had brought that out of him. Endless talking about what he'd done in the past, what he'd witnessed. Why he'd taken part in things that had hurt others. What he got out of it. The usual answers of *something to do* or *bored wasn't I*, wouldn't do here. No, he'd been questioned relentlessly. Then beaten if the answers weren't good enough.

He'd had time to think. To step back and look at himself. Look at his life. He'd always known on some level that what he'd been doing was wrong, but it had taken the shock of something like this happening to really drive the message home.

Goldie shifted on the bed, staring at the darkness above him. He could hear crying coming from the other side of the room. Probably the new lad. Goldie had been there the longest, so he'd seen this from the others as well. Late at night was when it finally hit them. The gravity of their situation. Four of them left now, all just lying there and waiting.

Things were different now though. Mealtimes had become more spaced out. There'd been no lessons in a while.

Maybe they'd not meant to go that far. But what had they expected? The Norris Green lad might have been in there only a few weeks longer than Goldie, but he'd not taken to it as he had. No, the lad had spent his whole time in there sulking, not listening, not doing as he was told. He was asking for it. He'd come back in after his

231

lessons in the evening, beaten and bruised. Blood staining the floor, curled up on his bed, moaning. Still, he'd gone back for more. Not just given in.

Maybe he'd just been harder than Goldie. More aware of himself. Goldie shook the thought away. The lad was thick as shit. Goldie knew there was only one way out of there, and that was to do as he was told. To hope against hope that he'd change enough for them to let him go. They'd always been careful — balaclavas over their faces the whole time. Full uniform to cover themselves. He knew one of them was a woman, but that wouldn't matter. The only time the lads saw them together was when three of them came to remove them from the room. One of them would have done the job just as well, considering they came tooled-up. A sawn-off shotgun in one hand, handcuffs thrown at them to bind themselves.

None of the lads were harder than a sawn-off shotgun.

Goldie had asked the man called Alpha repeatedly, endlessly, why he'd been taken. One time he'd actually given an answer other than *you deserve it.*

'Ever hear about National Service?'

'No . . . what's that?'

'Every lad used to have to do it. You'd reach seventeen and have to do eighteen months of military service. Didn't do it myself — bit before my time — but it worked. Gave people a sense of respect, of worthiness. Stopped being mandatory in 1960. No sign of it being brought back, so we're doing the next best thing.'

Goldie had received his worst beating since being in there for laughing in response. He hadn't meant to, sticking to his idea of keeping his head down and getting on with it, but he hadn't been able to help himself.

It was bollocks. This was far from National Service or whatever the fuck they wanted to call it.

This was torture.

The Norris Green lad being killed showed he was right to laugh back then. Because he'd got it spot on. There was no plan to set them free. Make them better. He no longer believed the lies. He no longer believed one lad had already been let go. He knew the truth now. Torture and death. Goldie had never been more sure of anything in his life. That lad was gone.

Two lads dead. And he wasn't getting out of there any different than them.

Things were happening though. He'd heard arguments. Raised voices outside, drifting into the barn as the wind swirled around the place at night.

All wasn't well.

Maybe he had a chance after all.

19

Rossi squinted into the sun as she watched Murphy walk away towards town and his lunch with Jess. The thought of the office canteen being the only thing on offer turned her stomach. She had to eat though, had to keep her strength up in the face of the seemingly endless days and nights on the horizon.

Not for the first time, she wondered how she'd got herself into this mess of a career.

She grabbed a sandwich and some fruit from the canteen on her way back up to the office, pausing to add two energy drinks from the vending machine outside the incident room. A balanced diet. Not for the first time that week, she thought of going to her parents' house for a proper meal. Proper food.

Pushing her way into the incident room, she stuck her head down, hoping to make her way to the poky little office at the back without being stopped. There wasn't much noise around her, everyone ostensibly getting their heads down and working hard. Others out there knocking on doors. Working their own cases. They covered such a vast area that a murder enquiry didn't really take as high a profile as it would have in the past. Especially the murder of someone young with a troubled record.

Rossi guessed she should feel sad or disappointed by the fact a gang of idiots driving into cash machines and robbing them should take a higher priority than a teenager's murder, but she knew the score now. Back when she'd first started — fresh out of uni with a sociology degree and a Marx-sized chip on her shoulder — she'd felt different. Fast-tracked within a few years into CID, the hope was to change the system from within. Three years on, all those thoughts of fighting against the system had gone. Now she was deeply embedded within it. Making excuses, justifying her decisions.

Rossi made it all the way across without interruption. She opened the office door, cringing at the sound of the creak in the hinges, just as every other time. For once, it was empty. No DC Harris. No Murphy opposite her. No Tony Brannon leering at her.

Bliss.

She sat down at her desk, removing her notepad and flipping over to a blank page. Opened the sandwich and ate with one hand, the other making notes.

If Murphy was going to bugger off for God knows how long in the middle of the day, it didn't mean she had to slack off as well.

She liked the process of making notes. Looking for something they'd missed, some hidden gem amongst the dirt.

So far, it had never happened, but there was always a first time. As her papa would say, *Chi non risica, non rosica.*

Nothing ventured, nothing gained.

Rossi plotted out what they'd learnt so far. The information didn't exactly fill her notebook.

The next step was logical. Find the man from the youth club.

She finished her sandwich and switched on her computer and waited less than a minute for it to boot up.

Dragging her mouse across, Rossi clicked on the database which would hopefully give her more information about Alan Bimpson. It would be difficult. They had a name and a rough age, but that was about it.

She searched for his name first, getting results from all around the country before narrowing her search to Merseyside. Three results. Unfortunately, it was three that could be disregarded instantly as being either too old — eighty-one and seventy-eight — or too young. Three years old. Rossi shook her head, thinking of a child called Alan.

Now that was evil.

Rossi turned to property records instead, finding two more matches. One thirty-two-year-old, which would be a little younger than they'd been told was the case but could be the guy. The other, fifty-two years old, born 1962. Last known address in Litherland, Quartz Way, which was on one of those new-build housing estates near Moss Lane, if Rossi was remembering right. Not bad, but nothing special — especially for a property developer, if Kevin Thornhill from the youth club was to be believed.

The door opened behind her, Rossi rolling her eyes at the break in her peace and quiet. She turned and raised a hand in greeting as DC Harris shuffled his way in to sit down at what was rapidly becoming his own desk. There'd been such a high turnover of different constables over the previous months that she'd given up even trying to build something resembling a good working relationship with any of them. Graham Harris seemed to be the exception, and had ingratiated himself into the dynamic Murphy and Rossi had created. He was quiet enough for it not to be a problem.

Didn't hurt that he was easy on the eye.

'Anything to report?' she said, swivelling her chair around to face him.

'Nothing useful. Gave up on the phone call. Couldn't make out anything really. Started ringing the number every half an hour instead.'

'Well . . . you never know. Suppose it can't hurt. My guess is that he's switched it off and thrown it by now.'

Harris shrugged, turning back around and dialling the number on his phone. Rossi watched as he dialled from memory before turning back to her screen, focussing on the latter Alan Bimpson.

Checking the land registry records was a first step. See if Mr Bimpson owned any farms maybe. Google his name, see if anything jumped out.

She went over her notes again. The narrative had been so different until the mysterious Ian had phoned the previous day. Yes, he'd known things about the way in which Dean Hughes had died. Details which hadn't been released. But the story he told seemed too fantastical. Five murderers. A strange farm where they were holding teenagers . . . it was all starting to sound ridiculous.

Then she thought of the events the previous year and realised that people resided in Liverpool, her city, who weren't the normal, everyday sort of killers; not the domestics, the druggies, the violent thugs who got unlucky with a single punch in town.

No, last year a serial killer had hit at the heart of the city and brought out the darkness which lay within . . . almost taking the life of her absent detective inspector.

'How long are land registry taking at the moment?' Rossi said, startling the detective constable from his staring competition with the wall.

'Not sure. Few hours, a day. Depends who's asking, usually.'

'I bet we could hurry that along.'

Harris turned his chair towards her. 'I've just been using Google. Takes less time and tends to give you the same info.'

Rossi nodded, 'Good thinking.' She switched to the search engine and typed in Alan Bimpson's name.

Thirty-odd thousand results.

She added more details to try and narrow down the results. She heard the dial tone from Harris's phone and the dialling of a number, but tried to ignore it. Read the top results and clicked on a few. A couple of newspaper articles which mentioned the local businessman and his donation to the local youth club, buried amongst much bigger articles about Kevin Thornhill and

238

his hope to create a place for disenfranchised youths.

Rossi returned to the list of results, ignoring the youth club articles and attempting to find something else.

She found what she was looking for, just as a voice echoed around the office which didn't belong to either her or DC Harris.

The Farm

Yesterday

It had felt like things were going back to normal. The little lessons had started again. The food being delivered wasn't an afterthought. They still looked like they were on edge when they came in to deal with them, but was bearable. The lads had begun to calm down, getting used to life in the Dorm again.

Goldie's patience had almost gone. Definitely with the lad from Toxteth. Introduced himself constantly as 'Holty', like in the third person or whatever. Not Tyler, as he had at the start, now it was all 'Holty', like they was mates or something.

Non-stop talking. *Holty reckons this is bollocks* or *I won't be doing any pervy shit, Holty doesn't do shite like that for anyone.* Goldie would just roll his eyes and — when he felt like a laugh — pretend to go for him. Just to watch him flinch back like a little rat.

The noise had started an hour before the other lads had begun to take notice. Goldie had sat up in the bed as soon as he'd heard the first voice. He knew the difference in the way the sounds from the voices carried over. He'd heard them shouting before, but this time it had been different. The low voices building over time. The occasional loud shout which emphasised a word or parts of sentences.

No . . . Can't do this . . . Not why . . . Don't get it . . . Listen . . . No...

The four lads crowded around the door eventually, straining to hear more, pushing and shoving each other. While the wood was solid, there were small gaps which let in some noise. None big enough to prise open though; Goldie had spent hours scrabbling around the edges trying to force it open, to no avail.

Still, you could hear them out there sometimes. Trampling around outside, watching them, perhaps. Not that Goldie knew for sure, there being no windows in the Dorm.

He shushed the others as he strained to hear more. The noise — argument, he now realised — had grown louder. Now they could hear whole sentences being blared out. From inside the farm.

'They're going mad. What they did to Dean is sending them bonkers,' Tyler said.

'Shut it and listen.'

'Holty was just saying, lad. No need.'

Goldie turned and looked at him, getting what he wanted as Tyler averted his eyes.

'This is our chance,' Goldie said, unable to hide the excitement in his voice. 'We all have to be on the same side here, understand?'

The other lads just looked towards him, their expressions blank.

'Listen. This is what we're going to do . . . '

★ ★ ★

Gamma had started it. All of them together for the first time in days, wanting to air her

241

grievances, as she'd put it. Like she would know what that word fucking meant, the daft bitch. Alpha knew who had put her up to it. Fucking Delta and his word-of-the-day bog roll. The wanker. Her husband, Tango, would go along with anything she said. Under the fucking thumb.

'We need to do something. I can't go on like this,' she'd said eventually, when they'd all settled down around the table. 'I can't get his face out of my head. It's always there, just needling me. Those little shits in there aren't helping either. I want out. I can't deal with all this any more.'

Alpha had tried to calm her down, but it hadn't been working. Not with everyone else suddenly piping up. If they'd just let him get on with things, everything would have been fine. It had gone downhill from there though. All of them getting on their high horses.

'I don't remember any of you saying any of this last Thursday,' Alpha said.

'Well, we were all in shock I suppose,' Tango said, fiddling with a lighter as he spoke. 'We kind of knew things like that could have happened, but when it's in front of you like that . . . it's different. I'm sure you felt the same.'

Alpha had slammed his fist on the table then, causing the others around it to flinch. 'No I fucking didn't. The kid wouldn't listen. Wouldn't learn. You all know that. He was given enough chances. He had to be dealt with.'

'He wasn't an animal, Alan,' Gamma said then, making Alpha sit back as she used his real name.

'I haven't been sleeping since it happened,' a small voice cut in. Omega, speaking for the first time. 'I know I said it was for the best, but it doesn't help. I keep praying, but it's no use. I keep seeing him, lying there . . . '

'You've . . . you've got to put that out of your head,' Alpha replied, brushing his hair back with his fingers. 'Remember what I said? Remember what the Bible says? What happened was unavoidable. They know the rules. We're making them better.'

'Would the auld fella agree, do you think?' Gamma said again, not letting it rest.

'He knew the score. This whole thing was his idea, remember.'

'That's what you say.' Gamma was on her feet by now, pointing at Alpha. 'But we've only got your word that he planned for this. Maybe he never wanted us to go this far. How do we know?'

Alpha had risen to face her then. 'Look, you all knew what you were signing up for. You all agreed — if things went that way, then that was just how it was going to be.'

'Did you let him go?' Delta was on his feet by then, with Gamma staring straight at him.

'Let who go?'

'The one we fixed. Did he really go home, or was that just what you told us? To keep us on board?'

'Of course I did . . . '

'Where is he then?'

Alpha shook his head, wanting them to stop it. Stop the questioning, the needling. It was all

243

going the wrong way.

'At home, last I checked.'

It had worked, once. One young lad released back into society. Changed. Better. Unable to identify any of them — Alpha had been sure of that. Even less likely to be able to point the police their way, anyway. He'd had no idea where he'd been kept for the four months it had taken to break him down and rebuild him. Four months of hard work, all leading to the point where they could send him back.

And it had worked. But that didn't mean Alpha could risk sending him out there. Not then.

Not with those first boys.

'Look. We know what we're doing works. You saw how he was when he left. But we couldn't be sure he wouldn't have been able to tell people what had been going on. Sure, we made threats towards him. Towards his family. But realistically, how long could that have gone on for?'

'You killed him . . . ' Gamma stumbled back and dropped into her seat. 'You're . . . you're a murderer.'

'No,' Alpha said, slamming his fist down on the table. 'What I did, I did for us all. Remember what the old man said to us. Collateral damage. In any war, it happens, and that's what we're in, understand? We're fighting against these kids. We're taking the streets back. But it takes time. Practice. I'm in it for the long haul. These first lot, these little bastards, they're just the first in a long line of kids we're going to be working with. But they aren't the ones to send back. Not yet.

We have to be tougher, stricter, harder. We have to grind them down more. So we can be sure. You all know that.'

'You're sick,' Delta said, moving towards the door.

'*I'm* sick?' Alpha shouted at Delta's back. 'I've seen you with them, what you've done. You're just as involved as us all. You enjoy it, George. I know you do. Hurting those lads gives you a thrill. A sense of power you're not getting out there.'

'For a reason. We all thought we were doing it for a reason. We didn't want to kill them.'

'Look,' Alpha said, softening his voice and moving towards Delta. 'I don't get anything out of it, honestly I don't. But it's the only way, surely you can see that?'

'We should have been told.'

'I did it all for everyone, so no one had to worry.'

'No,' Delta had said, turning to face Alpha. 'We should have been told, so we could stop you doing it.'

'We have to go to the police.'

'No. I'm not getting locked up for what he's done.'

'I can't live with this, can you?'

'If it stops now, we can.'

'We just let them go? What if they know who we are? What if they saw us one time?'

'Ever seen them without your balaclava covering your face? No. Don't worry about that.'

'They could still trace us.'

Alpha sat and listened to them go back and

forth. Hoping against hope that they'd change course. Come back to his way of thinking. But it was no use. They had already gone. All his hard work, gone to waste.

They were talking about the little scrotes locked up in the farm building as if they were deserving of compassion. They weren't. They were subhuman. Alpha knew that. He'd never had any doubt. He wanted to break them down, yes. Wanted to fix them. But, on that drive back, that kid, that little fucker who was only just eighteen, had shown him. Shown him that they couldn't be fixed.

'Wait. What are they doing?'

Alpha snapped back into the present, his attention taken by what they were all looking at; the small TV screen that had been set up in the kitchen, which showed the boys in the Dorm filmed on hidden cameras.

'They're doing something to the door.'

They watched as the four boys walked back from the door, going over to where one of the beds was, then Goldie, the oldest, pointing out where they should stand.

They watched as they lifted the bed and struck the door.

They heard the noise from outside.

Alpha grabbed his shotgun, motioning for the others to follow him. They moved slower than he would have expected.

'Come on.'

They trudged out of the kitchen, Alpha leading the way, almost running towards the Dorm.

246

He reached the door first, waiting a few seconds for everyone else to stack up behind him.

'Step away from the door,' Alpha shouted, hearing nothing from within. 'We're coming in. Everyone by their beds.'

Alpha shot a look towards Omega. Frowned a little at the expression he received back.

'On three . . . '

Alpha counted before snapping the lock back on the door, standing aside as Omega moved slowly and turned the key he'd been holding.

He opened the door, slow, precise. The hinges creaked as it moved inwards, darkness spilling out into more darkness.

'Stay where you are.'

Alpha took a step forwards.

Goldie's face appeared out of the gloom.

'Think fast,' Goldie said, before driving his forehead into Alpha's face.

The others didn't move quick enough, five versus four, but with Alpha already incapacitated, Goldie moved towards Omega, raising a fist towards him before launching a boot into his midsection.

Omega collapsed next to Alpha, the latter's vision blurred by blood which was gushing from his nose but running upwards as he lay on the floor.

Alpha could hear the cries from the others as they hesitated, not wanting to shoot.

Idiots, Alpha thought as he shook his head.

'Stop . . . ' Alpha gasped, choking on his blood. 'Now.'

Goldie turned towards him, a fistful of Gamma's hair in his hand, her balaclava already lost. 'We're just starting, mate.'

Alpha almost smiled, but instead concentrated on getting his bearings.

'Quick, come on.'

Alpha looked towards the new voice. Saw Tango, laid out on the floor, looking unconscious.

Alpha's hand gripped the shotgun which had slipped out of his grasp, turned to see the boys getting to their feet, pulling on each other to start running away.

'Don't, fucking, move,' Alpha said, standing up and levelling his gun at the boys. They shared quick glances, weighing up their options.

The new lad moved first. Alpha didn't flinch. Aimed and blew a hole in the boy's back. Shifted the gun back to the other three as the first boy fell to the floor, lifeless.

'It's all gone,' Alpha whispered. 'All of it.'

The next two fell quicker.

'One little piggy left,' Alpha said, staring at Goldie.

★   ★   ★

'You're going home now. You understand what'll happen if you tell anyone about what occurred here?'

A nod of understanding. Slow, deliberate. Alpha watched him, looked him up and down, satisfied. He took the scissors from the pocket near the knee of his cargo pants. Snipped the

248

cable tie binding his ankles together, before motioning for him to get out of the van.

The lad lasted five seconds on the outside before his old nature returned.

Alpha stepped back to let him walk away. The lad had looked down the road, the streetlights illuminating his face. Looked back at Alpha, and then grinned.

'Fuck you,' the lad had said, and spat in his face. He ran then, took off at a sprint.

Five seconds to confirm what Alpha had already known. That they could never change. Not really.

It took him around a minute to chase him down. Less than a second to plunge the scissors into his neck.

That's how the lad from Bootle had gone. On the side of a road in the north of Liverpool. Near the open fields between Crosby and Formby. Almost the middle of nowhere. Alpha had dragged his body into the woods there, burying it in a grave he spent an hour digging, hoping it was deep enough to never be found.

★ ★ ★

Alpha blinked a few times before wiping an arm across his face to clear his vision. Back in the kitchen, the bodies outside were already turning cold. The sounds were coming from in front of him, as the people he had shared the last year with shouted and bawled at each other. Desperation. Despair. The reverberations didn't make sense. He couldn't tell what they were

249

saying any more. It was just noise. Not real sentences until he really concentrated.

'We need to get out of here.'

'I can't believe they're dead.'

'We should untie this one. Just let him go.'

'He knows what we look like.'

'Our Father, who art in heaven . . . '

'Stop fucking praying. It's doing my fucking head in!'

Alpha tuned them out. The sound of his heartbeat became louder. Banging against his chest. The voice in his head. His own. Saying the same thing over and over.

Do it. Do it. Do it.

Alpha kicked the table back, raising the shotgun and standing up. He hit Gamma before she even had the chance to turn fully around. Alpha hit Tango square in the chest next. He turned and fired towards the door as Delta exited.

His heartbeat was the only sound as he took down Omega.

Bang. Bang. Bang.

God forgive them. God forgive me.

★ ★ ★

Darkness. Only darkness. No light, no escape. A hammer coming down towards him, then a wrecking ball. Pounding into him, knocking him off his feet in slow motion. Every bone cracking, every bruise, every organ shifted, all happening in turn so he could feel each one. Darkness, just darkness.

250

Goldie woke slowly, his eyes opening and closing like he was coming out of a deep sleep he didn't want to wake from. Tight eyelids, as if they were crusted over. He opened one a crack, trying to work out what was happening He tried to move his hand to rub his eyes. Couldn't move it. He tried the other hand and found the same result. Something was holding them in place, but he couldn't feel a weight on them, no hard resistance. His mind was confusing him, acting without going over options first. Working on instinct. Move this, feel that.

His legs wouldn't move.

Goldie's mind was cloudy, like walking through mist or fog. Trying to find his way along an unfamiliar street when he couldn't see more than a few inches in front of him.

His legs wouldn't move.

The pain was there, in the background, waiting for its moment to hit him full force. For now, it was just throbbing away in the distance, his head doubling in size with every pulse.

Goldie blinked. Once. Twice. Opened his eyes fully and came to know where he was.

On the rack.

His breathing became faster, rhythmic. In, out, in, out. The pulsing pain grew in his head, becoming heavier with each breath.

Two fingers entered his vision from above him. Clicking. Together.

'You with me?'

The voice came from behind him. Fragments of the events which had preceded the darkness began to crowd his mind. The noises from outside. The screaming.

Visions of blood, cascading in front of him.

'Wakey wakey.'

Goldie tried to form words, but his tongue felt like it had been removed. Just a gargle of noise escaping his mouth. It was still there, numb pain when he moved his teeth over the swollen form inside.

'You've taken quite a nasty knock to the head. Several, in fact. Probably best you don't try and talk for a while. Stay awake though. I've heard that's important.'

The noises. Banging around his skull, echoing and subsiding.

'You know . . . it wasn't my idea, this rack thing. Remember the old man? The one you and your shitty little mates tried to intimidate and scare? He was the one who began this whole thing. He suggested this as a punishment. For your crimes. Against him. Against us. Against our whole society. I remember the others didn't like the sound of it, but they just got swept along on the wave of actually doing something for a change.'

He remembered the other boys, lads, men. Falling where they were hit.

'It's a shame he didn't live long enough to see what he created here.'

It wasn't like in films, but Goldie already knew that. He'd seen real violence before. Inflicted it.

Not like this. Never like this.

'You . . . you kimmed 'em . . . '

'Please, if you're going to talk, try to enunciate. Yes, I killed them.'

252

'Aye . . . ?'

The form around him changed, moved. No longer behind him, now at his side.

'Because it was time. It wasn't working. Trying to help you boys was pointless. It was never going to work, was it?'

Goldie tried to speak, but the pain in his head was growing by the second. He could feel something dripping next to his ear.

'You would have left here and gone back to the way things were before within days. You're all the same. Nothing we did here would have changed that.'

Goldie shook his head but regretted it instantly. The pain which had been just below the surface now broke through. Exploding around him, filling his ears. He heard himself screaming but didn't remember telling himself to do so.

'Shhh . . . shhh . . . '

The pain didn't subside, but Goldie soon realised the screaming was making things worse. Tears formed and then snuck out the corner of his eyes.

'It's not my fault. You all have choices. You decide to go this way and end up here. It's your own decision to go down this path. I just can't take it any more. It's not right, what you all do. You make people scared to leave their houses. You frighten innocent people, you know that. All of you.'

The voice came closer.

Alpha. The man in charge. The only one Goldie had feared from the start.

Leaning over him as his eyes misted over with moisture, no amount of blinking clearing his vision, so that everything became blurred.

'You know what the worst thing is? You don't care. You don't care who you hurt as long as you're all having fun. Getting your kicks out of everyone else's misery.'

A breath, and then the man who called himself Alpha stood up. Goldie blinked some more, trying to clear his sight and failing.

'Well . . . no more. I'm going to make all of you sit up and take notice. Make you feel fear. Every single little scrote and scally in this city will be afraid. It's our turn now. The good people of this city. The ones who do everything right and get no reward for it. Who have sat back while you all take over. These are our streets and I'm taking them back. For us all. For me, for them. For everyone.'

Goldie tried to speak, but his throat hitched up on him. This was it. Every day in that hole of a room, the darkness, the only sounds coming from the others in the same position, every damn day, he had known. Known he wouldn't be leaving while still breathing. He'd lied to himself. Of course he had. Tried to think of a plan.

Then he'd come up with one on the spur of the moment. And Alpha had killed them all, sparing Goldie's life by not shooting him as well. He remembered throwing his hands up and the stock of the rifle striking him in the face. And again. His head being beaten before unconsciousness had taken him.

No. A bullet to his chest, to his head, to his

254

heart hadn't been the end.

There had been something else in mind for him.

His head was lifted up, the rest of his body still weighed down. Strapped down.

'This is the best I could do, but it'll work.'

Goldie looked to where Alpha had put something next to him on the rack. A large bowl, full of water. He started shaking his head, but it was no use.

It wasn't bad. Not at first. His head being forced underwater until he couldn't hold his breath any longer. Ripped back out, where he could suck in glorious air, before he was forced under again. Coughing and spluttering.

Each time underneath getting longer. Unable to breathe, in and out of consciousness. Drowning. He now knew what it felt like to drown. His mind playing tricks on him.

'Once more.'

The voice was ethereal. Not connected to what was playing out in his head. A different life, better than the one he had led.

Goldie opened his mouth, trying to breathe under the water, only succeeding in filling his lungs with liquid.

There was no return to the surface. No gasping, no air, no oxygen. Just darkness, seeping into him until it took over.

Goldie could feel nothing other than the pain in his body and his hope for release. An end.

The finality to sweep over him.

His last thoughts were just images. No sounds, no voices. Just his family. What was left of them.

Blurred and out of focus as his struggle stopped and his vision went black.

Gone.

★ ★ ★

Delta ran. For his life, for his future. Knowing there wasn't anything left back at that farm.

Alpha was going to kill everyone.

So he ran. Kept running, scared that he was going to be next. He had nowhere to go, having sold up his house to live at the farm full-time. No money, as he hadn't worked in months. All his savings being poured into this *project*.

All gone.

His old lungs couldn't hack it any more, so he stopped for a while. It was only then that he felt the pain. Put a hand to his shoulder, flinching as he looked at the blood which remained there when he took it back. He must have been hit when Alpha fired at him as he ran out the back door. He didn't know why he'd even gone back to the main house. He should have ran as soon as the boys had been killed. The upper hand they'd always had had now been ripped away, tearing a hole into the top of his arm in the process.

It was dark, the day's spring warmth now disappearing. Delta tried to stay away from the roads, scared that Alpha wouldn't stop at those left at the farm.

That he wouldn't stop until all of them had gone.

20

Murphy didn't bother with speed limits on the way back to the station. He picked his way through what traffic was on the roads, keeping all his focus on what was ahead of him.

He was there in less than fifteen minutes, but it felt like much longer.

Murphy's grip on the wheel tightened as he arrived on St Anne Street, the brown-bricked building appearing on the crest of the small hill halfway down. He shouldn't have taken off like that, not in the middle of the day. Not in the middle of a murder enquiry.

What had he missed?

It was like the months after his parents had been murdered all over again. Allowing his personal life to take over. It was supposed to be a fresh start, and the last year had given him the false sense of security that he could have it all. Be the husband, be the friend, be the man who could do it all.

Rossi's voice had sounded mixed. Fear and excitement. Breathless. As if she'd single-handedly solved everything whilst Murphy was off counselling some kid he wasn't even related to.

He kind of hoped that wasn't the case. Murphy wanted to be there for the conclusion of this one.

He parked up and was just about to leave the car when he glanced up at the rear exit and saw them. Two or three at first, then more. A mix of uniforms and detectives who had been working the Dean Hughes inquiry.

Rossi came out soon after, still trying to put her jacket on as she shouted orders across to stragglers who hadn't moved as fast as the first lot. She looked up as Murphy beeped his horn and changed direction, trotting across the car park towards him.

Murphy turned the engine over as she opened the passenger side door and sat down in the seat.

'Tell me on the way . . . '

'You don't know where we're going yet.'

Murphy followed out behind a yellow police van, the barrier to the car park already raised. 'You can tell me that as well.' He took one hand off the steering wheel to scratch at his beard. 'So, this 'Ian' just answered one of the phonecalls?'

'Yeah,' Rossi said, the same breathless excitement making her voice catch. 'You should have seen the face on Harris. Scared the shit out of him.'

'What did he say?' Murphy replied, not sharing the joke.

'Who, Harris?'

Murphy turned his head and gave her a look.

'Oh, right, yeah. He was scared. You could tell from his voice. I played on that a bit and got him to tell me what had happened.'

'Go on . . . '

Rossi blew out a breath and tapped a rhythm on her knee. 'The lead guy goes crazy, that we know. Shoots up the place apparently and our man Ian gets away.'

'We knew that.'

258

'Yeah. But now he wants to come in and help. Turns out he was hurt during his 'escape'. A graze by the sounds of it, but he's been holed up and losing blood. Didn't want to go to a hospital. Anyway, it looks like his conscience got the better of him.'

Murphy banged a hand against the wheel. 'So we're going to get him? Excellent work, Laura.'

'*Grazie.*'

'*Prego.*'

Rossi made a noise in the back of her throat. 'I knew you'd pick some words up eventually.'

'Just be glad it wasn't your usual bile.'

Rossi laughed, the sound cutting off as they began to slow behind the procession of cars and vans which were in front of them.

'Looks like we're here,' Murphy said after ten minutes or so of driving, lifting his foot off the accelerator.

They pulled in behind an unmarked car from the pool, a long line of cars in front and behind them.

They were going into the woods.

Childwall Woods was only around fifteen minutes from the city centre, but it felt like an entirely different place. Dense treelines on short roads, with immaculately presented, large semi-detached houses facing the outskirts of the woods themselves. Another example of the disparate versions of the city. The housing estates only a few miles away from middle-class suburbs.

There were a few entrances into the woods itself, with Rossi informing Murphy they had chosen the Childwall Abbey Road end to convene. Murphy looked up to the sky as the noise which the residents of Merseyside were now used to hovered above. Helicopters had become second nature to those in the city — deployed at a minute's notice and seemingly without thought. Murphy had little sympathy for those who constantly complained about the noise. He'd once lived on the flight path for Speke Airport . . . they had no idea. Murphy spoke in a low voice to Rossi as they reached the large group of uniforms and detectives near the short path which led into the woods.

'You take the lead. This is your shot.'

Rossi drew herself up, her black jacket tight against the open-necked white blouse underneath. 'No problem.'

Murphy watched the helicopter above as Rossi gave quick instructions. She had her phone open, giving details of the woods from a quick Google search she'd made on the way over. Murphy heard the words *thirty-nine acres* and *nature reserve* and chose to just follow Rossi and see where that took them.

They trudged off in groups of twos and threes. All on their guard. All a second away from calling for back-up, those trained in taser use going first. Everyone's hands on their belts.

The ground was soft but not muddy as they reached the woods, the relatively good weather they'd had the last month or so on their sides. The lack of rain hadn't dispersed the clouds overhead however, the light becoming progressively less bright as they entered the dense paths within the woods.

Murphy walked alongside Rossi, eyes shifting left to right as they moved slowly along the tracks, peering into the trees if they thought something looked out of place. Every now and again, they'd disturb someone walking a dog, or someone with binoculars around their neck. Bird watchers and nature lovers.

Somewhere, there was a man with a gunshot wound and a guilty conscience.

'Did he give any indication as to where he might be in here?'

Rossi shook her head to Murphy's question. 'Just that he was in the woods and to hurry.'

Murphy skirted around a suspicious-looking brown mark against the grey paving. 'He could have at least come out and met us on the main road.'

'He said he was too scared to do that. He thinks the lead guy is after him. And I wasn't about to argue.'

Murphy sniffed and went back to looking into the trees once more.

A shout from ahead drew them to a stop. A raised arm in the air, then silence assailing them through the trees.

Then the silence was broken. At first it was just voices, then hard shoes against the concrete paths as officers moved around them, moving forwards towards the commotion.

Murphy reacted slower than Rossi, who took off at a sprint, a pen clattering to the ground in front of him as it flew out of her jacket pocket. Murphy moved then, catching up to her quickly. They reached the point where the noise had begun, the treeline a blur of yellow as the flak jackets of the uniforms converged on one spot, eventually dispersing as the noise dissipated, just a few exchanges between breathless men and women.

The relative silence was ended by a single cry. 'Paramedic.'

Murphy pushed his way through a few bodies, aware of Rossi behind doing the same, coming to a small clearing past a few thin-trunked trees which had lined the path. Two uniforms blocked the view, but Murphy could see past them to what was slumped against the base of a tree. A man in his fifties at least, he guessed. Dressed in a T-shirt which was hanging off him and blue jeans which were already losing their original colour. The T-shirt he wore was once a faded green but was beginning to turn completely red.

Blood red. More brown than red, but unmistakeable all the same. As were the rips near the man's right shoulder, the T-shirt almost torn free on one side. The man's left hand was draped over the wound Murphy knew lay beneath. Seeping through onto his dirty hands. Three-day stubble and dark rings underneath his eyes.

Ian.

Or as Murphy knew him . . . George Stanley.

Murphy paced the path as four paramedics brought George past him on the stretcher. One of them was carrying an IV bag above her head, and they were making a show of holding the weight of what was now an emaciated man who had clearly gone at least a day or so without food or water.

George Stanley had said two words before finally accepting unconsciousness.

I'm scared.

Murphy wasn't sure of what.

'How do you know him?' Rossi said, standing close to him so as not to allow others to overhear their conversation.

'It was probably before your time. Ten years ago, his seventeen-year-old son was killed. I was still a uniform then, about six months before becoming a DC. It was pretty big news.'

'I'm trying to place it . . . '

Murphy waved a hand. 'Not important really. I was one of the first uniforms who spoke to him and his wife. Didn't take it serious, I suppose. Just some teenager who had gone missing. You know the score. When they found his body a couple of days later, it went a bit nuts. The local papers tried to insinuate we — the police — had done something wrong. Like we should have taken things more seriously. Things were a bit shaky, but thankfully upstairs didn't take much notice.'

'Teenagers go missing all the time.'

Murphy thought of Dean Hughes lying in the morgue at the Royal Hospital. 'Don't we just know it.'

Rossi began to walk, Murphy falling into step alongside her. 'How did he die? Murder . . . suicide?'

'Murder. Although that wasn't how it went later.'

Rossi frowned as Murphy looked down at her. 'I don't understand . . . '

263

'It was kids who did it. They got away with manslaughter charges in the end. Most were already out last time I checked. Moved away for the most part. Apparently it was bullying that got out of hand. No one meant for it to go that far, that type of thing. All we know is that Martin Stanley went to a party and on the walk home he was jumped by a few other teenagers from the same party. Pushed around a bit and then one of the group pushed too hard. They all panicked and tried to hide him.'

'Now . . . what? He's getting revenge on them?'

'Doesn't look that way,' Murphy said, slowing to allow a couple of uniforms to hurry past them. 'Dean Hughes wasn't one of those involved with his son's death, for one.'

'The same type of kids then. We need to find this place he mentioned,' Rossi said. 'This farm or whatever. If he has that past and is involved, I don't want to think about what the man who shot him is capable of.'

Murphy looked to the sky. Dark, angry clouds had formed since they'd entered the woods.

Rain was coming.

21

The hospital waiting room was almost empty. Murphy and Rossi took up two seats in the room, the occasional visitor joining them for short periods, but otherwise leaving them to discuss things without interruption.

There wasn't even a clock on the wall to count the seconds down.

Murphy's back had begun aching within minutes of sitting in the small seats. He was used to it though. Nothing in the world seemed to be made for anyone over six feet in height, never mind the extra four or five inches he carried around. A dull, familiar throbbing started in his lower back, one he knew would require more walking space than the small room could provide.

'I'm just saying, how hard would it be to just paint the walls a different colour? A nice deep red or a sky blue. Would really make a difference, I reckon.'

Rossi rolled her eyes at him as he complained. He thought it was a good idea, but she seemed unwilling to agree.

George Stanley had been sent into surgery an hour or so earlier, DCI Stephens making it clear that they weren't to leave until they'd spoken to him and found out more details.

'We should be doing something,' Rossi eventually said, breaking her ten-minute vow of silence.

'What can we do?' Murphy replied. 'We have someone who has already admitted to being involved in Dean Hughes's murder in custody. That's our best option right now . . . to get more answers from him.'

Rossi sighed and stood up, fidgeting with the broken water cooler, the water tap refusing to budge into a working position. There weren't any cups in there anyway.

'It just seems useless, sitting here waiting around. Could be hours.'

'Think of the overtime,' Murphy tried, forcing a smile on his face.

He received a harrumph and shrug in reply.

Murphy checked his phone again. Still no reply to the text message he'd sent Sarah when they'd first arrived. Another missed meal. Another missed conversation.

If she wasn't becoming used to his old ways, the job, she would be now. She'd never complained in the past, but Murphy got the feeling something was shifting.

Now the subject had turned to children, and when they were going to start having them.

'Let's lay it out again. From the beginning,' Murphy said, trying to bring Rossi back into it.

'If you want.'

'It might help,' Murphy replied, pulling out the murder folder. 'Dean Hughes's body is found on Friday morning. We speak to the vicar and the boys who found him. His mum says he's been gone for over six months, a letter was delivered to her saying he's safe and will come home soon. Enquiries lead us to the youth club.

We speak to a possible girlfriend, who turns out to probably be the last person to see him alive.'

Rossi banged out a beat on the wall with open palms. 'You sound like Poirot summing things up.'

'It helps.'

'I'm sure it does,' Rossi said, with a theatrical wave of her arm. 'Please continue, Hercule.'

'I thank you. We receive a call from someone calling themselves 'Ian', who says he was there when Dean Hughes died, and that some unnamed leader has gone berserk and killed more people. There's also more stuff about a farm and other teens being held. We find 'Ian', who turns out to be the father of another dead youngster. And he's been shot.'

'You're missing out the bloke from the youth club.'

Murphy frowned. 'Of course. How did I forget that?'

Rossi smiled thinly. 'It's this place. The drabness of it makes you dull and prone to memory lapses. And psychotic behaviour as well, probably.'

Murphy laughed, the sound echoing around the small space. 'Fine. So we have . . . '

'Alan Bimpson.'

'Alan Bimpson,' Murphy repeated. 'A bloke who rocks up at the youth club and tells the kids there what's wrong with them.'

'And probably worse. That Kevin Thornhill doesn't strike me as the most trustworthy bloke we've ever come across.'

Murphy yawned, stretching his legs out. 'Well

267

. . . we'll know more when we speak to Mr Stanley when he's well enough . . . '

'Which could be hours.'

Four, to be exact.

The surgery was successful and minor according to the surgeon. A quick bullet removal — the way he'd said it, as if it was the most common thing in the world — and George Stanley was arguing, first with the nurses, then with consultants about being allowed to speak to Murphy and Rossi.

Rossi, in particular.

'The second he shows any signs of distress,' the consultant said, playing his role perfectly as the harried medical expert who was just thinking of the patient, 'then I'm afraid any interview will have to be terminated.'

Murphy nodded along, each second inching closer to the door which separated them from the patient.

'No problem at all.'

The consultant made a show of heaving a big sigh and shaking his head before stepping aside.

Murphy blamed TV. Fiction was influencing everyone these days.

Once inside Stanley's room, the noise from outside was silenced quickly, the only sounds coming through the slightly open window from the traffic outside. Rossi excused the DC who had been stuck to George Stanley's side throughout his stay at hospital. Murphy wondered if he'd even been in the theatre with him.

'Mr Stanley,' Murphy said, allowing Rossi to

take the visitor's chair, standing at the foot of the bed instead. 'I'm going to repeat the caution which was said to you when you were found. Just in case you were unaware at the time.'

George Stanley gave him a dismissive wave, seeming to squint through him. Murphy repeated it anyway, never stumbling over the words which were now second nature to him.

'I want you to start at the beginning if you can.'

George Stanley winced as he tried to sit up a little more. Gave up trying after a few attempts. 'Have you found them yet?'

Murphy shared a look with Rossi. 'Let's just start at the beginning.'

'Fine,' Stanley replied. 'I was approached at the pub.'

'Which pub?' Murphy said, his own underused notepad in his hand.

'The George and Dragon in West Derby.'

Murphy nodded. He knew the place and made a note of it. 'Go on.'

'So, this old guy starts talking to me one night. I'd seen him there a lot. Used to give him a nod when I'd go in after work and that. It wasn't long before we were talking every night. The pub's quiet these days, with the smoking ban. So you get to know the same faces quite well. Anyway, soon we became a little group.'

'Who did? Who else was in the group?' Rossi said, laying a hand on the bed as she leant forward.

'Six of us, in the beginning. I don't know all their last names. There was Andrew. Then Bob and Joanne. Married couple. Don't think he worked any more but he used to be a brickie. She was working in the local supermarket.'

'That's three. Four including you. The old man makes five . . . who's the sixth?'

Stanley's pale face clouded over, to somehow become even more grey than it already was. 'Alan. Not that he ever really introduced himself. Joanne knew his real name though 'cause she saw him in the *Echo* one time.'

'Right . . . '

'He's the one who's done this,' Stanley said, using his good arm to point to his injured shoulder. 'I think he killed them all . . . '

Tears sprung up in Stanley's eyes, Murphy watching as he tried to blink them away.

'Okay. So how did it get to that point?'

'We just thought we were doing some good, you know? No one else was doing anything. The old man and Alpha had us all convinced. We'd have a few drinks and put the world to rights. About kids these days and that. Anyway, one day . . . I thought they were joking at first. But the auld fella says, we could do something real. Teach these kids a lesson.'

Murphy shook his head and made a note of Stanley's words. 'And that means more to you than most, doesn't it George?'

Stanley eyed him again, clockwork whirring behind his gaze. Murphy could almost see the pieces falling into place. 'It's you.'

It wasn't a question, it was a statement, and Murphy nodded in reply. 'Ten years ago now, isn't it?'

'Glad to see you've done well for yourself,' Stanley said, looking past Murphy now and staring at the wall. 'You had a bit of . . . what's the word . . . compassion about you. The rest of you lot we spoke to back then couldn't give two shits.'

'What happened?' Murphy said, wanting to move on.

'I was broken. I needed something, a purpose. You don't know how I was feeling. Those little bastards that killed my boy got out years ago. And now the streets are crawling with hundreds, thousands, just like them.'

'You wanted to make a difference,' Rossi said, soothing voice in play.

'Exactly,' Stanley said, his speech gaining a little strength. 'But we didn't know what to do really. That's when the old man told us of his plan. He said one night, 'I've got the tools, but I just can't do it now I'm old.' We'd all had a drink, and it seemed like a great plan.'

'What was the plan?' Rossi said.

'Alpha . . . Alan, I should say. He had this farm. Only it wasn't even a farm any more. He'd no animals any more, just the land. A few outbuildings and a little farmhouse.'

Stanley's voice grew quieter.

'The auld fella told us it'd be easy. Pick a few of these little bastards up off the street. Give them a bit of National Service, old-school style. Teach them some respect. I never expected it to go this far.'

Murphy stood up tall, blowing out a breath. 'Where's the farm, George?'

271

'I . . . I'm not sure . . . '

'Don't come over all coy now, George,' Murphy said. 'It's over. Now you have to help us. You're only guessing at what's happened. You don't know for sure. Don't have any more blood on your hands.'

Stanley let his head drop, exhaled deeply. 'It's out of the way. Near Netherley. I'm not sure what the name of the roads are or anything, but it's off Netherley Road. I know that.'

Rossi leant forward. 'Think you could draw us a map?'

Stanley closed his eyes. His hands shaking a little. 'I'm . . . I'm left-handed.'

Murphy stared at the bandage on his bloodied left shoulder.

'We'll get a map. I'm sure you can point with your other hand.'

Home

When they talked about what he was going to do over the next few days, they would use words like *manic, crazed, out of control*.

It was none of those things.

It was a specific plan. Put into place long before, without him even realising. He knew on some level it would come to this. It was a path he'd been travelling on for years. Each passing month, day, minute leading to the moment when he awoke from the daze he'd been living in. Woke and grasped what had been beyond his comprehension before then.

He had to do this.

Time was the only worry now. He had rushed from room to room when he'd first arrived. Sprinted up the driveway, almost breaking the key in the lock as he tried to open it quickly. He had to force himself to become calmer.

They would be looking for him. Sooner rather than later. He had no time, but he had to stay in control.

They would have Delta before too long.

That moment back at the farm, when time had slowed; those people he'd shared space and his life with were already fading. His conscience was clear. It was simple when he dwelt on any thoughts of it. Made perfect sense.

It was *his* job. Always had been. No one else was prepared to do it. Others had tried

— *snapped*, they called it — but never on the scale he was going to achieve.

Anger was there, of course. But there was no room for it. He'd been beaten down for so many years that anger, hurt, pain — it was all second nature. Things he'd acquired rather than been born with. He could hide it well, keep it safely locked away inside him. Methodical. Logical. That was his first nature. That was what he had been born with.

He planned. He checked maps. Made notes. Over the course of one day, he referred to old scraps of paper he'd kept over the previous months.

Group of boys — around five or six — maybe fourteen/ fifteen in age — one on a bike — Breckfield/Everton

Three boys, two girls — older than fifteen — Admiral St/ Toxteth

They were infecting the city. His city. Had been for so long now. And they'd just let them do it. Intimidation and violence. They didn't care about anyone, just themselves. Parasites who just scrounged around, making everyone else's life worse. Normal, hardworking people shouldn't have to deal with those types of no-hopers.

Well. No more. He was going to fix it.

He was sad about what had happened at the farm. Of course he was. He'd liked them, the others. He was glad in a way that not all of them had died. He was sure by now that Delta would have found his way to the police.

What could he tell them, really? That an old man in a pub had brought them together, given

274

them the tools to do what he thought would work, provided the place and the means, and then died. That they'd taken it too far, in some people's opinion. That they would never know if it would have worked eventually.

It didn't matter. It didn't matter even that Delta knew his name was Alan Bimpson.

He didn't plan on coming back from this.

What was there to come back to anyway? A lie of a life. No. He'd done enough before then, and he would do even better after this moment.

Over the next few days he would ensure his name and life was spoken about for decades to come.

Alan Bimpson stood up from the armchair in his living room, crossing the small space to the wooden coffee table in the middle of the room. All laid out on top, everything he would need.

He wasn't feeling nervous. He thought he would have been.

Alan Bimpson had used guns for so long, they felt natural in his hands. There were so many people like that, even in a country which seemed to openly shun firearms. Trained operators in weapons that would turn even the hardest guy out in town on a Saturday night to a piece of quivering dogshit on the floor.

Soldiers. Cops. Farmers. Hunters.

Enthusiasts.

Alan Bimpson hated the last group most of all.

He knew the power of these things. The assault rifle that took up most of the space on the coffee table. It had cut through three people with barely a breath being taken at the farm, so he knew its power. The handguns to either side. Close range, bullet in the head or neck or chest or stomach . . . it didn't matter. If it wasn't instant, blood loss would get you eventually.

He had knives, but hoped it wouldn't have to come to that. So messy.

Alan Bimpson had the experience. The know-how. He had the means and plans.

He had the targets in mind. He didn't know their names, but he knew enough. He didn't need to know a family history. They were all the same. He'd heard the '*mother*' of the boy from the previous week which had kicked this process into action quicker than he'd anticipated. He'd heard her all right. Simpering and crying about her lost child.

He knew the truth. He knew she barely cared about her children. Only about what they could mean for her monetary-wise.

All the same. They were all the same.

Scroungers.

Making everyone else's life a misery. Bringing up her horrible little bastard children to have no fucking respect. Only out for themselves, for what they could get.

He'd already forgotten her name.

There was no society any more. No neighbourhood. Just people either making the streets unclean with their presence, or too scared to leave the cocoon of their houses, safe in the glow of the box in the corner.

And not even homes were safe any more. Noisy neighbours, nasty neighbours, nosy neighbours.

Bastards, bastards, bastards.

He had the will.

When they talked about him in years, decades, centuries to come, they would never know what thoughts had run through his mind as he stood in his home that first evening, readying himself to leave. They could speculate, call it whatever they like, psychoanalyse it to death. A mental unhinging, a detachment from reality. A downward spiral into paranoia and despair.

It wasn't that at all. He knew what he was doing. He was conscious of his decision. It was the most unselfish act he'd ever commit in his life.

He took the last thing he needed. The gold chain, draped over a carriage clock on the mantelpiece. The cross on the end of it, glistening in the low sun.

It was time to clean up the streets.

22

They were in the supposedly nice part of the city. To look at, anyway. The police thought very differently.

The area of Netherley used to be predominantly farmland, green belt, countryside. Then they started building in the sixties; homes, flats, maisonettes . . . all for people to move there from other run-down parts of the city. The green faded and became grey and brown. Vermin-infested and crime-ridden. The flats were the worst. Built and pulled down in fifteen or twenty years.

They looked like a prison. Felt like one, Murphy guessed.

The eighties came and the flats were demolished, but the people were left behind.

Murphy stared out the window as they passed a group of young lads, openly drinking from cans of lager as the procession of police cars and vans lit them up with their headlights as they passed them by.

Both crime and youth unemployment were high in the area.

Things were better, Murphy had been told. Like everywhere in the city, crime rates had fallen. Meant very little for those who were still there, still stuck in the same position.

Out of the estates, it was different. When you hit the outskirts, the views changed, became beautiful. Murphy had driven around there often. Pulled up at the side of roads to look at horses in the open fields. The farms which survived pulling in a few passing motorists on their way out of the city, in the direction of Widnes.

The atmosphere in the car was thick with tension. They had only one man's word to go on, but everyone was expecting the worst. The firearms officers would be going in first, but that didn't stop the three DCs in the back considering the different possible scenarios which could occur. Murphy was having no trouble in tuning them out, but he could tell Rossi was struggling.

The amount of quiet swearing in Italian under her breath told him that.

'They're slowing up ahead.'

Murphy sat up straighter in the passenger seat, peering into the dull light to see if the lead van had turned off yet. They were going on sketchy instructions from the hospitalised George Stanley, but a few of the officers seemed to know where he meant. There were a few farms around the area, but the directions given seemed to pinpoint the place as what one uniform had termed 'The Old Manor'. Which didn't strike Murphy as a normal farm name.

'They're turning off,' Murphy said. The three blokes in the back of the car had gone quiet now.

'Almost there.'

Streetlights disappeared, bringing the lateness of the evening into starker relief.

They were going in blind.

Five minutes of winding around old, bumpy farm roads, travelling at no more than twenty mph, and the red brake lights signalled them to stop.

'We're here,' Murphy's radio crackled into life. 'Stay put until further notice.'

Murphy listened in as the firearms officers approached an unseen building, clearing the outside, then gaining entry. He thought he could see torchlight bouncing around up ahead as he peered through the windscreen. The car had become deathly quiet as everyone held their breath collectively, waiting. Waiting for it all to go wrong.

Murphy knew they'd be too late.

If George Stanley was right, if what he was saying was true, the man would be gone by now.

'All clear in main house. Three bodies, deceased on arrival.'

A quiet profanity came from the back of the car.

'Now moving onto outbuildings.'

Murphy waited, Rossi tapping out a beat on the steering wheel. He had the urge to tell her to stop, but controlled himself.

'Three buildings. One empty.'

Murphy had done firearms training. Many years previously. Hadn't enjoyed it at all. Didn't like the power of the weapons.

'Second building, one body. Deceased on arrival.'

Four. This would keep them occupied.

A few minutes later the final message came over the radio.

280

'Third building clear. Three bodies. Deceased on arrival.'

Seven bodies.

★ ★ ★

Murphy could hear them outside, the other uniforms, officers, detectives. Talking amongst themselves, some quietly, some louder than that. The level of swearing and taking of the Lord's name in vain would have made Frankie Boyle blush. Murphy stood with Rossi, surveying the scene in the kitchen of what they'd found to be the main farmhouse. They looked at it from a distance, suited-up in white forensic boilersuits in order to preserve any evidence.

He wasn't sure it was entirely needed.

'According to our Mr Stanley, one man is responsible for all this,' Rossi said, speaking for the first time without being prompted since they'd arrived there.

'Hard to imagine . . . '

'Not really,' a voice said, from behind a mask. Murphy turned to see the portly frame of a packaged-up Dr Houghton. 'You just have to see it.'

'What's your verdict?' Murphy said, moving back as a forensic officer bustled past him.

'These weren't the first to go,' Houghton replied, waving a hand across the three bodies who had fallen to the ground near each other.

Murphy gazed at each in turn, kneeling to get a closer look. The first, a white male who looked to be at least mid-forties from the greying hair, which was now matted with dark blood. His black T-shirt was torn almost in half, a dark hole in the middle of his chest, peppered by pellet marks. Flesh ripped apart. The second was a woman, the shirt she'd been wearing almost completely shredded. Her stomach was one open wound, a mass of red and pink as her insides tried to escape. Murphy swallowed back some bile before forcing himself to look at the third body.

'Looks like they were trying to leave when your man opened fire,' Houghton said from behind Murphy. 'Close-range gunshot wounds in a variety of places in their upper bodies and heads. Easy cause of death.'

'Except for him,' Murphy said, pointing to the third body of a man near the back door.

Houghton raised his eyebrows at the body. 'A shotgun or assault rifle can do a lot of damage.'

Murphy nodded, forcing himself to look at the body again. The face was empty of features, just a hole where they should be. Brain matter was strewn out behind his head, blood and gore filling out the rest of it.

'Have you been out to the other building yet?' Rossi said, her voice quiet in the small kitchen.

Houghton sighed, lifting his mask off his face. 'Yes. Three bodies, all died in the same manner. Gunshot wounds to the temple. Clean through.' They followed him outside, where he pointed a finger towards neat piles of brain matter which nestled on the floor near each body. Blood trails stretched across the concrete path which led towards the outbuilding. 'They'd been kept

282

inside, by the looks of things. Locks on the outside. They were shot just outside the building and then dragged back in. It was a massacre.'

Murphy had seen it already. Three young boys. Teenagers. None older than seventeen or eighteen. Their bodies a mess, the pain they'd experienced in death etched across their faces.

'It's small fry compared to what we found in the last building,' Houghton continued. 'One body. Tortured, by the looks of it. Won't know cause of death yet.'

Murphy rubbed a gloved hand over his face. Tiredness was battling against everyone there as the lateness of the night struck. They'd been at the farm for hours now, a quick glance at his watch telling Murphy it was closer to dawn than it was midnight.

'Any identifications?'

Houghton stifled a laugh. 'Nothing at all, David. Forensics will be able to tell you more on that. They're going through the rest of the house.'

'Okay, thanks Doctor.'

'This guy,' Houghton said, coming closer to Murphy and Rossi, 'this guy is manic, frenzied. I've not seen anything like this before. Seven dead, and six of them within a short space of time. He just took them out, one by one. Grouped together. It's . . . startling.'

'One got away. So we know he makes mistakes,' Rossi said, pulling herself up to full height, her soft accent becoming hardened.

'I hope you're right. Before we see any more of this,' Houghton replied, moving away as he spoke.

283

'Alan Bimpson,' Murphy said, turning to Rossi. 'We need to know everything we can on him now. He's our main suspect.'

Rossi nodded. 'I've got a bit, but not much. Possible addresses . . . '

'Let's get a team together. Put the doors through in the next hour.'

'Okay.'

Murphy rubbed his eyes, a stinging sensation hitting them. They say adrenaline gets you through the late nights as a copper, but they were human like everyone else. He needed sleep. Couldn't see it happening any time soon.

'Let's have a look at the third scene,' Murphy said finally.

Prepared himself.

The third building was no bigger than a large shed really. A single high-beam light had been set up outside, illuminating the thick wooden door which was being held open by a brick, placed there by a forensic officer, Murphy assumed. Inside, strip lighting lit up the small space, running down the middle of the room. Metal shelving ran down one side, empty crates scattered down the opposite side. The room was sparsely furnished, apart from the one object which took up most of the space.

'It's a rack,' Rossi's voice said from behind him.

Murphy nodded. He'd seen one before, but never in the flesh. True-crime books of serial killers had glorified the item for him. Various contraptions, built usually by hand, to inflict twisted desires.

Murphy exchanged a greeting with the last remaining forensic tech officer who was left with the body inside the room, clicking off the last few pictures. Then the body would lie there until another van arrived to take him to the mortuary.

To take his place alongside the seven other victims.

'I don't think it's too difficult to see what's happened to him,' Murphy said, walking around the body. The air grew thicker inside, as the smell hit, the body decomposing in the warmth of the small building. Rotting, biting at the back of his throat. Murphy tried not to swallow.

'He looks older than the other three.'

'Maybe. Perhaps he's just big for his age. No real stubble on his face.'

Murphy cast his eyes down the bare chest. Welts the size of fifty-pence pieces scattered across his chest like fallen leaves. Burns.

A soldering iron was lying on the floor near the rack.

Angry red marks fading to brown wrapped around his neck. Wounds which had bled but stopped short of gushing blood, no pooling around the body. Slash marks rather than punctures.

'This is wet . . . ' Murphy said, touching the surface of the rack.

'That'll be down to this,' Rossi replied, pointing towards a half-empty bowl. 'He drowned him.'

Murphy shook his head. 'I think they call it water-boarding.'

'Jesus . . . '

His trousers, blue jeans with no belt, had been

left untouched. Dirty brown stains on the knees. He had been left in the restraints.

'He shoots everyone else . . . why the difference here?' Rossi said, lifting various items off the metal shelves and placing them back down soundlessly.

'Personal grudge? Fun? I don't know.'

The forensic officer began packing away his camera, left the room without a further word. Murphy moved to the top of the body, leaning over the head to stare at the scarred shaved dome.

'Some of these aren't even fully healed. He's been here a while, I'd guess,' Murphy said, fighting against the urge to move the head to a straight position.

'Well, Dean Hughes was here almost seven months.'

'Right.'

Outside there was a burst of laughter, quickly muted by low words.

'This won't be the last,' Murphy said, standing up straight and hearing a crack in his back as he did so. 'Whoever did this has unravelled.'

'Or this was always his plan . . . '

Rossi hummed under her breath.

A shadow fell across the body lying prone on the rack. Murphy turned to see DS Brannon standing in the doorway.

'Jesus . . . '

Murphy looked back at the victim once more before walking towards DS Brannon. 'Warrant in yet?'

DS Brannon continued to look past Murphy

towards the rack. Wide-eyed, turning pale in the dim light. Then the smell hit him, making him shoot his hand to his mouth. Retching sounds followed, before Brannon started to shake and pull himself together.

'Brannon? You with me?'

'Yeah,' DS Brannon said, switching his gaze towards Murphy, shaking his head. 'Sorry . . . erm, it should be here soon.'

'Good. The boss here yet?'

DS Brannon nodded, struggling to keep from looking over Murphy's shoulder again.

Murphy shoved his way past him, walking back towards the main house. He didn't stop to see if Rossi was following him. He wanted to speak to DCI Stephens alone. Murphy knew what was going to happen next and didn't want to lose time.

He found her in what they'd decided was a living room, but was so sparsely decorated it could barely be described as such. A few wooden chairs and an open fireplace, unstocked with wood or any other kind of fuel. A few newspapers on the floor underneath the boarded-up window which faced out onto the driveway. Old and already yellowing. DCI Stephens was listening to a breathless DC Harris as he spoke ten to the dozen, bringing her up to date with what they'd discovered so far.

Murphy cleared his throat, causing DC Harris to excuse himself. Murphy and DCI Stephens stood opposite each other for a few seconds, just sharing a look between themselves. The quietness blanketed over them.

'What the hell . . . '

'I know,' Murphy said, lifting a hand. 'It's not what we were expecting.'

'You can say that again . . . '

'We think we have a name for the guy who did it. Alan Bimpson.'

'So your DC Harris says. Warrant is in. You can put his door through as soon as possible.'

'Good.'

'I've spoken to the Super. I think you know this calls for a major op. We'll be getting all the resources we need. A statement will be made to the press shortly, not that many of them will be awake for it.'

'Twenty-four-hour news these days . . . '

DCI Stephens waved a hand at him before sliding it through her shoulder-length hair. Tension was battling with tiredness in her face. Murphy expected the same look was being mirrored back at her.

'I don't think I've ever had one with this many before.'

'Closest I've come is a house fire. That was four . . . but it wasn't like this. This is something else. I've got officers out there who are not handling it.'

DCI Stephens nodded. 'Then you need to get a handle on them, David. I won't have anyone going off with depression or anything like that. I'll be heading the operation but you're still the one in charge. I'll just be liaising with you a lot more. Any media goes through me. I want you to make sure that lot out there don't leak a thing to the press.'

'I can try . . . '

'You'll do more than try. I want this locked tight. Nothing gets out until we have Bimpson locked up. I don't want panic spreading. Organise a team. Whoever and however many you need, you've got it.'

Murphy blew out a breath. 'No problem.'

DCI Stephens started to leave, before Columbo-ing back. 'One more thing. Not everyone can function without sleep. Make sure you put them in shifts. Same goes for you.'

Murphy kept his mouth tightly sealed, breathing deeply through his nostrils.

Whatever his boss said, he wasn't going home.

23

People were already getting snappy with each other. Most of those who had been at the farm the previous night were still working away in the incident room. The sun was beaming through the windows; it was the warmest day of the year so far, bringing with it complaints about heat and comfort.

Murphy and Rossi were taking turns to get cold drinks from the vending machine. Too busy for arguments.

The operation had now taken over the main space, leaving Murphy without the comparative silence of his own small, shared office space as he and Rossi were forced to join the team out on the main floor. The dawn raids on the two properties in the name of Alan Bimpson had come to nothing. Items taken away to be processed, dozens of witness statements taken from neighbours and a lot of crime scene tape strung around the homes.

Excitement had quickly turned to worry as the first word had leaked out in the press. Every major media outlet was descending on Liverpool like locusts. A big story was brewing. Had already occurred. Seven bodies in one place.

It would be rolling news for a few hours at least.

'Maybe we'll get that stupid bint from *Sky News* doing those interviews on the street.'

'Who's that?' Murphy said, turning to Rossi.

'You know the one. Dark-haired, tight-faced. Always asking ridiculous questions and being dead insensitive.'

'I don't watch it,' Murphy said, turning back to the murder board.

'*Mannaggia* . . . Why did you ask who I meant then? It wouldn't matter if I gave you her name, you wouldn't know her anyway.'

Murphy rubbed a hand over his face, scratching at a stray hair in his beard. Probably a grey one, he thought. He'd seen them creeping in more often. 'I don't know. Just leave it.'

'Fine. What's next then?'

Murphy sighed, thinking of his side of the bed at home. It hadn't been slept on much the previous few nights.

'We've got two cars registered to him from the DVLA. We'll have a picture of him soon, hopefully, from what we've got from the house. We need to speak to George Stanley again.'

'At least we know where he is . . . '

'Yes. We do. And . . . ' Murphy was interrupted by a fast-approaching DS Brannon barrelling across towards them.

'Shit. Shit. Shit,' DS Brannon said as a greeting. 'We may have a problem.'

Murphy shook his head, his brain seeming to rattle in his skull. 'Go on . . . '

'Kevin Thornhill has been reported missing by his wife.'

Murphy frowned. 'The youth club guy?'

'Yes, the youth club guy,' DS Brannon almost sneered back. 'I rang one of the volunteers, who

291

says she turned up for work but couldn't get in. Kevin usually opens up at nine . . . '

Murphy didn't wait for him to finish his sentence. 'We can't really be dealing with that kind of thing right now, Brannon. If you haven't noticed, we've got six people on the board.'

'You don't think it could be linked?' DS Brannon said, looking towards Rossi as if for support.

Rossi looked away.

'Look, if you want to have a quick run down to the youth club, be my guest. But at the moment, we're concentrating on what we have here.'

DS Brannon looked as if he was about to argue, before thinking better of it and leaving without another word. Murphy stared after him, his eyes blurring as they gazed for too long.

'It's a bit of a coincidence, don't you think?' Rossi said, snapping Murphy's attention back.

'And probably nothing more,' Murphy replied, turning back towards the board. 'We can't be wasting time on stuff like that.'

'Still . . . '

'Enough,' Murphy snapped, causing a few heads at the surrounding desks to lift up in interest. 'Concentrate on what we have here. It's plenty to go on.'

'Okay, okay. I was just saying . . . '

'I know,' Murphy said, cutting her off with a raise of his palm. 'We're all knackered, but let's not start on each other. Now, where were we?'

Rossi looked at him for a second before speaking. 'George Stanley.'

'Ah. Yeah. We need to speak to him again.'

'Maybe you should . . . *we* should, take a break first. Get a couple of hours' kip or something?'

Murphy sighed, then looked towards DCI Stephens's office. He could see her through the open blinds, talking on the phone. No doubt she was speaking to the Superintendent, trying to placate him.

'You go first. We'll take turns. Get back here between twelve and one though. I'll take the afternoon shift.' Rossi didn't wait for him to change his mind, just turned on her heels, grabbed her coat and left.

He watched her leave. Jealous that she was about to get a few hours' kip.

★　★　★

Murphy snapped to attention as the buzzer sounded. He pushed open the door to the ward at the hospital, the doors locked to keep out stragglers, but also coming in handy as an extra deterrent now that George Stanley's story had turned out to be true.

Outside Stanley's private recovery room sat two bored-looking constables in uniform. They gave him a nod as he arrived.

Murphy's weathered and bearded face was all the ID he needed these days.

He entered the room to find DC Harris playing cards with George Stanley, who was sitting up in his bed, holding cards in one hand, having to place them down to pick up another one from the deck.

Harris stood as Murphy entered, but Stanley barely looked up at him as he crossed the small space.

'Just passing the time, sir,' Harris said, guilt fleeting across his face. Murphy shook his head to let him know he hadn't been doing anything wrong.

'Bet it's getting boring being in here, isn't it, Mr Stanley?' Murphy said, taking Harris's seat and letting the DC lean against the windowsill.

'Yep,' Stanley replied, still staring at the cards in his hand. The plastic bag on the drip running into a cannula on his hand was almost empty, the tape holding the tube in place turning up at the edges. 'How long do you reckon I'll be in here?'

Murphy shared a look with Harris. 'I thought you might want to stay in here a bit longer. Given where we'll be taking you when you're recovered.'

Stanley stopped splaying his cards and dropped them to the bed. His face fell, his chest hitching up a little. 'Oh, right. Yeah,' Stanley said finally, voice catching in his throat. 'How long do you reckon I'm looking at?'

Murphy blew out a whistle. 'Could be a long time. Kidnapping, abduction, false imprisonment, assault, torture . . . that's before we even get to the murder part.'

'I didn't have anything to do with that . . . '

'Dean Hughes was murdered whilst you watched, George. Do you understand that? And then there's the others. You were a part of the whole thing.'

Tears sprang up in George Stanley's eyes. 'It wasn't supposed to happen . . . '

'Yeah, well it did,' Murphy replied, standing up from the seat. 'And now you'll have to face up to that. Before we get there though, you can start making amends.'

Stanley nodded slowly, rubbing his eyes free of tears with his good hand. 'How?'

'We need to find him.'

George Stanley began shaking his head, before Murphy cut in.

'I don't want to hear anything about you not knowing where he is or any of that bollocks.'

'Okay,' Stanley replied in a quiet voice. 'What . . . where do I start?'

'At the beginning. The first meeting you had with him. Who was there?'

'I saw him a couple of times, with the old guy in the pub. He was just there, you know? One day. He spoke to the auld fella like he'd known him for a while. Soon, there were five of us. It was obvious really who was leading the whole thing, but we were just excited at first.'

'Who was leading it?'

George Stanley breathed out, long and loud. 'Alan Bimpson. We just went along with what he was saying.'

Murphy leant on the bed stand, not taking his eyes off George Stanley. 'Tell me about the first.'

'The auld fella was having problems with some teenagers hanging around his house. He'd come into the pub shaking most evenings. They were terrorising him. He'd been to your lot loads of times, but nothing had been done. At first I

295

thought we were just going to knock a few heads together, but they wanted more.'

'Who did?'

'Alan and the auld fella.'

'What was the auld fella's name?' DC Harris said, the sudden interruption causing Murphy's head to snap towards him.

'I don't know. People used to call him Major, like that guy from *Fawlty Towers*. Remember that show?'

Murphy ignored the question. 'So, the *Major* comes in telling his tale of woe. Some kids are messing up his garden or whatever . . . '

'They were doing worse than that.'

'Never mind,' Murphy replied, dismissing Stanley. 'You think you're all going to beat up some kids . . . '

'They were hardly kids . . . '

'And instead you, what?' Murphy said, ignoring George Stanley's interruption. 'You kidnap them and lock them up at a farm?'

'Well . . . they already had one there.'

Murphy shook his head. 'What are you talking about?'

'We found out later that Bimpson and the auld fella had picked one up already. Some lad who they caught trying to break into a house or something. He was the boy we put outside the church. Dean Hughes. We came in for the big lad.'

Murphy thought about the victim tied to the rack. 'Black guy? About six two?'

'That's the one.'

Murphy nodded. 'So, he could take Dean

Hughes alone, but needed help with the bigger lad. Sound about right?'

George Stanley nodded.

'What happened next?'

'It . . . we took a few more,' Stanley said, his chin tucked into his chest. 'I watched, mostly. We had cameras set up and that.'

'Yeah, we found those.'

'Just to see what effect we were having, nothing more than that. There was no paedo stuff going on or anything.'

'Well done you,' Murphy replied, holding back a round of mock applause. 'What was the plan? Beat the shit out of them, until what . . . they gave in and became choirboys?'

'Something like that.'

'Did it work?'

Stanley lifted his head. 'We thought it had, but Bimpson made fools of us. One of the first ones they brought in, he was a changed guy. Respectful, disciplined, willing. We were going to let him go.'

Murphy laughed once. 'I don't believe this . . . '

'It's true,' Stanley replied, his voice raised. 'They never saw our faces, barely heard our voices. It was done like clockwork. Bimpson was supposed to take him home. We'd keep an eye on him of course, but that was the plan.'

'What happened?'

'He never made it. Bimpson killed him. We found that out the other night.'

Murphy was struggling to keep up with the story. Tiredness and incredulity scrambling his synapses of understanding. 'Right . . . and your story is he killed Dean Hughes?'

'Well . . . we were all there, but it was him who took it too far. The lad wouldn't listen. He'd never listened. No matter what we did, he was still the same disrespectful little bastard he had been since we picked him up. He was only quiet when he was in the Dorm. When we tried to teach him, he turned. Bimpson just lost it. But we were all involved.'

'What happened to the auld fella . . . the Major?' DC Harris said, again surprising Murphy with his question.

'Bimpson told us he died of a heart attack. Wasn't exactly shocking, as he was getting on a bit. We never saw him after we took the first lad. He was always ill.'

'So Alan Bimpson was closest to the old man then?' Murphy said, sharing a look with DC Harris.

'Oh, definitely. He'd talk about him all the time.'

'And he never mentioned an actual name?'

George Stanley shook his head. 'It never came up.'

Murphy waited a beat. Tears had dripped down George Stanley's face as he talked, but his voice had remained calm.

'You're not sorry. Are you?'

Stanley looked up and caught his stare. 'Of course I am . . . '

Murphy laughed, once, loud. 'You enjoyed giving them something back. Getting revenge for your boy.'

298

Stanley's hands were shaking, small movements which Murphy would have missed if he wasn't watching him so closely.

'They did terrible things to people,' Stanley said after a few seconds' silence. 'It was time they got a taste.'

'You understand it's gone too far?'

Stanley nodded. 'No one deserves to bury their child. I know that better than anyone. This'll help though, right? They'll know I helped.'

Murphy stood up straight, the now-familiar crack in his back accompanying the movement. 'I need to find him. We need to know where he is.'

Stanley looked towards the ceiling. 'I don't know what to tell you. I don't know where he lives, or where he might be. I thought he was chasing me, that's why I hid in the woods. He's not all there now.'

'You're telling me . . . '

'He changed. He was going downhill for weeks. More violent with them, less willing to listen to reason.'

Murphy moved closer to the head of the hospital bed, leaning on the safety railing so he was only inches from George Stanley's face. 'Tell me.'

The tears were flowing more freely now. George Stanley's shoulders shuddered in time with each drop.

'I don't think he's finished.'

The Youth Club

The youth club was quiet, the evening session long over and a new day on its way. The only sounds he'd heard as he entered the building were birds beginning their morning calls.

He shouldn't even be there. There'd been a phone call at his house from his *primary investor*, as he liked to call himself, telling Kevin he had to urgently speak to him. Four o' damn clock in the morning.

Kevin Thornhill was sitting in his office, sweating in the crowded space, beads of perspiration emanating from somewhere on his forehead and then roving down his face, gravity doing its job.

But it wasn't warm in there. It was cool enough that he needed a jacket. He would have put one on — if it wasn't for the six foot two, stocky-shouldered, crew-cut, scarred-face man pointing a rather large shotgun at his chest.

There was fear. Of course. Kevin could feel it trickling down his trouser leg. But there was also something else. A knowing. There were facts he could understand, even as bile rushed up his throat, threatening to escape. And with that knowing came the knowledge that this was it. This wasn't something he could talk his way out of. There'd be no going home, going back to normal. Not for him.

When they say that time stretches out for you

when you're in a life or death situation, they're lying. Kevin Thornhill could feel every minute, every second, passing him by. Passing by with his inaction, his ineffectiveness. His body's refusal to talk, to negotiate. The silence grew around him, cocooning him, restricting him. His breath grew short, shallow, in and out, in and out. Hitching finally, as his body began to react in different ways.

They talk about a fight or flight reflex. Kevin Thornhill wasn't responding to either.

They were right about being frozen.

Frozen, scared shitless.

His brain still ticked over. Thoughts banging into each other in there. Bumping and banging and running into each other in there. Inside, where it didn't count. It was adrenaline, something told him that. A word coming out of the ether in block capitals. Adrenaline. Then it was his son and daughter. Pictures, not words. They were much younger than the twenty-somethings they were now. It was them at five and seven. Ten and eight. Newborns.

They talk about your life flashing before your eyes. They were wrong. He couldn't think straight enough to put things in order of his life history.

He thought of his wife long after the word adrenaline. Then felt a pang of guilt that she wasn't one of the first thoughts he'd had.

He wasn't saying anything. The man with the gun. Pointed at his chest. He was mute. Just staring, staring, staring . . . almost right through him.

The knowledge of what was to come That's where it came from. The staring eyes. The calmness, the ease with which he faced him down.

The difference in him, the man he thought he knew.

Another word . . . acquaintance.

Benefactor.

Family.

Kevin tried not to think of what they'd called him after his first talk with the kids.

Nutter.

He almost winced at the word.

Maybe they should have taken that jokey nickname a little more seriously.

Still he stared. And Kevin Thornhill couldn't help but stare back. Lost in the man's gaze as his brain ticked ever on. Words, pictures.

Why couldn't he talk?

At least babble a little?

Beg for his life, for the sake of his family? If he loved them he would, surely? Why couldn't he make himself talk?

Fear, fear, fear. He's afraid. He knows, he knows, he knows.

He was going to die.

Finally, the man Kevin Thornhill knew as someone other than Alan Bimpson spoke.

'You told them about me.'

Not a question. Kevin Thornhill's brain — seemingly the only working part of him now, other than his bladder — told him that. No inflection at the end of the sentence, no question mark.

'It doesn't matter anyway. It just means less time for me to do my work.'

Kevin Thornhill opened his mouth. He didn't remember sending the signal for that to happen, but it was there. He tried to speak, but instead his mouth just gaped and closed.

'No need for you to say anything, Kevin. I know everything you want to say.'

His voice was so calm. They could have been discussing something dull or routine. If Kevin Thornhill had had even a semblance of hope at that moment, he might have believed everything could still be okay.

'You've been trying to help these kids. I know that. But you know the reality of the situation.'

The man Kevin Thornhill knew as someone-fucking-better-than-this-*Alan Bimpson* . . . took a short step forward, his hardened, unshaven face coming even closer.

'You know the truth. You can't stop them. They'll never change. You know why? They don't want to. They're happiest making others unhappy. That's what they do for fun. They laugh at you, Kevin. They come here for the free stuff, the roof over their heads when it's pissing down outside. Then they leave here and go out on the streets and carry on doing what they always do.'

He wanted to shake his head. Say no. That it wasn't true. That they were doing good work there. Helping to give these kids a chance at a different life.

But Kevin Thornhill still couldn't speak.

'I decided you'd be the first only a couple of hours ago. Take away the ridiculous notion at the

303

source. Drive them out like rats, make my job easier. They won't understand, not really.'

A moment of silence.

'Of course . . . I say the first, but there have been others. All leading to this. My final act. I want you to understand, I'm not doing this because I want to. Not really. It's just that . . . they'll blame you. Think you had something to do with it all. I can't have that. Your kids deserve better than to be put through that kind of attention. This is just so they can have a better life. They can mourn you, but then get on with their lives. You'll never have to look them in the eye and wonder if they believe you. That you didn't know who I really was. What I really am.'

Kevin Thornhill swallowed. Another part of him finally coming to life. Acidic, sour, bitter, burning the back of his throat.

He so badly wanted to talk. To say anything. His brain had given him a million and one things to say, but they wouldn't come out.

They would think he tried. His family wouldn't believe that he just sat there, mute, frozen, unmoving. Afraid. He'd always presented himself as someone who could face down anything. He wasn't a fearful person. He'd lived through worse things, he'd always say. Lived in dodgy places, dealt with dodgy people. Scary people.

The gun. Those two words appeared in his mind.

That's all it was.

The last three words Kevin Thornhill heard came next.

'I'm sorry, kid.'

* * *

Alan Bimpson slumped down the wall once Kevin Thornhill stopped breathing. Became someone else for a brief moment. The ghost he'd left behind. Once the gargling and gasping had finished. When Kevin's heart finally gave up trying to pump blood around his body, succumbing to the trauma created by the shotgun wound to his chest.

He was crying. His cheeks wet with tears. Silent, not sobbing.

It wasn't supposed to be this way. They were going to make a difference, all together. And now he had been left alone.

It was a trial. Redemption. He had to make up for the wrongs that had been committed. Clean up the streets . . .

But he knew he didn't really believe in it. When Alan allowed himself to drift, to just allow his mind to clear and think logically, it didn't make sense. What he was doing, what he had done.

He was a killer.

He was worse than them.

It was too late. He was too far gone. His mind closed up again. Put those doubting thoughts in a box and left it in a corner. Hopefully never to be opened.

He was alone. In the quiet. Kevin Thornhill's decomposing body feet away from where he was slumped to the floor, holding a sawn-off shotgun he'd been given by an old man with a grudge.

Tired. So damn tired. The mix of emotions

305

driving him on autopilot. Exhilaration and despair.

He was gone.

Time. He had no time. Why had he come here? Killed the only person he had a slight trust in.

Back in the box.

The sun was beginning to peer through the windows in the corridor outside the office, the door moving almost imperceptibly in an unseen draught. He stared at the blur of the outside world through the windows from his position on the floor, willing it to go dark again.

He preferred the dark. In the light, his true nature was undeniable. And that was what scared him now.

Himself. What he was capable of. Cold-blooded murder.

They deserved it. That was the truth. Everything he'd done, everything he would do, they deserved it and more.

He closed his eyes, allowing the rising sunlight to bathe him anew.

Resolve. Resolution.

The end.

24

The sun was high in the sky but still shining through the windscreen as DS Tony Brannon drove over the speed limit. Weaving in and out of slow-moving traffic with the practised air of an experienced driver, he leant over to the glovebox and opened it to find his sunglasses.

Oakleys. They made him look good as he dangled one arm on the rim of the window, one palm on the steering wheel.

If he could get his weight down, he'd be a catch. He knew that.

Not that he ever had any problems getting women back to his apartment outside the city centre. It was near the university — and there were plenty of inexperienced students who were impressed by his tales of bravery and selflessness as a cop.

He could never get them to stay long after the first night though. He was undecided on whether that was a good thing or not.

There were also the naive girls at work. New ones all the time, coming in to do admin jobs or newly passed-out uniforms. They didn't know of his reputation, so he could use his greatest asset.

He could talk, he could make them laugh. Charm and confidence went a long way, even when three stone overweight with the eating habits of a small orang-utan.

Brannon overtook a slow-moving Fiat, giving

the wanker signal to the auld fella behind the wheel when he received a beep in the process. He was driving down Muirhead Avenue, the main road which bordered the Norris Green estate. He loved the houses down there, the large semi-detached dwellings, trees lining the road. Any other location, and it would be a nice area to live. Brannon knew better though. He knew the scum which lay behind the closed doors.

It was even worse once you turned off the road and entered the estate proper. Then it became more apparent, even from the roadside. Decrepit houses, decrepit people. Aimless single mothers and their horrible little offspring. Little Jayden or gorgeous Chantelle. Skanky names for skanky kids. All designed to end up making his life a misery as soon as they could start answering back.

He fucking hated the job sometimes. Having to deal with scallies almost exclusively, it seemed. And every day there seemed to be another one popping out.

Brannon hated driving alone. It led him to moments of frustration like this as he let his thoughts run away with themselves, imagining dealing with them the old-fashioned way. Couldn't do that any more. No more beatings in the back of a van to let the little bastards know who was in charge. Getting them back to the station and giving the drunken dickheads a hiding.

Political correctness gone mad.

Murphy was the worst type of this new breed of detective, Brannon thought. Too eager to please. Like a fucking modern Dixon of Dock Green. Wanting to know everyone's name, everyone's problem. Being the problem solver. Problem was, the knob had the memory of a goldfish with dementia sometimes, so could never do the job he wanted to do.

Big fella though, Brannon thought as he reached the end of Muirhead Avenue and turned right onto Dwerryhouse Lane. He tried to avoid antagonising him as much as possible.

Brannon knew he shouldn't be checking this out alone. He knew it was all connected. Something had happened to Kevin Thornhill and Murphy had dismissed it out of hand, just because it was Brannon who had brought it to him.

Well, he was going to make a mug out of him. Again. Murphy had got away with fucking up the previous year, but Brannon had just been waiting for his chance. Brannon knew Murphy wasn't the same guy he was before his parents got snuffed, but didn't give a shit.

He wanted DI. Soon. He'd earned it. He wanted the extra money and of course, the power that came with it. If Murphy had to be seen as a screw-up for it to happen, fuck him. Wouldn't be his fault, so it wasn't like Murphy could blame him.

Brannon pulled the car over outside the youth club and got out. The sounds of the playground drifted over the metal railings of the school on the other side of the road. He inwardly shuddered at the noise. He fucking hated kids. Especially the scallies that lived around there. He had no idea how Kevin Thornhill put up with them. Must do his head in.

The youth club was closed up and quiet. No answer when he knocked on the door and then banged on it for good measure. He was starting to think he was wrong, that something might have happened to Kevin, when he spotted something in the window. The reflection, to be more precise. Brannon turned around and walked towards the car which was parked a few yards away from his.

Kevin Thornhill's car.

Brannon banged on the door louder.

'Kev? It's Tony. Open up, mate.'

Nothing.

Brannon kicked at the bottom of the door and instantly regretted it. Solid, probably metal.

'Shit.'

His Asda shoes didn't exactly give him much protection.

Brannon limped around the side of the building to where Thornhill's office windows were situated. The blinds were shut on most of them, but he tried peering through each pane anyway. The sun shining behind him made it difficult to see anything beyond his own reflection.

'Kev? Are you in there?'

Now he thought about it, just because Kev's car was here, didn't mean he was. Kev had always had more luck than he had with women, so it was more likely he'd got some bit on the side up this way and slept in. Brannon almost laughed out loud at the thought of Kev waking up late and realising what had happened.

'Must have been quite the sess — '

The muttering under his breath stopped as he heard a noise coming from the front of the youth club. Brannon turned and began moving back there.

★　★　★

He'd heard the banging but hadn't been able to distinguish it from the vivid dream he'd been having. Alan Bimpson heard the voice but still didn't marry it to the outside world. Instead he tried to stay in the cocoon of the dream world. Malleable to his own wishes. He could have anything he liked in there, any situation he could possibly imagine.

His own subconscious was trying to mess with that, but it wasn't winning; the images of darkness and blood attempting to overpower his dreams being replaced by the good within him.

The banging stopped. The voice was closer than before.

His eyes snapped open. Blurred vision at first, along with an ache in his neck. The realisation of the small arsenal he'd been cuddling up to next to him. The shotgun lying to one side, a pool of blood zeroing in on its position.

In a matter of milliseconds it all came back to him.

More banging. On the windows in the corridor. Accompanied by a more insistent voice, then the sound of laughter.

He shouldn't be there. Not now. Not when he hadn't finished.

311

Alan Bimpson had made a mistake. He wasn't supposed to make mistakes, not this character — this man — he'd created.

He got to his feet and grabbed the gun from the floor. Gathered up his rucksack which he had lain on, the weapons inside the reason for the ache in his neck, and walked out of the office without looking at the body he'd left there.

Whoever was out there wouldn't stand in his way.

Alan reached the front entrance, sliding the bolts across in silence, and then the key he'd left in there the previous night.

He was sweating already. Heart pumping, hands shaking. A million thoughts running through his mind.

Bimpson opened the door, sunlight streaming through and into his face so he had to shield his eyes.

He span to his left, the shotgun held in both hands.

'Kev . . . wait, who are you? What's going . . . '

Bang.

25

Murphy was taking a breather and the chance to grab a coffee from a dodgy-looking vending machine in the hospital corridor. Eighty pence and it tasted like boiled shite.

Should have gone for the hot chocolate. More difficult to get that wrong.

Officers had spoken to the landlord of the George and Dragon pub where the group had first met, but he hadn't been able to give them an actual name for the 'Major' character. More detectives would be out to question the regulars when the pub started filling up somewhat during the evening, but Murphy wasn't holding his breath.

He walked over to where DC Harris had sat down in a small waiting area, just a few plastic chairs bolted to the ground near a desk with a bored receptionist behind it, rummaging through her handbag. The seats were empty other than the two detectives, silence permeating the corridor.

'Lunchtime,' Harris said, looking at his watch and gesturing towards the receptionist.

Murphy nodded and took another swig of his coffee, grimacing at the taste.

'Any closer to finding him?' Harris said, his hands clasped together between his knees as he leant forward opposite Murphy.

'Nope,' Murphy replied, placing the plastic cup of coffee on the ground. 'Where do you even start with something like this? Guy could be anywhere.'

'At least we have a picture.'

Murphy murmured his agreement. He'd confirmed with George Stanley that the Alan Bimpson who had been featured in the local paper and who had been visiting the youth club were one and the same person.

'I expect it'll be all over the media soon enough. We have a witness, so it's not like we have to worry too much about mistaken identity.'

'DCI taking over that?'

Murphy nodded, bending down to pick up his coffee before deciding against it. He needed a kip. Just a few hours would be nice.

'So, has he been talkative at all while you've been watching him?' Murphy said, interlocking his fingers behind his head and stretching.

'Not really. Just keeps saying he never meant for any of this to happen. Told him I couldn't really discuss it as he was still under caution. Then he slept for a bit. Guess he didn't get much the last few days.'

'Guilty conscience can do that to you.'

'You think he'll get charged with murder?'

Murphy thought on it for a few seconds. 'I imagine so. Probably just for Dean Hughes. He'll have a whole list of other charges on top of that though. He'll get life, even if they don't get the murder charge.'

'Doesn't make sense at all. Why would someone like him get involved in all this? He lost his kid and then takes someone else's, as what? Revenge?'

314

'Grief makes you think and do things differently. Especially when it's forced upon you. Having something — someone — taken from you screws with your brain.'

Murphy attempted to keep Harris's eyes on his own, but the DC found the ground more of interest.

'Not that it makes it right or understandable,' Murphy continued, talking more to himself than DC Harris. 'But it makes you think, if nothing else. George Stanley had his whole world ripped from underneath him when his son was killed. Then to see those responsible for that given light sentences and being able to move on, it must have done something to him.'

'Doesn't mean he shouldn't be punished just the same,' Harris's reply came after a few silent moments. 'Now we have a nutcase with a gun on some kind of rampage.'

Murphy let the last comment hang in the air. They were just waiting for something else to happen now. For Alan Bimpson to make his next move, most likely. He would have gone to ground, Murphy thought, knowing the scene at the farm would have been discovered not long after his actions.

Especially considering George Stanley was alive.

Murphy pondered on that fact. It didn't fit the profile of someone who was experienced in this type of thing, leaving a witness like that. It spoke of someone acting on impulse, a burst of anger, rather than months of plotting. Or maybe he was wrong and Alan Bimpson had just been unlucky.

'He won't have gone far,' Murphy said, causing DC Harris to finally look up from the floor.

'What makes you say that?'

'Because I agree with Mr Stanley. He's not finished. I don't believe this was the endgame, the scene at the farm. I think it was the beginning. He's been slowly disintegrating until he tried to wipe them all out. Now he's gone off on one, he could turn on anyone.'

'Surely he'd try and get as far away as possible? He'll know we're looking for him.'

Murphy shook his head. 'They never do really.' He rubbed his eyes, trying to free the tiredness, thinking about possible targets. 'Alan Bimpson quite plainly has young people — certain types of young people, anyway — in his sights. Which means he could become bolder in his abductions, or just cut straight to murder. Also, those who he believes are protecting them? God knows what he's thinking . . . '

Murphy stood up and, scuffing his shoes against the linoleum floor, walked away from the increasingly horizontal DC Harris. He reached into his pocket as he walked, taking out his mobile phone and bringing the screen to life.

Just the four missed calls from Sarah.

He'd spoken to her the evening before, telling her he would be working through the night once they'd discovered the scene at the farm. Still, he should have called her before then, the time now getting on for midday.

He pressed the call button once he'd messed around with swiping the screen. He swore things

316

were better when everything had a proper button on it.

'Hey,' Sarah's voice came through the earpiece and Murphy relaxed. Not angry. He would have got a more formal greeting if that had been the case.

'Hey, you.'

'Still there?'

'Yeah, hopefully I'll get a few hours this afternoon. Could do with some sleep, to be honest. Bloody knackered.'

Murphy could hear the noise of traffic in the background as Sarah took a second or two to respond.

'Not surprised. You've been working for over a day. What's going on? I saw something on the news earlier about a scene out near Netherley . . .'

'Believe me, you don't want to know right now. Let's just say it's a multiple and we're still looking for the guy.'

'Jesus . . .'

'No need to take the Lord's name in vain. What kind of Catholic are you?'

'A recovering one.'

The instant response made Murphy laugh out loud, causing a passing nurse to shoot him an admonishing look.

'That's my joke.'

'Well . . . you don't own it.' The traffic noise dissipated as he imagined her stepping onto a quieter street or inside. 'Listen, I'll be home later. We still haven't finished our conversation.'

Murphy's smile fell from his face. 'Bit of a bad

317

time at the moment for that type of thing.'

'Don't give me that,' Sarah replied, with what he imagined was a grin on her face. 'You've discussed worse in the middle of bigger cases . . .'

'I wouldn't be sure of that.'

'So stop trying to get out of it,' Sarah continued, as if she hadn't heard him. 'I'll let you get some sleep first, but we are talking about it. Also, I want to hire someone to come and finish off the decorating. God knows when you'll get to it.'

'There you go again, taking His name in vain.'

'We'll speak later. I'm having lunch with Jess, and she's bored of listening to me on the phone.'

Murphy leant with his back against a wall, alcohol gel dispenser next to his elbow. 'Tell her I said hello.'

'Will do. Speak to you later. Love you.'

Murphy replied in kind, then spent a few seconds trying to hang up before realising the call had already ended.

One day he'd get the hang of the thing.

Murphy ran a hand through his rapidly diminishing hairline and closed his eyes for a moment, the stinging sensation becoming almost too much. He felt old, the previous thirty-odd years conspiring against him. A relatively young man, as he'd been called ever since making DI by the time he was thirty. Every year that had followed had felt like four. He was chasing forty but felt closer to fifty.

Such was the life.

How could he be a father when a sleepless

night made him feel as if he was lugging a suitcase of a body around, full of heavy, tired bones? Murphy was pretty sure one of the prerequisite terms for accepting parenthood was the knowledge that sleep was a distant memory for the first twelve or so months.

Murphy rubbed his temples, slowly opening his eyes to reveal the hospital corridor once more. Not for the first time, he repeated his focus mantra while he narrowed his eyes, almost straining the pain away. Pushed himself off the wall and made his way back to DC Harris and the waiting area. To his work. To the long hours of waiting around, hoping a mistake hasn't cost you a case. Or a body.

Harris's back was the first thing Murphy saw as he entered, but he already knew something was wrong. Rigid shoulders, one arm rising up before flopping to his side.

Plus, he could hear his raised voice, shouting into the phone.

'Where . . . ? Tell me fucking where . . . ? He's gonna go mad if you don't tell me . . . don't put her on . . . no . . . '

Murphy's brow furrowed as he moved slower, his shoes making no sound on the floor as he reached DC Harris and stood to his side.

'Hello, boss . . . no, he's just on the phone or something . . . okay . . . I understand . . . fucking shit!'

Harris had turned only slightly, but the sight of Murphy at his shoulder had caused him to jump a foot in the air and drop his phone. Calmly, Murphy bent down and picked it up, the back of the mobile phone still sliding across the floor, but otherwise intact. Murphy lifted the phone to his ear, DCI Stephens's voice screeching through the speaker before it had even reached his ear.

He waited for a gap in her speech before speaking. 'It's me. What's happened?'

Ten seconds later, he was running.

26

Rossi cursed more often than she would ever tell her parents, even more so given it was in their mother tongue. There was something about the Italian language which gave swearing much more . . . *gravitas*.

Swinging her car around, when she was only yards from her house and the comfort of her own bed — a few hours' kip and a shower being her top priority at that moment — was all the reason she needed to start a crescendo of foul language to fill the space in her car.

'*Cazzo . . . mannaggia tua . . . figlio un cane . . . pezzo di merda . . . FICA.*'

She just wanted to go home. Shut herself away for a while and rest. She couldn't though. That gnawing feeling in the pit of her stomach wouldn't allow it. She'd known as soon as she'd left the station, pulling her car out onto St Anne Street and pointing the way home.

Rossi stuck two fingers up at someone beeping their horn as she finished the U-turn in one swift movement, a quick glance in her rear-view mirror telling her she'd had plenty of time.

Probably.

Fucking Brannon and fucking Murphy.

It had started as soon as Brannon had announced the disappearance of the youth club bloke. Wheels turning and turning. Coincidences that don't just happen.

321

She catastrophised things, according to her ex, a psychology lecturer. That had been his major issue at the time. Some word that she'd never heard used in that way suddenly becoming his go-to move whenever they'd argued.

Rossi had pretended to know exactly what he'd meant the first time he had said the word, telling him to go fuck himself and storming out the room — then pulling out her phone and googling it as soon as she was upstairs.

Cazzo.

He was probably right though. She did have a tendency to see the bad in everything. Pessimism was just her default setting — why set yourself up for disappointment, when if you thought something bad would happen and it didn't you could feel great? It was win-win, as far as she was concerned.

So what if sometimes that led to thinking the worst of every situation?

That's why she wasn't lying in bed at that moment though. Why she was driving across Queens Road and up the East Lancashire Road towards Norris Green.

Rossi had seen the worst in the situation, and imagined the possibility DS Brannon could be walking into a place he couldn't handle alone.

A sexist would call it woman's intuition, but it was more about experience and logic. Rossi just knew something was wrong about the whole thing.

If she was truthful, making sure Brannon was safe was more about making sure David Murphy was covered, rather than Brannon's safety. She couldn't really care less about him, but Murphy deserved help . . . and if something happened to Brannon, she knew where the blame would lay.

Rossi slowed as she turned down Lower House Lane, the dual carriageway quiet for the time of day. A couple of minutes later, and the church appeared on her left, the youth club behind it.

She parked up on the street rather than pulling into the side road, noticing Brannon's car outside the youth club. Got out of the car and started walking, the only noise coming from the few cars which passed on the main road a few yards away.

Rossi walked around the corner onto the side street where the youth club was, catching sight of herself in the driver's side window of Brannon's car.

The reflection made her pause.

She heard Brannon shout, but was locked on the reflection of a man exiting the youth club. Holding what looked very much like a shotgun and a rucksack.

Her throat clogged up.

Staring at the reflection of the man, who was only looking towards where Brannon's shouts were coming from, she willed herself to turn around. Shout. Do anything to stop what she knew was about to happen.

Rossi had heard witnesses say they froze in situations like this. Had sniffed and sneered outside interview rooms as she discussed cases with other detectives. All believing that they would act differently if they were involved in the

323

same circumstances.

She'd been wrong. Obviously. She couldn't move. Laura Rossi, detective sergeant in North Liverpool CID, was just as cowardly as all those others she'd mocked over the years.

Now she knew. Fear rooted you to the ground. Panic stopped your voice from shouting out. Horror crawled around your veins and kept you still, hoping you hadn't been spotted.

It took a second to think all those things. In that time, Brannon's voice had become closer. Her own private movie, playing out in a blurred reflection of a car window.

In two seconds, her thoughts began to flurry.

Do something. Say something. Anything.

Stay still. The wolf can't catch you if you're completely still.

Rossi looked away, down at her inert feet mocking her with their immobility.

Turn around. Face him. Stop Brannon from walking into a face full of pellets. Death.

Rossi looked up, past the window, to the church which backed onto the side street.

Nel nome del Padre, e del Figlio, e dello Spirito Santo. Amen.

Rossi turned and took in the tableau. The man holding the shotgun with two hands, level with his chest, waiting for Brannon to come into view.

Brannon about to turn the corner of the building. Shaking his head in slow motion.

'Brannon, get back.'

Both heads shot towards her scream, but she barely saw the man turn the shotgun her way as she began moving.

Leaning over, willing her legs to move faster, quicker, to get around the car to put a barrier between her and him. Between her and death.

She couldn't hear.

Rossi had one hand on the bonnet as she began to run. Felt, rather than heard, the glass shatter on the car.

Pain.

Turned as she fell down. Saw the man holding the shotgun move backwards with the recoil.

Brannon stood motionless at the corner of the building, disbelief drawing his face downwards. Not a perfect O. She recognised the look.

Looking down at her white shirt revealed where her jacket had flown open as she'd fell.

Thinking it probably wouldn't be white for much longer.

Ave, O Maria, piena di grazia, il Signore è con te. Tu sei benedetta fra le donne e benedetto è il frutto del tuo seno, Gesù. Santa Maria, Madre di Dio, prega per noi peccatori, adesso e nell'ora della nostra morte.

Amen.

PART THREE

PART THREE

Home

Six Months Ago

His dad had lived there since he'd married Mum. Forty-odd years in the same house. He couldn't imagine anything worse. Settling anywhere. The same walls staring back at you every day. Familiarity with every surface, every crack, every fucking piece of brick in the place.

He was the only one who'd wanted to move when they'd been kids. His brother and sister had been happy enough to just carry on in the same house as normal, but not him. Constantly complaining about not having his own room, the same four walls surrounding him forever. He wanted to go somewhere else. Four bedrooms, so he could have his own space.

His dad was his best friend.

It helped they liked the same things. Same taste in music, films. They'd sit and watch whatever movies were showing on the TV that had cost a fortune back then, whilst his mum would make herself busy doing whatever mums did. The other two in their rooms, or out with friends.

He wasn't interested in anything like that. He was happy enough just sitting with his dad when he'd come home from work smelling like paint and hard graft.

When he was really young, he'd spend hours

just picking flecks of paint out of his dad's rapidly thinning hair.

He'd got too old for doing that kind of thing far too quick for his liking.

It was the seventies, going into the eighties. Liverpool FC were flying and dad's favourite player had been Emlyn Hughes. He left and it became Alan Hansen. Tough defenders who weren't afraid to stick their heads on the line.

His dad was everything.

Now that man was lying on the sofa, bought on tick twenty years before. Still spring in the cushions. One arm lying across his chest, the other behind him. His legs dangling off the end.

His dad looked old for the first time.

Pale and loose-skinned. Lined and weathered.

Old.

Dead.

He knew without checking. No rise and fall of his chest. Already going cold. Stiff.

When he was about to leave school, his dad had sat him down and had a serious conversation with him. He'd noticed the changes. The giving up. He'd never been a great student. Quiet, reserved. He'd finally made friends with people his own age and they were more interesting. What they could get up to at the weekend. Which girls were more likely to let you cop off with them. It was the early nineties, Liverpool was coming out of the desolation of the eighties and the job market wasn't exactly welcoming to a sixteen-year-old lad with no qualifications. He didn't much care anyway. His dad had noticed the scrapes, the bruises. The

330

marks of late-night fights and drinking cider in parks. His parents had always been lax with their youngest, letting him set his own time to get home by at the weekends. Still, their sighs and groans on a Saturday afternoon had been getting longer and more annoying, so he'd seen the *talk* coming.

His dad had been watching *Grandstand* on the TV. Just the two of them, him still sweating out the two or three litres of cider he'd drank the night before, his dad sat with the *Liverpool Echo* on his knee, a cup of coffee in his hand.

His dad had just started talking. Telling him stories he'd heard before about his own childhood. The stuff he'd got up to with his own mates in that period after the war had ended and the fifties heralded change that never really came. How a stint in the army had made him a changed man, how never really knowing his own dad had marked his life in numerous, significant ways.

'You need to find something in your life,' his dad had said to him years before. 'Something you're good at. I don't want you turning into one of those little bastards on the streets, making everyone else's life a misery. You're better than that.'

Now his dad wasn't waking up. No matter how much he shook him. The rush, the adrenaline of what they'd done that evening had worn off. The years they'd discussed what they'd do if they were in charge, the time they'd begun planning what they'd finally found the people for. The look on that *little bastard*'s face when

331

they'd pulled him in the van. Scared shitless and looking more like a little boy, rather than the old teenager who had tormented his dad for months.

When his mum had died, he spent most of his free time with his dad. Not there though, not at the house. At the local pub, mostly. During the evenings, after he'd finished up work for the day.

His dad was still his best friend.

Even after he'd retired, become a little slower as he left his sixties and entered the decade of death, they were still close. They still shared the same taste in things, the same views.

Everything was going to shit. That was view number one. Things had been different years ago. Of course, there were scallies around, they're like rats in London . . . never more than a few feet away from one. But it was different now. They were different now. At least back in the day there was a pretence of respect. Now they just didn't care. Wanted to drag everyone down to their level.

His dad's arm was shifting his weight over where he'd moved it, looking for a pulse. He'd fall off the sofa if gravity was allowed to do its job. A car passed by outside the window, lighting up the darkness within the living room for a few fleeting seconds with its headlights. The light faded away and he blinked a few times to get used to the gloom again.

It was cold. His dad didn't believe in having the heating on past a certain time. It had gone three in the morning when he'd arrived, so the house had become cold.

When his dad had told him of his idea, he'd

initially nodded along as if it was possible. He knew it wasn't really, not these days. They seemed fearless, these young lads out there every night, not caring at all about consequences. He doubted locking them up and giving them a lesson using violence alone would have any effect. Look at how many get banged up in Walton and come out unchanged. If prison didn't make a difference, what chance did a forty-odd-year-old property developer and his retired father have?

That's why we need a team.

The pub was always quiet during the evenings they'd meet up for a few pints. Watch the mid-week footy on the new flat-screen Brian, the landlord, had installed, hoping to attract a few more punters. Only a few regulars, those hanging on despite the smoking ban and the supermarkets charging a tenner for a whole crate of lager, rather than the two-fifty a pint it was there now.

It was easy to get on speaking terms with those there. Soon, you know who shared your beliefs, your politics. You know which ones to avoid because everything came back to immigration and you're not interested in racists. You want the old-school ones. You want the ones who remember a time when respect was earned and not expected. You want the ones that want to do something about it. Who don't want to just sit around and piss and moan about how everything was better in the old days, when you could leave your door open and no one would rob you . . . conveniently forgetting that no one had fuck all to steal back then anyway.

No. You want the ones with a clear idea. Maybe a personal grudge. They've been broken into by kids who got nothing but a slap on the wrist. You want the ones who were sick and tired of good, honest working men and women being forced to pay for Chantelle down the road to spew another kid out of her nethers, the father some snot-nosed dickhead who wouldn't know how to support his own head if it wasn't attached to his bony shoulders . . . just so she could get more money from the dole.

They made a list.

You wanted anger, but directed in the right places. The focus had to be on those in the wrong. They didn't care that they'd had a shit upbringing, which probably explained their behaviour as teenagers. No. They were becoming adults, they had to learn personal responsibility for their actions.

Him and his auld fella. Something to concentrate on rather than the fact they'd just lost a mother and wife. It had been exciting in those early days, checking the regulars out, see if any fit.

A few hours before he'd walked in to find his dad lifeless in his living room, they'd taken the second one. The one his dad wanted. The one who had made his life a misery the past few months. The one who hadn't listened to his dad, who'd scarpered as soon as he'd come around himself.

He'd been a perfect choice.

It had been too much though. It was obvious

now. He'd killed his own father because he hadn't planned it out properly. He shouldn't have been involved in this part. He could have visited the farm he'd bought for the land a few years previously and left, almost forgetting about it.

His dad should have been in bed. Not outside his own house, shouting the odds with some scally.

He stood in the darkness, just looking at the lifeless, breathless body that used to be his dad. His best friend.

Wiped away a tear which had snuck out of his eye. Moved over to the window and took out his mobile phone. Dialled for a pointless ambulance and waited.

Waited for this part to be over, so he could go back to the farm and finish what they'd started.

27

Murphy arrived at the scene within five minutes of hanging up on DCI Stephens. Dozens of cars blocked the road up towards the back of the church, so he dumped his own car on Dwerryhouse Lane and ran the last part there. Almost punched a uniform who tried to block his path but settled for shoving his warrant card in the dickhead's face without breaking stride.

As he got closer, he realised it probably wouldn't have been a good idea anyway. Firearms officers were dotted about the place, casually standing around with guns slung over their shoulders, just waiting to be used. An ambulance was pulled up at the side street which led down to the youth club. Murphy slowed down to a fast walk and tried to see beyond the multitude of people who seemed to have taken up residence in the road, the uniforms and plain-clothes milling about together.

Brannon.

He almost grabbed the fat bastard there and then, but instead followed where Brannon was looking towards and caught sight of Rossi's black boots.

Please, please, please. Not another one.

Murphy took in the scene in a glance. Brannon's car; smashed windows and a hole in the passenger side door. Four paramedics, two of them standing to the side doing nothing. DCI

Stephens shouting into her phone on the other side of Brannon's car.

DS Laura Rossi lying on the floor, oxygen mask over her face, the white blouse she'd been wearing earlier now splattered with red. Her jacket lying off to her side. Murphy shrugged off the feeling of wanting to pick it up, to make sure it didn't get dirty.

He felt a hand on his shoulder and turned to find Brannon, ashen-faced and shaking.

'It was so quick . . . so quick.'

Murphy stared down at him, not replying.

'She was just there, I couldn't do anything. I didn't even know she was here.'

Murphy shrugged his hand away and moved closer to Rossi. Concentrated on her chest. Made sure it was rising and falling. Moved further forward as he couldn't tell.

'You let her get shot . . . '

'No! He missed, he fucking missed . . . '

Murphy wasn't listening. Saw the blood on Rossi's top and saw only red. Pushed Brannon against the car, gave him a left hook to the body and watched him crumple to the floor.

Murphy heard DCI Stephens shouting from across the road but ignored it and moved towards Rossi.

One of the 'standing around, doing fuck all' paramedics moved to block his path, but then thought better of it.

Now he could see her properly.

'How is she?' Murphy said, surprised by the sound of his own voice.

'Lucky.'

337

Murphy turned towards the paramedic who had answered him. The female half of the Olympic 'standing around, doing nothing' team of two. 'What did you say?'

'Few inches to her left and her head would have been blown off. As it is, just a bad flesh wound. She'll be all right. Who are you, anyway?'

Murphy didn't reply, instead moving towards Rossi again, ignoring the paramedic who was doing something to Rossi's shoulder and who tried to stop him.

'Laura, *come stai?*'

Murphy watched as Rossi's right hand came up and shifted the oxygen mask away from her face.

'Good try,' she said, Murphy almost missing it as she spoke under the noise, 'but your Scouse accent makes it sound shit.'

Murphy smiled, patted her leg and then stood up. DCI Stephens was stood over Rossi, her face stern and straight.

'Over here, now.'

Murphy shrugged his shoulders towards the horizontal Rossi and trudged off in the direction DCI Stephens had gone, past Brannon's car and towards the end of the side street. Murphy noticed for the first time that there were officers milling around the entrance to the youth club. A glimpse of a forensic tech confirmed it to him. He passed Brannon, being helped up by a uniform who couldn't keep the smirk off his face. Murphy didn't return it.

'What the hell do you think you're doing?' Stephens said, once they'd put some distance between them and the others on the scene.

Murphy shrugged. 'He deserved it.'

'You're making a bad situation worse. Go home.'

'In a minute. Kevin Thornhill?' Murphy said.

She nodded. 'Dead a few hours. Nice big hole in his chest. Our man seems to have sat with the body for a while.'

'Listen . . . '

'No,' DCI Stephens interrupted, pulling her jacket closer around herself as a cool wind whipped down the street. 'I'll be doing the talking.'

Murphy held up his hands.

'Brannon told me he came to you this morning with this information — that Kevin Thornhill hadn't been seen — and you dismissed him. Told him to go looking for him if he was bothered. You knew there was a connection, but didn't think to join the two things . . . '

'I couldn't be sure of that . . . '

'Nonetheless, you sent a man down here on his own. Into God knows what situation.'

'He didn't.'

Murphy and DCI Stephens turned to see a pale-skinned version of Rossi holding off a tutting paramedic who had his hand pressed to her shoulder.

'DS Rossi, go back to the ambulance,' DCI Stephens said. 'You're going to the hospital.'

'I will, although I'm fine, really. Just need a patch-up. Shock, more than anything. But don't be too hard on our DI. He told me to come

339

down and back up Brannon. Had a change of heart after Brannon had stormed out.'

Murphy swallowed. 'Laura, you don't need to . . .'

Rossi held up the hand on her good arm. 'No. It's okay. It just all happened so fast. No one was to blame.'

Murphy tried to hold Rossi's gaze, to try and communicate something, but she turned and leant on the paramedic. 'Let's get me sorted so I can come back and get the *bastardo* who did this to me,' Rossi said, before walking away.

DCI Stephens watched her walk away before turning back to Murphy.

'Is that true?'

Murphy thought for a second, before deciding not to answer in any other way but with a shrug.

DCI Stephens sighed and rubbed the bridge of her nose. 'Look, DI Burrows is working the scene in there. Let him get on with that. Alan Bimpson's face is going to be all over the news and social media within an hour now he's shot a copper. It's going to get busy later. Take the chance to get some sleep. I'll clear things with Brannon.'

Murphy began to argue, but DCI Stephens cut him off.

'Not a discussion. We've all been on for too long. Go home, get some sleep and be back in later. You'll get a call if you're needed.'

Murphy considered arguing further, but the look on DCI Stephens's face made his mind up.

He took one last look at the youth club, and walked back to his car.

The drive home had been a blur as tiredness swept over him and the image of Rossi lying there in broken glass and her own blood crowded his mind. It was only mid-afternoon, but it felt like the middle of the night, darkness threatening to swarm over and around him.

Murphy sat in the car for a few minutes once he reached home, his head resting against the steering wheel, trying not to close his eyes and fall asleep right there. He forced himself to turn off the radio, which had been talking about the events of the previous few hours on a loop. The same tiny crumbs of information being offered repeatedly, over and over.

Murphy knew what would come next. Nationals. They had it all now. Multiple bodies, a cop shot in the line of duty. The man responsible still on the loose. He expected that idiot from *Sky News* would be showing up any minute now to interview concerned locals live on TV.

It took a few goes, but he finally got the key in the door and opened it up, shifting post on the mat further into the house.

'Sarah?'

If the unattended post hadn't been a big clue, the silence which followed was. Not home from work yet.

He pulled himself upstairs and ran the shower. He'd planned to put in a separate cubicle, but for now was happy enough with the one over the new bath. Murphy undressed in the bedroom and padded back through to the bathroom, wincing as he climbed into the bath, his rib injury from the previous year reminding him it still wasn't right. All it took was lack of sleep and it acted up.

'Getting old . . . '

He let the hot water roll over himself, leaning on the wall in front of him, stretching out his tired limbs.

One man. Alan Bimpson. Victims totting up and all over the place. Had a thing for teenagers, scallies in particular. Wanted to get back at them, so was now killing them.

Oh, and those who helped him in some way. The others at the farm.

Murphy washed and dried himself off before drawing the curtains in the bedroom. Just a couple of hours, he thought, that's all he needed. He set the alarm to go off at five p.m. and didn't bother getting under the covers. Curled into a large ball and closed his eyes.

Brain still ticking over. Not stopping. Never stopping.

Murphy woke to the blistering sound of an alarm and a hand shaking his shoulder.

Shoulder. Rossi.

His eyes snapped open, which was his first mistake. Pain shot behind his retinas as he squinted against the low light coming through the curtains and door.

'You have to go back in?'

Sarah's voice was like a screech, even though Murphy knew she'd spoken softly.

'Yeah,' he managed to reply, the effort of opening his mouth and forming words exhausting him all over again.

A couple of hours was never enough.

'Okay. You're eating first though. I'm making your tea. You can tell me what the hell is going on then.'

Murphy tried to bury himself into the bed but Sarah whipped back the bed covers, exposing his naked skin to the icebox the bedroom had turned into since he'd been asleep. He hugged the bed harder but gave up. Swung his legs over the side of the bed, then lifted his torso up. Snatched up his mobile phone to check for missed calls or messages. Nothing.

'There's clean clothes on the door,' Sarah said, her voice drifting in from the landing as she reached the stairs.

Murphy grunted a thanks and got dressed. Like he had a choice.

He shuffled down the stairs, the smell from the kitchen making him realise he hadn't eaten in hours.

A silent meal of egg, chips and beans shared over the smaller kitchen table followed, with Murphy happy that Sarah allowed him to wake up properly before asking questions. But as soon as he forced the last forkful of beans down his throat, she was on him.

'What's happening out there? It's all over the news, you know.'

Murphy stood and placed his dirty plate on the side, leaving the dishwasher loading for Sarah to do when he left.

'We don't know much at the moment . . . '

'You know enough. Should I be worried?'

Murphy turned and attempted a smile. Sarah didn't look impressed.

'Some guy. Killed some teenagers and now seems to be working his way through the scally phonebook. He killed a youth club manager this morning and . . . '

He stopped, not wanting to say the next part. Knowing he had to.

'What . . . ?'

Murphy opened the fridge, reached for a can of Diet Coke and opened it. Took a swig, grimacing at the sudden cold. 'Brannon had gone down there. He was mates with the guy . . . '

'The killer?'

'No, the youth club one. Laura followed him there.' He drank a little more. Swallowed. 'She was shot.'

Sarah put her hands to her mouth. Murphy spoke before she had a chance to respond.

'She's okay. Grazed her if anything. She got lucky. It was my fault.'

'Don't be stupid . . . '

'No,' Murphy said, slamming the Coke can down on the kitchen counter. 'It was. I sent off Brannon on his own without thinking. The youth club manager had a connection to the case and I didn't even think. Laura did though. She shouldn't have been there.'

'She's going to be okay though. So just don't screw up again and it'll be fine.'

Murphy leant against the counter, palms flat on the surface. He moved forward to rest his forehead on the cupboard in front of him. 'It's not that easy.'

'Of course it is.'

344

He heard Sarah's chair scrape backwards. Soon, her arms around him, her head resting in the nook between his shoulder blades.

'It'll be okay. You were just tired, that's all. They overwork you when it gets like this. You won't make a mistake again, I promise.'

Murphy leant back, letting her arms fall away. He made to turn, then decided against it. 'It's this sort of thing I'm talking about, Sarah.'

'What do you mean?'

Murphy screwed his eyes tight, rubbed against his eyelids. 'This. My job. My career. I'm thinking of too many things. The last time this happened . . . '

'Don't . . . '

'I can't do it. Not now. I can't be a father. I'm only just hanging on as it is, Sarah.'

He heard her move away. Risked turning around, but did so slowly.

She was turned away from him, her blonde hair almost to the middle of her back now she'd let it grow. Perfectly straight, full of life.

'I need this, David. We need this. We're never going to move on if we don't start planning ahead. Everything is day-to-day with us. I need more.'

Murphy crossed the room, placing his hands on her shoulders. 'That's not true. Everything's fine. Why change it, anyway?'

'It's not fine,' Sarah said, pulling away from him as her shout echoed around the kitchen. 'You came back to me last year, yeah. Great. But it's like we're on a cliff. Right at the edge. One gust of wind, and we're on the rocks again.'

'I don't feel that way,' Murphy said, taking a step forward.

'Yes, you do. I can see it in you. The way you look at me, the way you are.'

Murphy shook his head, stepping backwards now. 'I don't need this right now . . . '

'When, then, David?' Sarah said, turning on him. 'When the timing is all set for you to make your grand decisions?'

'How about when there isn't someone killing a bunch of people in Liverpool?'

Sarah breathed out, not looking at him any more. Staring at the floor, slowly shaking her head, arms wrapped around herself.

'I'm sorry,' Sarah said, 'but I'm just tired, David. Tired of feeling like we're not moving anywhere. Like you're scared of doing anything in case things screw up again.'

Murphy moved towards her. 'It's not that. It's not that at all. Look, it's just that . . . if I'm going to do something as huge as bring a life into this place, I want to be able to do it right. I want to be there, not out all hours with other people's kids when things have gone wrong for them. I want a kid that will recognise me. Right now, being a DI, I'm at the front. The boss to those under me, the punchbag for those above.'

Sarah looked up at him, eyes dry. 'Change things then.'

'I'm trying,' Murphy replied, pulling Sarah towards him. 'First, let me catch the bad guy so we can all sleep well at night.'

Sarah laughed, muffled against his chest. Pulled away. 'You need to stop watching those

American cop shows.'

Murphy laughed back. Hugged her tight, kissed her.

Then left.

Because that was what he did. He always left her.

28

Murphy had just closed the front door when his phone started playing *Money* by Pink Floyd in his pocket.

He regretted ever asking Sarah how he could get one of those song ringtones on the thing. Now he was stuck with probably his least favourite Floyd track. He could ask again, he supposed, but he hated giving her any excuse to take the piss out of his technology failings, or his taste in music.

'Murphy,' he said in time with the beeps as the central locking on his car unlocked.

'It's me,' Rossi said, her voice already set on *angry*. 'Come get me.'

'Wait a second,' Murphy said, opening the car door and performing the 'getting into a tight space when you're six foot four' dance. 'What's going on, where are you?'

'I'm still at the Royal.'

Murphy knew Rossi's feelings on hospitals, so wasn't exactly surprised by her tone. 'They've cleared you to be released already?'

'Like I care. I'm fine, just a bit scraped up. Are you on your way?'

'Hang on, maybe you should . . . '

'*Mannaggia* . . . I'm not sitting around here any more. Come pick me up. I'll be waiting outside.'

The phone went silent, Murphy still sitting in the driver's seat with it clamped to his ear, trying to speak to emptiness. Muttering under his breath, he placed the phone in the hands-free set on the dashboard and started the car up.

When in doubt, don't argue with the angry Scouse-Italian woman. Always a good motto to live by.

Murphy dialled the office and reversed out of the driveway as it rang. A DS answered, putting him through to DCI Stephens as well as any efficient receptionist.

Another cutback. At least this one hadn't really affected anyone.

'Stephens.'

'It's Murphy . . . '

The sigh filled the car with static. 'David, I thought I told you . . . '

'Yeah, I got a few hours and feel fine,' Murphy said, looking left and right, waiting for a break in the traffic. Bloody rush hour. 'What's the latest?'

'Nothing as yet. We're getting CCTV pulled, but there's nothing that close to the area. No witnesses as yet. The Super has pulled together every resource we can get. It's going big.'

'News?'

'National.'

Murphy puffed his cheeks and turned onto the main road after spotting a gap. 'Great. Live?'

'Just updates now. Local are going big on it. Expect Pete Price to have a particularly angry phone-in show tonight.'

Murphy made a mental note not to tune in. 'How big is the team?'

'Me and DCI Carnaby from Sefton are nominal heads, but the Super is taking over main

349

duties. We've got four DIs from Sefton coming over, two from Knowsley. A whole bunch of DSs and DCs, and about six million uniforms out there looking for him.'

Murphy shook his head. 'You know that saying . . . '

'Too many chefs spoil the scouse?'

'Almost.'

'There's not much we can do about it. It's the way of things now. They're worried we've got a Moat, or that bloke in Cumbria. It's all about armed response now. Bringing them in from all over, from what I can tell. They're not telling us much.'

That's what this situation needs, Murphy thought. More guns.

'I'm on my way in. Be there soon.'

DCI Stephens hung up without another word, Murphy turning on the radio and skipping through the stations. The only station not talking about it seemed to be talkSPORT, which was something, he supposed.

He settled on Radio Merseyside, where the usual football chat at teatime had been replaced with a serious-sounding bloke who was taking calls about the day's events.

'I just want to know what they're doin' to keep our kids safe, you know? If even the bizzies are gettin' shot, what will that mean for the rest of us, like?'

'I understand your concerns, Kim, and I share them. What are the police in Merseyside doing to keep our children safe this evening? We'll be back with more of your calls, the real voices of

Liverpool, right after Listen *by Beyonce.'*

Murphy turned back to talkSPORT.

The Royal Hospital was undergoing massive change, money pumped in to renovate the whole place, turning it into something a private facility would be envious of. Sarah had told Murphy it would all be private soon enough anyway, so it hardly mattered.

Rossi was waiting at the front entrance, as he'd expected. Folded arms and narrowed eyes, jacket pulled tight across herself.

To hide the bloodstains, Murphy guessed.

He pulled up, parking in the taxi point and getting out of the car, leaving it running. He trotted over to Rossi who was steaming towards him, her head down.

'Get back in the car,' she shouted across at him. 'I'm not a bloody invalid.'

Murphy stopped, thought for a second, then opened the passenger side door anyway. Waited for her to give him the evil eye and then get inside, Murphy shutting the door after her.

'How are you feeling?' Murphy said, as he got back in the car.

'Fine. Shouldn't have even gone to the place. Was expecting them to at least replace some of the blood I lost. Superficial, they reckon. Looks worse than it is.'

Murphy turned to look at her before driving off. She was perhaps paler than usual, her dark Mediterranean complexion a little faded. Scrapes and cuts which had been cleaned up on her face, and a bandage across one hand. The white padding which had been used to dress the wound on her shoulder was poking out the top of her jacket.

'Do you want to go home?'

'No,' Rossi said, pressing the button which let the window down, 'back to the station. I've got a clean shirt there.'

'I'm not sure that's a good . . . '

'Just drive, will you,' she replied, lighting up a cigarette and blowing smoke out the window. 'I'm okay, honestly. I'd be the first to try and blag some sick pay. I'm sure the boss needs all the heads she can get.'

Murphy turned to the front, thinking. 'Okay. But you're on desk duty for now. If we get a call-out, you're staying there.'

'Fine. Let's just get going. I don't want to miss anything else. I'm sure you don't, either.'

Murphy pulled out of the hospital car park, the traffic even busier down there near the city centre. It took a good couple of minutes, and Rossi lighting another cigarette, before he was able to pull onto the main road of Prescot Street. It was only a short drive back to St Anne Street, but the rush-hour traffic added at least fifteen minutes to the journey. The silent journey. Every time Murphy thought to say something, he tried it out in his head first, and it just didn't sound right.

He spoke when they pulled into the car park behind the station. The number of vehicles there had tripled since he'd left that day, people coming in and out of the building. The media were probably still mostly camped outside the scene at the youth club, but that hadn't stopped a few turning up at the CID offices, hoping to

352

get someone willing to speak off the record, he guessed.

'Listen, about earlier. What you told the boss . . . '

'Don't . . . '

'No. I have to. You shouldn't have done that. If something comes up because of it later on down the line, it could screw up things, case-wise. I could have defended the decision, you know that.'

' "Case-wise'? What do you mean?'

'If they found out you hadn't been sent there, well . . . it gives cause for a defence lawyer to give another angle. *Cop gone rogue* kind of thing.'

'We haven't even caught the prick yet, David.'

Murphy turned at the sound of his name.

Rossi never used his name.

He went to speak, but Rossi cut him off.

'It'll be fine,' Rossi said, flicking her cigarette out the window and winding it up. 'Look, they're just looking for a reason to get you, you know that. If they hear you endangered a copper's life . . . you wouldn't last long. Brannon for one would never tire of it. You owe me, that's all.'

'*Ferrero Rocher?*' Murphy said, turning to her and smiling.

'A big box. Now let's get in. See what the score is.'

Toxteth

Liverpool 8

He waited around the corner in the van he'd driven down there the night before. White, nondescript. Bought for cash, weeks earlier, with bogus details. Some dodgy garage out in Bootle.

Doesn't matter how hard they tried, you couldn't keep the dodgy ones out of Liverpool.

He had no doubt he wouldn't last long with this vehicle, but it would do for the rest of the day, he thought. They had his picture — the radio had told him as much. He checked the news sites online, using the phone he'd have to throw away sooner than the van. There was his face, staring back at him from a four and a half inch screen.

He wasn't top news story on some of them. Not yet.

He would be tomorrow.

The sound of sirens kept coming and going. It was getting more difficult to see anything of interest, as more and more people turned up for a gawp. He was parked a good distance away, off the main road, facing towards the side street behind the church. There was a pub a little further behind him, rapidly filling up with punters all eager for a gossip. Probably hadn't seen business like it in years.

He should get some credit for that.

Parasites breeding parasites. The area was full of them. Kids killing kids over supposed gangland arguments that spiralled out of control. Innocents in the crossfire, not considered until it was too late.

Kids. That's all they were. They might be adult in age, but that was all they were. Kids. Not taught properly.

He so wanted to start here. The cesspit of Norris Green.

Probably shouldn't have done Kevin Thornhill first. There was no way he could do anything there now. Place was crawling with coppers.

He took his notepad out. Pulled his beanie hat further down to cover his head as another police car squealed past. They'd start on the area soon enough, looking for witnesses. A bloke sat in a van a few hundred yards down the road, staring towards the scene, was likely to get someone's attention.

He scanned the list and picked the place.

Liverpool 8.

Toxteth.

Home of the riots in '81. The butt of many a joke in the more affluent suburbs in the city. You didn't want to end up there — that's where everyone was on smack or crack, or whatever was the go-to drug of choice for the disenfranchised youth of that decade. Bad life choices, bad parents. That's where you'd end up if you screwed around as a kid, didn't make the right decisions. Just a wealth of unemployed scum, with no future to speak of.

That's what some liked to say.

He knew differently, of course. There were many who weren't like that in the area. Some had a greater sense of community, rallying around to try and give the place a better rep. It half worked. Still an area of low house prices and racial tension, high unemployment and derelict streets; houses torn down to pave the way for redevelopment that took years to occur.

It'd been a long time since he'd had to drive through the streets, the years in between giving him pause.

Single-mindedness only went so far.

They talk about being on autopilot — doing things without even realising you're out of control. They would be wrong in his case. He knew every step, every thought that turned into action.

He just didn't want to stop.

He ditched the van once he was away from Norris Green. Left it for someone to find and spend hours scouring. They'd find his DNA and fingerprints all over it, but he didn't think it would matter much. Not with his face currently being circulated on every news channel going.

He was trending on Twitter. Number two and three, under some boyband he thought he may have heard of but wasn't sure. Still, number two wasn't bad.

#AlanBimpson
#Liverpool
#WeLoveYouHarry

He was in a silver Focus now. '51 plate, so it had some miles on the clock, but it was doing the job. He didn't want to stand out too much and he was already running out of vehicles not registered to him.

He thought of his '12 plate Audi Q5 being taken away from the driveway of his house.

He liked that car.

Toxteth still bore the scars of the eighties, true, but there were many signs of change in his eyes. Newer buildings, rebuilt shops.

Window dressing.

You couldn't hide everything. Not entirely. He'd gone online months before, checking the crime rates in different parts of the city. Toxteth wasn't as bad as somewhere like Anfield, but it was still up there. Especially for anti-social behaviour, which was what interested him most.

He turned off Park Road, going in search of more closely knitted areas. Signs of the council estates which always drew the worst examples. Modern new-build houses competing for space amongst the older houses. Post-war, pre-war. No real signs of life.

The evening was drawing in, the sky overhead darkening as the May daylight struggled. He began to think the papers had been lying to him all this time. The streets of the poorer areas weren't littered with the destitute, the vermin. They were dull, soulless. Or maybe he wasn't looking properly. Every other time they'd wanted to pick up someone new for the farm they'd never had any trouble.

He carried on further, dusk turning into evening around the time he started feeling hungry again. The satiation from the drive-thru meal he'd had earlier finally wearing off.

Then he spotted them.

Two of them. Grey jogging bottoms tucked into black socks, black trainers. The North Face black jackets. The archetypal scally. Uniformed-up, one hand down the front of their kecks, as if constantly worried someone was going to come along and steal their dicks. One was wearing a woollen hat, pulled low over his head as if it would magically hide his face. The other was more brazen.

He became aware of his hands sliding down the steering wheel as the sweat began to drip from him. One minute the air inside the car had been unnoticeable, then it was stifling, making it hard for him to breathe.

He watched them as he drove well under the thirty mph limit on the deserted side roads. Peering through his windscreen as the lads strolled about, sometimes looking around them, sometimes staring lifelessly into their mobile phone screens.

They walked across the road ahead of him towards the play area, which he knew was a popular place for them to hang around in until the early hours. Bereft of young kids and harassed parents, it became their playground. They each took a swing as he pulled up near the park entrance. One took out rolling papers and a small tin, began making up what he presumed was a spliff. The light from the flame as the one in the hat sparked up illuminated his hard face for a split second before flickering out.

He shook his seatbelt off as they started passing it between them, taking long drags before exhaling slowly into the now fully darkened sky.

He wanted to knife these two. Hear their screams, their surprise. Then their death.

It was ones like these, taking over what should be good, nice places for young kids to play. Fouling these areas with their mere presence. Nothing better to do on a cool May night but sit in a kids' playground, getting stoned or whatever. No-marks. No-lifes.

There was a skill to using a knife, a certain expertise that needed to be gained before you could use one successfully.

Or two at the same time.

He shook his head and instead removed the assault rifle from underneath the blanket where he'd hidden it from plain view on the back seat. The shotgun was to the side of him, but he left that in the car as he slipped out.

The handgun was still safely tucked into the shoulder holster, as always.

He crouched low as he approached, before realising that might bring too much attention if someone was walking past or behind him.

He would start with these scallies and then whoever came next. The ones who came to defend them. Those who complained about them endlessly but turned into bleeding hearts when someone finally did something about the problem.

They were the problem.

Alan Bimpson's night of violence was about to begin.

The youths were oblivious to his approach, the

sickly sweet aroma drifting from their direction nullifying the senses which might otherwise have saved their lives.

The one without a hat didn't even turn around when he loaded up and charged the M16.

Single-burst rounds. Not like those video games or war films these wankers played around with. The rifle butt tucked into his shoulder with barely any recoil.

The one with the hat took a bullet to the face as he turned at the noise. From ten feet away, Alan Bimpson barely blinked as the boy's face ripped apart under the force of a single bullet entering high up on his cheek, just underneath his eye. Flesh and bone melting from the heat, flipping him backwards before he even had a chance to breathe one last time.

The one without the hat simply stared at his friend's body as it catapulted backwards. Watched the blood quickly run out of his destroyed face as a ruined mass stared back at him.

Alan Bimpson didn't think he'd turn around. Walked forward a few steps and put three quick rounds into the back of his head. In a line. Top, middle and bottom. Traffic lights, blood, death.

He took out the ear buds as Mr No-Hat fell forwards, landing on his friend's upturned, dead hand.

Alan heard voices from outside the play-ground. Laughter, he thought.

Thirty-round magazine. Four gone.

Still time to play.

29

As Murphy and Rossi entered the incident room, the tension dissipated for a few seconds as a half-hearted round of applause broke out. Rossi took it as Murphy expected her to.

'Shut it, you lot. It's not like I was actually shot properly.'

A few comedians made some jokes, others shared words of support, but within a few minutes it was as if their colleague hadn't almost had her head blown off hours earlier, as everyone went back to concentrating on the job at hand.

Staring at screens, talking on phones, making notes, staring at screens a bit more. This was detective work in the twenty-first century. Murphy made his way towards his office, checking the murder board as he went, noticing it had been expanded by the joining of three cousins as more and more information had arrived.

He checked his messages as he reached his desk, ignoring anything that didn't have *very urgent* attached to it and pulling out the preliminary reports from the scene at the farm the previous night.

One in particular stood out. Murphy picked up his phone and dialled.

'Houghton,' came the reply after a few rings.

'It's Murphy. Just got your message.'

'Ah, didn't think it would take this long . . . '

Murphy ignored the sarcastic tone. 'Is this certain?'

'As certain as we can be right now.'

'Jesus . . . ' Murphy said, letting out a sigh.

'That's an operative word to use in this situation, yes. Our lovely local vicar . . . '

'Reverend,' Murphy corrected.

'Yes, yes, of course. We found a few personal effects during the sweep of the rest of the house. Led us to a lock-up garage, just past the entrance to the farm. It looks like that's where all the deceased kept their vehicles. An enterprising fellow down here ran a few checks and provided his name. That, and a couple of credit cards in his name, means we're pretty certain.'

Murphy thought back to his conversation with Reverend Andrew Pearson, looking for any memory of something being *off* with him. Came up with nothing.

'He seemed . . . normal,' Murphy said after a few seconds of silence.

'I'm sure they always do,' Houghton replied.

Murphy ended the call, leant back in his chair and swept a hand through his hair. He took the files out with him as he left the office, making his way over to the murder boards to read the latest. Rossi was still showing off her war wound to a few of the female detectives, so he left her to it, sitting at an empty desk as close to the boards as he could manage.

Eight new victims to join the one that was already placed there. Nine in total.

And whoever it was surely wasn't done yet.

'Laura,' Murphy said, extricating her away

from a gaggle of nosing constables. When she finally reached him, he told her about the reverend's involvement.

'Jesus . . . ' Rossi said when he finished.

'That seems to be the popular reaction,' Murphy replied.

'What does it mean?'

Murphy didn't answer straight away, trying to fit the new information in with what was already known.

'Not sure yet. We need to find out what's happening first.'

Rossi nodded slowly, Murphy watching her as she processed the new info before she moved across the room to an empty desk and computer. He beckoned one of the detective sergeants he knew from the drugs team over. 'Trev, you all right mate?'

'Not bad. Moved over to help you lot out. Seems like we've got quite the nutcase going here.'

Murphy grimaced. 'You can say that again. What do you know about what's been going on? Can't see Stephens in here . . . '

DS Trevor Vaughan wheeled his chair over, looking over his shoulder as he got closer. 'Been sent home. If you'd seen the state of her by five o'clock you wouldn't have been surprised. Dead on her feet. Super is on his way for a tactical meeting at seven to tell us the latest. I've heard we'll be turning it all over to firearms, and that we're just here to help out with the dogsbody-shite.'

'Where did you hear that?'

363

Vaughan looked over his shoulder again and leant further forward. The world loves a gossip. 'They're apparently already out there. They don't want to let this guy go on a spree. Getting texts off uniforms who reckon they're being moved from certain areas in the city.'

Murphy was about to respond when Detective Superintendent Gareth Butler sashayed into the incident room. Sashayed being the correct way of describing his method of gaining people's attention quickly. He didn't even need to speak, just move his hips.

One of those blokes who has a presence about him, Rossi had said to him once. Murphy spotted her across the desks, looking from the Super to Murphy in one slow glance.

A raise of the eyebrows, and nothing needed to be said.

'Murphy, Stephens's office please,' DSI Butler said, without breaking stride or gaze on the six feet ahead of him.

'Sir.'

Murphy swivelled in his commandeered chair, wishing as usual for at least five more minutes than he ever got. Took in the murder boards once more, trying to memorise the information held on them, taking note of the new names and committing them to memory.

1 — Dean Hughes — Age 18
2 — Joanne Meadowcroft — Aged 45
3 — Robert Meadowcroft — Aged 47
4 — Unknown — Aged 40–55
5 — Michael Wilson — Aged 17

364

6 — Tyler Holt — Aged 17
7 — Unknown — Aged?? (Body not found)
8 — Joshua Gold — Aged 18
9 — Kevin Thornhill — Aged 52

Murphy scrubbed out the *Unknown* next to number 4 and replaced it with Reverend Andrew Pearson's name.

Murphy swallowed and gathered up the folders, giving the nod for Rossi to stay where she was as he walked after the Super.

There was silence behind the door which DSI Butler had closed behind him and his two assistants. Murphy knocked anyway, knowing those in power always liked this little play.

'Sit down, David,' DSI Butler said as he entered. 'Let me just get set here.'

Murphy took the chance to read some more of the reports he'd been sent. Top line, all of them except the guy found on the rack had died of gunshot wounds. As expected.

Rack Guy hadn't fared as well. Tortured first.

Murphy scanned the rest of the reports, but they were startlingly bare. Some references to malnourishment or weight loss, old injuries, new injuries.

'So . . . DCI Stephens has been given a few hours off, so I thought it best, given the major incident that's happening right now, that I come along for the ride. I know you've been leading the murder investigation into the first victim, David, but I'm sure you're aware that things have moved on from there . . . ?'

Murphy nodded. 'Of course.'

'Good. There are multiple firearms officers in the area now, waiting to be sent to any incidents that occur. We're holding a press conference in the next half an hour, asking for help and all the usual things. You'll still be needed I imagine, but from now on, this is a major incident, so the usual protocols have been put into action.'

Just what he thought, more people involved. 'Sir,' Murphy said, 'with all due respect et cetera, I've been working the case from the beginning, so I'd like to still be highly involved.'

DSI Butler steepled his fingers together and appeared to give it some thought. 'I'm sure you're aware that we're now talking about something that goes above your level, Detective Inspector.'

Murphy made to speak, but DSI Butler held up a hand as he stood. 'We'll keep you as involved as needed, David, but this has become a situation that requires different techniques. Don't worry, you'll be kept up to date with all developments.'

With that, DSI Butler left the room, not waiting for Murphy to stand up and speak any further.

'We're out, aren't we?' Rossi said from the doorway, as Murphy looked past her, watching DSI Butler leave.

Murphy turned to her. 'Officially we're still involved, but it's now a major incident. There'll be command levels, all that bollocks. Unofficially . . . '

Rossi smirked. 'We're going to do our job.'

'Always,' Murphy replied.

366

Murphy stretched and checked the time again. Only early in the evening, but already the few hours of sleep he'd caught that afternoon were fading into memory. The fact that he'd done nothing but stare at screen after screen, report after report, wasn't helping.

'Coffee?' Rossi said, without looking up.

'No, don't bother. You found anything?'

Rossi shook her head. 'He's got property, but it's all under the company's name. Nothing about him personally. DVLA can't match the cars we know are his, as they're all registered to the company. Alan Bimpson exists, but at the moment we know *molto poco* about him.'

'Probably not his real name.'

'What makes you think that?'

'Why else would you go to the trouble of hiding so much information? Why wouldn't he own any of these things personally . . . his house, his car?'

'I know the answer to that,' DC Harris said from the open doorway to their office. He looked, at last, older than the young boy Murphy always thought he resembled. Losing sleep hadn't agreed with him.

'Go on,' Rossi said, leaning back in her chair and accepting the energy drink Harris held out to her.

'It's a security thing. If anything happens to the business — if he's found liable for anything personally — he can pretend he has no assets, so he wouldn't be able to pay fines or whatever.

Saw it in the *Echo* about some dodgy investors last year.'

Murphy pursed his lips. 'What if the company goes down though?'

DC Harris shrugged, collapsing down into his chair.

'He's probably paying himself a nice wedge as a director, or something like that,' Rossi said. 'All the cars, the houses and that, they go through the company. Then he gets a pot of money to store away.'

'In which case . . . '

'We look at who's listed as a director of the company and go through each name,' Rossi said with a smile.

'Exactly,' Murphy replied.

'Onto it,' Rossi said, leaning forward and tapping away at her keyboard.

'Any more from our man at the hospital, Harris?' Murphy said, turning towards the DC.

DC Harris shook his head. 'Doctors said it's best Stanley rests now. Left a couple of uniforms with him, but he was sleeping anyway.'

Murphy heard commotion outside in the main office but ignored it. 'Any news on him being released so we can get him charged and that?'

DC Harris was trying to peer around the office door. 'Maybe tomorrow,' he said after a few seconds.

Murphy's phone started buzzing in his pocket. Pulling it out, he saw Sarah's name flash up. He swiped the screen, feeling pleased with himself when it worked first time and answered. 'Hello, was just about to ring . . . '

'What's going on? Are you there now? Are you okay?'

Murphy sat up straighter, the concern and breathlessness in Sarah's voice worrying him. 'What's up? I'm fine, just at the station . . . '

'Oh, thank God. I thought you'd be there.'

Murphy scratched at his beard, shifted the phone from one ear to the other and watched DC Harris stand up and begin to walk out of the office. 'Where, babe?'

'I'm watching it on the news now. It's gone nuts on Sky and it's on the BBC News channel as well. They're saying there could be up to ten people dead.'

Murphy was still frowning as DC Harris came back in, beckoning them to join him outside. 'I don't understand, Sarah. Who's dead?'

'That guy you're after. He's been in Toxteth. He's shot people, David.'

Murphy reached the office door and looked across the now-manic incident room.

'I've got to go, Sarah. I'll call you later.' Murphy stabbed at the end call button on his phone and rushed out the room across the main office, an empty chair banging to the floor as he made his way without abandon. 'Someone want to tell me why I'm finding out from a member of the public about what's been going on?'

Rossi turned to him, moving a step away from the DS she'd been talking to. 'Because we didn't know. Press found out first. They were filming there when it kicked off. Firearms are on their way now.'

369

'How many?'

Rossi shook her head. 'No idea.'

Murphy stood still for a second, then made up his mind. 'Rossi, stay here. Harris, come on.'

30

You can't choose the last words you ever say to your child — and that's what they are, no matter what age — as they leave the house. Off to school, off out with friends. Off to work, or on a date. You don't think of them as last words. Just another part of the ongoing conversation, the never-ending role as a parent.

Two lads went down first in Toxteth. Dead before they hit the ground, as the saying goes. Took longer than that, of course, but it's the little things you tell yourself.

Matthew Collins and Cameron Wilkins. Colly and Wilko to their mates. Seventeen and eighteen years of age. Still living at home.

Colly was the first to be hit by Alan Bimpson's gun. He'd left home only half an hour earlier, meeting up with Wilko after the older lad had texted him.

Got some. Outside in ten.

Colly lived with his mum and two younger sisters, an older brother who lived away. That's what they told the two girls anyway — Millie and Leah. They didn't need to know that their twenty-year-old brother, the man of the house in many ways, was doing five years inside for being caught dealing class As. It was a stitch-up, he'd told Colly. Wrong place, wrong time. Didn't matter to the bizzies, or the courts though. One look at where he lived told them all they needed to know. Liverpool 8, fuck 'em. All the same. Liz Collins knew the score though. Just get your head down and power through. Hope for the best. Knowing this was about as *best* as it was ever going to be. Four kids, all to the same dad though. She wore that badge with a bit of pride. At least she only got fucked about by the one bloke. Listened to his lies, then threw the bastard out when Matthew was born. Made the mistake of letting him back in, before fucking him off again when Leah was about to turn one.

Now Matthew was getting older. Making the same mistakes as his brother. She'd played the game before so knew the signs.

'Where are you going?' she shouted to him before he left that evening, hearing him coming down the stairs like a herd of elephants. 'Hope it's not out.'

Her son, seventeen years old, but only a little boy of four a moment before. Years flitting by without realising.

'I'm just meeting Wilko. Be back in a bit.'

'Don't be spending any money,' Liz said, pausing the Sky box. 'You still owe me leccy money.'

'I know, I know,' Matthew replied, shifting on his feet now, pulling his jacket together. 'I'll get some while I'm out if I can.'

'You better. Not having you leech off me forever, son. Need to stand on your own two feet a bit more. Stop taking the piss around here or I'll sling you out.'

'Yeah, yeah, Mum. Whatever. I've got to go.'

'Course. Your mates are always more important. Just like that brother of yours. I swear, if

372

you're getting into trouble . . . '

'I'm not . . . '

'Don't, I'm not stupid. I know what you're up to. Think on, son. Don't be like him, you hear me. Be back early. We can watch a film or something.'

'Yeah I'll try, Mum. See you later.'

Liz watched her son leave the room, the faint musk of aftershave hanging in the air after he left. Shaking her head as she imagined what he was doing out there.

Matthew 'Colly' Collins at least had a family who cared. Cameron Wilkins was sick of his own home. The succession of uncles and stepdads getting to him after a while. The last one was sticking around though. And unfortunately he was the worst of the lot.

'Where the fuck do you think you're going? There's dishes in the sink.'

'Just out,' Wilko replied, eyeing the bloke who had taken over his house in the past six months. 'I'll do them when I get back.'

'It's all right love, I'll do them . . . ' his mum began.

'Don't be soft, Karen. He needs to learn.'

'I said I'll do 'em,' Wilko said, itching to get out and smoke a bit, but never wanting to back down to the prick. Greg Shaw. Who the fuck was called Greg, anyway? 'God . . . why don't you ever listen.'

'Don't fuckin' talk to me like that . . . '

'Or what?' Wilko said, coming further into the living room. 'Do something.'

'You want to watch your mouth, or I'll fuckin' shut it for you.'

'You gonna let him talk to me like that, Mum?' Wilko said, looking past the dickhead who thought he could just come in and be the man of the house. 'Mum?'

'Stop fighting, boys,' his mum answered wearily. 'There's no need for it.'

'He started it. Coming in here and acting the big man,' Wilko said, clenching a fist. Wondering what it'd be like to knock the knobhead out. 'He shouldn't be ordering me about.'

'I'll do what I like in my house, you little shit,' Greg said, stepping towards him. 'You should remember that . . . '

'It's not your house . . . '

'I fuckin' pay the bills,' Greg said, his voice now bouncing off the walls. 'If it wasn't for me, you and your mum would be on the streets. You'd do well to think on that. My roof, my fuckin' rules. You hear me?'

'Mum . . . are you gonna let him say this?' Wilko wanted so much for her to stop this. To stand up to this wanker.

'He's right, Cameron. You do need to show a bit more respect to Greg. He's been more of a father to you than your own.'

'I can't believe this,' Wilko said, zipping up his jacket. 'I'm gone. You can both fuck off. I'm done with the both of youse.'

The slam of the door timed with Greg sitting back down on the sofa, letting out a heavy sigh. 'He needs to learn, love. You've let him get away with murder over the years, you know.'

'I know,' Karen replied, shaking her head. 'He's needed a male figure in his life for ages.'

'He'll come around,' Greg said, stretching out and kicking his shoes off into the middle of the floor. 'Do us a cuppa, love. Parched here.'

Two boys, one classed as an adult, one still a child really. Both teenagers. Only a few months between them. Smoking weed in a kids' playground on a weekday evening. Nothing better to do with their time. Black jackets, hoods up. Black trainers and trackie bottoms on. Knowing exactly how they looked to others, doing it on purpose. Enjoying the looks on the faces of those who were afraid of them.

The only bit of power they really had.

Matthew's mum heard first.

Liz was just putting Leah back to bed for the second time when her mobile started going downstairs. She took the stairs down two at a time but still missed it. Checked the missed call and rolled her eyes when she saw Elaine's name there. Probably just wanted a moan about her useless husband again. She ignored the next call as well, but when the phone went again, she frowned and picked up, not used to being tried this often.

'Hello,' she said, trying to sound breathless.

'Liz, it's me. Have you heard what's going on?'

'No,' Liz replied, already bored. 'I've been trying to get Leah to sleep, but she's not going down. Can I ring you back?'

'Listen, there's something going on down by Granby Street. A shooting or something.'

'Another one? I'll ring you back later, yeah. It's just I've got to get this child down at some point.'

'It's not the usual. Apparently it's some mad bloke shooting people in the street. They reckon he's already done in three or four.'

Liz stopped. 'Where did you say it was?'

'Pat from next door reckons it's to do with that bizzie getting shot today, but I reckon she's talking shite. I turned around to her and said she should stop listening to that gossip from over the way, you know the one who robbed the wheelie bin from number twenty-three and thinks she's got away with it.'

'Where was it, Elaine?' Liz said, her voice louder now.

'Granby Street, apparently. The park down there. Two lads went first, they're saying. Place is crawling with bizzies. God knows how anyone will be getting any sleep tonight if they're out there all night. Not like they're going to be quiet, is it . . .'

Liz had stopped listening. One night, around two or three months earlier, she'd had a knock on the door. Just as she was getting to the end of an episode of Corrie or something like that. Her son stood next to a copper in full uniform, hat underneath his arm. Stern look on his face. All *Matthew has been caught drinking and smoking where he shouldn't be* and *caution this time, but don't let it happen again.*

Caught in a kids' playground, at the bottom of Granby Street. With that lad he was always with.

'Oh no . . .'

'What's up Liz? Hello . . . hello?'

Liz had already dropped the phone to the floor.

376

Sometimes, a mother just knows.

Cameron Wilkins' mother didn't know. Not until the police officer knocked on her door an hour or two later. She'd been watching the news, just like everyone else in the city was by that time. Shaking her head, alongside Greg, at the state of Liverpool these days. Not like back in the day. She couldn't remember if she was thinking those things, or if it was just absorbing what Greg was saying over and over. Scallies this, scallies that. Drugs and gangs. The end of society. Jeremy Kyle generation.

'Are you Karen Wilkins?'

'What's he done now?' Karen replied, expecting the worst she could imagine. Already resigning herself to having to go down the police station and retrieve that stupid son of hers.

'Can I come in?'

'What's going on now?' Greg said, having scraped himself off the sofa and entered the hallway. 'If it's that little shit, he's on his own. Not helping him out any more. Isn't that right, Karen?'

'I'm afraid it's a bit more *delicate* than that. Let me come inside and we can talk.'

Karen had begun to calculate things in her head by then. 'Be quiet, Greg,' she said, stepping aside and letting the uniformed copper inside, followed by a short woman with tied-back blonde hair.

It was when Karen saw her face that she'd realised for certain.

Her son had lain dead on the soft tarmac of the play area for the past couple of hours and she

377

hadn't known. Hadn't felt a thing.

You can't choose the last words you say to your child as they leave the house. Not really. Otherwise you'd never let them leave, thinking over and over about what you should say to them. Final words of love, of wisdom. Some morsel of comfort that will get them through the time they spend away from you.

Matthew Collins. Colly to his mates. He wanted to do something with his life. Run his own business. Not sure what kind, but he liked the sound of being his own boss. When he was younger, he'd gone through a spate of asthma, his mum having him up to Alder Hey a number of times when he'd gone grey around the mouth. Not enough oxygen getting into him. Worried her sick.

He'd been stopped and searched by police more times than he could remember. One street caution for cannabis possession. Another for being in a fight he couldn't remember any more.

His mum had washed the blood from his school shirts, tried to talk to him, but it was like having a conversation with a brick wall. He'd almost been nicked for robbery, but the charges had been dropped.

His two younger sisters doted on him. They would light up when he entered the room, the small amounts of time he deigned to spend with them the highlight of their week.

Cameron Wilkins was an only child, but was close to his cousins. He would have ended up in prison. No doubt about it. First arrest at thirteen for shoplifting and assaulting a security guard.

Since then, numerous charges that were either dropped or led to a few months in the youth courts. Referral orders, the usual punishment.

His dad had been locked up for ten years for almost killing his mother. He was now out, but not allowed near either of them.

Cameron didn't know what he wanted to do. Maybe get some girl pregnant so they could get a council house together. He heard being a spark or a welder paid well, so kept meaning to look into that.

He loved his mum. They'd been close. Things had changed as he got older, but that was what it mostly boiled down to. He wanted to see her happy. His mum knew that.

She clung onto that. It was all she had left.

A memory of love.

31

Princes Avenue in Toxteth was only a few minutes away from the city centre, and even with the traffic building up as they got closer, Murphy and DC Harris managed to pull up to the end of the busy street within ten minutes of leaving the CID offices in St Anne Street.

Them, and around a million other coppers, it seemed.

The scene in the distance was a sea of red and blue lights, endless marked cars parked, abandoned almost, along the usually busy thoroughfare of Princes Avenue. Then there were the other vehicles, civilian ones.

They *had* been abandoned.

Murphy pointed out a spot by the old church halfway down. 'We'll walk from there.'

Harris parked up and they both got out of the car, avoiding the seemingly endless stream of people moving in the opposite direction to them.

'Whole area is being evacuated,' Harris said, turning to him. 'By the looks of things, anyway.'

Murphy allowed a couple to pass by them, one holding a swaddled baby to her chest as they hurried by, heads down. 'Yeah, looks that way. Here's the helicopter now.'

The familiar soundtrack to the city's residents hovered high overhead, before moving further forward and around, then coming to a standstill up ahead.

'Near Granby Street, that is,' Harris said, still moving forward through the thickening crowd. People were flowing across the entire road area, the dual carriageway becoming a sea of faces illuminated in the growing darkness.

Murphy pulled Harris by the jacket sleeve and pulled him away from the right-hand side of the road and into the centre where the crowd was thinner, skirting the grassy area which separated the roads going in either direction.

'When we get to the cordon, just say nothing, okay?' Murphy said.

'Sound.'

Someone had tried to set up police tape across the road but had deserted the task, so it flapped across the ground in the cool breeze.

A line of police vans and cars was keeping back those who'd stayed behind to see what was happening. Memories of 1981 came back to Murphy; of being a very young child pulled back from the window by his mum and dad as he watched police battling with the disenchanted and abused on the streets in Speke. Not as bad as it had been in Liverpool 8, but those 'riots' had reached even the outermost corners of the city.

'DI Murphy with St Anne Street,' Murphy said, holding up his ID to a suited-up sergeant who was standing closest to the bank of vehicles. 'What's the situation?'

'Sergeant Mason,' he replied, not bothering with a handshake or anything as formal. 'Some nutter with a gun killed a couple of scallies on the other side of Granby Street. Looks like

381

there's been more as well. Couple of Indians have just been taken to hospital.'

Murphy looked around, moving past the sergeant. 'No command centre yet?'

'No,' Sergeant Mason replied. 'We've only just arrived and it's all a bit chaotic, as you can see. We've got the civs out of the area and firearms are down the streets now to see if he's still here. Didn't fucking help that the press were here at the time. All over the bloody news already. Nothing we can do about that. Are you here to sort that kind of thing out or something?'

'Something like that . . . ' Murphy replied, the vibration of his phone distracting him. 'Excuse me.'

Murphy retrieved his phone, 'Murphy.'

'It's DSI Butler. I've just been told you're on the scene there . . . '

'I am,' Murphy replied, motioning for Harris to go and speak to a few of the uniforms who were standing close to the back of a police van. 'It's a bit hectic down here, as you can imagine.'

'I can. SFOs and AFOs are there though, so you don't need to be getting yourself too close.'

'Just came down to see if it was linked to our Alan Bimpson case. I'm guessing it is?'

There was a dark laugh from the Superintendent. 'I'm assuming you haven't seen the news just yet then? It's our man all right.'

Murphy looked towards Harris who was beckoning him over. 'Well, I'll make sure to watch the next bulletin,' he said into the phone and then hung up, jogging over to where Harris and a few uniforms were standing.

'What's going on?' Murphy said, as he reached them.

Harris stepped aside, revealing an older man, his make-up starting to run and hair not as coiffed as Murphy imagined it would have been thirty minutes earlier, still holding a microphone.

The cameraman sat beside the reporter, looking bemused by the whole thing.

'These two were doing a live report on the BBC. Our guy came a bit closer than they were expecting.'

Murphy eyed up the reporter and didn't bother to ask him what had happened, turning instead to the cameraman. 'DI Murphy. You are?'

'Simon Ridley.'

'Great. That thing next to you,' Murphy said, pointing to the tablet which was resting next to his camera, 'reckon you can show me the footage you took earlier?'

'Of course. I imagine it'll be on YouTube already. It's gone mad on Twitter, so someone will have uploaded it.'

'Good, get it on there for me.'

A few minutes later and Murphy was holding onto the tablet. DC Harris hovered over his shoulder, watching. It was a normal outside broadcast at first, the news ticker moving across the bottom of the screen keeping people updated on what was already being told to them by the person on camera.

'Why did you choose here to do the piece?' Murphy said, not taking his eyes off the footage.

'You know how it is . . . ' Simon the cameraman answered.

Murphy did. Any chance to link something violent to this part of the city, still synonymous with the eighties and its battle within itself.

'Here it comes . . . ' DC Harris said.

At first, it was just a few glances to the side, as a couple of bangs happened off-screen. Could be mistaken for fireworks or something. Then screams, growing louder as they got closer to where they were filming on the corner of Granby Street. Some people running past a few seconds later. The report then cut to the newsreader in the studio, split-screen, so the on-the-ground reporter could be seen to begin to lose his composure. Wondering why all these Scousers are running towards him, screaming. Then the bangs happened again, the unmistakeable sound of automatic fire. That's when the reporter hit the ground, the camera still upright, filming empty air. Slowly, it turned and zoomed in, as the newsreader back in the studio adjusted her glasses on the left-hand side of the screen and leant forward. The camera closed in on the scene and captured Alan Bimpson walking slowly towards them. He was a few hundred yards away, but with the close, tight shot the cameraman had made from zooming in, he filled the screen. No close facial features but unmistakeably him. Bimpson was almost sauntering down the road, sometimes aiming his rifle at those running away, sometimes relaxing his arms and glancing behind him.

He spotted something to his right, stopped and aimed his rifle. Cushioned the recoil in his shoulder as the screaming ends.

Then the gunman saw the camera ahead of him, causing him to stop in his tracks. He cocked his head a little and started to move forwards again.

'Get the fuck out of here knobheads, he's shooting everyone!'

The screen cut back to the safety of the studio, where the newsreader adjusted her glasses again, then apologised for the language used.

The video ended.

'This all you got?' Murphy said, handing the tablet back to the cameraman.

'Yeah. We took your man's advice and got out of there. Hung around a bit further up the road and watched him get in his car and leave. Cool as you like.'

Murphy rubbed his right hand across the back of his neck. 'Okay. Someone will take a proper statement, but,' Murphy turned to the seemingly whiter-haired reporter, 'relax. He's not coming back any time soon.'

The reporter stiffened as he was spoken to, just nodded in response.

Murphy turned and walked a few feet away, studying the houses on the Princes Avenue side. Old Victorian buildings, standing with purpose.

'What now?' DC Harris said, zipping his black jacket up and running a hand through his hair, all in one movement.

Murphy looked around, at the myriad vans and cars. 'Firearms will blanket this area, but he's long gone. Not much we can do here. We need to find out more about Bimpson himself. Find out what's driving him.'

'Back to the station then?'

'Can you think of anything else?' Murphy replied, looking down at the young DC.

Harris shook his head. 'We're not exactly going to do much here.'

'Area commander will be here shortly,' Murphy said to Sergeant Mason as they walked past him. His hair was sticking up at odd angles, where it had been messed with.

'Okay,' Mason replied, frowning, and placed his hat back on his head. 'Where are you off to?'

Murphy just smiled and carried on walking.

Hopefully, he thought, to do something more productive than stand around looking like a misplaced ornament.

Bootle

He didn't think he would make it out of Toxteth, but by some miracle he had. The news cameras turning up hadn't been part of his plan, but it hardly mattered now.

He wasn't coming back from this.

He left the car abandoned near the docks and picked up another he'd left there. A small, white Rover hatchback that had cost a couple of hundred quid cash, the seller not bothering to ask questions or see ID. All the details he'd used had been fake anyway, so it wouldn't be traced back to him.

He imagined they'd find the other one eventually, but by that time the night would be long over. All he cared about was being able to move north of the city without being stopped.

He drove through the city centre, the sirens and shouts coming in through the open side window. There would be roadblocks set up, he reckoned. But it was too soon for that.

It had only been ten minutes since he'd left Toxteth.

The first two had gone down fast. Then, well . . . things had become a little blurry for him. He remembered screaming, shouting. The click as his rifle had run out of bullets. Then, the camera across the street, realising he'd made his way up Granby Street and was near Princes Avenue. He seemed to recall talking, but didn't know about

387

what. He was just focussed solely on the task at hand, forcing his forty-odd-year-old body to move quicker than it had in a long time, as he worried about being outflanked and stopped.

He didn't worry about the sounds of people hitting the pavement. They deserved it. For all their bluster about wanting the place to be different, Toxteth and the rest of Liverpool 8 was a stain on his city. All the talk of regeneration, yet all he saw was boarded-up houses, steel shutters, and new-builds which already looked crumbling under the strain of housing the scum.

If they couldn't teach the children themselves, they didn't deserve to live. It was as simple as that.

He took out a few of the worst. Those older teenagers who were nothing but a blight on normal life.

The ones who had killed his mother and father by their actions.

Now it was the next stop. Bootle, to the north of the city. Where the lad who had pretended he could be reintegrated successfully into society came from. A stupid little prick who'd thought he could fool him into thinking he'd changed.

He'd shown him.

Now it was time to take out a few of his friends.

It wasn't hard to find suitable targets in that part of the city. It was full of them. He drove the old car out of the city centre onto Derby Road, turning off on Strand Road and driving towards the New Strand Shopping Centre. He would park the car there and rest for a while. Let the events of earlier reach the ears and eyes of the population in Bootle and then see who still wanted to come out and play.

It was dark outside, as his watch — the facia had cracked at some point, but he couldn't recall it happening — ticked over past ten p.m. The late May evening gave up the ghost of its preparation for summer evenings and allowed the cover of darkness to fall over him.

He checked his weaponry, closed his eyes for a few seconds, spoke to his dad in his head and then left the car.

It didn't take long to find them.

A group of five or six, pushing and shoving each other, laughing and shouting as they walked down Stanley Road from the direction of the Marsh Lane junction. A big Lidl shop on the corner with a car park which Alan Bimpson headed towards, empty of cars apart from one or two. He briefly considered the manager and their assistant finishing off inside, a hard day's work behind them, a late night and broken sleep ahead, only to do it all over again the next day.

Then he saw the gang approaching him. None of them over the age of nineteen, he guessed. One perhaps as young as thirteen or fourteen. Swaggering, staggering. Arrogant, self-satisfied. Blind to the danger, too brash and confident. They'd heard of what had happened in Liverpool 8 and wanted to prove something . . . that they were different. That some old guy couldn't scare them straight.

They came towards him, which was commendable. Until he took the now fully reloaded rifle out of the backpack he had slung over his shoulder.

'Shit. Fuck! It's him, on your fuckin' toes . . . '

He didn't really take much pleasure in killing these scummy bastards, with their baggy jeans, jogging bottoms, hoodies, caps, black jackets, shaved heads; shouting in their broken speech patterns. Shooting them in the backs, as they ran away from him, dropping like flies, one after the other. Looking down the rifle for better aim, met at first with silence, then by screaming coming from behind him.

The junction was busy, but he found he had no appetite for more. He stood instead, observing the reaction from those who stayed to watch what unfolded. Most ran, the sounds of his gunshots tapping into their fight or flight responses and choosing the latter. The others . . . they stopped to watch what would happen next, as if he was the star of a new reality show.

They took out mobile phones and started filming and taking pictures, from what they thought was a safe distance across the main road. Holding up their phones to record the moment when they were in his presence.

He wheeled around, wide-eyed as he took in the one, two, five, ten separate people doing this. Filming him, filming this. Later to be played back on the news, no doubt with a warning before it was shown. Zooming in on the broken bodies which lay on the edge of the Lidl car park, blood pooling around them. Turning the screen red. Blurred out on TV — but the viewers at home would know what was there.

He wanted to go, leave, to get away. They didn't understand. Would never understand.

'Why are you doing this? Please stop.' A woman's voice came from a few yards away. Alan Bimpson turned, saw the light of a camera phone and snapped back.

He needed to think. 'I need to go back. To where it all started. I need to go back.'

He dropped the spent rifle on the ground, moved out of the car park and began walking, as those ahead of him scattered. Moving to the other side of Stanley Road, as if a few more yards of distance would save them if he decided to take care of them as well.

The shotgun in his backpack banged into his shoulder blades, so he removed it, holding it loosely in one hand as he walked, the shouts and screams drifting behind him as he left them to run and hide.

Another group ahead of him on the now almost-empty street. Four of them, all looking the same. He wanted to make them disappear, make them all disappear, but he couldn't do it. One group down, more to gawk and replace.

'Bang. You're dead. Bang. You're dead.'

Two of them on the ground as he pointed the shotgun at them, scrambling around to run. A third taking to his heels as soon as he'd come close to them.

One stock-still, shaking. Quivering.

'You. If you come with me now, I won't kill or hurt you. Just come with me now.'

The lad in front of him trembled, looked left and right, but the shotgun under his chin

391

snapped the attention back to Alan Bimpson.

Bimpson tensed as he heard sirens coming towards them. 'Now. You need to drive me somewhere.'

32

The major incident room back at the station was already starting to resemble a ghost town as Murphy and Harris entered. All available officers were on the ground, showing their faces, keeping a presence going.

It was a manhunt now. That was according to the Breaking News ticker on the rolling news channels. A couple of detective constables Murphy didn't recognise were sitting in front of the TV screen showing the footage, just staring.

Murphy kept walking, finding Rossi back in their office. He watched her from the doorway for a few seconds, seeing her wince as she reached across her desk for a file.

'You shouldn't be here.'

'I knew you were there,' Rossi said, without turning around. 'I was just doing it to wind you up.'

'Course you did,' Murphy replied, moving around her desk to his own. 'Anything new?'

'Not really. I've got a list of the company directors being sent over ASAP. Other than that, we have a picture of him in the *Echo*, with no name or any real information at all, a list of the properties the property company owns, and that's about it.'

'Well, we should have more soon enough. Plus, the whole of Merseyside Police seems to be out there. He's not going to get very far.'

DC Harris appeared at the doorway. 'They've got his car. Followed him on cameras, but lost him near the docks . . . '

'Let me guess . . . firearms are now in that area?'

Harris nodded. 'Found nothing but dead bodies and the injured in Toxteth.'

'How many?' Murphy asked, bracing himself.

'Four dead on scene. Six injured. Two critical.'

'All young?' Rossi said, turning around in her chair. 'I mean, were they all teenagers?'

Harris shrugged. 'Not sure.'

'They won't be,' Murphy said. 'He's gone nuclear now. Anyone in his path is a threat to him.'

'What makes you say that?' Rossi said, breaking the top off another energy drink.

'I saw it on the video. He didn't even pause when he shot at one point. It's anyone and everyone now. He'll either burn out quickly, top himself within a few hours, or we'll catch him somewhere and shoot him before he kills himself. It's what always happens.'

'Always? Can't remember this happening before . . . '

Murphy drummed his fingers on his desk, 'Not here, no. But elsewhere. He'll have had a cause — probably still thinks he does, but it's too public now for it to be controlled. That's key now. There's little we can do here, other than hope he's caught before anyone else gets in his way.'

Only two hours later, Murphy's hopes were extinguished.

Reports started coming in quicker this time. Multitudes of people ringing any emergency number they could get hold of. 999 was picking up calls every few seconds, the CID offices were getting calls direct.

'Where exactly is it?' Murphy asked, to someone who had finally put the phone down.

'Bootle, sir.'

'I know that you div, I meant where in Bootle?'

'Oh,' came the red-faced reply. 'Stanley Road and Marsh Lane junction. The Lidl on the corner.'

Murphy thought about it, then moved to where Rossi was standing, watching the TV. 'Any news from the ground?'

Rossi shook her head. 'Nothing yet, but it's only happened in the past half hour or so. Look at these idiots,' she said, pointing a finger at the screen. 'Just standing around, filming.'

On the TV was a video of the scene, shot by a passer-by and given to the news channels rather than the police first.

Such was policing in this age.

'Why are they just standing around filming the thing?' Rossi said, her voice getting more high-pitched as she continued watching. 'Either get the hell out of there, or do something.'

Murphy didn't get it either, this prevailing wind of change that was occurring where everyone was suddenly recording events themselves. 'It's like slowing down to see a car accident on a motorway. You know you shouldn't but you can't help yourself. Now everyone has a camera in their pocket, so it's just the next step from staring to recording it.'

'Sick is what it is.'

Murphy stared at the screen, watching as Bimpson turned and spoke to the camera. He looked different than in the picture they had of him. More drawn in the face, older, dark circles under his eyes. His hair wasn't gelled back and in perfect position now. The cap he'd been wearing had been discarded, revealing an unkemptness which didn't seem to suit him. The backpack he was carrying was making him walk a little bent over, as if the effort was becoming too much, as if the gun in his hand was heavier.

'Wind it back . . . can you do that on this one?' Murphy said as he kept watching. 'Well?'

Rossi was fiddling with the remote, 'Can't remember if we lost Sky Plus in the last cuts . . . ' she replied, finding the rewind button and pressing.

'Good. No, too far. Right before he turns. That's it . . . '

Murphy and Rossi watched in silence as something was said by Bimpson to the camera.

'I need to go back. To where it all started. I need to go back.'

Rossi paused and rewound it again, playing it a few more times.

'What do you think that means?'

Murphy shook his head but took out his phone. Found the number he wanted and started calling.

'Stephens.'

Murphy had expected a tired voice to come through, but DCI Stephens sounded bright, alert.

'It's Murphy. Are you following what's going on?'

'Yes, of course. I'm about to meet with DSI Butler to talk strategy going forward.'

Murphy pursed his lips, surprised a little. 'Oh right. It's just . . . there's something in the latest video that's on the news.'

'From Toxteth?'

'No,' Murphy replied, wondering when the media became the forefront of information in policing. 'The Bootle one. Bimpson says something to the camera . . . '

'Of course,' the lie came back. Murphy wondered when it had become easier for his boss to do that. 'Remind me what he said again.'

'He says he's going back to where it all started . . . '

'We'll discuss that in the meeting, I'm sure. For now, see if you can find out any more about this guy. That should keep you busy.'

Murphy stared at the phone display as DCI Stephens ended the call. 'Well . . . I think that pretty much settles it,' he half mumbled to himself.

'Settles what?' Rossi said, eyes still locked on the TV screen.

'We're to continue our efforts in finding out more about Bimpson.'

'We knew that anyway.'

Murphy tucked his phone back into his

pocket. 'There should be more we can do . . . '

'Like what?'

Murphy shrugged, walking the floor space next to where Rossi was perched on a desk. 'Like, anything. Why have we been left to it, here on admin duty basically? Does it really matter what we find out here?'

'You never know . . . '

'I think we do,' Murphy replied, stopping in front of Rossi, shaking his head as she tried to peer around him.

'Look, once this guy started shooting people in the street, what did you expect? They're hardly likely to let us knock on doors without firearms officers going in there first . . . '

'Shoot first, ask questions later . . . '

'Whatever,' Rossi said, standing up and walking back to the office. 'I've already been shot at once today. I'd prefer it if I didn't have to do that again, and I certainly don't want it happening to you either.'

'What's that supposed to mean?' Murphy said, following Rossi across the room.

'You're a bigger target,' Rossi replied, sitting down at her desk. 'He's hardly likely to miss you, is he?'

'Cheeky.'

Rossi hushed him, pointing at her computer screen. 'Details are in on the directors. A lot of names on here.'

'Let me look.'

Murphy squatted next to Rossi's desk as they read the names on the screen. None jumped out at him at first glance.

Rossi staring at the side of his face made him look twice.

'Thornhill . . . '

'A Kevin, which I imagine is our dead youth club guy. And a Simon . . . '

'I'll ring Brannon,' Murphy said, moving around to his desk. 'Find out the score. Bit strange that Kevin was a director of that company.'

Rossi leant over her keyboard and began typing. 'I'll check out the other names. See if we can eliminate a few straight off.'

Murphy rang Brannon from the desk phone, wondering if he'd even answer, let alone speak to him, given what had happened earlier in the day.

It could have been worse . . . he could actually have broken the fat prick's nose like he'd wanted to. Silver linings . . .

'Yeah.'

A glorious way to answer the phone. 'It's Murphy.'

'Called to apologise?'

Fuck's sake . . . 'Yeah, that, and some actual important stuff.'

'Look, I'm with Kevin Thornhill's missus at the moment. Can it wait?'

'No. Listen, we've just got the list of directors of Alan Bimpson's property firm back . . . '

A sigh. Murphy could almost smell the cheese and onion breath. 'And?'

'Kevin's name is on there.'

Silence. 'That could mean anything or nothing.'

'There's also a Simon Thornhill.'

399

A hand over the mouthpiece, ill-placed as Murphy could hear a muffled voice say, 'Who's Simon? Right . . . didn't know that . . . ' Static shifted as Brannon took his hand away.

'Apparently Kevin had a brother. They weren't on the best of terms.'

'We need to know where he lives. He might be in danger as well.'

'Hang on . . . ' This time the hand was better at its job, as the line went silent for a good thirty seconds. Murphy chewed on the end of a biro as he waited, cracking the lid. 'You still there?'

'Of course.'

'No one knows where he lives. No one really knows anything about him. Kevin's missus met him once, years and years ago. He didn't even go to the funerals.'

Murphy removed the biro from his mouth. 'What funerals?'

'Fucking hell, do you not look into these things or something? Kevin's mum passed away last year, then his dad a few months later. Broken heart they reckon. He was getting on, like.'

'And the mum?'

'That's another story . . . '

Murphy sat forward, dropping the pen on his desk.

'Tell me it.'

33

Sarah was already sick of spending her evenings alone. Although she was under no illusions; she knew the score with David Murphy. A big case came in and he was gone, like he was never really there anyway. She'd laugh and say they were like ships passing in the night, but she was getting a bit bored with the line.

It was always the same with him. Once the big conversations started, he stuck his head in Crosby beach and pretended not to listen. Same with any kind of job around the house. There was always a time limit to everything.

She picked paint flecks out of her hair as she waited for the kettle to boil. Radio Merseyside was broadcasting on the kitchen radio, giving her wall-to-wall coverage of what was happening in Liverpool that evening.

It was ridiculous to even conceive of the idea that David was involved with this type of event. The idea that he would even be near this guy — someone shooting people in the street, for Christ's sake — was beyond real.

She didn't know if she liked the feeling.

Sarah moved her lesson plans to one side of the table and sat down, staying near to the radio, preferring the local voice to the one coming from the TV in the living room. She drank a cup of tea without thinking about it, concentrating on the sound from the radio.

'Unconfirmed reports say more than three dead, with more seriously injured. Police are advising people to stay at home and only make journeys within the city if necessary. Now, the weather.'

Sarah wondered how many people even listened to the local radio any more. Couldn't be that many, not with six thousand channels on TV to choose from. Mainly old people, with nothing but nostalgia keeping them loyal.

Oh, God, she was one of those people. Getting older constantly, she thought, a dramatic eye roll for no one's benefit but her own thrown in for good measure.

She finished drinking, rinsing her mug and placing it in the dishwasher. Still the same feeling, as always. Unable to marry her two separate lives together. BD and AD. Before and After David.

She'd never considered a dishwasher before. Just wasn't on her radar. Now she couldn't live without it. No clue how she lived before it existed in her kitchen.

It was the small things.

Sarah moved back into the living room, curling up on the sofa with a fresh cup of tea, flicking between the news channels as live shots of her city appeared across them both. Big news, blood sells.

She knew that only too well.

Maybe she just needed more friends. More hobbies. She'd tried a few things, but nothing really appealed. And after a day teaching primary school kids she could barely be arsed to sit

402

upright, never mind do anything else.

At least she had Jess. That was one good friend. True, she'd been David's mate first, but the two saw much more of each other without David now.

'Speak of the devil . . . ' Sarah said under her breath as her phone rang, Jess's Facebook profile picture flashing up on her screen.

'Hey, was just thinking about you . . . '

'Have you seen what's going on? Fucking crazy out there!'

Sarah smiled. 'Yeah, it's David's case. Or was. I'm not sure what he's doing now with it. Not seen him on TV at all, so I don't think he's in Toxteth.'

'It's so weird. I've just driven back from town and the roads are dead. Everyone hiding away.'

'It is after nine . . . '

'Is it? Bloody hell, later than I thought. You know how it is. Once you start working, it's hard to stop.' Jess's voice went muffled as she shouted, 'Peter?'

'Yep. Is he out again?'

Jess came back on. 'Seems like it . . . Peter?'

Sarah held the phone away from her ear as Jess seemingly tested her voice level.

'He'll be out with his mates somewhere, I imagine. No clue as to what's going on.'

'Yeah,' Jess replied.

Sarah frowned. 'You all right?'

'Yeah, course. Just don't like him being out when all this is going on . . . '

'Oh, don't worry about him, Jess. He'll be fine. It sounds like this guy is heading to south

403

Liverpool anyway, from what they're saying here.'

'I suppose you're right. I'll try ringing Peter, see if he answers. That's if he hasn't sold this phone as well.'

Sarah hung up after saying her goodbyes, unable to stop the thoughts entering her head. She knew more than Jess did, she got that now. Jess wasn't aware that some bloke was targeting teenagers, and that now he seemed to have taken his crusade to the streets.

She tried ringing David, just to get peace of mind, but there was no answer. Left a message, but didn't expect a call back soon.

Head in the sand. Head in the job.

Everything would be waiting for him when he returned. When it was all over.

Until the next time.

★　★　★

Sarah shouted at the phone to shut up before realising she'd fallen asleep on the couch. If it hadn't rang repeatedly, she probably wouldn't have woken up, but there were only so many times the stupid song she used as a ringtone could play before she had to stop ignoring it.

She picked it up, expecting it to be David, glancing at the TV as she opened one eye a crack.

'Hello?'

Breathing on the line, nothing for a second, then a noise she'd never heard before. Almost a cry, a sob, a bark.

404

'He's been taken, Sarah . . . ' Jess eventually managed.

Sarah sat up, still waking up. 'Who, David? What are you talking about?'

'No. Peter. No one is listening to me.' The crying was back, but it sounded more like sobbing than the horrible barking noise of before.

'Calm down, Jess. What's gone on? What's happened to Peter?' She looked towards the TV screen, saw the word BOOTLE appear and shook her head.

'His mates have just turned up. They've just been in Bootle . . . '

There were sobs now, stopping Jess from talking as Sarah began reading the text on the TV screen.

Further shootings in Liverpool. Bootle area. Reports suggest at least three dead.

'Oh no . . . ' Sarah murmured, her hand going to her mouth.

'I can't find him. They say he was taken.'

Sarah looked around the empty living room. 'Taken?'

'By him. The police aren't doing anything . . . '

'Have you tried David?'

Jess choked back, more crying. 'Yeah, loads. No answer. Going straight to voicemail.'

Sarah stood up, her legs still a little wobbly from the unexpected sleep. 'I'll ring direct. See if I can get hold of him. Don't worry, Jess. We'll find him. I'm coming round to yours now.'

'Thanks, Sarah,' Jess replied. 'Tell Bear that I want everything done. The works.'

Sarah ended the call and began scrolling for the direct line to David's office. Finding it, she dialled and waited.

'Rossi.'

Sarah brushed a hand through her hair, checking the mirror in the hall for a second before pulling her boots out of the shoe rack. 'Hi Laura, it's Sarah.'

'Hi Sarah. Sorry, he's not here. Have you tried his mobile?'

Sarah paused in the hallway, one boot on unzipped, the other hanging limply in her other hand. 'Where is he?'

'He's gone to chase up a lead. As you can imagine, we're a bit swamped here. What's up?'

Sarah breathed in, pulling on her other boot. Began telling Rossi of Jess's phone call.

When she was done, platitudes over, she left the house.

Hoping everything was going to be okay.

Hoping David wasn't going to be in danger.

Hoping against hope. Against reality.

34

While his wife was still sleeping on their sofa, having not yet been woken by Jess, Murphy continued listening to Brannon on the phone.

'I can't believe you don't know this . . . '

'Get over it, Brannon,' Murphy barked back. 'I don't have time for fucking about. What happened?'

'Jesus . . . it's outrageous this.' A long sigh which sounded as fake as Brannon's intermittent tan. 'Kevin Thornhill's mum went first. She was out shopping and got mugged. Had her nose broken, but it brought on a heart attack. She died a month or so later, from complications with the surgery she had afterwards. The scrotes who mugged her were never found, even though there was CCTV of the attack . . . '

'I remember that,' Murphy said. 'Caused quite a shitstorm. Seemed to disappear eventually . . . '

'Yeah, except some of us don't forget easily. His dad especially. He died not long after. Stroke or heart attack. I forget which. It's not been easy on the family, and now this.'

Murphy thought for a second. 'Do you know what the brother looks like?'

'No idea. Hang on . . . '

The phone went silent again. Murphy tried to use the time to make things fit but couldn't place the pieces together.

'There's no photos of him here, but Kev's

missus knows what he looks like she reckons, although it's been years. What for?'

'Throw the news on and see if she recognises the picture of Alan Bimpson that's been released.'

'You're not thinking he's — '

'Just do it, will you?'

'Fine. Wait there. Got it on now. Jan, do you know that face, do you recognise it?'

Murphy waited as a muffled response came.

'She doesn't think so.'

Murphy's shoulders slumped. 'Okay, no problem. Could just be a coincidence then.'

'Right you are. Listen, we'll need to talk to the boss when this is all done. I've got some grievances . . . '

'Yeah, yeah,' Murphy replied, ending the call before Brannon could go on any further.

'What's that all about?' Rossi said from behind him.

Murphy swivelled in his chair. 'Something or nothing. Can't quite decide yet. Any news?'

'We've had word from on the ground. Bootle is clear. Our man isn't there any more. They're trying to trace him now.'

Murphy laced his fingers together behind his head. 'I hate this. Feel like a spare part just sitting around here.'

'Tell me about it.'

'Then we need to do something,' Murphy replied, sitting forward. 'Harris, get in here.'

DC Harris came scuttling back in response to Murphy's shout. 'Yeah.'

'You're with me again. We're going to check

408

out some of these directors' addresses. See if we can get a lead on Bimpson.'

'Okay . . . '

Murphy could see the reticence plastered all over the young DC's face. 'Don't worry. First sign of trouble, we'll be out of there before anything can happen.'

'No, it's fine. Honest.'

'Tell your face,' Murphy replied. 'Let me just clear it with the bosses.'

Murphy lifted the phone and dialled DCI Stephens's number. As he explained the situation, he watched Rossi print off the list of addresses they currently had for the directors for Bimpson's property firm.

'David, we're quite busy here. What can I do for you?'

'We're going to head out and see if we can track down some info about Bimpson's property firm. There's a list of directors, so we're going to see if there's any of them who might know where he could be . . . '

'We're pretty much decided on where that is, David, but you're free to check things out.'

Murphy stood up. 'Where do you think it is? What have you got?'

'Calm down, David. It was you who gave us the lead. We looked at what he was caught saying in Bootle on camera. We reckon he's going back to the farm. We're getting set for a long night.'

Murphy thought about it, tried to make the piece fit. If he chewed off one end and forced it in, it kind of worked.

Kind of didn't.

'If you think that's what he means, sounds like a plan. We'll do this lot here then, keep us busy.'

'Good.'

The call ended, Murphy taking the proffered piece of paper from Rossi and motioning to Harris to follow him.

Something wasn't right.

★ ★ ★

Rossi found the information before too long. Trying to find a link between Alan Bimpson and the directors named at his company, it had become even more obvious that Bimpson was a blag name, a pseudonym used to keep his identity a secret from the beginning. Going back even further than when this case started, to when he'd first invested in the youth club and Kevin Thornhill's vision.

But it still didn't make sense. Had he really been planning the events of the last few months for that long? Rossi checked the date on the photograph, the single one they had held before he'd become the star of the new reality show in Liverpool.

Scousers Shooting Scallies.

Rossi didn't think even Channel 5 would take that show. Never mind ITV2.

The date was over eighteen months before. If Bimpson had started taking teenagers seven months before, Dean Hughes being the first, it made little sense that he would have started using a different name in his official records that far back. There could have been a whole host of

410

reasons that he'd given the *Liverpool Echo* a different name, but would he have used one for his own company?

Rossi chewed on the end of the pen she was holding, before spitting it out when she realised she'd picked it up out there in the main incident room.

'Don't know what they're carrying . . . '

She went to her Internet browser and typed the property firm's name into Google, waiting for the inevitable deluge of results that always came. Resisting the initial urge to click on the firm's website, she instead clicked on the images tab.

It was there, a few scrolls from the top of course, but there all the same.

A picture of them all together. A major deal announced of some kind, in one of those magazines that only the trade would normally see. Now these things always end up on a website no one ever visits.

The phone rang on Murphy's desk, Rossi glancing at it before looking at the picture, clicking on the site it was attached to and waiting for it to load. She stood up, answering the phone to the stricken and upset Sarah, replacing the handset when she was done.

Torn.

Rossi hated talking to DCI Stephens, avoided it as much as possible. A probable reason she had never really fought to make DI was because she could do without having to speak to her too often. It was much easier that Murphy was her buffer. It was nothing against the boss — Rossi

411

just felt there was always a study being taken. An *are you as good as me, or better?* type of scrutiny. It was always the same with women in the police. Stupid, but true.

Rossi couldn't be arsed with all of that. Was constantly being told about it, but just didn't care. She stopped being competitive about stupid stuff back in school.

She picked up the phone anyway and called DCI Stephens.

'Stephens,' the voice almost barked back at Rossi over the phone.

'Er, hello . . . it's DS Laura Rossi.'

'Yes.'

Wasn't even a question. A statement of a yes. *Mannaggia* . . .

'Yeah, I've just had a call from the mother of the boy Bimpson is supposed to have taken . . . ' Rossi said, hoping the little lie wouldn't come back on her.

'Allegedly. We're still looking into it, but I have to say the witnesses aren't exactly the most solid we've ever had . . . '

'Right . . . it's just that the lad who's supposed to be taken is Peter White. It's Murphy's godson.'

'Oh . . . '

'So that might be worth looking into a bit more then?' Rossi said, trying to keep her voice flat and calm.

'Yes. For David's peace of mind of course. In fact, why hasn't he called me instead?'

Rossi almost lied for no reason, forgetting Murphy had already cleared it with the boss that he was going out.

412

Already forming a habit of lying for her DI. Not good.

'He's out isn't he . . . doesn't know that he's gone.'

There was a beat of silence, then DCI Stephens said, 'Okay. Let's keep it that way. I don't want him going all rogue cop on us. Got enough on our plates. Any news on finding out more about our man?'

Rossi remembered the photograph she'd just found online. 'Possibly. Just checking it out now.'

'Good. Okay. Right, well I'm being called back, so just call if you find anything of actual help.'

Rossi ended the call, still holding back the Italian curses that were threatening to be spewed out at her boss. Never a good idea to call your boss a bitch, even in a different language.

She walked back around the desk, moving her mouse so the screen came back to life. The website was on there, the photo at the top something entirely different. She scrolled down, trying to find the photo she'd found in her search, wading through a couple of dozen news items about various housing deals and market information from around the country. It was an old site, the newest item having been posted almost a year earlier, which made Rossi wonder what had happened in the meantime.

Another one bites the dust.

It was almost buried, in between a report on interest rates and the housing prices in Bristol, but there it was.

Aspire Properties announce multimillion deal to build properties in the North West.

There, smiling across the whole board, were the directors of the property firm, all dressed smartly, suited and booted, standing on what looked like some sort of wasteland.

A quote from one of the directors.

'This is a great opportunity for us to create a new community,' Simon Thornhill told us this week. 'We're all really looking forward to creating new homes for first-time buyers. When I first started this company over ten years ago, I always envisaged that this would be what could be achieved. I hope it's just the start of many of these new, small communities we can help to build.'

Shit.

Rossi looked at the picture again, looking across the faces to find Kevin Thornhill. Found him near the middle, his arm around a grinning, full-haired, shaven man in his thirties.

The last year or so had not been kind to Simon Thornhill.

Or, as Rossi and Murphy, had come to know him, Alan Bimpson.

35

Murphy handed the list of four names and addresses over to DC Harris and put his seatbelt on. Turned the radio to BBC Merseyside, and listened to the growing fear and revulsion echo around him from the speakers.

'Where are we going first?' DC Harris said, as Murphy drove out of the car park, turning left onto St Anne Street, past a scrum of media which had assembled. Most shouted unanswered questions at the car, others stared at phones and tablets, probably wishing they were closer to the real action in the city.

And Murphy didn't mean Concert Square.

If it bleeds, it leads.

'The obvious, I suppose. Simon Thornhill. If anything, I'm not sure he'll even know about his brother yet.'

'This address is familiar . . . '

'So we can at least tell him about that,' Murphy continued, not listening to DC Harris mumble under his breath. 'What's the address?'

'Eaton Road in West Derby. I swear there's something about that road name . . . '

'It's about ten minutes' walk away from where we found the first victim. That'll be all. Either that, or it's the fact that Melwood is just up the road from there.'

'Yeah, must be,' DC Harris replied, tucking the piece of paper in the side pocket on the

415

passenger side door. 'So we're just going to knock and see if he's in?'

Murphy allowed a marked police car to speed past him at the junction, lights flashing but no siren. He didn't think the late-night caution of not using them would be needed that night. He couldn't imagine many people in the city would be having early nights. 'Yeah, just see if we can fill in the blanks about the other people on the list. See if we can track down Bimpson in case things don't go as planned elsewhere.'

'Sound.'

Murphy's phone vibrated in his pocket, but he ignored it again. He knew it'd be Sarah checking up on him. Resolved to call her back when he parked up. He drove down Everton Valley with ease, traffic much quieter than it usually was, even at that time of night.

'Roads are dead . . . ' Harris said, from beside him.

'There's something in that sentence that might tell you why,' Murphy replied, driving past first Goodison Park, then Stanley Park, and wondering if there was ever a time when the possibility of a football stadium being built there wasn't being widely discussed. Wondered what would happen now Anfield was going to be expanded instead.

Onto Queens Drive, passing only a car or two on the entire journey.

'Spooky,' Murphy said, as the combination of a usually busy A road as Queens Drive and lack of bodies on the streets became starker.

'Almost like a ghost town,' Harris replied.

416

'Yeah,' Murphy said, peering into the distance at what looked like the flashing blue and red lights of a marked car. 'Think there's something going on up ahead though.'

Murphy slowed the car as they passed. A couple of uniforms talking to a group of four teenagers as they leant on a garden wall, hands out to their sides as one by one they were searched, pockets turned out. Harris put his window down at just the right time to catch one particularly hard-looking kid of no more than fifteen shout, 'We'll sort him ourselves. Not like you lot are gonna do anythin' abar 'im.'

Murphy carried on driving as Harris pressed the switch for his electric window. 'Guess there'll be a fair bit of that about tonight,' Harris said, staring ahead. 'Load of scallies thinking they're a match for a man who's proper tooled-up.'

'You're not wrong. Which is why it's hopefully coming to an end already. Just hope they're right about the farm being where he's headed. God knows where else he'll be if not.'

Murphy turned left onto Alder Road, another leafy part of the city that was often overlooked, past Alder Hey Children's Hospital. A car passed them by on the opposite side of the road, the first they'd seen in a while.

For such a normally busy city, the almost-empty roads were telling their own story.

A couple of minutes later, Murphy was checking house numbers on Eaton Road, finding the one they were looking for in the darkness only by Harris switching on his torch and shining it at the doors, the streetlights not giving enough illumination to see the houses properly.

'That's the one,' Harris said, Murphy pulling into a space between two parked cars a little further on. 'Nice house.'

'They all are down here. West Derby was all right until a few years back. Getting worse though.'

Harris murmured agreement as he got out the car, leaving Murphy alone for a few seconds as he took his seatbelt off and went to follow him. Thinking on, he grabbed his usual kit, hoping DC Harris was also holding his.

They passed a few houses, leaving the bigger semi-detached ones behind as they found the one they were looking for — a smaller relation, but still sizeable. A red-painted garage door separated the house from next door, who had built an extension over their own.

'Lights are on,' Harris said, as they approached the front door.

Murphy checked his watch but couldn't make out the dial. 'What is it . . . about midnight now?'

Harris pulled out his phone, something it hadn't occurred to Murphy to do. 'Ten minutes before.'

'We're lucky then.'

Murphy walked behind Harris up the short paved driveway, the cracks numerous, the desperate need for replacement becoming more apparent by the footstep.

Murphy noticed the curtain twitching to his right, as Harris, having already reached the front door, turned to look at him. Murphy stopped, peering into the front garden at the overgrown weeds, back at the cracked, flaking paint on the windowsills, only slightly illuminated by the light from within the house.

Dead flowers in a pot next to the front door.

'What's up?' Harris said, his voice low, his right index finger on the doorbell, pressed down.

'Not sure . . . ' Murphy replied, still taking in the facade of a house that didn't really say *named director of a massive property firm.*

'Doorbell's not working,' Harris said, turning back around, clenching a fist and knocking rapidly on the old wooden door.

'Sound like the rent man,' Murphy said under his breath, using the line his dad used to say.

'*You do anything for family . . . you just hope it works both ways . . .* '

Murphy swung his head back around to where Harris was standing, one hand in the air, ready to knock again.

'Harris, get back.'

Harris turned, a look of confusion passing across his face, before the door seemed to explode in front of him.

Murphy looked up at the sky, on his back for some reason, ears ringing. Blinking against clouds that were filling his vision, pulling himself to his feet. Tried to work out what had happened, failed.

The noise from Harris, lying a few feet away from him, pulled him to his senses.

'Shit . . . Harris, Harris, are you okay?'

Murphy got to his knees, taking off his jacket. The smell of spent shotgun shells and gunpowder assailed him as he tucked the jacket under

Harris's head. Light spilled from the now-open doorway, showing Murphy the damage.

The blood spilling from Harris's open mouth as he tried to breathe through it, producing sounds Murphy hadn't experienced in a long time.

The sound of the dying.

★   ★   ★

Inside the house, as DC Graham Harris choked on his own blood, Alan Bimpson — as he liked to be called now — tried to calm himself. Used the dimmer switch on the wall of the living room, leaving the door open rather than closing it behind him.

'I hate interruptions,' Simon Thornhill said, his switch back into Bimpson mode complete again, following his earlier slip. 'Now . . . where were we, Peter?'

Peter White let his head drop down into his chest, blood dripping onto the beige carpet.

In his mind, the feeling of loneliness and abandonment returned.

He was going to die here. He knew it on every level.

No one was going to save him.

Peter

It didn't matter that his mum was a well-paid lawyer. It didn't matter that they lived in a dead nice house, didn't even matter that his godfather, the only real male role model he had, was a bizzie. A detective inspector, whatever that meant, at that.

None of those things mattered.

It wasn't his background that made him want to do stupid shit with his mates. That stuff just meant he could always rely on having the gear that he needed. The right clothes, the right trainers. The latest game for his computer. The latest computer, for that matter. He'd got a PlayStation 4 months before any of his mates had convinced their mums to get one on tick from BrightHouse or wherever. Always had a new North Face jacket if he wanted one. Still got pocket money at seventeen, even if the amount had gone up over the years.

Wanted for nothing.

Didn't matter.

When he was out with his mates, doing whatever he liked, all of them taking the piss out of each other, out of other people, there was nothing else he wanted to be doing. It was a laugh. Better than being in school, bored out of his head as someone went on and on about something he had no interest in.

Yeah, they probably went too far sometimes.

Smoked a bit of weed and got pissed. Scratched up people's cars for a laugh. Threw a few bricks at houses which they'd been told paedos lived in, without ever really knowing if it was true.

Once, him and four other lads had found a car badge broken on the pavement. Just sitting there, smudged on one side, shiny on the other. BMW, he seemed to remember.

They'd started arguing over who got to keep it, until Wardy had walked over to an Audi which was parked on the other side, taking the penknife he always carried with him, and prised off the badge. Holding it aloft in the sky, yelling at the moon. The rest of them pissing themselves laughing at the sight.

By the end of that night, they had a holdall full of car badges they'd ripped off every car they could find. Even jarg cars like Ford Escorts and those stupid little Micras. It didn't matter. They wanted to get them all.

Tonight, he'd only been with the lads for half an hour when it had happened. They'd been walking into Bootle to meet up with some birds Wardy said were up for a bit. Peter knew they'd be skets, but didn't care. He wanted a laugh, anything to take his mind off what was going on at home.

They'd heard about what was going on, over in Liverpool 8, but it barely registered with them. It was somewhere else, not happening to them.

Didn't matter.

Then they'd heard the bangs.

Instead of doing what everyone else would, they ran towards them. Each of them egging each other on, laughing even as they got closer. Saw people up ahead with their phones out, filming something up by the Lidl on the corner.

Peter had seen the man first.

Pulled everyone else to a stop. His feet were frozen to the ground as the man walked right towards them. The shotgun in his hand making Peter's eyes grow wider, his breath shorten and heart start banging away at his chest wall.

Frogmarched away.

Why him? There were three others he could have chosen, but it was him. Always fucking him.

He'd driven once before. Wardy's cousin had nicked some car one night, was offering everyone a go for a flim. Peter thought five quid was worth it to drive a car, even if it was some shitty little Clio. He'd let Wardy's cousin start it up and then sat behind the wheel.

Now he was driving with a shotgun pointed at his chest. A sweaty and shaking man who couldn't stop talking to himself sitting next to him.

Peter swallowed again and again, his mouth hanging open as it seemed to fill endlessly with moisture. Hands moving about the steering wheel as he drove, trying to remember to change gear as he moved up in speed.

'What's your name?'

Peter tried to breathe normally. 'P — Peter.'

'Okay, Peter. Don't do more than thirty. They'll stop us and I'll have to kill you. I don't want to kill you here. Not here. I need to get home . . . need to get home . . . '

The man trailed off as he spoke, once again murmuring under his breath to himself.

Every now and again he'd shout a direction. 'Next right. Next left.' Each time, Peter slowed, hoping he wouldn't crash into a wall.

On the other hand, maybe that wouldn't be such a bad idea. Wondered if he would have enough time to speed up and smash the car into one before having his head blown off.

After what seemed like twenty days, but was more like twenty minutes, the man stopped talking, breathing in and out heavily, like one of those weird martial artists.

'Park here,' he said, pointing to a grass verge. Peter aimed but missed, leaving the car half on and half off the kerb.

'It'll do.'

Peter kept his eyes on the road ahead, scared to look to his side. The man shifted next to him, the car door opening and shutting in one long movement. Then he sensed his door being opened and sneaked a glance to his right, saw nothing but black trousers and black boots.

'Out. Walk by my side.'

Peter willed his legs to move, but it didn't matter anyway. The man was bored of waiting, he imagined, as he was grabbed by the shoulder and forced out the car, tripping over his own feet before righting himself and walking.

He tried to take in details of the house, just in case. Saw nothing special. Nothing that jumped out at him.

Peter's mind went blank as he tried to think of something, anything. What would Uncle David do?

He had no fucking idea.

Instead, he allowed himself to be led through the front door, into a room on his right, the darkened room lighting up with a click. The furniture looked old, decrepit. Old people smell came wafting towards him, as dust sprung up in the air.

'Over there. Sit.'

Peter shuffled towards an old wooden chair which had been placed in the centre of the room, indentations from where a coffee table had once stood dotted in four places in front of him as he sat.

The man moved around him, pulling his arms back and wrapping something around them, attaching him to the chair. Tight, too tight, around his wrists, cutting into them, pain shooting through them up into his shoulders.

'Don't move.'

The same went around his ankles, trapping him against the chair legs. All the time, a part of his mind was telling him to do something, kick out, scream. Anything.

The thought of a bullet entering his chest stopped him.

'There. Done,' the man said.

Peter tried to speak, but it came out as a whisper.

'Speak up, lad,' the man said, standing in front of him now. 'Can't hear you.'

Peter swallowed and tried again. 'Wh — what are you going to do?'

'We're just going to have a talk. That's all. It's all going to end now, I know that. You know it as well.'

Peter shook his head. 'I don't understand . . . '

'Course you do. You're just too thick to realise. It's because of people like you. Stupid little kids like you. That's why we're here.'

Peter's throat felt like it had grown twice the size, a lump the size of a ball suddenly stuck back there.

'This house . . . this house is where it all started. When you took my mother away from me . . . '

'I . . . I didn't . . . '

'Shut up,' the man said, slamming something against Peter's head. His vision went cloudy, starry, then slowly cleared. He felt something wet slowly fall along the side of his face.

'Speak when spoken to. Something else you're not taught these days, just like so many others. I tried to help you, you know that? Tried to make you all see the errors of your ways, but you weren't having it, were you? No, you just want to piss around, fucking with everyone's lives. Well . . . not any more. No. You'll all be shitting yourselves now, won't you?'

Peter choked back as tears sprang from his eyes. He didn't understand, didn't get it. What was happening? What had he done?

'Yeah, you cry now, but what about when you're destroying people's property, eh? What about when you're beating up some kid for daring to be different to you? Where's your fucking tears then?'

Peter screwed his eyes tight, willing the room to disappear. To be transported back to his own house. Anywhere. Anywhere but there. He could hear the man's breathing, closer to him now. If he opened his eyes, he knew he'd be there, centimetres from his face.

'What about when you're knocking old women down in the street, robbing their handbags and laughing about it? You don't think I didn't know? I knew what you all did when she was lying there, helpless, breathless. You laughed and thought it was all just one big laugh. Spat on her as she lay on the ground. What had she ever done to you, what the fuck could she possibly ever have done to you lot?'

'Please . . . ' Peter said, his voice hitching around his sobs. 'I don't know who you think I am, but I haven't done anything wrong . . . '

'Oh,' the man replied, his voice louder now. 'That's always the line, isn't it?' His voice became mocking. ' 'I didn't mean it. I didn't do nothing wrong.' Bollocks. You know what you're doing and you enjoy it. We let you get away with it, little by little over the years, and now we're paying the price. Well, no more.'

Peter heard movement, then the sound of the door swish along the carpet. He opened his eyes a little, seeing headlights play across the window. The man returned to the room, peering outside through the curtains, stood still for a minute . . . maybe two.

'You're all going to get it,' the man said, without turning around. 'You're all going to see what happens when you push us too far.'

Peter thought he heard voices outside, the bubble of hope forming in his stomach quickly diminished by the sight of the man raising up the

427

shotgun he was holding in his hand and leaving the room again.

Footsteps outside the house. Peter tried straining against the binds that were tying him to the chair, but there was no give. Tried bucking against the chair, but it was solid wood, barely moving as he pulled against the weight of it.

The bang when it came . . . he thought that was it. Thought he was gone. So loud, so deafening, it felt as though it had happened right next to him. As he opened his eyes, slowly, carefully, the room was still empty, still the same. If there'd been an explosion, it hadn't happened in there.

He cried out, but made no noise, just a horrible, gargling sound in the back of his throat as his cries were drowned out. The man returned to the room, spoke but made no sense. What had he done?

Then Peter heard the voice.

Outside, bellowing, shouting for help. Telling someone to get there fucking fast.

Peter breathed in, tried to contain himself. Didn't think he'd get more than one shot. Knew there was a chance he'd die either way. Decided it didn't matter if he tried or not.

Finally, he shouted at the top of his voice.

36

Murphy's hands shook as he tried to decide what to do first. Taking his phone out of his pocket, he dialled 999 and tried pulling the dead weight of DC Harris away from the open doorway.

'This is Detective Inspector David Murphy with St Anne Street CID. I've got an officer down, firearms present . . . ' he reeled off the address and stopped talking as he managed to move DC Harris around to behind the front garden wall.

'Just get everyone you can down here now,' he shouted into the phone.

Murphy pulled pepper spray from his belt loop, looked down at the can and, thinking of the man in the house, almost laughed.

Then a shout made him stop short.

'Uncle David . . . it's Pe — '

Cut off without a sound that he could hear out there. Murphy was on his haunches, listening, a trail of blood leading towards the house as Harris's shortening breaths tried to force their way into his chest. He reeled around, looking at the houses opposite, the odd light on here and there. One snapping on, then going off just as quick.

'Harris . . . can you hear me?'

Murphy turned Harris on his side as the DC began to shiver uncontrollably. 'Wh — What's going on?' came his response, the effort it took

429

making Harris's eyes glaze over.

'No . . . ' Murphy shouted into Harris's face. 'Stay awake, you hear me? I need you to stay awake. The ambulance is on its way, you're gonna be fine, you believe me?'

Tears rolled down Harris's cheeks as he tried to nod. Murphy grabbed his right hand, squeezing it in his bearlike grip.

'He . . . he . . . he shot me,' Harris said, his voice barely a whisper.

Murphy tried to smile. 'He did, but he's obviously a shit shot. Missed that massive head of yours by a mile.'

Murphy stood, looking back towards the house. Somewhere on the periphery of his senses he heard a phone ring.

Mind made up.

'You stay here, okay? They'll be with you any second now.'

★   ★   ★

Rossi remembered her car was still in Norris Green around the time she reached the car park and started looking around for it.

'*Cazzo!*'

A uniform who had been standing nearby jumped out of his skin, almost off the ground, which would have made her smile at any other time. Right then though . . . right then, it was different.

'You need to take me somewhere,' Rossi said, moving around to the passenger side door of the marked car the uniform had been standing next to.

430

'Erm . . . yeah, sure,' the guy said, wearing bemusement as if it was his normal expression. 'Just . . . erm . . . who are you?'

'Detective Sergeant Laura Rossi. Pleased to meet you, I'm sure you're doing a great job, wife and kids? Blah blah blah. Now get in the fucking car and drive. Pretty please, with a fuckload of sugar on top. Eaton Road, West Derby. Stick the noise and lights on.'

A few seconds later they were hurtling towards West Derby, Rossi answering questions as they tried to break the land speed record on West Derby Road.

'Don't worry,' Rossi said, as the uniform gave her a wide-eyed look when she mentioned the case she was working. 'You won't have to get out the car. At this rate we'll probably beat them there.'

She tried ringing both Murphy and Harris once again. Still no answer. Rossi had recollections of the year before, when Murphy had managed to put himself in a dangerous situation without realising. That he was doing it again was nothing short of what she had come to expect from him. It was almost as if the universe was trying to tell him something. She hadn't got there in time last year, but things had still been okay.

But that particular bad guy didn't have the weaponry this one did.

★ ★ ★

Murphy's shoes struck a loose paving slab, loosening it further as he moved towards the open door. He noticed the light had dimmed in

431

the front room, the small paved garden underneath the large bay window not as illuminated as before. He lifted the can of pepper spray level with his shoulder, his telescopic baton extended out and in his left hand.

Being a former boxer came in useful sometimes. It meant he was used to needing both hands to fight.

He mentally calculated the door opening, deciding it might be a tight fit, but that he should be able to move through it without opening it any wider and further announcing his presence. What he was going to do once inside the hallway, he didn't know, but at that moment he was just taking it one step at a time, trying not to think about the bleeding DC a few feet away and listening for any sound which came from within the house.

A voice. Low and staccato. Further inside, not by the doorway.

Concentrating on his breathing, Murphy kept moving forward, holding his breath as he crouched a little, crossing the threshold, and stopping as he made it inside. He tried to stop himself from hurtling through the door, head down, spraying pepper at anything that moved and hoping for the best.

Instead, he looked through the open living room door, the light inside dim and uninviting.

'Peter?' Murphy said, moving forward a step. 'Are you okay?'

'He can't talk right now, detective. Why don't you step inside so we can see you?'

'I'd rather hear from Peter,' Murphy said,

holding the baton a little way out from his body, finger ready on the pepper spray, trying to work out where Alan Bimpson's voice — or rather, Simon Thornhill's voice — was coming from in the room beyond.

'I'm afraid that's not going to be the case, David. I can call you that, right?'

'Call me what you like, but let me hear from Peter.'

A high-pitched wail made him jump back against the wall.

'You asked . . . now come in here.'

Murphy moved slowly, shuffling against the wall and around the doorframe, the wood-panelled door still blocking Simon Thornhill and Peter from view.

He stood strong when the scene came into view.

Peter was tied to a chair, hands behind his back, jacket ripped open on one side, revealing a dark T-shirt underneath. One trainer had fallen off, lying a few inches from where his black-socked foot was flat to the floor. One side of his face was dark red, crimson drying blood crusting on his cheek and jawline. His hair was matted from the wound which had caused it. His eyes were red and puffy from crying, the smell of ammonia filling the air as the dampness of Peter's trousers became apparent.

'What a horrible little coincidence this is for you, detective,' Thornhill said. 'How did you find me?'

Murphy ignored the question, his attention fixed on Peter. 'It's all right son. It's going to be fine.'

From the way his head lolled forward onto his chest, Murphy could see Thornhill had grabbed him somewhere a man never wants to be mistreated, the hitching breaths relaying most of the story.

The gun being held to his godson's head — the closest thing to a child he'd ever had, the boy he'd known since he was nothing but a scan picture.

Murphy locked eyes with Thornhill.

'I think you need to stop now. Lower the gun, we'll talk. But you need to let this boy go.'

Thornhill stared back for a second, then laughed. 'He thinks we should stop now? Now?'

Murphy stared again, inching forward towards Thornhill. 'Yes. In a minute, two, tops, this house is going to be surrounded by firearms officers with itchy fingers, just hoping to put you down. Let's not go through that, hey? Let's me and you just walk out of here without any drama and your guts on the floor. How does that sound?'

Thornhill seemed to ponder for a second, lips pursed as he looked towards the ceiling. 'Erm . . . how's about no. How about, instead, you drop those silly little things you're holding, or I put a bullet in the boy's head.'

Murphy stayed still for a second, watched as the finger around the gun's trigger tightened a little and then dropped his baton and pepper spray.

'Good. You see, finally, I've got your attention. For years we tried to tell you what these little bastards were doing to us, but no one listened. Well, we've got your undivided attention now, haven't we?'

434

'It's just you left now, Simon,' Murphy said, noticing a flinch in Thornhill's face as he called him by his name. 'No one else. And you have my attention, yes. So, tell me, what do you want to talk about?'

Thornhill pushed the gun further towards Peter's head, making the boy lean over to one side, almost toppling over the chair. 'I want to talk about these little pricks and why you've let them get away with murder. Every fucking day, the little parasites. And then . . . then as soon as a few of us get together and start trying to do your fucking job for you, you come after us. It's not right . . . it's not right . . . '

Murphy inched another step forward. 'Right. But this isn't helping, can you see that, Simon?' Another flinch. 'You need to step away from the boy and look at what you're doing, Simon.'

Murphy didn't even see the gun raise to the ceiling, but he heard it go off, almost diving towards Peter a split-second later, before working out what had happened.

'My name is Alan Bimpson. When I'm doing this, it's Alan Bimpson. Understand?'

Murphy nodded. Watched as the gun went back to Peter's head.

'How did he know your name, your voice? Why did he call you uncle?'

Murphy breathed in. 'He's my godson.'

Another laugh. 'See. You see now? Even having someone like you in his life wasn't enough.'

'He's done nothing wrong.'

'Has he shite. Look at him. Dressed like them, hanging around with his little gang. He's exactly like them. A little scally for a godson. How proud you must be.'

'It's not like that . . . '

Thornhill waved the gun in his direction, Murphy holding his breath and almost closing his eyes.

'It doesn't matter how it is. I can see it clearly. I know how this ends. I've seen it before,' Thornhill said, looking past Murphy and through the window. 'They'll think I'm crazy. That we were crazy.'

'They can think what they like,' Murphy said, risking another step forward. He was now only a few feet away, unarmed and with no backup.

Other than that, things were going well, he thought.

'Only you can stop this, Si — Alan. What's it going to be? Are we going to walk out of here and you can talk to me somewhere else, all about your . . . your grievances?'

Thornhill looked past him again as sirens began sounding in the street. Peter's sobs filled the silence, as Murphy tried to make some eye contact with him, to let him know everything was going to work out.

'It's not right. This used to be a good city. A good country. Now we're infested with this lot of work-shy, lazy bastards.'

'They're not all like that . . . ' Murphy said. 'Not even most of them. Think of the positives . . . '

'There *are* no positives. Live on the streets a bit, detective. You'll see what it's like then. Have your family targeted by scum like these and then

436

see how you feel. No . . . '

The room didn't need a light any more. The amount of red and blue flashing across the three of them in the living room was overwhelming.

'They killed them. Both of them.'

'I know, Alan.'

A sharp laugh. 'You should be cheering me on. My fucking mum. And dad as well. Didn't give a fuck about either of them. Just let them die.'

'So this is about revenge, for you?'

Thornhill ran a shaking hand through hair which was plastered to his head by sweat. 'No. No, no, no. It's more than that. It has to be. It's a mission . . . yeah, a mission. Someone has to sort them out. An eye for an eye . . . '

The room fell almost silent, save for the deep breaths Thornhill was making, like a bull ready to charge.

'Please,' Murphy said, lifting his hands up. 'Just talk to me some more. We can make this right . . . '

'I want you to see this,' Thornhill said. He dropped the shotgun to the floor before placing his hand inside his jacket to bring out a handgun. 'You have to tell them all the things I've said. Maybe things will change.'

Murphy watched as the gun levelled.

Bang. Bang.

* * *

Rossi hadn't got there in time. She could see that instantly. The road packed with cars, two ambulances, a row of uniformed officers. AFOs

437

with guns drawn, pointing towards the house.

She leapt out the car as it came to a stop, running towards the house ahead.

'What's happened?' she shouted into the face of a uniformed sergeant. Then she saw DC Harris being loaded onto a stretcher by two paramedics, one of them pumping his chest.

She ran to his side, shrugging off the restraining hand of the sergeant.

Gunshots, then shouts from the firearms officers, made her glance towards the house.

Silence fell as the firearms officers walked slowly towards the building from where the shots had sounded.

Watched as Murphy emerged with a struggle. Almost falling under the weight in his arms.

'He's one of us,' she screamed. 'Don't fucking shoot, he's one of us.'

Murphy went down on one knee as he was surrounded by officers. Rossi tried to push past, but her way was blocked. She looked past the shoulder of the burly armed officer who was standing in her way. Tried to listen to what was being said. Snippets. That was all she got.

'Get paramedics over here.'

'Let him go now. We've got him.'

'Come on, just let him go. He's all right . . . '

'Move away . . . '

Epilogue

She was going to bury her own son.

The thought ran through her mind over and over. It wasn't right. It wasn't the correct order of these things. You're not supposed to do it this way. She was supposed to see him get married, have grandchildren. Grow into an adult. Make mistakes. Make more mistakes. Argue with her more. Make up, laugh, and be happy. Live a life. Look after her when she was older. All that circle of life bollocks.

It wasn't supposed to be like this.

She'd been hounded for days by the press but hadn't said a word. Didn't want to make things worse than they already were. Didn't want the judging eyes of people on her. Knew she couldn't resist clicking online to see her exclusive interview — the comments underneath left by those who didn't care about what they said and what effect it could have on her, on anyone. She'd already read enough. Even though they weren't mentioning her or her son's name, people still felt able to pass judgement on the families of every victim. All sixteen of them. Leaving hate-filled comments they thought were common sense.

She'd had nothing better to do. Just waiting around for this day. The day she put her son in a coffin, said goodbye as he was burned to ashes, and then a buffet at some function room.

439

It didn't make sense.

She didn't believe in God, not one that could take a child away from its mother, but she didn't know if he did or not. They'd never really spoken about it. She didn't know if he wanted a secular funeral, or a proper religious one. She'd ransacked his room, trying to find some evidence of a belief in there, but only found unmarked blank dvds which contained nothing but porn and downloaded music, and a whole host of dirty washing.

In the end, she'd played safe and gone with middle-of-the-road religion. Nothing over the top. Not full-blown catholic style, but religious enough to cover herself. No church, just a crematorium.

She was burying her child. It didn't matter that he was basically an adult. He was her baby. Nine months growing inside her — she barely remembered that now; sixteen hours of labour — she remembered that. Then years of watching him grow into the young man he always would be.

The priest, or vicar — she could never tell the difference — droned on for a good fifteen, twenty minutes. She imagined he'd had his hands full with teenage funerals lately. He still managed to make it sound like he hadn't said the same things at those ones though. He'd never met her son, but you wouldn't know that. Managed to convey the sadness that hung over the gathering.

He'd asked if she wanted to say something, but she'd said no. Didn't want to lose it up there,

440

under the staring eyes of those watching. She asked a friend to read a poem she'd always liked. She didn't know if he would have liked it.

Probably not.

She tuned back into the vicar-priest's words as she could tell it was coming to an end. She knew what was going to happen next. The coffin would move around, be wheeled away through the curtains, never to be seen again.

'As we say our final goodbye to Peter David White, please stand for the song chosen for this event by his mother, Jess.'

★   ★   ★

Murphy watched from the back of the cremato-rium, Sarah on one side, Rossi to the other. Sarah holding his hand, Rossi giving the occa-sional elbow squeeze.

He wanted to be down there, on the front row, next to Jess. But she'd made it quite clear that he wasn't wanted.

He shouldn't be there.

When he thought back to those last moments, as Simon Thornhill pulled out a handgun from a shoulder holster, squeezed the trigger and put a bullet into the brain of his godson, then stuck the gun in his own mouth and fired . . . when he thought about those seconds, milliseconds even, it was always much slower. He was able to cover those few feet quicker, made it in time to stop.

Instead, he'd watched as Peter slumped over, the chair falling with him. Blood pooling around his head. He'd cut him free, using the penknife

441

he'd been keeping in his back pocket, knowing Thornhill would make him drop his police weapons.

Weapons . . . it almost made him laugh. They were nothing when facing a man holding the ultimate.

Carried his body out the house, knowing.

He was gone. It was his fault. He should have saved him. Standing there at the back of the church, the last words Jess had spoken to him the previous day, as he tried to comfort her, still rang through his head.

Come, but after that, we're done. You should have saved him. It's your fault.

He knew on one level it was just misplaced anger. That she was blaming him just so she could blame someone. Anyone.

It didn't matter. Peter was gone.

And nothing was going to bring him back.

DEAD GONE

Luca Veste

When DI David Murphy and DS Laura Rossi are called to investigate the murder of a student at the City of Liverpool University, they find a letter from her killer attached to her body detailing a famous and deadly unethical psychological experiment that had been performed on her. Convinced at first that the murderer is someone close to the victim, Murphy dismisses the letter as a bid to throw them off the scent . . . until more bodies are found, each with their own letter attached. Meanwhile Rob Barker, an admin worker at the university, is dealing with his own loss. His partner has been missing for almost a year, with suspicion firmly pointed at him. And as the two seemingly unconnected events collide, Murphy and Rossi realise they are chasing a killer unlike any they've faced before . . .